Burke's War

Bob Burke Suspense Thriller 1

a novel by

William F. Brown

CHAPTER ONE

Like millions of business travelers before him, Bob Burke found himself staring absently out the window of a 767 as it came in to land at Chicago's O'Hare airport. Unlike all the others, however, as the suburban buildings passed beneath him, he watched a man murder a woman on one of the rooftops below. No one believed him, of course, but that didn't matter. He knew what he saw, and Bob Burke wasn't the kind of guy to let a thing like that rest.

He was returning home to Chicago from a quick business trip to Washington, D. C., on a United Airlines flight, sitting in a window seat up in First Class. It was late afternoon. The weather was perfect and visibility was unlimited. The 767 was on final approach and he enjoyed a bird's-eye view of the sea of houses, shops, and offices that composed Chicago's western suburbs. It's hard not to look down as the world passes by. Makes a man feel a bit like God, he thought, or a 200-mile-per-hour voyeur, anyway. Then, in those next few seconds, his life changed forever.

The roof was on a big commercial building — maybe an office or warehouse of some type. It was big, flat, and covered with that light-brown pea gravel that roofers use for ballast. Whether on a rooftop like this, in a jungle, an arid desert, or on a high mountain trail, the first thing that catches an infantryman's eye is movement. In this case, the door to the building's emergency stairwell suddenly flew open and a dark-haired woman ran onto the roof, looking as if the hounds of Hell were snapping at her heels. She wore a soft, thin white dress that billowed around her. Right behind her came a tall man in a dark suit, running even faster. She appeared pale and petite, almost delicate, and the man was twice her size. The woman turned and pointed at him, screaming and clearly terrified as he closed in, laughing. After all, she could run as fast as she wanted, but the roof was literally a dead-end for her.

She took a few more steps, stumbled, and fell. That was all the man needed. Her white dress, arms, legs, and gravel went flying in all directions as he jumped on top, straddled her, and wrapped his fingers around her throat. They were long and thin, and Burke thought they could circle her neck two or three times over. She fought back with a fierce determination, struggling to get away and finally struggling to breathe; but he was too big and too powerful for her. Terrified, she opened her mouth and tried to scream, but he leaned forward with all his weight, pressing down on her throat, slowly squeezing the life out of her. Besides, with the roar of the big airplane passing overhead, she could have screamed her lungs out and no one would hear her anyway.

That was the moment when the woman's head turned. She looked up and saw Bob Burke's face in the airplane window. For that brief instant, he must have offered her some thin ray of hope, and she moved, made a sound, or did something to alert the man in the dark suit, because he also looked up and saw Burke staring down at him. From his expression, the man didn't appear one bit concerned. He didn't stop or even pause. Instead, he squeezed even harder and strangled the life out of her as Burke watched. Cold? Cruel? There wasn't a hint of alarm or panic in the bastard's eyes and he appeared to be enjoying it. Why not? There was nothing the man on the airplane could do to stop him.

Over the years, Bob Burke had watched a lot of people die. He probably even killed more than his share; but that was during two wars, and this wasn't Iraq or Afghanistan. He was flying in a 767 over suburban Chicago, and for a second he forgot where he was. He unbuckled his seat belt, stood, and shouted, "My God, that guy's killing her," and pointed out the window.

His Vice President of Finance, Charlie Newcomb, sat next to him on the aisle. Burke grabbed Charlie's arm and tried to pull him over to the window to look, but Charlie was forty pounds overweight. His ample butt was scrunched into his seat with his seatbelt fastened tightly around him, so there was no way Charlie could move fast enough to see anything on the ground before it passed out of view. As a last resort, Burke leaned out into the aisle, caught the flight attendant's attention in her galley jump seat, and yelled for her to come and look, but that proved to be an even worse idea.

It had been a lovely late spring afternoon in Washington DC when he and Charlie hailed a cab outside the Pentagon and headed back to Dulles with their tails between their legs. There was a hint of cherry blossoms and azaleas in the air and the usual late-afternoon thunderstorms were already building over the Potomac to the northwest. In Chicago, the air would seem cool and crisp, but there was much more on the two men's minds than the weather. Their corporation had just taken a crippling blow, compliments of the US Department of Defense bureaucrats and the old Washington political "two-step."

Slumped in his seat in First Class, Bob Burke tried not to think about it. He was well into his second complimentary scotch, one of the few benefits that still came with a first-class ticket. The pilot was finishing a series of long, looping turns to the north and back east until he had the big airplane pointed at the suburban cities of Wheaton, Glen Ellyn, Addison, Indian Hills, and finally at O'Hare's runway L–110. Twenty miles out, the cornfields were replaced by emerald-green fairways, white sand traps, big-lot subdivisions, curving streets, cul-de-sacs, sprawling houses, three-car garages, freshly mowed lawns, and swimming pools with tall fences. The two-lane country roads widened to four and even six lanes, and gas stations, branch banks, and strip malls popped up at the increasingly frequent intersections.

He was finishing his first year as President of Toler TeleCom, a small, high-tech telecommunications and software-consulting firm located in suburban Chicago. He and Charlie were in town to pitch what was supposed to be a routine renewal of their DOD contract to design and build encryption and recording devices for the Defense Department, only to be told that the DOD procurement gnomes had suddenly decided to "go a different direction," as they so pleasantly put it. With a smarmy smile and the scratch of a pen, Toler TeleCom lost its largest contract to Summit Symbiotics, a company they had never even heard of. "Lost" was a generous way of putting it. "Stolen" was more accurate.

After West Point and twelve years carrying out the toughest infantry, Special Ops, and Delta Force assignments the US Army offered, Bob Burke could read people like a hunting hawk and his survival instincts were honed to a razor's edge. After all, that was why Ed Toler hired him. But when a disaster like this struck, different men react differently. Bob chose to stare out the airplane window and replay the DOD meeting over and over again in his mind, trying to find any subtle nuances or "tells" he might have missed the first time; Charlie spent the flight bent over his laptop with his eyes dancing across the spreadsheets in Summit's winning bid, desperate to find some faint ray of hope. Why not? Charlie was a bean counter. He still believed that answers could be found in his neat rows and columns. Bob knew better. The DOD decision reeked of politics and bullshit, not numbers. In that arena, the answers were in what Burke saw in a man's eyes, what he heard in his voice, and what he felt in his handshake. That was why he knew they were screwed the moment he heard the DOD procurement team say they were accepting Summit Symbiotics' proposal instead of Toler TeleCom's.

It was a setup, of course. Either the smiling DOD procurement people had been told what their decision was to be by the big brass in the Pentagon's Inner Ring, or Summit left a briefcase full of cash or a job offer on someone's desk. Call it a campaign contribution, a kickback, "pre-retirement profit-sharing," or an old-fashioned bribe, but Summit submitted an impossibly low bid. In hindsight, it was probably all four. Everyone knew Summit would more than make up the loss through a string of subsequent Change Orders. Well, shame on the DOD, and shame on a top-notch Army combat commander and tactician like Bob Burke for not anticipating a trap, allowing himself to be blindsided by such an obvious tactic, and not being ready with his own countermoves. It was one more painful lesson that bureaucratic warfare on the Potomac could be every bit as nasty and to-the-death as the many firefights he engaged in during four tours in Iraq and Afghanistan. In the "desert," the bad guys carried AK-47s and RPGs, but the US Army gave him a gun of his own and let him shoot back.

"Man, this is *so* bogus," Charlie continued grousing, mostly to himself, about Summit's proposal. "This thing doesn't even meet half of the specs."

"Of course it doesn't," Bob replied calmly enough.

"We got screwed, Bobby, plain and simple. How could the Feds be this stupid? I can show you the stuff that got left out of their bid. They'll come running back with overruns and Change Orders before spring and the Feds will have to accept them, because they can never admit they made a mistake this bad. You watch. No way is this gonna stick. Those bastards!"

"It's Washington, Charlie. It is all about politics and payoffs now, not competence," Bob answered as he drained his glass of scotch and held it up so the flight attendant in the galley could see his smiling face. "But we knew that a long time ago, didn't we? Our mistake was going after the DOD business in the first place."

"That's not your fault, Bobby. Trying to stick our snouts in the Federal trough was Ed Toler's big idea. He was a great guy, but you inherited his mess."

"Charlie, Ed's been in the ground for two years now. If the Army taught me nothing else, it's that you can't keep blaming your predecessor, not if you had enough time to change things. The only thing I regret is that it's going to cost a lot of good people their jobs."

The flight attendant, Sabrina Fowler, finally sauntered over holding another double scotch, but she wasn't very happy about it. She looked at her watch and said, "We land in fifteen minutes, and both of you guys are looped."

"Not him." Bob glanced at Charlie with a pleasant, anesthetized smile. "He's fine."

"Gee. That is so funny," she answered, deadpan, having already heard that sophomoric act too many times before. "Look, I've been on my feet since 6:00 this morning, and I don't need another standup comic. Which of you is driving?"

"The Grinch next to me," Bob lied. "We'll behave, honest."

"Okay," she said as her eyes narrowed and she set the new glass on the armrest. "But if I get any blow-back, you'd better never end up on my flight again. Got it?"

"Yes, ma'am," Bob answered with a winning smile. He detested the unnecessary business expense of flying in First Class, but every now and then, there were advantages.

As the flight attendant walked away, Bob picked up the fresh scotch and downed half of it. He heard the whine and squeal of the 767's landing gear coming down, and turned back to the window. Below, the big airplane flashed across a verdant suburban golf course and he saw a guy slice his tee shot into the woods, while his pals hit on the "beer-babe" in the drink cart. On the next green, an overweight foursome plumb-bobbed their bad putts. In rapid succession, the big houses and golf courses gave way to smaller houses, apartments, two-story office buildings, low-rise warehouses, and large distribution centers, as the jet dropped lower. They were the disposable shells of modern American commerce — the leased, multipurpose buildings that housed the vast majority of today's suburban businesses. No one enjoyed living in a house or playing golf beneath a low-flying 767, but it wouldn't bother a guy running a loud forklift or a clerk-typist sitting in a cubicle beneath a thick, insulated acoustical tile ceiling, which is why buildings like that crowded around a noisy airport like O'Hare. One thing that most of them had in common, however, was a large, rectangular roof. It could be white, black, or different shades of brown, depending upon whether it was made of one of the newer high-tech single-ply plastic materials, or layers of old-fashioned coal-tar pitch and black tarpaper. If the roof was light brown, it was usually "ballasted" with an inch or two of loose, round pea gravel for protection.

Bob let his eyes roam across the buildings below, while Charlie continued to rant about Symbiotics' proposal. Bob tried to ignore him, but then Charlie hit a hot button. "Angie's gonna crap when she hears we lost the contract, isn't she?"

"Don't worry about Angie. It's me she's gonna hammer, not you," he quickly replied.

Charlie looked over at him. "Oh, you don't look worse for the wear, Bob."

"Trust me, that woman knows how to leave bruises and scars where you can't see them," he answered with a knowing smile. Angie was Bob Burke's volatile and soon-to-be-ex-wife. She was Ed Toler's only child. When Ed founded Toler TeleCom, he made Angie his Vice President in charge of absolutely nothing, with a big salary and a bigger expense account. As soon as he met Bob, however, Ed realized his new son-in-law would make an infinitely better successor than Angie ever could. He began working on Bob to give up his Army career and join Toler TeleCom as his Vice President of Operations — a real job with real responsibilities. Initially, Bob laughed it off, but the cold, hard truth was that he was burnt out from almost continuous high-stress combat in one Third World country after another. You are what you are, and you are what you do, he knew all too well. So, in the end, he accepted. He was more than ready for a change and threw himself into his new career with no reservations. That was about the same time Ed Toler reached for the shiny brass ring of DOD business. Two years later, when Ed got sick and went in the hospital, never to come back out, he named Bob the new company President over his one-time heir apparent and successor, Angie. Their normally incendiary marriage had flamed out months before, but when the Old Man put Bob in control instead of her, that did it. All of Ed's managers, the unions, and the banks quickly agreed with Ed's choice, but Angie never would.

"Think she's gonna sue us again?" Charlie asked.

"Probably. That girl's always had more lawyers than brains."

"And the sense of humor of a scalded cat."

Bob smiled pleasantly enough, knowing Charlie couldn't know the half of it, and turned back to his scotch and the window. The big jetliner dropped lower and lower, but his mind continued to be elsewhere. All things considered, it was dawning on him that his decision to get out of the Army might have been a mistake. True, Special Operations was a savage, no-holds-barred world, but it was important and invigorating, and he was exceptionally skilled at it. He loved the men he fought alongside. That was a cliché, but they were brothers and that bond would never break. And after a day like today, he'd rather be fighting on the Amu Darya River in Afghanistan than the Potomac. Sadly, it might even be safer.

Below, dozens and dozens of commercial, office and light-industrial buildings stretched toward the horizon. To his left, he saw a tall white municipal water tank. Painted on its side in bright green was the profile of an Indian chief in a full war bonnet. Almost directly down, between the airplane and the water tank stood a three-story, blue glass office building. That was when he saw the woman in the white dress run out onto the roof. He would never forget the image of her running, stumbling in the loose pea gravel, nor of the man in the dark blue business suit chasing her. He appeared older, with graying temples, a white shirt, and a rich, red-striped tie. He looked almost dignified, like a politician on a Sunday morning news show, one of those preachers from South Carolina on cable TV, or a jungle cat on the prowl — calm and under control as he ran her to ground. In that instant when she looked up at the airplane and at Burke, the man in the dark suit looked up at him too; their eyes locked on each other's and his sadistic expression burned itself into Burke's brain. Then, as quickly as the two figures appeared below, they were gone from his view.

Desperate to stop him from killing her, Burke unbuckled his seat belt, stood, and tried to step over Charlie to get into the aisle, but that accomplished nothing. Sabrina Fowler, the flight attendant, leaped out of her jump seat in the galley and dashed down the aisle to their row.

"Mr. Burke, get back in your seat. Now!" she ordered. Like a good middle linebacker, she cut him off and boxed him in. Her knees were flexed, her weight was evenly distributed on the balls of her feet, and she stood in a perfect "triple-threat" athletic position to stop him cold. She placed the palm of her hand against his chest and shoved him back into his seat before he could get one foot into the aisle. Wherever he thought he was going, he wasn't going to get there.

"You told me you'd behave." She glared down at him.

"Come over here and look." He turned back and pointed out the window, his jet-black eyes flashing. "There's a woman being killed down there!"

"I don't think so, now fasten your seat belt!"

"I'm serious. Come here and look," he tried to convince her.

Her patience exhausted, she said, "I *knew* I shouldn't have given you that third drink!"

"But he's strangling her."

She leaned forward and got right into his face. "Buckle that seat belt, or I'll have you arrested when we land. You got that?"

Finally, he complied and snapped the belt in, but he continued to argue with Charlie and with her. "You saw her, didn't you, Charlie?"

"Bob, I was over here with my nose in a spreadsheet. I didn't see..."

Reluctantly, Burke turned back to the flight attendant. "Look, ask the captain and the rest of the crew up in the cockpit. They must have been looking out there too. Or ask the other passengers on this side of the plane. Someone else must have seen it."

"I'm not about to ask anybody anything until after we land."

"Okay, but I want to talk to the police as soon as we do."

"Oh, that won't be a problem, Mr. Burke," she answered sarcastically. "I'm sure they'll want to talk to you, too. Now sit down, and shut up!"

CHAPTER TWO

O'Hare Airport resembled a large octopus thrown onto the ice from the upper deck of a hockey arena, its legs splayed out in all directions. After the 767 landed, the pilot took a long, circuitous route around the taxiways to the other side of the big terminal, leaving Bob Burke to wonder if Gate C-28 was in Illinois or Wisconsin. As soon as the seat belt light went off, he tried to step over Charlie and head for the exit door; but Sabrina Fowler, now much-less-than-friendly, would have none of it. She stopped him with a long, pointed index finger before he took two steps up the aisle.

"Oh, no, you don't." She jabbed him in the chest again and drove him back into his seat. "You neither," she said as she turned her wrath on Charlie.

"Me? What did I do?" Charlie asked.

"You're with him, that's enough."

With a heavy sigh, Burke returned to his seat, looked out the window, and waited, knowing it was now far too late to try to help that woman, if he ever could.

After the last of the other passengers "deplaned," Sabrina finally returned, gave him a thin smile, and motioned for them to gather their bags and follow her. On the ramp beyond the exit door stood two uniformed Chicago Police Officers and Detective Lieutenant Ernie Travers. Big and beefy, Travers wore a cheap, blue business suit that hung on him like a wrinkled old sack and might have come from the "2-For" rack at JCPenney. Hard to blame the man, Burke thought. When you do "cop work" these days, bloodstains, sweat, food, coffee, and rubbing up against the criminally unwashed will turn most of your clothes into throw-aways. Besides, with Travers's body type, he needed a roomy fit to cover what Bob Burke immediately recognized had to be a large handgun in a shoulder holster under his arm, as well as the handcuffs, notebook, two-way radio, and all the other assorted cop-crap that even a plainclothes officer was required to carry these days. The Army solved that problem several wars earlier by issuing their men cheap utility fatigues, but that was not an option for a police detective.

Travers stood in the center of the ramp outside the airplane exit door, with his arms folded across his chest, carefully appraising Bob Burke as he approached. Bob was doing the same thing, and they both knew it, noting Travers's hands, his body language, and looking into his eyes. Observing things like that was the way Burke was trained, and apparently Travers was too. For the briefest of moments, their eyes met and the first spark of mutual recognition passed between them. The beefy Chicago cop was a head-and-a-half taller, at least sixty or seventy pounds heavier, and twenty years older. For the same reasons, Bob figured he must look very ordinary and even a bit dorky to the big cop. Of average height and weight, Burke was more fit and trim than his professionally-tailored suit revealed. The shirt collar and cuffs on Ernie Travers's were graying and frayed and his ugly green-plaid tie must have been a throw-in with the suit, while Bob Burke's entire outfit appeared expensive and new. His shirt collar was unbuttoned and his silk tie hung loose at the neck, but that was typical of most other businessmen passing through the terminal late any afternoon. Like the others, he carried a briefcase; but his was thick and well worn, as if it weren't for show and he actually carried things inside that he might use for business. The same was true for his watch. It was a cheap, black-faced Timex army model with an olive-drab, nylon wristband. Look as he might, Travers could not see any tats, earrings, or gaudy "bling" hanging around this man's neck.

"I understand you want to talk to the police," Travers said.

"Yeah, well, it's a little late for that now," Burke replied, realizing this would be a massive waste of time. "I saw a woman being attacked back there…"

"Back there? You mean in the airplane? Back in coach?" Travers quickly asked.

"No, no, outside, on the ground. I was looking out the window as we came in to land, and I saw a man chase a woman across one of the rooftops. He knocked her down, jumped on top of her, and started strangling her."

Travers studied him for a moment. "You were looking out your window, and you saw this happening as your plane came in? I guess you have pretty good eyes, Mr.…."

"Burke, Bob Burke."

"You got some ID, Mr. Burke?" Travers asked as he held out his hand, looking both bored and angry in equal measure.

Burke complied, pulling out his wallet and handing Travers his driver's license and a business card.

Travers studied them both for a moment. "What brings you to Chicago?"

"I live here, in Arlington Heights, as you can see from the address on my IDs."

"And this business of yours, Toler TeleCom?"

"It's in Schaumburg. We design and install advanced telecommunications systems. Some are business applications, and some are highly-classified projects for the Defense Department."

"Highly classified? And you're the company president. I'll bet that requires a pretty-good security clearance, doesn't it?" Travers asked, thinking Burke might not be a total nut as he slipped the driver's license and business card into his shirt pocket.

"My clearances are about as high as you can get, always have been."

"I'm sure," Travers said as he leaned closer and recognized the smell of booze. He looked into Burke's eyes and could tell he was well toasted. "What's that, bourbon?"

"Actually, a couple of scotches, neat," Burke replied.

"A couple? He drank three, and they were all doubles," Sabrina Fowler chimed in.

"Ah, another country heard from." Travers turned toward her with a thin, unforgiving smile. "And you were working First Class? Miz..." he asked as he read her nametag. "Fowler? Which means you're the one who served him all those drinks, and the one I have to thank for saving me from that hot meatball sandwich up in the office?"

"Oh, give me a break, Lieutenant," she answered angrily.

Travers turned his stare back on Burke. "Look, it's late and I'm tired. I'll give you a one-time free pass if you're straight with me, Mister Burke. Did you *really* see something down there, or is this a few too many scotches talking?"

"You got a lie detector?"

"No, and I don't have a breathalyzer on me either." Travers glared.

"Guess we're even then." Burke glared right back. "Detective, I know what I saw; so are you gonna keep standing here busting my chops, or are we going to go back there and look?"

"Back there? Exactly where do you suggest 'there' might be, Mr. Burke?"

That was when the pilot and the rest of the cabin crew came down the aisle behind them, carrying their bags and hoping to squeeze through and head for their hotel, but Travers held up his hand like a traffic cop and stopped them at the door. "Captain Schweitzer," Travers said, reading the pilot's nametag, "give me some help here. This gentleman says he saw a woman being attacked on a rooftop as you came in to land.

From the time you were low enough for him to see something like that until you reached the runway's outer lights, that's gotta be what? Four or five miles, at a couple of hundred miles an hour?"

"On a clear day like today, yeah. And maybe a mile wide," Schweitzer replied.

"Okay, let's say four square miles, maybe more," Travers concluded, as he turned back toward Burke. "That's half the suburbs north and west of here."

"The building wasn't that far back, Lieutenant," Burke countered. "We were pretty low by then, a couple of hundred feet or less, I'd guess."

Travers cocked his head and studied him for a moment. "What? You fly airplanes too?"

Burke crossed his arms across his chest, looked up, and gave the big cop a thin, irritated smile. "No, but I've flown enough *in* them — jets, props, and helicopters, low and fast — so you might say I know what things look like up close and personal like that."

Travers took a second, closer look. He saw a collection of scars on Burke's hands and face, and recognized the distinctive class ring on his finger. "A West Point ring knocker?"

"Uncle's Reform School on the Hudson, class of '99... What about you? The MPs?"

"Good guess. Iraq, both wars, but I was in the reserves, 'summer help,' as we called it. Something tells me you were neither, right?"

"Me? Oh, I spent twelve years in the Signal Corps."

"Signal Corps?" Travers scoffed. "You don't look like a telephone guy to me."

"Funny, I hear that a lot," Burke said with an embarrassed smile. "Signal loaned me to the Infantry right out of the Point. I was in a mech battalion, the Rangers and some other things."

"Some other things?" It was Travers's turn to smile. "What? Delta? Special Ops? With the ring and twelve years in, that would make you what? A captain or major?"

"A major," Burke said, deciding it was time to change the subject. "What about you, Lieutenant? You still in the reserves?"

"Me? Oh, I'm a full colonel now, making sure Illinois doesn't get invaded by Wisconsin with the rest of us 'weekend warriors,' Major."

"No. no, it's plain old mister, now, Lieutenant. I hung up the uniform and the rank three years ago. You gung-ho types can have all the excitement now."

"Gung-ho types? Boy, have you got that wrong," Travers laughed.

"In six months, I'll have my twenty-five in and then I'm gone. However, it does sound like you spent some time flying around. Unfortunately, we have one hell of a lot of rooftops out there, Mister Burke."

"Agreed, but this was an office building, maybe three stories tall, all blue glass. Almost everything else out there was flat and low, only one- or two-story, so it stood out."

"True, but that doesn't matter." Travers frowned, thinking. "If the building is out to the west, it's outside airport property and way outside my jurisdiction."

"Your jurisdiction?" Burke snapped angrily. "Look, I saw a woman being murdered back there. What the hell does jurisdiction matter?"

"Nothing to you, but it opens up a world of legal complications," Travers said, as he looked away, embarrassed, knowing Burke was right. Frustrated, he turned his attention on Charlie, Sabrina, and the other crewmembers. "Any of you see anything?" he asked hopefully, but all he got in return were shrugs and one loud complaint.

"Lieutenant," the flight attendant whined, "I got an outbound to Orlando, first thing."

"I'm sure you do, Miz Fowler, but I got a real nice couch up in my office that should help you take a load off those sore feet of yours. By the way," Travers turned his head and eyed Charlie for a moment, "is this guy with you?"

"I'm his Vice President of Finance."

"Ah, a bean counter. Isn't that nice," Travers replied, deadpan. "You can come too."

"You've got to be kidding," Sabrina pleaded. "I didn't see a damned thing."

"No, but you're the only independent set of eyes I've got and since you poured all those drinks, you're coming." Travers turned back to the pilot. "You too. I have some maps up in my office, and I need you to show me the flight path."

Before the City of Chicago opened O'Hare in 1963, it annexed the airport and a narrow corridor of land through the northwest suburbs to physically and legally connect it to the city. The Federal Transportation Security Administration, or TSA, held sway inside the airport's security checkpoints, in the terminal's baggage areas, and on its taxiways. The Chicago Police Department's jurisdiction began outside the checkpoints, and included any non-Federal criminal acts that occurred anywhere on the airport property or within the corridor back to the city. While that seemed like a simple division of labor, it did not account for the hundreds of uniformed and non-uniformed private security guards, county cops, state police, Forest Preserve District police, a dozen separate suburban police departments, US Air Marshals, airline security, and miscellaneous rent-a-cops, who spent most of their time tripping over and frustrating each other. Anyway, that was how Ernie Travers saw it.

With Travers in the lead and his two uniformed officers bringing up the rear, their small procession worked its way down the long concourse to the main terminal and up a flight of stairs to the small CPD Airport Security Office. It was in the "low rent" district deep inside the second floor. With no windows, a beautiful sunrise or sunset, torrential rain, a blizzard, or even a tornado was only a rumor in here. The office featured a cramped reception area, several small work cubicles, a conference room, and a tiny kitchen barely big enough for a coffee pot. The desks and file cabinets were a mixed bag of US government surplus repainted in an institutional gray. Someone had scrounged a few airline travel posters and taped them to the walls. Cheesy? Perhaps, but the romantic beaches, palm trees, and snow-capped mountains helped hide the faded green paint.

As depressing as the small office was, it was a plum assignment for a Chicago cop, because it was as far from the department's big headquarters at 3510 South Michigan Avenue as one could get. Out of sight and out of mind, and without the bureaucrats, the politicians, and the press breathing down your neck, it was the perfect terminal assignment for a senior detective with one too many bullet holes and a history of bad chest pains like Ernie Travers. He trooped everyone inside his conference room, pausing for a moment at his secretary's desk. Burke saw him lean over, whisper something, and hand her his driver's license and business card, no doubt to check him out. Burke smiled, knowing that she was about to fall into a very deep DOD black hole.

The conference room's far wall was taken up by a large aerial photograph of the northwest suburbs. The airport sat at the center, with runways pointing out in all directions. Travers motioned for Captain Schweitzer to join him at the map. "Show me your approach, what you came in over."

The pilot quickly found Runway L-110, and drew a line to the west with his hand. "We were on autopilot, Lieutenant. I may have looked out the front windscreen a couple of times, but my eyes were focused on the instruments, not the ground. Sorry."

"Okay, thanks a lot, Captain. I appreciate the help. You can go."

"Me too? Can I go?" Sabrina Fowler asked hopefully.

"Nope. You're staying."

"Why? I told you I didn't see anything."

"Sure you did; you saw him," Travers replied. "Okay, Mr. Burke," he said as his hand swept across the map. "I assume you've seen more than a few aerial photographs…"

"Too many, Lieutenant," Burke answered as he stepped forward.

"You were on the left side of the plane, looking down at an oblique angle, so I figure this is about what you would have seen," Travers said as his finger drew a line across the map. "Anything look familiar?"

"Finally starting to believe me, huh?" Burke answered.

"I never said I didn't, but you don't make it easy."

Burke smiled as he stepped closer and let his eyes run across the aerial photo. "The rooftops do look about the same, don't they?" he said as he tried to picture it all in his mind. "The one that woman was on was light brown. Maybe some kind of gravel?"

"They call it pea gravel. It protects the surface on some kinds of roofs."

"The office building was blue, three stories tall, and I remember a big water tower not too far away, almost in line. It was white, with some kind of green stuff on it," he said as he pointed to a circular shape. "There! That's the water tower. You can see the long, circular shadow it throws."

Travers stared at the aerial photo. "Figures," he moaned.

"What's that mean?"

"Well, for starters, it ain't Chicago."

"And it ain't Kansas, either, Toto. So what?"

"That's Indian Hills. Let's say we tread a little softly out there, that's all."

"A *little softly*?" Burke questioned.

"Chief Bentley doesn't appreciate outside agencies coming into his town. There was some history between him and my predecessor, so I avoid the place whenever I can. Sometimes, he's not a problem; sometimes he's a pain in the ass."

"Sometimes?"

"It's his town, not mine." Travers shrugged. "But if you don't like the way I am handling this, I can drop you off at TSA and you can tell them your story. Of course, you might end up sitting down there all night, getting put on their 'disruptive passenger no-fly list,' and find all of your nifty security clearances put on hold, but if that's what you'd prefer...?"

"No, no," Burke answered, resigned to his fate.

Ernie Travers's secretary walked into the room. "Did I hear 'Indian Hills,' Ernie? You aren't going to drive over there unannounced, are you?" she asked as she slipped him Burke's driver's license and business card, and shook her head "no."

"Yeah, well, I'll see how it shakes out, Gladys," he answered as he slid the cards across the table to Burke. "If I need to make a stop, I'll radio in and have you call the Chief for me."

"Bentley? You want *me* to call that moron?" she asked.

"I hear he likes to schmooze with secretaries."

"Ernie..." she groaned. "The guy's a blowhard, and that little pit bull of his, Bobby Joe, is a creep. If he so much as touches me again, I swear..."

"You have my permission to deck him," Travers answered. "If he doesn't want to cooperate, tell him I'll turn the whole thing over to the FBI or the state cops. His choice."

"No matter, he ain't gonna like it," she said as she walked away shaking her head.

"All right, folks, let's go for a ride," Travers said firmly as he glanced at Sabrina Fowler again. "All of us. Looks like you all have your carry-ons, so bring them along and we'll throw them in my trunk." Now she was *really* furious, mostly at Burke. Travers led them out the Airport Security Office's back door into a lower service area where a large, dark-blue unmarked police cruiser was parked.

After they threw their bags in the trunk, Travers opened the driver's side door and pointed at Burke. "You ride shotgun. Maybe you'll recognize something as we drive. Miz Fowler, you and Mister Newcomb get in the back. I'd put Burke back there with you but I'd have to ask one of my Patrol Officers to sit in the middle for crowd control, wouldn't I?"

"That is so un-funny!" she steamed as she climbed in the backseat. "It smells back here!" she growled at Travers.

"It's a police car; they all smell."

"I'm sending you my dry-cleaning bill. I don't even want to touch anything back here."

"You'll be fine. We have it hosed out every shift, just for the stewardesses"

"I'm not a stewardess; I'm a Flight Attendant!"

"Of course you are," Travers cut her off, trying not to smile, as he started the car and drove toward the airport exit. "Now, let's go find that water tower, Mister Burke, and that blue-glass office building of yours."

CHAPTER THREE

Ernie Travers took the Kennedy Expressway East, got off at the first major exit, Mannheim Road, and headed south. Mannheim was a busy commercial boulevard lined with strip centers, motels, and large office buildings. As quickly as he got on, he got off Mannheim onto Route 19 and headed west. This was another bustling commercial road, which ran along the airport's southern boundary, but the early evening rush hour traffic had already slowed it to a crawl, giving them time to talk.

"Coming in on L-110, as you did, you must have passed right over those buildings up ahead, Mister Burke," Travers began. "It's getting dark, but I'll keep driving west toward that water tower. You sound off if you see anything."

After five minutes, the tall municipal water tank appeared in the distance. Floodlit, it now stood out against the dark sky like a giant white mushroom, except for the profile of an Indian Chief in a full war bonnet painted on it in dull green. Above the Indian's head was a crescent of letters that was supposed to spell "Indian Hills." As they got closer, Bob could see that the water tank had seen better days. Its bright-white paint was now a dingy pale gray, and showed numerous white splotches that were someone's attempt to cover a generation of graffiti. To add to its sorry state, the once-proud Indian chief now sported an eye patch, a cigar drooping out of his mouth, and a town name that read, "Indian Losers."

"Your pal, Chief Bentley, isn't going to like that," Charlie snorted from the back seat.

"Nah, it looks like that stuff's been up there for a while," Bob Burke commented. "I suspect he got used to it a long time ago."

"And I suspect you're right." Ernie Travers smiled. "But big town or small, the cops tend to care about the things they get paid to care about."

A brief flash of light drew Burke's attention to his left. He turned and saw it was the lights from the busy highway reflecting off an office building. "There!" he said as he pointed across the front seat. "That's it."

"Great. That's Indian Hills, all right," Travers said as he continued down the road and turned into a large, well-landscaped business park. In the median stood a decorative blue metallic sign with large brass letters that read "Hills Corporate Center." Farther on, at the end of the second cul-de-sac to the left stood the three-story blue glass office building that Bob had seen from the airplane. He was positive it was. On the upper corner of the front façade stood the bold, black letters, "CHC" in an ornate, Gothic script. On the ground, at the entrance to its parking lot, was a matching sign that read "Consolidated Health Care" and "An SD Health Services Company" in smaller letters below.

Travers drove into the far corner of the building's parking lot, parked in the outer row of spaces, and picked up his radio microphone. "Mobile One to Base… Gladys, you'd better call your pal the Chief and ask him if he can meet us at the Consolidated Health Care building in the Hills Corporate Center business park."

"Ten–four, Lieutenant" came her less-than-enthusiastic reply. Travers leaned back in his seat, rubbed his eyes, and tried to relax.

"Been a long day?" Burke asked.

"They don't make 'em short anymore." The police detective shrugged.

"I know the feeling," Burke commiserated.

"Well, one way or the other this shouldn't take very long."

He was right about that. No more than five minutes later, two white police cars swung into the parking lot, one behind the other, drove around the perimeter, and pulled in next to them, one police car on each side. Both carried the latest, low-slung light racks on their roofs, and the same green Indian chief's head Burke saw on the water tank. The one on the left also bore the words "Chief of Police" in large gold letters beneath the Indian. The other car simply read "Police Department" in black.

"I'll bet he's got all the latest toys from the 'Cop Shop Christmas Catalog,' too," Bob quipped as he saw four radio antennae on the Chief's car roof and trunk, and a set of thick, heavy-duty, black-wall tires. "Perfect choice for an 'O.J. Simpson car chase.' "

"Behave," Travers told him as the driver's side door of the police cruiser opened and out stepped what must be the Chief himself. He wore a set of crisply laundered khaki slacks and shirt, complete with four silver stars on each collar.

"Maybe I was in the Army too long, but why does every Chief of Police, whether he's got two cops under him or twenty thousand, have to wear as many stars as George Patton?"

"You've never been to a cop convention, have you?" Travers answered.

Bentley had on a pair of silver-lensed aviator sunglasses, like the pair Ponch wore on *'Chips,'* and reached back inside for a brown, round-brimmed 'Smokey the Bear' hat. The driver's side door on the other car opened and out stepped a miniature version of Bentley: shorter and fatter, but wearing the same aviator sunglasses. There was a lone stripe on his shirtsleeve, marking him as a junior patrolman, and a nametag that read "B. J. Leonard." He may not have much police experience, Bob thought, but he saw all the *"Dukes of Hazard"* reruns. His legs were spread, there was a smirk on his lips, and his right hand rested on the butt of a long-barreled .38-caliber Colt revolver he carried in a holster low on his hip as he stared in at Burke.

Bob almost laughed aloud as he watched the Chief hitch up his pants. "Is this *'Smokey and the Bandit'* or what?" he asked.

"Careful," Travers warned. "That old bastard ain't Jackie Gleason," he said as he opened his own car door and got out to greet the Chief. The two men shook hands politely enough as Bob joined them.

Bentley eyed Burke as he approached. "Loo-tenant, your girl told me you got some kinda problem you want to see me about? Somebody thinks they saw something up a roof?"

"That's right, Chief, and I appreciate your taking the time to help us resolve it."

"Well, I know you're the 'new boy' over there at O'Hare, but this here's Indian Hills and you're a long way from airport property, you know."

Burke saw Travers's eyes flash, but he managed to keep himself under control. "True enough, Chief, but I figured you'd rather take a nice, quiet look around with me than have the TSA and FBI digging in your shorts."

Bentley's eyes narrowed as he realized he'd been out-slithered. "No, no. I guess there's no need to get them Feds involved. We always try to cooperate with our neighbors, even the airport. Now, what seems to be the problem?"

"Mr. Burke here was looking out his window as his plane came in to land, and he says he saw a woman being attacked up on the roof."

"Before we go traipsin' in there, you got some ID, Mr. Burke?" Bob pulled out his wallet, showed Bentley his driver's license, and handed him one of his business cards. Bentley handed the wallet back, but studied the business card for a moment. "You're in the phone business?" he asked as he slipped the business card into his pocket, and then turned, hands on hips, and stared up at the blue glass building. "Loo-tenant, this here's the CHC headquarters. They're a fine, upstanding member of our Indian Hills business community, and I'm not sure I want them gettin' all disturbed over some kind of wild accusation."

"Well, Chief, I'll be happy to pass it over to the FBI, if that's what you want."

"No, no, we don't need none of that." Bentley quickly backed down and turned to face Travers. "So, what exactly is it you want?"

"I'd like you to take us inside for a quick look around, if that's okay, Chief?"

"You want to go inside... and take a look around?" Bentley seethed, but realized there was little choice. "All right, we'll go inside and get this bullshit over, if that'll settle it. But you be real careful in there, you hear me. This here's *my* town!"

With Bentley in the lead and Travers close behind, their small group headed up the landscaped front walk. Burke followed the two cops, with Charlie and Sabrina Fowler behind him, and the Indian Hills patrolman taking up the rear. He barely gave Sabrina enough room to squeeze out of the back seat between him and the car, leering at her as she brushed against him.

She jumped and glared back at him, hands on hips. "Touch me again, little man, and you'll walk crooked for a week!"

"Bobby Joe, get away from that woman!" Bentley snapped at him. The patrolman backed off, but he followed Sabrina up the sidewalk like a street dog in heat, his eyes never leaving her butt and his hand never leaving his revolver.

They reached the building and passed through its tall revolving glass door. Inside, Burke found himself in a spacious, two-story atrium lobby, with expensive black marble walls, a white travertine floor, gleaming brass fittings, and lush interior plants and trees. The building appeared to have two wings, connected by a second- and third-floor landing and elevator lobby that looked out over the open atrium. In the center of the lobby, sitting like the final battlement guarding the castle keep, stood a circular black marble reception desk, whose base sat a foot or two off the floor. Sitting behind it was a young, blond-haired woman. The nameplate in front of her read "Linda Sylvester." Wide-eyed and nervous, she watched as this odd group of people approached.

Chief Bentley was obviously no stranger here. He walked right up to her desk, leaned his meaty forearm on the tall counter, and asked, "Linda darlin', I don't suppose Tony's in, is he?"

"Well, uh, let me call upstairs and..." she replied, flustered.

"Ask him if he can drop down here for a minute and help me clear up a little problem."

The receptionist picked up her telephone, pressed some buttons, and gave a hushed, cryptic message to someone. "He'll be down in a minute, Chief," she said, as her eyes darted around at Travers, Sabrina, Charlie, and finally came to rest on Burke. He smiled at her, but that only seemed to make her even more uncomfortable. She quickly looked away.

After a few awkward minutes, Burke saw the lights change on the elevator panel on the far wall behind her. With a soft "ding," the set of polished brass doors quietly opened and two men stepped out into the lobby. The one in the lead was thickset and muscular. He wore a sharkskin blazer, dark gray slacks, and Italian loafers, and had a noticeable bulge under his left arm even larger than Ernie Travers's. He wore a monogrammed black shirt, open at the neck, with a half dozen gold chains and medallions hanging down his chest. His big hands, thick neck, barrel chest, and powerful upper arms gave him a look of an over-the-hill bodybuilder, but Bob's attention went to his dark, hooded eyes. They quickly scanned the group of strangers, slicing, dicing, and evaluating each one until they came to Burke and Travers. The other man was taller and thinner, well dressed in a conservative dark blue pinstriped suit. He wore a crisp white shirt with a burgundy tie and a matching handkerchief in his breast pocket. The monogrammed cuffs were accentuated by a pair of blue sapphire cufflinks which matched the lobby walls. His black hair was combed straight back off his forehead and there was a fashionable touch of gray above each ear. From his amused smile, Burke concluded he thought he was the one in charge, although the goon next to him might disagree.

The instant Bob saw him and those cynical cold gray eyes, he recognized him. Undeterred, the man returned Burke's stare, much as he did when the airplane flew over, and a moment of instant recognition passed between them. Bob pointed at him, and then turned toward Travers.

"That's him. That's the guy I saw up on the roof strangling that woman."

"Whoa now! Hold on a minute, boy," Bentley exclaimed, holding up his hands, but the man in the suit did not skip a beat.

"Oh, that's all right, Chief," the man said with a condescending smile as he continued walking toward them, pulling down his French cuffs. "You say you saw *me* on the roof? *Strangling* a woman?" He laughed. "It appears someone has a *very* vivid imagination."

Bentley stepped between them. "I'm real sorry about this, Dr. Greenway..."

"Help me out here, Tony." Greenway ignored Bentley and turned toward the bodybuilder. "The roof? Do I even *know* how to get up there?"

"You? I freakin' doubt it," the big man grunted.

"Why don't you introduce us to our visitors, Chief," Greenway continued confidently.

"Well, uh, this here is Lieutenant Travers from the CPD unit over at O'Hare," Bentley began. It was obvious to Burke from the furtive glances the three men exchanged, that they knew each other well, and that this was a little game they were playing. "Doctor Greenway is President of CHC, and Mister Scalese is his Head of Corporate Security," he added as he motioned toward the muscle in the sharkskin jacket. "Dr. Greenway, Travers here says that these folks were looking out a window on a flight comin' in from DC about an hour ago, and they saw somethin' up on your roof."

"On our roof? How very remarkable," Greenway countered with an unapologetic smile. "I'm sorry, but I don't believe we've been introduced. You are Mister…"

"Burke, Bob Burke." Burke answered as his tired frustration turned to anger. Maybe it was the all-too-knowing glances between Bentley and the other two, or Greenway's supreme arrogance, or the condescending expression on his face, but Bob knew this was a charade.

"And you say you saw a woman being attacked up on our roof?" Greenway asked. "Well, I'm shocked!" he added as he turned toward Scalese as if for help. "What did she look like?"

"You know damned well what she looked like," Bob answered.

"I do?" Greenway answered, feigning innocence.

"She was tall, with dark hair. She was wearing a flowing white dress, and it was blowing in the wind until you knocked her down and jumped on top of her."

"Oh, really! And when did all of this happen?"

"Maybe an hour and a half ago."

"Well, that answers that. I've been in meetings all afternoon. Chief, I have no idea what this man is talking about. It must be some other building."

"I know what I saw." Bob's jet-black eyes flashed ominously.

"And I'm sure you think you do," Greenway countered. "But this is a private building. Our roof is closed to the public. I assure you I was not up there, and neither was anyone else. Isn't that right, Tony?" Greenway smiled and turned toward Scalese.

"That's right, Doc. We keep those doors locked and nobody goes up there unless it's a contractor or something. The only way to get inside the building and up to the roof is to walk past our receptionist, and we've got lights, cameras, and locks on everything else."

The young receptionist was listening to every word, looking back and forth between the three men like a spectator at a tennis match, not knowing what to think. "A white dress?" she finally spoke up. "I think Eleanor was wearing a white dress when I saw her come in this morning, Dr. Greenway, and..."

"That's enough, Linda," Greenway cut her off. "No doubt that is in style these days and you can find them all over town, but I'm not going to have my staff involved with these outrageous accusations." Scalese also sensed the danger and walked behind the reception desk, grabbed the young woman by her arm, none too gently, and led her away down a side corridor before she could finish what she was saying.

"Who is Eleanor?" Bob quickly asked.

"One of our employees, but she has been in the same meetings, and she is none of your business," Greenway answered, but Burke could see the first cracks in that once-confident façade. "If you want anything else, I suggest you talk to our lawyers. I'm sure you understand. Isn't that right, Chief?"

"Uh, yeah, that's right, Dr. Greenway," Bentley said.

Bob knew he had reached a dead end. "Since you said the roof's locked and no one's been up there, do you mind if we take a look? Maybe I'll see the right building."

Greenway stared at him for a moment, his eyes narrowing as he thought it over, debating.

"What can it hurt?" Travers asked.

Finally, Greenway relented. "All right," he said as Scalese returned. "Be my guest. Anthony, would you mind accompanying these people to the roof?" Scalese glared at him, as if he thought Greenway had lost his mind. Reluctantly, he motioned them toward the elevators. They all got in the small cab. When the doors closed, Bob found himself standing side by side between Greenway and Scalese against the back wall. The Italian was bigger than him by six inches and at least sixty or seventy pounds, and they were all muscle. Greenway was even taller, but much thinner. From the smug expression on his face, he knew Burke was on a fool's errand.

They got off at the third floor. Scalese led the group to a thick steel fire door at the end of the hall. He hit the panic bar with his meaty forearm and the door flew open. On the other side was a clean, well-lit emergency stairwell. One set of risers went down to the lower floors, while the other continued up to the roof. With Scalese leading, they marched up. At the top, they came to a small landing and a second, thick fire door. Scalese hit that panic bar too, and the door flew open, outward, onto the roof. So much for "locked doors," Bob thought. They stepped over a high threshold onto a thick, six-foot-by-six-foot rubberized walk-off matt. In front of them lay the open expanse of brown pea gravel, but there was no body now and no blood to be seen either. Most of the pea gravel appeared to have been raked and neatly leveled, but in several areas it had been disturbed and pushed around, including a spot near the center of the roof, where flashes of the underlying black-rubber roofing could be seen.

"That's where the woman was." Bob pointed. "That's where you killed her."

"Where I killed her?" Greenway laughed, having regained his confident bravado. "I don't know what you were drinking up there on your airplane, but you have a fantastic imagination, Mr. Burke. There was a roof leak up here, and I believe that area is where the repairmen were looking around and running their tests. Isn't that correct, Anthony?"

"Yeah, it's hard to find a leak on these flat roofs, and they still ain't done."

"Mind if I look?" Bob asked.

"You are persistent; I'll give you that," Greenway said with a thin, wary smile. "But I don't suppose it can do any harm. Be careful where you walk, though. We wouldn't want any more problems up here, would we?"

Bob walked slowly to the disturbed area in the center of the roof, bent down, and looked closely at the surface; but he could see nothing wrong. There were scrapes on the black membrane of the roofing material below the gravel, but that meant very little. What he did not see was any blood or scraps of her white dress. He raised his head and looked around at the rest of the buildings. This was the right one, and this was where Greenway killed her; Bob was positive about that. Unfortunately, more than enough time had passed for him to get rid of the body, but not enough for him to clean absolutely everything. Burke knew it, and so did Greenway. He could see it on the doctor's face as he rejoined them at the stairwell.

Travers turned toward Charlie Newcomb and Sabrina Fowler. "You two got anything to add? You see anything?"

Charlie shook his head, but the flight attendant had been waiting for an opportunity like this. "See, I told you I never saw a damned thing! That guy's nuts." She pointed at Bob. "Now can I go home?"

Greenway smiled. "Well, are you satisfied now?" he asked.

"No," Bob said as he turned toward Travers and Bentley. "Are you going to get a search warrant?"

"A search warrant?" Bentley exploded. "For what?"

"For a body. Look, I know what I saw, and I'll bet she's somewhere in this building."

"On that ridiculous note, I'm afraid I'm going to ask you to leave — all of you," Greenway cut him off. "I tried to be cooperative, but you finally exhausted my patience."

Travers put his hand on Bob's shoulder and tried to lead him toward the door. "There's no grounds for a search warrant, Mister Burke; we would never be able to get one."

"You're damned right you wouldn't, not in my town!" Bentley added.

Bob turned toward Greenway. "All right, do you care if we look around the rest of the building?"

"This time, yes I do. It's full of trade secrets and proprietary information, so I must say no, Mister Burke. Please leave my building."

Bob stopped arguing, because he knew it would do no good. It was time to make a tactical withdrawal, lick your wounds, and wait to fight another day. That was what he would do. He bit his tongue and quietly followed Travers and the others as they returned to the emergency stairwell, walked down to the third floor, and took the elevator to the lobby. Standing against the rear wall, he looked at Greenway and Scalese again. The expression on the doctor's face was triumphant, but the expression on his Chief of Security showed something altogether different, Bob thought. Scalese looked angry, and it wasn't only at Bob Burke.

In the lobby, it was Ernie Travers who finally broke the awkward silence, as he turned back to Greenway and said, "Thanks for your cooperation, Doctor. You too, Chief, thanks for your time. As you can appreciate, it's something we couldn't ignore."

They nodded, but Bentley couldn't leave well enough alone. "Well, I hate to tell you I told you so, Loo-tenant," the Chief chortled, exchanging knowing glances with Bobby Joe, "but I told you so."

Bob was livid as he turned back toward Greenway. "Well played, Doctor; but we both know what happened up on that roof, and I'm not the only one," he said as he looked at Scalese.

Greenway straightened his suit coat again, and looked back at Bob with a thin, knowing smile. "I doubt that, Mr. Burke, but you have a nice day, anyway."

While his patrolman, Bobby Joe, escorted them out the front door, Chief Bentley remained behind, leaning on the reception desk in the CHC lobby, watching as Burke, Travers, and the others left the building through the big revolving door.

When they were gone, Bentley motioned for Greenway to step closer, grinned and placed Bob's business card on the top of the reception desk. "You ain't got nuthin' to worry about, Doc. He's some kinda 'telephone guy.' He works for one of those damned phone companies."

Greenway started to pick the card up, but Scalese pulled it out of his hand and took a close look at it. "Toler TeleCom," he said. "I'll see what else I can find out about him."

Travers drove out of the CHC parking lot and they rode in silence until they reached Mannheim Road. It was Sabrina Fowler who spoke up first. "Are these games finally over? Can I go home now?" she demanded in a huff.

"Yes, you may, Ms. Fowler," Travers answered politely, "and I appreciate your help. I'll take you out to your car. How's that sound?"

"All right, but don't spend all night doing it," she said as she turned her red-hot glare on Bob and Charlie. "Next time you idiots decide to fly, book American or Delta; you might not survive another flight with me."

Travers drove them back around to the main airport terminal and dropped Sabrina Fowler off at her car in the airline crew parking lot. She quickly got out, turned, and flipped Bob and Charlie the bird as she slammed the door behind her and walked away. Travers drove back to the airport terminal and stopped opposite the exit doors from Arrivals.

"There's a shuttle bus to your lot every ten minutes," he told them.

"You mean you're not gonna drive us out to our cars?" Charlie asked.

"No, but I'm not flipping you the bird either."

"That guy Greenway is getting away with murder, Ernie, and you know it," Bob said as he got out of the car.

"Maybe... hell, I'll even give you a probably," Travers admitted. "But you haven't given me much to work with, you know. There isn't a shred of evidence that says Greenway's done a damned thing, him or Scalese, and you don't have any other witnesses to back you up."

"No, but I know what I saw, and things like that don't go away. Neither do I."

"I'm not sure I like the sound of that, Mr. Burke. I'll keep my eye on them and do what I can. If somebody did get killed up on that roof, sooner or later a body will show up. They always do, but you need to stay out of it. Do we understand each other?"

"Oh, I understand you perfectly, Lieutenant." Bob smiled as he closed the door and backed away from the car. Travers didn't look very happy about it, but they both knew there was nothing he could do.

As they waited for the shuttle bus, Charlie said, "This has been a very interesting evening, Bob, but you gotta forget all that stuff. We got big problems of our own. I went over all the numbers and the spreadsheets and we gotta focus on the business thing in the morning, both of us, or we're finished."

"Yeah, I know," Bob reluctantly admitted, knowing Charlie was right, but he was having a tough time getting rid of the image of the woman in the white dress on the roof. He kept trying hard to convince himself that he must have been wrong about what he saw and it was the scotch talking, but he knew it wasn't.

"First thing, Bob. We gotta talk, first thing."

"First thing," Bob agreed. First thing. The business problems they were facing were huge, and they must be his top priority, his only priority. He knew that, but the look in that bastard Greenway's eyes as he strangled that woman refused to go away. It was for him to see every time he closed his eyes. Travers and all the rest of them could try to convince him otherwise, but he knew what he saw. The only question that remained was what he was going to do about it.

CHAPTER FOUR

After Bentley left and the bright-red taillights of two Indian Hills police cars disappeared down the Hills Corporate Center entry road, Dr. Lawrence Greenway and Tony Scalese stood on the front sidewalk of the blue glass Consolidated Health Care building and continued to argue. "Are you out of your freakin' mind, Doc?" Scalese stepped closer and tapped Greenway in the chest with his forefinger. From most people, a tap in the chest with the tip of a finger would get your attention. From Tony Scalese, it could leave a bruise or break a bone.

Greenway was half a head taller. He glared down angrily at the muscular Italian but did not dare to do much else as he pulled down on his shirt cuffs and tried to compose himself. "Aren't you forgetting yourself, Anthony?" he asked.

"Me? Forgettin' myself?" Scalese's angry eyes flashed.

"Yes, I think you're forgetting who you work for."

Scalese leaned in closer and poked Greenway in the chest again, harder this time, driving him back a step and his confident arrogance along with it. "No, Doc! You're the one who's doin' the forgettin.' I work for Mr. D, not you, and he told you to keep a low profile — no waves, no cops, and no more freakin' dead bodies. Why'd you think he put me here?"

Chagrined, Greenway answered, "I did what I had to do."

"Like hell you did. I heard what that guy Burke said, and I can see it all over your face. It's a damned good thing there weren't any more witnesses, or this whole thing would be over. Now who was it?"

"It was Eleanor... Eleanor Purdue," Greenway finally admitted.

"Like the receptionist, Linda Sylvester, said. Why am I not surprised, Doc?"

"What choice did I have? I caught her in my office going through my files. She had one of those little miniature cameras."

"A miniature camera, huh?" Scalese backed off a half step, thinking.

"Yes, and with that bastard O'Malley's Grand Jury starting next week, you know what that means as well as I do."

"You think she was turnin' that stuff over to O'Malley?"

"What else could it mean? Let's hope it didn't get that far."

"Hope?" Scalese flared. "Maybe we'd freakin' *know*, if you hadn't gone and killed her."

"She did not give me that option, Anthony. She was photographing the Medicaid billings and the test results from India — taking pictures of the spreadsheets, and I chased her. We ended up on the roof."

"And you strangled her up there, like that little prick Burke said you did."

"Yes! But she didn't give me any choice, I swear it."

"Maybe not, but you loved doing her anyway, didn't you, like all the other ones."

"No, those were accidents. I... I lost control. With Eleanor it was different."

"Different?" Scalese asked as he stepped closer again, well inside Greenway's space. The doctor flinched and Scalese smiled. "She was playing you. When you had her on that big leather couch of yours with her feet up in the air, you thought you were screwin' her; but she was the one screwin' you, Doc! You sure it wasn't that she got a little too frisky for you?"

"How dare you?"

"How dare I? What? Are you really that stupid? You think I don't make it my business to know everything that's goin' on around here? That's why Mr. D put me here."

"My private relations are none of your business... or his."

"They are when you're playing on our dime, Sport. Besides, the way you parade the hired help in and out of that little office love nest of yours, do you really think it's some kinda goddamn secret? Even I saw the bruises on her wrists last week, and so did every other broad in the place. What? You like it a little rough with 'em now?"

"You bastard!"

"Me? Hell, you think those women don't talk to each other? Sooner or later, it was all gonna blow up in your face. Now, tell me; how the hell did she find all that stuff?"

"I... I was looking over some of the files and financial reports... I guess I left them out."

"Files? You told Mr. D there was nuthin' on paper no more. You told him you burned everything they could use against us."

"Look, Tony, I can't keep everything in my head, you know. I needed some spreadsheets to keep track of the numbers, to make sure everything balanced."

"Spreadsheets? Numbers?"

"Don't worry, it was all coded, and..."

"Coded? With the FBI, the NSA, and all the rest, you think the Feds ain't clever enough to figure 'em out?"

"I'm sorry. They were on my desk and..."

"You know, Doc, when the Feds finally got Capone back in the '20s, it wasn't for murder, gambling, or running booze, it was for taxes... and you still think they're only 'some spreadsheets,' 'some *numbers*' you left out on your desk?"

"I know, I know, it was careless of me."

"You moron! When Mr. D..."

Greenway was in a panic now. "Oh, come on, Tony. I was in a hurry to get to Glenview for a speech. I got down the road a couple of minutes and realized I forgot my notes, so I turned around and drove back. She had the sheets spread out on my desk and was flipping through them, taking pictures with some kind of little flash camera, when I caught her."

Scalese held out his hand and waited. Reluctantly, Greenway reached into his pocket, pulled out a small, rectangular, silver camera, and gave it to him. Scalese held it up and examined it carefully. "This ain't something you pick up at Walmart to take pictures of the kids at the beach, Doc. It's a Minox, one of the new digital models — very nice, very sophisticated, and very expensive." He turned it on and looked at the small display window. "Looks like she took forty-five shots. That's a lot of pages, Doc, a lot of spreadsheets... unless she was takin' some of you and her doin' it on your couch."

Greenway was almost a head taller than Scalese, but it was no contest. He was slim and athletic, like a dancer, while Scalese was bulked up, with muscles on top of his muscles and a crazy-mean look in his eye — too much prison time, too many weights, and way too many 'roids. Regardless of the reason, Tony Scalese was intimidating.

"Well, at least I caught her before she did anything with them," Greenway offered.

Scalese's forefinger shot out again and poked Greenway in the chest, hard. "You don't know shit, Doc! A camera like that means she wasn't no amateur. What else did she get her hands onto? And who the hell is she working for?" Scalese asked as he poked him again and pushed him backwards. "You don't have a freakin' clue, do you?"

"I tried to get it out of her, but she wouldn't tell me."

"Maybe she couldn't talk too well, while those long, manicured fingers of yours were wrapped around her throat. You ever think of that, Doc?"

"She was my problem, and I took care of it."

"Took care of it? Took care of it! Is that what you call it?

"She got away from me in the office and ran up there. What else could I do?"

"You coulda called me, that's what you coulda done. I'd have made her talk; but no, you get your rocks off by strangling women."

"I think you are forgetting yourself!" Greenway bristled angrily. "This is *my* company and *my* operation."

"Your company? *Your* company? You're the one doing the forgettin', Doc. You were bought and paid for a long time ago."

"I told you I'll take care of the problems, and I did."

"Like you did today?" Scalese asked sarcastically. "First, you let a snoopy bean counter you were bangin' get her hands on our books — the real ones! Then you got a witness involved."

"Him?" Greenway scoffed. "Bentley slipped me his card before he left. The man works for a 'communications' company, for Christ's sake. He probably installs telephones."

"Maybe, but there were two more who heard him, plus a Chicago police detective, our pal Bentley, and our own receptionist. What's next? A TV news crew and film at 6:00?"

"You were there. He'd been drinking. Nobody believed his story."

"That Chicago cop ain't like Bentley. How do you know what he believed?"

"Bentley told me Chicago has no jurisdiction here. He said he can control it."

"Bentley told you that, huh?" Scalese's finger jabbed him again. "You know, he's a lot like you; he's got an over-inflated sense of his own worth."

"Bentley won't say anything."

"Not with what *we* pay him; but the others are risks we don't need."

"What about Linda, the receptionist? She said she saw Eleanor this morning. I can talk to her if you want. You know, make sure she keeps her mouth shut."

Scalese turned and glared at him. "No! I know how *you* 'talk' to them; and you stay the hell away from her. I already told her to keep her mouth shut and not to talk to nobody. That Purdue broad wasn't' workin' alone, you know. With a camera like that, she was probably snoopin' around for that bastard O'Malley or the FBI, gettin' information that's gonna put us all down in the Federal pen in Marion, if we aren't careful."

"Don't you think I know that!"

"For her to take a risk like that? She musta really been out to get you."

Greenway glared back at him but said nothing.

"Let me tell you somethin', Doc." Scalese closed in on him again. "I can do jail time. I've done it before and I can do it again. But a good-lookin' guy like you? They're gonna love you in there, but they'll be the ones playin' *doctor,* not you. Don't worry, though," he said as he slipped his hand into his jacket pocket and pulled out a 9-inch stiletto. He flicked the blade open and held it up in front of Greenway's face so that the light from the lobby reflected off its razor-sharp blade. "You'll never see the inside of a prison or a courtroom. Mr. D will take you on a little fishing trip out in the lake long before that ever happens."

Greenway stared into Scalese's cold, dark eyes and began to sweat. "Look, Anthony, we're on the same side here. We're partners. I'm not going to do anything to upset things."

"Wrong! You already did, Doc." Scalese cut him off, grabbing him by the lapel and pulling him closer. "You don't seem to understand. There's a lot at stake here, millions, and the people I work for take things like that deadly serious. You ain't supposed to be goin' around killin' people or tryin' to get rid of bodies. That's *my* job, remember? You're supposed to stick to the hip and knee replacements, the padded bills at the clinics and nursing homes, and push the meds. I'm here to handle 'security.' "

"I know, I know, Tony." Greenway kept trying to back away, but Scalese tightened his grip on his lapel, and stayed up in his face.

"Mr. D ain't gonna be happy when he hears about this," Scalese told him.

"Look, uh… Who says he has to?"

Scalese laughed. "Who says he has to? Don't go diggin' yourself in deeper than you already are, Doc. You said you got everything under control. Okay, what'd you do with the Purdue broad? Where did you put her body?"

Greenway shrank back. "In… uh, in the third floor mechanical room."

"The third floor mechanical room?" Scalese laughed derisively at him and shook his head. Finally, he let go of the lapel on Greenway's suit coat. "You really are a piece of work, Doc," he said as he closed the stiletto and dropped it in his pocket.

"I wrapped her in a plastic sheet the painters left and stuffed her behind the air handler. I was going to get rid of her tonight, after the janitors left."

"In a plastic sheet the painters left? Yeah, you got things under control, all right."

"It was only temporary. Most of the staff's already gone. No one was going to find her up there. I was going to get rid of her later tonight, but then I got that call from Bentley."

"So, it's a good thing they didn't search the building like that guy Burke wanted them to do, isn't it?"

"That was never going to happen."

"No, because you 'took care of everything.' " Scalese snorted.

"All right!" Greenway lost his temper. "You think you're the *big expert*' on getting rid of bodies. *You* handle it! After the janitors left, I was going to put her body in her car and dump it over on the West Side. If you've got a better idea, why don't you do it."

"I will; and you don't need to tell me how to get rid of a stiff, Doc. But the next time you need somethin' done like that, call me first — and there better not be a next time, because I'm getting tired of cleaning up your messes."

Greenway studied him for a moment before a thin smile crossed his lips. "Okay, Tony, how much do you want?"

"How much? Oh, let's say, fifty 'large,' " Scalese answered and watched Greenway's smile fade. "You can always do it yourself, of course; but if I do it, there won't be no blowback. Mr. D don't want no more waves and he don't want to hear no more stories."

"You aren't too subtle, but I get the message, Anthony." Greenway began to recover his confidence. "Fifty thousand? I can do that... I assume that will buy your complete discretion?"

"My *complete discretion*? Oh, no, that's only for the body. If you want it to stay between you and me, you better make it a hundred."

Now, Greenway's smile was completely gone. "A hundred? All right, Tony, *"no problema,"* as 'your people' would say. A hundred 'large' it is, and now I own you."

Scalese looked at him and laughed even harder now. "You own me? You got balls, Doc, I'll give you that much. You got balls, all right... but next time, keep 'em in your pants."

CHAPTER FIVE

While the offices of Consolidated Health Care were in a modern, three-story, blue-glass building in a beautifully landscaped office park in a trendy suburb west of O'Hare, Toler TeleCom's offices ran more to the dumpy and practical. They were located in a boring, two-story, thirty-year-old-brick office-warehouse in an area of Schaumburg behind the big Motorola plant that featured more of the same. The company offices filled the front half of the building, while their warehouse, equipment storage, and trucks occupied the rear half. Each of the two buildings projected exactly the image that their owners wanted for their companies.

The morning after his O'Hare Airport fiasco, Bob Burke arrived at the Toler TeleCom offices a few minutes after 8:00, much later than usual, more hung over, and psychologically black and blue from having asked, "You moron, what were you thinking!" over and over again to himself in the mirror. Still, he knew that the best cure for a flood of self-doubt and self-pity was to jump right into the deep end and start swimming.

Yesterday's business suit was gone, replaced with faded blue jeans, a button-down Oxford cloth shirt, an old tweed sports coat, and a pair of well-worn Asics running shoes. As he walked through the front door and across the small lobby, he gave a hurried nod to Margie Thomas. She had been the company's receptionist, "gatekeeper," and corporate pit bull since Ed Toler founded it. She and Angie Toler never got along, due to one perceived slight or another, and Angie retaliated by trying to get the bean counters to cut the position and replace her with a tasteful little sign and a buzzer. Ed Toler told them "no" a long time ago, but that did not stop Angie from continuing to try. To Ed, a smart receptionist was the company's public face, its first line of defense, and invaluable. That was one of the many things that Ed got right.

Margie watched him over the top of her glasses. "Casual Tuesday?" she muttered under her breath. "I must've missed the memo."

Ignoring the comment, he trudged on into the company's administrative offices and took the first quick right past the desk of Maryanne Simpson, his Executive Assistant and Ed's long before that. Whether in government or business, most managers put their own offices in a distant corner, usually at the end of the longest hallway, around a few corners, and well out of sight from virtually everyone. That type of "boss cave" was exactly what Ed Toler refused to have. He put his own office,

Maryanne's, and the main conference room up front in the center of the larger space, where all the main hallways intersected. Like the other managers' offices, the corridor door walls were glass, and his door was rarely closed. "How else can you know what's going on?" Ed said. "I want to see what my people are doing, and more importantly, I want them to see what *I'm* doing. I can't think of running this place any other way." Neither could Bob.

As he tried to slip past Maryanne's desk and through the door to his office, she looked up and snapped her gum at him. Like a warning shot across the bow of a ship, that was her usual way of getting people's attention. "You've got visitors," she warned, glancing toward his closed office door. He frowned, knowing she understood his standing order about no visitors before 9:00 a.m. She returned his unhappy look and shrugged, "The little one didn't give me much choice. He is a pushy bastard, as you'll see. And don't ask, I've already taken them coffee, twice."

Bob opened his office door and stepped inside, where he found two men waiting for him. One was his old "pal" from O'Hare, Chicago Police Department Lieutenant Ernie Travers. The other was someone he recognized from local TV news — a small, fastidious little man in a conservative blue suit, turtle-shell glasses, and a bow tie. He was Peter O'Malley, the US Attorney for Northern Illinois. The image Bob recalled was of the man behind a bank of microphones on the steps of the Federal Courthouse — presumably behind a short lectern or standing on a very thick phone book. This morning, however, O'Malley was sitting stiffly upright in Burke's chair, behind Bob's desk, looking like it was "bring your kid to the office day." Ignoring the fact that Bob had just walked in in, O'Malley continued flipping through the pages of Bob's desk calendar. Maryanne was very particular about how she sorted and stacked papers, correspondence, and telephone notes on her boss's desk when he was out, and it was obvious that her neat piles had been mussed and rummaged through. Figures, Bob thought. That was why nosey, mouthy little jerks usually became standup comics or lawyers.

Bob chose to ignore the provocation, for the moment, anyway. He set his briefcase on his round conference table and looked over at Travers. "Hi, Ernie," he said. "Long time no see."

The big police lieutenant was as far away from O'Malley as the small office would allow. He stood by the sidewall, arms folded across his chest, eyeing the gallery of photos and plaques hanging there. Most were standard company PR stuff that Ed Toler left behind. There were shots of a few of their big jobs, of Ed shaking hands with customers, of key staff, and various plaques and awards that the company received over the years, but those weren't the photos Ernie Travers was looking at. Almost lost in the dense sea of color were two framed ones along the far edge, which were of Bob Burke in the Army. The others were full of bright colors, but the scenes in these two appeared beige on dusty, dull beige. The top one dated from the first Iraq war — the good one. Travers looked closer and saw a young, smiling Lieutenant Robert Burke kneeling in the center of two or three dozen laughing, grinning American soldiers in full battle dress. Behind them sat two big M-113 Armored Personnel Carriers, an Abrams tank, and an empty, rock-strewn desert. It was an interesting shot, but the other photo drew Travers' attention even more. It was of a smaller group of eight heavily armed men — American Special Ops soldiers, he immediately guessed — set against a craggy, snowcapped mountain range. They wore scraggly beards, baggy pants, shawls, and the flat "pakol" hats that the native Afghans wore. To a man, they looked older and more scarred and battle-worn than the other group. Their smiles appeared thin and forced, but the eager young men in the first photo had won their war. They had kicked ass in a matter of days and would soon be on their way home from their first and only tour. On the other hand, the men in the other photo were on their second, third, or even fourth tours, trapped in a war that ground on and on and ended up kicking everyone's ass. Travers leaned closer and studied the small man in the center. He leaned on a long-barreled Barrett M-83 sniper rifle, and above his beard and mustache, Travers recognized Bob Burke's hard black eyes.

"Interesting," Travers commented.

Burke frowned. "Those two were my wife's idea, not mine."

"No surprise there."

He and Angie argued about them many times. "They are *exactly* what you need to impress your customers and get things off on the right foot, Bobby," she insisted. "You should put up more, plus all the medals and flags. You know what I mean." He did, but he didn't agree. With her, he rarely did. "They only impress the wrong people," he told her until he finally gave up arguing. With Angie, he learned to pick his battles, which he rarely won anyway. Besides, he could take them down later, when she wasn't around. Unfortunately, she anticipated that move and took the precaution of mounting them to the wall with heavy-duty butterfly dry-wall screws. Smart girl, as usual. To get rid of them, he would need to tear half the wall down.

Travers's eyes met Burke's for an instant and Bob saw the man's embarrassment, not over the photographs, but for being there in the first place and for the man sitting behind Bob's desk. Travers motioned toward the first photo from Iraq, "I remember you said you were a Ranger in Iraq, and Mech Infantry?"

"Seventh Cav," Bob acknowledged with a slight nod of the head.

"Yeah?" Travers turned and smiled. "I ran the MP stockade right behind you guys. We were the ones stuck with all those prisoners you left behind in the dust. What a mess."

"War always is."

"This other one doesn't exactly look like the Army drill team at Fort Myer. What? Afghanistan? Special Ops?" Travers looked at him and asked, but all he got in return was an embarrassed shrug. "I know, I know. If you told me, you'd have to kill me," Travers laughed.

"Oh, Major Burke doesn't need to be that coy around us, does he?" O'Malley finally spoke up, not bothering to look up from the papers on the desk. "I read your 201 File."

"And anything else you can get your hands on." Bob turned his hard, humorless eyes on the little man. "Now, get the hell out of my chair."

"Perhaps you don't know who I am…"

"And perhaps I don't give a rat's ass if I do, Mister O'Malley. If you don't close my calendar and get the hell away from my desk, you'll be lying outside in the grass after I toss you through the window. You got that?"

O'Malley looked up at him for a moment, apparently surprised, but he slowly got to his feet and closed the cover of the desk calendar. "To quote your friend Travers, 'interesting.' " O'Malley then walked around to the front of Bob's desk and plopped in one of the guest chairs, while Bob went the other way around and retook his own desk chair. "As I was saying," O'Malley continued without skipping a beat, "I read your personnel file, or at least I tried — West Point and twelve years of extremely distinguished, highly-decorated service that anyone would be proud of. Unfortunately, all of the good stuff appears to be redacted. Imagine that. Over the years, I've examined more than my share of Army personnel files. I've got to tell you, I've never seen one with so many black lines and deletions."

"Really? I had no idea, Mister O'Malley; I was but a simple soldier, doing my duty," he answered, straight-faced. "But if you don't like the redacts, maybe you should call the Attorney General in

Washington. I'm sure he can get you a clean copy."

"I did." O'Malley chuckled. "That's what *he* sent me."

Bob tried not to smile. The office door opened and Maryanne Simpson walked in carrying a large cup of coffee, an urn, and two extra-strength aspirin, which she handed Burke. They exchanged knowing glances as he swallowed the aspirin dry. "Another refill, gentlemen?" she asked. They both shook their heads, so she quickly retreated and closed the door behind her.

Bob finally looked across at O'Malley. "All right, tell me what you want."

"To the point — I like that. As you apparently know, I am the US Attorney for Northern Illinois. My jurisdiction covers half the state plus parts of Wisconsin and Indiana. While it appears you have some very *unique* skills and training, I assume you did not go to law school, did you, Mister Burke?"

"No, while you were doing that, I was doing *that,*" Bob nodded toward the two photos on the wall, "and getting myself *redacted,* of course." He smiled, thinking Angie might have been right for once, about the photographs anyway.

"I guess I deserved that, didn't I?" O'Malley replied. "And I apologize if I came on a bit strong. The job of a US Attorney is to investigate and enforce Federal law within his jurisdiction. That covers a multitude of sins, literally, including graft, official corruption, income tax evasion, organized crime, Medicare and Medicaid fraud, tampering with Federal witnesses, and occasionally even murder, which, unfortunately, is what brings me to your office this morning, Bob… you don't mind my calling you Bob, do you?"

"Tell you what," Bob answered as he took another sip of coffee. "Let's leave it Mister Burke and Mister O'Malley. We aren't friends, and you aren't going to be here very long."

"We can play it your way, if that's what you want… Mister Burke. I understand you were involved in an incident over at Consolidated Health Care last night. Lieutenant Travers filled me in on the details. He said some good things about you so I asked him to introduce me." O'Malley picked up his briefcase and laid it across his knees. As he did, Burke glanced at Travers, who gave him a helpless shrug in return. O'Malley pulled out a set of glossy photographic prints which he began laying individually across the front edge of Burke's desk, one at a time for dramatic effect.

Bob leaned forward and took a quick look. There were six

photographs. They were headshots of women, brunettes and one dishwater blonde, all in their twenties or thirties. Three were formal portrait or studio shots in color, perhaps from a high school or college yearbook. The next two were also in color, but casual snapshots. One was slightly out of focus. It showed a woman holding a can of beer over her head, dancing in a crowded bar, while the other was of a younger brunette in a bikini at the beach. The last photograph was a stark, black-and-white police mug shot of a disheveled brunette, front view and side, holding a placard in front of her with a booking number. Bob looked closely at each face, figuring they were the real reason O'Malley came to see him this morning, but he said nothing.

"Do you recognize any of those women?" the US Attorney asked.

Bob reached out and touched one of the portrait shots. "This one," he immediately answered. "And this one," he added as he pointed to the woman in the bikini at the beach. "It's the same woman, the one I saw Greenway strangling on the rooftop yesterday." O'Malley's eyes lit up as if he had won the lottery. "However, before you wet your pants, it was getting dark and I was looking down through an airplane window as we flew by. Her hair is a lot shorter in this picture, and Greenway was on top of her, leaning forward, and partly blocking my view. That might cause you some problems with a good defense attorney."

"Let me worry about that." O'Malley dismissed the concern with a wave of his hand. "First impressions are usually the right ones, and you sound very positive."

"Oh, I am. I'll never forget her eyes. Things like that stay with you."

"I'm sure. And you are certain it was Greenway?"

"I might forget my wife's birthday or our anniversary, but I'll never forget the look on that bastard's face. It was him all right."

"Excellent," O'Malley commented. As the US Attorney looked down at the photographs again, Burke swore he could hear the wheels turning inside the man's head. "What about these other women?" he asked. "Do you recognize any of them?"

Bob leaned forward and looked at the photos a second time, finally pointing to the one on the far right, the one of the young woman in the bar, dancing with a can of beer. "This one. She looks like the CHC receptionist. What was her name?" he asked himself, trying to rub the headache out of his temple. "Sylvester, Linda Sylvester. Yeah, that was it. I saw it on the nameplate on the reception desk."

"Very good," O'Malley smiled, sounding pleased. "She's a fairly new hire and a friend of the dead woman. As I'm sure you realize, a receptionist can be a valuable source of information on any business these days. One way or another, everyone and everything passes by their desks, going in or out."

"I'll have to remember that, but she looks like she knows how to have fun," Bob replied, staring more closely at the photograph, and her face.

"That photo is seven or eight years old. She has a daughter, is divorced now, and started working at CHC a couple of months ago."

"Last night, when I said that the woman on the roof was wearing a white dress, she looked at Greenway and said, 'That was what Eleanor was wearing.' And she looked scared."

"She should be... and so should you. These people are not to be taken lightly," O'Malley warned, and then turned toward Travers. "Lieutenant, would you mind stepping outside for a few minutes?" Travers couldn't move fast enough, as he quickly excused himself from the room.

When Burke and O'Malley were alone, the US Attorney leaned forward. "What I'm about to tell you must be held in strictest confidence, Mr. Burke. I have impanelled a Federal Grand Jury, which is looking into Organized Crime and its role in the massive Medicare and Medicaid fraud in the Chicagoland area. This is not penny-ante street crime. It involves tens of millions of dollars, money that is being denied to the poor and elderly in this community who badly need it. By definition, Grand Jury proceedings are secret. They must be, if we hope to crack the syndicates who are perpetrating the crimes. I am telling you these things in order to enlist your cooperation with my investigation, but the specifics of the case must remain secret."

"Sure. So who was she?" Bob pointed to the dead woman's photo.

"Eleanor Purdue. She is, or was, head of accounting for CHC. She's scheduled to testify to my Grand Jury next week, but she appears to have gone missing. She was supposed to meet me last night and turn over more of their financial and business records, but she never showed. Then, when I saw the TSA report regarding what you allegedly saw and the details of your subsequent visit to the CHC building, some very unfortunate pieces fell into place."

"You think that's why Greenway killed her?"

"Him or the people he's working for. No doubt about that. You see, Consolidated Health Care began a dozen years ago as a storefront clinic serving the homeless and indigent in one of the worst neighborhoods on Chicago's infamous South Side. Greenway bootstrapped it into two or three more clinics, all legit and doing good work. For what he did back then, 'Larry' Greenway, as he was called, should be commended. Unfortunately, clinics like his on Medicaid and Medicare funding live hand to mouth. When the wrong people knocked on his door and offered to fill his pockets with cash and build him a dozen more clinics, he never looked back. In the best of circumstances, the ill-trained and badly overworked HHS financial management staffs in Springfield and Washington can't keep up with the paperwork. When you flood them with clever scams, slick accounting techniques, and massive overbilling, it's no contest. That was when 'Larry' Greenway became Doctor Lawrence Greenway in two-thousand-dollar suits."

"French cuffs, Italian leather shoes, and silk ties?"

"Only the best. The man you saw last night is not the same one who worked down on 63rd and Cottage Grove six years ago. His operation remains centered in Chicago's inner city, but he now has 22 clinics in five cities and three states, and is heavily into prescription drugs, switching the good stuff with substandard foreign concoctions, shoddy medical devices, neck and back trauma, physical therapy, 'mobility' devices, outpatient surgery, traffic accidents, in-home services, and anything else they can dream up. Those are the 'soft' medical services that are very hard to police, and wide open for fraud. Unfortunately, it's like stealing candy from a baby if you don't care whom you hurt."

"I assume that's where the guy with the gold chains and muscles comes in?"

"His name is Anthony Scalese, 'Tony Scales,' in Mafia-ese. He is an underboss and occasional muscle for Salvatore DiGrigoria, 'Sally Bats,' who is the current Capo of what used to be the Accardo–Giancana crime family here. Unlike New York, there's been only one mob 'family' running Chicago since Al Capone, even though it's now split into three branches of the DiGrigoria family."

" 'Tony Scales,' 'Sally Bats' — I thought they only talk that way in the movies."

"No, they're all too real. In the late 1970s, a burglary gang was dumb enough to hit Tony 'Big Tuna' Accardo's house in River Forest while he was vacationing in Palm Springs. Reportedly, Accardo was one of Capone's gunmen on St. Valentine's Day in 1929. Anyway, these burglars really messed up Accardo's house. Sal DiGrigoria was one of his lieutenants. He was called 'Sally Bats' because he liked Louisville

Sluggers, and not to play baseball. Within a month, all six burglars were hunted down and savagely beaten to death. The word is that Scalese is every bit as vicious, but his weapon of choice is a 9-inch stiletto, not a baseball bat."

"I don't have a nickname, Mr. O'Malley, and I don't scare easily."

"I gathered that, but I wanted you to understand the kind of people you're dealing with. Remember, many of the top city, county, and state officials around here, especially the police, and that includes your friend Sheriff Bentley and half the other elected officials in Indian Hills, have been on their payroll or taking campaign contributions from their 'front' businesses like CHC for years. If they can't buy someone, they're pretty good at intimidating anyone who gets in their way. If that doesn't work, people disappear."

"So you think that's what happened to your witness?"

"It's beginning to look that way. I have a fallback meeting with Eleanor tomorrow night, and there's the Grand Jury hearing on Tuesday. I hope she shows; but if she doesn't, I'll know she was the woman in the white dress you saw on the roof."

"My money says it was; and from the expression on Linda Sylvester, she knows it, too."

"They were friends. Did she say anything else to you?"

"No, Scalese hustled her out of the lobby before she could."

"They can be very scary people for a young woman," O'Malley reflected.

"But it was Greenway up on the roof strangling her, not Tony Scalese."

"That has me puzzled too. I know she was trying to get more documents to turn over to us. I told her to be careful, but maybe Greenway caught her. Then again, that man has raised sexual harassment to an art form. Eleanor told us he's chased, seduced, or raped half the women in the place; unfortunately, Eleanor included. That's why most of them are terrified of him, but not Eleanor. With her, it turned into a white-hot hatred and burning desire for revenge. In the end, that might have caused her to take one risk too many. Or maybe he went after her again, I really don't know."

"None of the other women have done anything about it?"

"They're too scared. Like Purdue and Sylvester, most of his employees are single women and they are very vulnerable. That's who Greenway hires and he pays them well. Besides, who can they can complain to? The Indian Hills Police? Chief Bentley? Or CHC corporate? Old Sal DiGrigoria? With Scalese backing Greenway up, the women put up with it and hope he picks on someone else. They learn to never go anywhere alone, especially not to his office, or they start carrying pepper spray or a box cutter in their purses."

"Sounds to me like you need to talk to Linda Sylvester," Bob told him. "You said they were friends, and she might have been one of the last people to see Eleanor alive."

O'Malley leaned forward and looked across the desk at him. "If I go over there and try to question her or call her in front of my Grand Jury, they'll be on her before I get out of my car. I would have to go in with badges, warrants, subpoenas, and Witness Protection, but Sylvester may not even know anything. No, that'll only scare her off and I'll end up with nothing."

"It didn't scare Eleanor Purdue."

"Eleanor has no kids or family in the area, and she was out for revenge for what Greenway did to her. Sylvester's a whole different story. She has a young daughter, and apparently, Greenway hasn't gotten around to her yet. That makes all the difference. That's why I need your help."

"My help? I've already told you everything I know — you, Travers and Bentley," Bob said. "So I don't know what else you think I can do."

"You can talk to Linda Sylvester. She heard what you said last night. You're a Good Samaritan who saw something and is seeking the truth. Unless I miss my guess, that girl needs someone to talk to about now; and maybe she'll open up to you. Perhaps you can nose around, remember a few more details than you did before, you and your finance man, Charlie Newcomb. That will rattle them a little, even if you have to make it up."

"Excuse me, don't they call that perjury?"

"It's my ball, my court, my game, and I'm the one who makes all the calls."

"I don't work that way."

"You will, Bob, you will; because you don't like what happened to Eleanor Purdue any more than I do, and you are in a unique position to help me stop them."

"Maybe, but if they're as dangerous as you say they are, why should I get involved?"

"Because I can get that Department of Defense contract back for you. Guaranteed. One phone call, and I can get that Summit Symbiotics proposal tossed out and yours reinstated. But if you don't help me, you'll never see it again." O'Malley leaned across the desk, his eyes cold and calculating. "I know all about your business problems, Bob. I know about the DOD contract, how you got screwed, and what's been going on between you and that crazy wife of yours. My people have only been checking you out since last night, but in another day or two, I'll know everything there is to know. Everything. If you help me, I can be very, very appreciative. Or I can be your worst enemy. It's your choice."

"That sounds like a threat."

"In Chicago? I prefer to call it reality. As I said, I'm up against some very bad people and I am asking for your help to bring them down. Besides, you don't like them either, especially Greenway. You saw him. You know what I'm talking about, and I think you want to bring him down every bit as much as I do."

Bob stared at him, his eyes as cold and hard as O'Malley's. Finally, he shrugged and said, "I'll think about it."

"I thought you might. The key is Linda Sylvester. Maybe if she sees you again, that might loosen her up and get her to talk."

O'Malley finally stood up, put the photographs back in his briefcase, and looked down at Bob's desk chair. "That's comfortable; I think I should get one of those," he said as he snapped the briefcase shut with a flourish. "Stay in touch, Mister Burke. Call me if anything comes up or you get any ideas. I have an army of people I can call in to help you, but you need to let me know. Chicago isn't the kind of place where you want to be out there on the high wire working alone without a net."

CHAPTER SIX

When O'Malley finally closed his briefcase and left, Bob Burke leaned back in his desk chair and ran his fingers through his hair, scratching an itch that refused to go away. He would rather have kept his old Army buzz-cut, but Angie pouted for at least a month, sticking out her lower lip and whining, "Bob-by, 'Army hair' is ugly. It makes you look like a dumb goober." That girl knew how to pout, almost as well as she knew how to do many other things, too. Unfortunately, that was only the beginning of her personal "Project Bobby." She dressed him in custom-made $2,000 suits, handmade $200 shirts, and $150 ties, and he became her personal Ken Doll. He hated the clothes even more than the haircut, but he was stuck wearing the business suits she bought until the day she walked out. Since then, he only wore what he wanted to wear, and the hair was next on his list.

He met Angie when he was on leave at Hilton Head. He was a tired, burned-out grunt and she was nine years younger with no "off" button. She relit fires he forgot he had; and for the next two years, they were as hot as two teenagers on Prom night. Like a moth drawn to a flame, he couldn't resist her or her father's subsequent job offer, so he put in his retirement papers and never looked back.

Ed Toler desperately needed decisive new leadership to move his company forward and found in Bob Burke exactly what he was looking for — someone who knew how to lead and who valued the company and its people as highly as he did. Angie was his only child and would inherit the business, but she was hopeless as a business manager. She liked good things and good times but she always viewed the company as her personal cookie jar. Ed knew that as soon as he was gone she would be digging into it with both hands and would run the company right into the ground. Bob Burke, on the other hand, hit the ground running. He learned the business from the bottom up and provided Ed the succession he so desperately sought. Unfortunately, that put Bob and Angie on a bitter collision course from which their marriage would never survive.

Well, it was too late for regrets, and he never fretted over things he had no control over. There were meetings he needed to schedule with key staff over the DOD contract and he needed to put in some serious face time with his accountants and lawyers. There were also two idiot congressmen with whom he needed to have some blistering phone calls. In the end, Bob realized getting screwed by the colonels at DOD was largely his own fault. Not having been forewarned by the politicos was all on them, of course, but he knew you get no more than you pay for with a congressman. Obviously, Summit Symbiotics spent a lot more on them than he had.

However, the first thing he needed to do was talk to Charlie. One of Bob's favorite quotes was from Dirty Harry who said, "A man's got to know his limitations," and Bob Burke was painfully aware of his. He was a decent manager, a people person, and a good leader. What he was not was a finance or numbers man, and there was no need for him to try to become one. All that was necessary was for him to know what he didn't know, and then hire people who did. That was where Charlie Newcomb came in. He was overweight, sloppily dressed with at least one shirttail hanging out, and had more pens and pencils in his shirt pocket than an MIT electrical engineer. For the next two hours, he and Charlie remained bent over Bob's conference table, staring at lines of red numbers. While Bob made the occasional phone call to their bankers, lawyers, and some of their larger remaining customers, Charlie continued to comb through spreadsheets as his fingers pounded his laptop's keyboard. By 3:00 o'clock, you could see the desperation in the room running down the walls.

"We're toast, aren't we?" Bob finally concluded as he let his subconscious doodle on a yellow legal pad. That was what he usually did when he was thinking; but this time, he came up with nothing, and so did the doodles.

"Bottom line?" Charlie squinted at the machine. "By the end of this fiscal year, we need to either go out and find $1.5 million in new business… or right now, today, begin to shed $500,000 in current, hard-dollar expenses. There's a continuum of choices in between, of course, and maybe we can get a couple of loans, but those are the most workable numbers."

"I expected something like that."

Charlie nodded, finally asking him, "You sorry you got out of the Army?"

"Every minute of every damned day," he answered with a smile. "But no, not really. It was time. I was burned out, and I needed to get away from all that."

"I think I understand. Do you think there's any hope we can get the DOD contract back?"

"I plan to talk to them, light a fire under our congressman, yell, scream, and generally raise as much stink as I can, but I'm not optimistic.

Maybe we can get a piece of the business back, or get Symbiotic to throw us a bone and subcontract some of it to us, but none of that's gonna do very much in the long run," Bob said with a heavy sigh. "Wait a minute, though. Aren't we insured? What if we kill one of us? Would that help?"

"The corporate Key Man insurance policy? Actually, I was staring at the ceiling last night and came up with the same idea," Charlie answered. "It would only get us about halfway there, and the survivor would have to go to jail; so, no, I'm afraid we're going to have to shed a lot of payroll and expenses, and not you or me."

"It isn't the payroll shedding that bothers me. We were small and efficient before, and we can get that way again. It's letting a lot of good people go that I hate. That's not why I took this job. I wanted to build the business up, not tear it down."

"You know, it really would help if we could get Angie off the payroll."

"Angie?" Burke laughed.

"Her salary and her 'expenses' are a big nut we've been carrying ever since Ed died."

"We'd need a hit man, and we could never afford one who was good enough."

"Or brave enough to try?" Charlie added, and they both began to laugh. "It would be like going after a big grizzly bear; what if he missed or only wounded her?"

"Actually, I was thinking more like Godzilla, in the last movie."

"The one with Matthew Broderick, the last scene, where Godzilla kept on coming and coming?"

"Yeah, but Angie's more determined."

"And Godzilla's easier to get along with."

"Hey, that's my almost, soon-to-be-ex-wife you're talking about!"

"Speaking of which, when are you gonna call her?" Charlie dared ask.

Burke slumped back in his chair. "Why did you have to remind me, when things were going so well."

Fortunately or unfortunately, he didn't have to. His intercom buzzed and he heard Maryanne Thomas's nervous voice say, "Bob? You'd better duck. Angie's on her way back, and she doesn't look very happy."

"Oh, shit," the two men muttered in unison.

The dreaded Angie did not wait to be let in or announced. The door flew open and slammed into the sidewall, and she stormed in and began reaming him out before it stopped swinging.

"You moron! You are such an asshole!" she glared, directing her full ire at Bob.

"You need to focus on one insult at a time, Angie; it's more effective that way," he managed to get in.

"Don't make jokes, Bobby." She glared at him. "You lost the DOD contract? The goddamned DOD contract?"

"That's… That's not fair, Angie," Charlie tried to interject. "Bob didn't…"

"Shut up, Charlie!" Her hand cut through the air like a knife and silenced him. "No one was talking to you," she said as she turned her hate-filled eyes back on Bob. "Why don't you get out of here and stop fighting me, while there's still something here that someone would want to buy. You can take your pet toad with you and those gung-ho Army photos on the wall too."

"Hey! Putting those up was your idea not mine," Bob countered with a half-smile. "If you don't like the interior decorating, blame yourself, not me."

"Stop interrupting!" she snapped as she closed in, pointing at him with a sharp, angry finger. "And don't worry, it's all gonna get redone, real soon. My father may have thought you were the son he never had, but I hate to break the bad news — I'm an only child!"

"I am well aware of that, Angie dearest."

"Besides, you don't know shit about high tech."

"Neither do you. I never wanted the company, and you know it. That was your father's idea, because he figured it was the only way he could 'keep you in the style to which you became accustomed,' as he put it. He knew you'd blow through the whole thing in five years and there'd be nothing left — no money, no company, and no jobs — they'd all be gone."

Hands on hips, she glared down at him. "You're missing the point. I'm his daughter. It was supposed to be *mine*, not *yours*, and it's none of your goddamn business what I do with it."

"That's not the way your father looked at it."

"No? Well, you should have stayed in the damned Army. Eating out of cans and blowing things up are about all you were ever good for."

"Oh? There was a time you thought the list was a little longer than that."

"Don't flatter yourself. I'm not nineteen anymore, this isn't the backseat of your Chevrolet, and frankly, I've had better. See, I grew up, Bob, and so have my tastes. So I'm calling a board meeting. You have until close of business today to resign. If you don't, I'll take the company from you and you'll end up with nothing!"

"A board meeting, Angie? You've tried that before," he shrugged. "It didn't work then, and it won't work now."

"This time it will. When you lost that DOD contract, you've got everyone scared."

He ran his hands through his hair and took a deep breath. "What do you want, Angie?" he asked in disgust. "I need to be spending my time getting it back, and shaking the trees for some new work, not sword fighting with you. You know that, and so will the Board."

"I already have proxies on 47%."

"Got the union guys to drink your Kool-Aid?"

"Maybe, and by the board meeting, I'll have a lot more. If that doesn't work, I'll get the banks to call your notes."

Bob sat up, looked at her, and shook his head. "Why would you do that? Your father spent his life building this company. This isn't an ego thing for me. All I want is to see the company back on track and profitable again."

"It's supposed to be *my* company, Bobby. *Mine*! He was *my* father, not yours, and I don't have a big emotional attachment to the place like you do. In fact, I don't have an emotional attachment to much of anything anymore, except money. An appraiser friend of mine told me, 'It don't matter what you think or what you want; a business is worth what it'll fetch in dollars — not a penny more and not a penny less.' "

"An appraiser? What happened to the tennis pro at the club and the bartender at the Hilton?" he asked sarcastically. "But it's nice to see you're getting your business advice from someone with a little substance for a change."

"Very funny. I need money, Bobby, and I don't give a damn how I get it. However, if you and your numbers genius here can figure out a way to buy me out..."

"Buy you out? Sure, we can talk about that after we get things back on course."

"No. Too bad, so sad, but I'm not waiting. If you can't come up with the money right now, I'm taking over and I'll sell the damned thing."

Angie was her father's biggest frustration. With her high-spending lifestyle, he knew she would do exactly what she said she would do — cash the company out as soon as he was gone. He was not about to let her do that and tried his best to get her to care, but it was hopeless and they fought about it constantly. When Angie dragged Bob home the first time and introduced him to her father, he thought she was putting him on. Every other boy she brought home was a moron whom Ed immediately hated. But a career Army officer, West Point, ten years older than she was, sensible, polite, and someone he could actually carry on an adult conversation with? It had to be a put-on. She must have rented him from central casting, Ed thought, and that was before he learned about Bob's skills and combat record. He knew he dared not gush, much less act like he approved. That would kill the romance for sure. Once it became clear that Bob was real, and that he and Angie were serious and actually planning to get married, Ed approached him about leaving the Army and joining the company.

"I don't know a damned thing about business, Ed, much less telecommunications," Bob told him, but it didn't matter.

"Hell, Bob, I can buy all the techies, lawyers, and MBAs I want. I have an office full of those. What I can't buy is a leader, someone who can step in and run this place. The company is its people. You know how to read 'em, motivate 'em, hire 'em, and fire 'em, and that's something that can't be learned from a class or out of a book. One of my old friends, Larry Benson, once told me there were only two places that teach leadership like that — the Boy Scouts and the Army. As far as I know, you and I are the only two alumni of both of those that I see around here, and I ain't lookin' for an Eagle Scout."

The title Ed gave him was Vice President but Bob's first assignment was on a truck as an installer trainee, then bench repairman, and finally as a salesman, calling on customers and prospects, learning the business lines from the bottom up. After two years, he was well on his way toward understanding field and headquarters operations when the old man died. That forced a serious shortening of the management-training ladder and Bob found himself in charge.

Ed hoped that Bob might be able to tame Angie and control her, or at least slow her down, once they got married. Unfortunately, that was as hopeless as it ever was. The way she spent money, keeping it all in the family was probably the only way any man would be able to afford her. "Hell," he said, "it's all gonna be hers in the end anyway. Maybe she'll figure that out before she drives you nuts, too." Nice in theory, but she never did.

The headstrong young tigress did, however, make one hell of a lover on the weekends while Bob was still in uniform, but their marriage quickly proved to be an emotional disaster. For the first two years, Bob worked his way up through sales, marketing, operations, and management while the old man got sicker and sicker. He saw their marital train wreck coming too and realized that if he did not take steps to protect the family business and its people, a vengeful Angie would soon destroy everything in her path. Ed and his attorneys spent a long weekend out of town, supposedly duck hunting up in Wisconsin. When they came back, he finalized the outline of a clever stock distribution plan that would solve the control and liquidation problem, or so he thought.

For most of the past decade, Toler TeleCom did plain vanilla, commercial communications and security systems work. It was steady, predictable, and profitable, but Ed longed to take a shot at the big time — the prestigious and lucrative defense contracting market. Angie was on the Board of Directors too, holding her late mother's shares and seat, and she fought with her father constantly about the direction they should take. To her, the company was little more than a cash cow to support her increasingly expensive tastes, and she never wanted him to venture beyond their comfortable, mainstream, Midwest base.

"Those I-495 Beltway bandits are going to eat you alive, Dad," she warned. "It's all politics back there, and you know it. You're gonna lose your butt!"

"Well, it's my butt to lose, isn't it?"

"For the moment." She glared at him.

"Angie, a business grows or it dies; but it can never stand still. Besides, I built this company for all the good people who work here, not only for you."

"Well, it's gonna be mine, whether you like it or not, isn't it?"

"That all depends on whether or not you finally grow up."

The week Ed got his test results and knew he was headed for the hospital, probably for that last time, he named Bob Burke President and CEO, promoting him over four other Vice Presidents, including Angie. They were already separated by then, and Ed's new stock distribution and succession plan gave Bob controlling interest in 27% of the company's stock, via a loan that he would be required to pay back if he ever tried to sell the shares. The same was true for the other recipients. He pegged the security for the loans to the value of the stock at the time of distribution, effectively tying everyone's hands. Ed put another 26% of the stock into a trust for the other salaried employees, based on their positions and seniority. Their existing 401K and its board would manage that trust. Similarly, the company's blue-collar craft union pension plan got another 24%. That left Angie with 23% of the outstanding shares, including her mother's, which she already owned.

Ed's stock distribution plan was diabolical. Angie's 23% effectively froze her out of control of the company. Both the union and the white-collar trusts could only be voted as blocks. Even if Angie got the blue-collar union with its 24% to join with her, or the salaried white-collar employees with their 26%, she would still fall short unless she could attract the support of *both* the management trust and the unions. As Ed well knew, the likelihood of that happening was slim to none. On the other hand, with 27%, Bob retained control of the company so long as he continued to hold the support of either the union or the other managers. In addition, his grant of shares prohibited each of those groups from selling more than 20% of their holdings in any one year, and the company retained the right of first refusal to buy them. So Ed could rest easy knowing that his darling daughter could continue to live her ridiculously stylish lifestyle on the company's dividends and earnings, but that was all she would get. She could yell, scream, and file lawsuits to her little heart's content, but she was powerless to cause the company any serious damage, sell it, or break it up.

That was, until the DOD contract blew up in Bob Burke's face.

CHAPTER SEVEN

Angie finally left. So did Charlie. Bob shook his head and reached for the bottle of twenty-five-year-old Macallan single-malt scotch in his bottom desk drawer, and poured himself three fingers in a heavy cut-glass tumbler, neat. Drinking scotch in the middle of the afternoon wasn't something he did regularly, but Ed had left it as a "special" present. "A tot of this golden nectar can even make a rotten day feel a little bit better," he wrote on the card. The Macallan did help during some bad times, as Burke well remembered, so why not now? He spun his desk chair toward the window, propped his stocking feet on the credenza, and leaned back with the tumbler sitting on his chest.

Normally, this was a great way to end a day — looking out the window into a glorious afternoon sky through the amber glow of a fine glass of scotch. Not today, though. Ever since he boarded the airplane in Washington, D.C., to return home, he felt as if he were on a downward spiral, helplessly spinning downward faster and faster. Most of that was a result of the loss of the DOD contract and the convulsions that would cause within the company, but Angie's visit, her threats, and O'Malley's visit all contributed. Charlie was right, however. The business deserved every bit of his attention. He owed it to the people who worked here, but he couldn't give it. Not today. The images of Eleanor Purdue being strangled on the Consolidated Health Care building roof and the look on that bastard Greenway's face kept popping up inside his head, and they wouldn't go away. Neither would Peter O'Malley's offer. While he was in the Army, Bob Burke never liked politicians, not that he gave them much thought. They expected career soldiers to avoid politics and politicians whatever their ilk, and Bob Burke never wasted time on things he could not do anything about anyway. Since he became a civilian and tried to manage a business, his opinion of them steadily worsened. O'Malley was one more classic example of the breed — a self-centered egomaniac one should never trust, and whose concern stretched no further than his own re-appointment, the front page of The Tribune, and an eventual run for political office. Mayor? a seat in the Senate? Even Governor. Politics. It was the nature of the beast these days. But like a well-executed judo throw, a Nageaza, the question was, how could Burke use O'Malley's own ego and bluster against himself?

As he downed the last of the scotch, he heard a hurried knock on his door and Charlie burst in holding his laptop in front of him with one hand, while still beating on the keys with the other. "Bob," he said without waiting for an invitation, "I did some digging into Summit Symbiotics..."

"You too? I tried for a while, but all I got was garbage, PR crap, and a migraine."

"It took some serious database mining to get past all that. No offense, but techie stuff like that's well below your pay grade. Besides, you're too old to even try."

"What do you mean too old?" Bob asked as he spun around and sat up.

"Seriously? The next time you have a system or database issue and I'm not around, go to the mall and find a twelve-year-old with an iPad, or a sixteen-year-old freshman at MIT. You're a dinosaur when it comes to this stuff, and it absolutely isn't worth your time." Finally, Charlie took his eyes off the screen, looked down at Bob's desk, and saw the bottle. "Macallan? Twenty-five-year-old? You're way too cheap to buy good swill like that. Where'd you get it?"

"Ed Toler left it for me... for medicinal purposes, of course."

"And you've been holding out?"

"There's another tumbler on the bookcase and plenty of shots left in the bottle. Pull up a chair and tell me what you found."

Charlie didn't need to be asked twice. He filled his glass and took a chair on the other side of Bob's desk. "I went back through Symbiotics' proposal, and pawed through their corporate papers. Their office address is a PO Box in D. C. and they incorporated in Delaware. It's cheap, very pro-business, and the state makes it hard to access the documents and then drill down through the layers to get at the real ownership."

"Nothing unusual there."

"True, but what *is* unusual, is that Symbiotic only incorporated thirty days ago. All of the reports and papers — all of them — their Annual Report, the PR material in the proposal, even the Articles of Incorporation and the official filings are very light on names and photographs of officers, staff, places, preceding corporations, and *anything* that they have actually done, including contracts, projects, previous customers, and all the rest."

"Thirty days?" Bob asked. "I remember the crap we went through, all the hoops DOD made us jump through to even be allowed to submit. How the hell did they give a start-up outfit like that such an important contract?"

"How? Well, if they really are legit, maybe they're an off-book spinoff from some major corporation that did a lot of DOD work. As far as I can tell, though, Symbiotic has no corporate linkage to anybody. Okay, then I wondered if maybe DOD knew the people? I mean, they could be some good tech people who quit somewhere else, DOD knows them, and they're doing it at a loss to get a foot in the door. Who knows? I suppose it happens."

"It happens? No, Charlie, shit happens! That was our contract. Who are they?"

"Precisely! You and I are in the business and we know most of the techies in our little niche. It's a small fraternity, especially if they are doing military telecom work, right? Well, I looked through every piece of paper I could find, and dug out the names of every one of their officers and key technical people. Guess what? They're all lawyers! Every goddamned one of them. I looked some of them up in Martindale-Hubbell, the national directory of lawyers and law firms, but I didn't need to. Most of the ones in the Symbiotic papers have their law firm affiliations written below their names. Obviously, someone plugged them in to fill the required slots, but there isn't a telecom exec or manager in the whole bunch."

"Lawyers?"

"Yep, lawyers, and it gets worse. You remember the firm Angie used when she tried to contest the old man's will — Gordon and Kramer downtown. Well, guess who Summit's registered agents are? Gordon and Kramer. Summit Symbiotics is a Delaware corporation, which is a subsidiary of Summit Industries, also a Delaware corporation, which is in turn owned by — you got it — Summit International, a Delaware holding company, with murky layer after murky layer. However, for a Federal bid and contract, they must be registered. After digging, and digging, and digging some more, I finally found a list of their ownership and Board of Directors. Naturally, it consists of eight of the top partners of Gordon and Kramer."

"No tech people?"

"Actually, they have two. They even put their photos in the annual report standing in front of a huge satellite dish array in the desert, complete with horn-rimmed glasses, lab coats, and clipboards, trying to look like they knew what they're doing."

"Out in the desert?" Bob scratched his head. "I don't get it."

"Neither do they. My guess is, they threw a paper-signing party in Vegas and took some promo shots outside town at that big satellite dish array at the UNLV research center."

"So, who are they?"

"You remember that guy Randy Person and his pal Harry Ingersoll?"

"The two guys we fired? You gotta be kidding!"

"Nope, I'm serious as an undertaker."

"Person and Ingersoll... as I remember, one of them gussied up his résumé and the other was so abrasive that no one would work with him. Total zeros, both of them."

"That's them. We fired them last summer. As usual, to avoid being sued, nobody outside the office knew about it. One morning they were here, the next morning they were gone; because that was best for everyone, right?"

"Why do I sense a migraine coming here?"

"Migraine? Oh, this one's gonna twist your shorts good. What's the common thread?"

"I'm getting a sick feeling you're gonna tell me it's Angie."

"Give the man a cigar. She knew all about those two. I'm sure you discussed their termination at the board meeting, right? When we let them go, they became a couple of techies she could hire cheap. And Gordon and Kramer are her lawyers."

"Strike two," Bob groaned.

"Finally, for a two-out, top of the 9th, three-and-two hard-cheese 'I bet you can't hit this' fastball on the inside corner, when I dug deep enough into the papers and tax records of that holding company in Delaware, she's listed as the freaking Chairman of the Board!"

Bob stared at him, speechless, unable to breathe, feeling as if something sucked the air out of the room. "That's gotta be a mistake. Why would Angie do something like that? Are you sure?" As he looked across the desk at Charlie, he could see he was.

"You know her a tad better than I do, of course," Charlie smiled, "but I got the impression she never liked one pair of shoes, if she could get two."

"Or six, or ten."

"Not that I fully understand the intricate working of the female mind, especially hers; but she's already tried to force you out a couple of times, running straight at you through the board. When that didn't work, maybe she decided to make an end run, go for the DOD contract, and put you and the company out in the cold. Do you think she could be that malevolent, that clever?"

"Angie? You bet your knutchkies she could; but why would she tear the house down around herself? That's lose-lose, for us and for her... isn't it?"

"No, anything but, Bob! Think about it. She'd have the new company, which she would be in complete control of, a handpicked board, her own staff, and she'd have the new DOD contract; albeit with no way to carry it out, but that doesn't matter. After she wrecks Toler TeleCom, she can come back here and cherrypick whatever tech guys she needs."

"You're right," Bob said as he slumped back in his chair. "Why didn't I see it?"

"Because your mind doesn't work like that. If she can force you out at this new board meeting, that's even better. She can skip a few steps, merge the two companies, and have it all."

"We've got to get that DOD contract back."

"It's our only chance."

"Yeah, but I'm so damn tired right now. I feel brain-dead. After that woman on the roof, and then Greenway, and O'Malley... I can't focus."

"You've got to," Charlie answered as he closed his laptop and scooped up the papers strewn across Bob's desk. "I'll admit you have other 'woman problems' right now, but the really *big* problem is with the live woman you married, not the dead one on the roof."

"Yeah, I get it. It's time for you to go back to your office and think, and it's time for me to make some phone calls."

"You'd better reach out to the Trustees of both of the pension plans, and the banks."

"I know, but I'm starting with George Grierson."

"The lawyer? Yeah," Charlie agreed. "He should probably be first." With that final ugly thought, Charlie drained the last of his scotch and left Bob alone with his phone.

Three hours later, he tossed his pen on the desk and shook his head. Pension plan trustees, bankers, and lawyers — he felt drained. Angie had them in a vice and was tightening it as fast as she could. Still, he looked down at the yellow legal pad sitting in front of him. It was covered with doodles, but there was not a serious thought about Toler TeleCom to be seen. He had drawn dramatic sketches of airplanes, water towers, and police cars, plus the intricate, overly stylized initials "CHC." This was getting him nowhere, he realized, as he turned and looked out the window. Angie and the DOD contract might be his big problems, but the woman on the roof refused to be pushed aside. Every time he closed his eyes, she was there, lying on her back in the brown gravel, staring up at him, with Lawrence Greenway's long fingers wrapped around her throat. She was there, hovering front and center in his conscience, and she was not going away until Burke did something about her.

Reluctantly, he pushed the pad of paper away, opened the keyboard drawer to his desk, and turned his eyes to his computer monitor. The Army spent years and tens of thousands of dollars teaching him to act on instinct, to trust his gut, and to make life-and-death decisions on a very short list of facts. After six months on this job, his sharp-edged tactical training was being dulled by computer searches, too many meetings, and mountains of e-mail. Sad but true. Now, there wasn't a problem he needed input on or an issue he could create, or even think of creating, that Google wouldn't bury him under a mountain of useless online information in the time it took to type it into a search engine. It was paralysis-by-analysis, the usual cause of stagnation in the business world, and it drove him crazy.

However, the second critical skill the Army taught him was to know your enemy. His fingers dropped to the keyboard and he typed in 'Consolidated Health Care.' He barely hit Enter when a cascading list of newspaper and magazine stories filled the screen. Below the search box it said, "About 11,370 Results. 0.27 seconds." Wow, he thought. In the new age of information overkill, it became incredibly easy to hide things. All you have to do is leave it out in plain sight halfway down a list like that. Who would ever find it? Still, he knew he must try. Jumping around from subject to subject, from corporate information, to press releases, to newspaper and magazine stories, he could see CHC ballooned up in a very short time from one inner-city clinic to a major Medicare provider in the "urban" Chicago area and surrounding states, but O'Malley's numbers were already out of date. They did $87 million in business last year, primarily Medicare and Medicaid, with a staff of five hundred and twenty-five employees at seventeen corporate and clinic locations, plus several new drug-manufacturing operations in India and Pakistan. No wonder Chief Bentley went into protective overdrive when Burke and Travers came knocking. No question, CHC must be Indian Hills biggest employer and taxpayer.

CHC's website was very slick, with beautiful, full-color photography, professional shots of the Indian Hills headquarters, the clinics in the city, and their new pill factory in India, as well as a long list of departments and subjects. Funny, but the more Bob saw, the less he knew. Digging through their official corporate reports and filings, he saw the same multilayered structure with interlocking corporations and holding companies that Charlie noted with Summit Symbiotics. Like everything these days, domestic or foreign, from cars and refrigerators to corporations, it was damned hard to tell who owned what anymore, where anything was made, what it was made of, and whether it might kill you if you ate it. The most frequent answers now seemed to be China and "You really don't want to know."

Their website was an electronic version of their annual report. Taking a cue from Charlie, he clicked to the back pages, where he saw what he was really looking for — the names, photos and bios of the Board Members, Principal Officers, and Executives of CHC. Front and center on almost every page was the smiling, debonair face of Lawrence Greenway. He was the President and CEO, apparently a child prodigy who was born and raised in Chicago, and earned a Doctor of Medicine from Loyola and an MBA from the Kellogg School at Northwestern. Not exactly chopped liver, Burke thought, and not to be underestimated. There followed some headlines and a collage of photographs showing the truly pioneering work Greenway did at his inner city clinics and what they were now doing overseas.

On the last few pages, he saw the photographs of the other Officers and Department Heads. His eyes immediately picked out the photograph of Eleanor Purdue. As O'Malley said, she was CHC's Chief Financial Officer and head of accounting. However, looking through the rest of the list and at the other photographs, he did not see Salvatore DiGrigoria, Tony Scalese, or anyone else with so much as an Italian last name. Figures, Bob thought.

Returning to the long page of Google search results, he found a list of press releases and news stories, mostly related to Lawrence Greenway's recent testimony in front of US House and Senate hearings on Medicaid and Medicare fraud and abuse. In several of the photos, Greenway appeared to be sitting comfortably in front of a bank of microphones at a witness table in one of the hearing rooms. Dressed in his usual impeccably tailored suit with his raven hair slicked back, he looked to be the confident lord of everything he surveyed. From the exhibition he put on in his corporate lobby the day before, Burke doubted the senators or congressmen at that Washington hearing could lay a glove on the man.

As he glanced through the accompanying articles, he found

himself in a quick double take. Rather than dodge questions or mutter platitudes, Greenway took the offensive. "Shame on you!" He sat at that hearing table and wagged his finger at the assembled congressmen. "You're the ones who wrote this horribly crafted legislation, not we in the medical services industry. All it does is invite fraud and abuse from our competitors. To top it all off, you take massive campaign contributions from the very people you're supposed to be regulating. That makes a mockery of the entire process."

Well, you can't accuse the man of not having chutzpah, Bob thought as he found himself laughing aloud. It was as if Greenway was daring the congressional committee to come after him, convinced that they couldn't touch him. He was probably right. He was slick, and he believed he was bulletproof. Interesting.

The flurry of news stories and press releases that followed the hearings appeared to have been generated by CHC's corporate public relations staff. They were designed to get the company's version of the facts out first, to brag about all the good things they did, and to spin them in the print and electronic media far ahead of anything that the legitimate press might manage to dig up on Greenway or CHC. Even if they did, CHC's PR people would jump on any real story or question and bury it under a blizzard of subsequent misinformation. However, while Greenway might think he was bulletproof, Bob wondered if that was the way Salvatore DiGrigoria looked at all this unwanted publicity. The Mob usually preferred to stay way below the radar, not to tweak Congress, and not to get their faces plastered all over the morning newspapers. No, he thought, that was not something Old Sal would have appreciated, which may be why he sent in his pet pit bull, Tony Scalese.

Bob leaned back in his desk chair and stared out the window again. It was all so obvious, he thought. He spent less than a day, a few hours really, and was he the only one who could connect the dots? Lawrence Greenway was a crook on a massive scale. Graft and corruption with federal contracts was nothing new, but Bob drew the line at murder and was determined not to let Greenway get away with it.

The sun was going down. He was not accomplishing a damned thing here in the office, and he knew he needed some fresh air. He turned the monitor off, locked his desk drawers, pulled on a blue nylon windbreaker, and headed for the door.

Downtown, on the 32nd floor of the Federal Building, US

Attorney for Northern Illinois, Peter Francis O'Malley III, was also staring out his office window into the setting sun. He leaned back in his desk chair, his stocking feet propped up on his window ledge, thinking, and getting even angrier than Bob Burke. Finally, he spun the chair around, and glared up at his assistant, FBI Agent Mike Hanover, who stood in front of his desk like an obedient Doberman, waiting patiently for his master's orders. He had worked for O'Malley for six months, ever since O'Malley received his Presidential Appointment to the position. O'Malley was the third US Attorney for whom Hanover worked, and while six months was not a long span in a government position like this, Hanover had already learned to detest the intense, miniature Irishman. Today was one more painful lesson as to why.

"I don't give a rat's ass, Mike! Keep digging until you find something, and don't come back until you do. If that smartass Burke won't jump in front of Greenway's train, then I guess I'll have to throw him there and see what happens."

"Chief, we've been digging, but the guy's clean. He's a war hero."

"Find something, goddammit! I want leverage. Dig up some dirt on him or his company or that slut of a wife of his — I don't care which or how, only when. And don't worry about him not being dirty; he will be when I get through."

CHAPTER EIGHT

Angie lay naked on a lounge chair on the massive pool deck of her father's big house — now her big house — in Winnetka, finishing what was left of a bottle of the best Riesling she could find in his wine cellar. Decisions, decisions, she complained, unable to make up her mind whether to spend what was left of the afternoon out here finishing the wine, or go to the club for an early evening "tennis lesson" with Klaus the "pro." Ever since Bob moved out, there was no one around to pester or harass when she got horny. That bastard! Fortunately, at that moment her housekeeper Consuelo stepped out the rear kitchen door and cautiously approached her. Angie's temper was notorious, and the hired help knew she did not like surprises.

"Mee-sus Burke," Consuelo said softly, "there's a Mee-ster O'Malley at the front door to see you. His card say he is the US Attorney…"

"Yeah, I know who he is."

"He does not have an appointment, so I told him you were unavailable."

"No, you can send him out here," she answered as she put on her dark sunglasses and made a half-hearted effort to cover herself with a huge Turkish towel, leaving some of the more delicious areas partially exposed.

"Si, Mee-sus Burke," her housekeeper smiled hesitantly. "And… it is almost 4:00 now. I be leaving soon, so I put your salad in the refrigerator."

"That's fine, Consuelo. Bring us a couple of your special Texas Teas before you leave, *por favor*, and make his strong enough to peel paint."

Several minutes later, Consuelo returned, escorting a short, handsome man in an expensive blue suit.

"Pardon me for not getting up, Mr. O'Malley, but that might be a problem."

"I completely understand, Mrs. Burke," O'Malley laughed as he took the lounge chair opposite her. "A beautiful woman like you should take advantage of the sun while you can."

"Flattery only works on me if you're trying to get in my pants, Mr. O'Malley, and I don't think that's what you're trying to do, is it?"

"No, no, not at the moment," he laughed.

"That's good, since I'm not wearing any."

Only then did O'Malley realize how quickly this woman put him off his game, and that almost never happened to him. The sun was behind her and shining uncomfortably into his eyes, while she wore dark glasses, and he could not see her eyes at all. Did she plan it this way? Knowing what he already knew about her, he wouldn't be surprised. That was when the housekeeper returned and placed a tall icy glass in front of each of them.

Angie raised her glass toward him. "To the wheels of justice, Mr. O'Malley, may they not run over your foot," she said as she took a sip from her glass.

He laughed as he tipped his glass up and took a big swallow, suddenly coughing as the potent mixture of almost straight tequila hit his throat. "Sorry about that," he told her. "Must have gone down wrong," he added as he coughed a few more times.

"Sometimes Consuelo doesn't measure very well."

"So it seems. Anyway, I'm Peter O'Malley, I'm the US..."

"I know who you are."

"That didn't sound very warm and friendly, Mrs. Burke."

"You can call me Angie, and let's say I'm not a huge fan of the US Government at the moment."

"Ah, the DOD contract your company lost."

"Lost? We didn't lose anything, it was stolen; and unfortunately, it isn't my company at the moment, as I suspect you already know. Is that why you are here? Are you launching an investigation of Summit Symbiotics and those colonels over at DOD procurement?"

"No, no," he smiled as he picked at the seam of his trousers. "Actually, I'm here for some information on your husband."

"Bobby? He's not here and I doubt he is coming back. As I'm sure you know, we aren't exactly on the best of terms at the moment, business or personal. We've separated."

"So I hear. I actually spoke with him this morning in his office regarding a murder he claims to have witnessed last night. I know that has nothing whatsoever to do with your company, but frankly, he wasn't as friendly or cooperative with my investigation as I hoped he might be."

"That doesn't sound like him; he's about as 'straight arrow' as they come, but he doesn't like being pushed around."

"So I understand. But tell me something; you are separated, why not divorced?"

She shrugged and looked around at the pool and the house. "You know, I guess I haven't found the time."

O'Malley nodded. "Still hoping?" he asked. She smiled back, but volunteered nothing so he continued. "Anyway, I asked my staff to take a look at his Army records so that I could get a better handle on the man, you know."

"And you didn't learn very much, did you?"

"Frankly, I've never seen so much redacting and blank pages in my life. The last half of his career appears to be completely classified."

"Even to a big-shot US Attorney? I'll bet that got you mad."

"Frankly, it did; but it also made me very curious. What can you tell me about him?"

"You mean what did he do in the Army, in Iraq and Afghanistan?" she laughed.

"Well, yes, that would certainly help, and anything else you know about what he did."

"Me? Not a damned thing. He never opened up to me or anyone else outside the service as far as I know. Maybe to my father, but he's long gone now. So I suspect you know more about that part of his life than I do. To tell you the truth, though, I couldn't care less, never did. That was his 'guy' thing, him and his pals, and I was permanently locked out. I could have the rest of him, but never that. When you tell that to a 'tender' young bride, especially one like me, it really hacks them off. So I said, 'screw you!' You have your little secrets, and I'll have mine."

"Interesting… You know, there's a wall of photos and plaques in his office…"

"Awful, aren't they? My father left all that crap. I tried to get a decorator…"

"No, no not those. One shows your husband with his troops in Iraq. The other one is of him and what could only be a Delta force or CIA Special Ops team in Afghanistan."

"And you're thinking to yourself, 'When I met that guy in the office, he didn't look like much, did he? Pretty ordinary, in fact.' "

"West Point, Rangers, Delta Force? I'm surprised he was big enough to get in."

"He told me he ate a lot of bananas and stood up straight," she laughed. "The other guys in that photo look like a bunch of low-lifes you wouldn't want to meet in a dark alley, while Bobby looks like the supply clerk who gave them a case of beer so he could get in their photo and get some free drinks at the VFW back home."

"Now that you mention it," O'Malley smiled.

She shook her head. "Well, that's not the way *they* tell it."

"So, you met them?"

"Most of his Special Ops guys were at our wedding. Vinnie, Ace, Chester, and Lonzo — those four I will never forget. They were his senior sergeants, and they have that magical bond he said only soldiers in a war can share. They remain intensely loyal to each other, and to him, even now. No matter what they were doing, they came to the wedding, at least the ones who weren't dead or off on some other god-awful mission somewhere. Apparently, they all think they owe him big time, and they'll tell you, they'd go to war with him all over again, any place, anytime."

"So, they talked to you about what they did, what he did?"

"Oh, God no! All I got was a comment here and a look there, enough for them to let me know I should appreciate what I was getting. They all have nicknames, you know, for operational security. They call Bobby 'the Ghost,' or 'Casper,' because they said he could 'disappear' and you'd never even know he was there. And whether he had a gun, a knife, or only his bare hands, I got the idea that *he's* the one you wouldn't want to run into in a dark alley."

"Really… But with a distinguished career like that, why did he get out?"

"I am vain enough to think it was for me, but I doubt it. We were the hottest thing on the planet for a year or two, but it was the Army itself and the war that finally drove him out. It never seemed to end, and he lost too many classmates and friends in something that meant less and less to him the longer it lasted. He often said that if the Pentagon refused to study history, at least they could read some Kipling."

"Kipling? You're kidding."

"Nope. He's a very interesting man, undoubtedly the most interesting man I've ever met. I think if they had left him out in the bush with his men chasing the bad guys, he'd still be there; but that wasn't going to happen. The higher he got in rank and responsibility, the worse the bullshit became, until he couldn't take it anymore. He was on the list for Lieutenant Colonel, which I'm told was pretty remarkable for his age, and on the fast track for stars. That was when he and I hooked up, and my father made him an offer he couldn't refuse — me, the company, a fresh start, the whole enchilada." She paused and looked across at O'Malley for a moment. "All right, Peter, your turn. What do you want from me?"

"A glass of wine with a beautiful naked woman, what else could I possibly want?"

"Almost naked, Peter. With me, there is a magical difference."

"What more could life possibly offer?"

She smiled. "What more? I've been told that an evening around my pool under the stars with a fine bottle of wine can be most memorable," she smiled coyly.

"I'll have to work on that," O'Malley said as he leaned back, smiled, and straightened the crease in his slacks. "Unfortunately, the timing is very bad for me. You see, Bob holds the key to a very important prosecution I'm working on. He claims he saw a man strangling a woman to death on a roof..."

"The airplane thing, when he was landing at O'Hare?'

"Word travels fast. Yes, the woman was supposed to testify in front of my Grand Jury this week, but she's disappeared and I fear the worst has happened."

"I thought Bobby went to the police and told them what he saw. What's the problem?"

"There's no 'problem,' per se. However, I was hoping he would agree to be a tad more 'creative' regarding who and what he saw. Unfortunately, he wasn't interested in stretching his memory quite that far."

Angie looked across and laughed at him. "You wanted him to lie, so you could nail some perp, didn't you?"

"Well, I would phrase it a bit more delicately than that," he tried one of his most buttery smiles. "The man I am investigating is a sexual predator."

"How nice," she grinned. "I didn't realize sex was a federal crime now."

"Normally, it isn't, but this man has a long track record of sexual harassment and rape involving his employees, and we believe a number of murders as well. My main interest is his involvement in a massive Medicaid and Medicare fraud scheme; so, this is hardly a matter of my trying to 'nail' an innocent man."

"Regardless, Bobby's not wired that way, and he doesn't like to be pushed."

"I understand that, but I need his help to pressure the individual involved, so I can elicit his testimony against the criminal network he is involved in. In the end, what your husband may or may not have seen on the roof won't matter very much. He's simply leverage. As I said, I hoped your husband would be a useful means to a very necessary end, and I came up here to see if you could give me any hints as to how I could get him to do that."

"If that's why you came all the way up here, you wasted a lot of gas. He's gonna do what he wants to do, and what he thinks is right. If you want to change his mind, you need to give him a good reason. So, good luck with that, Mr. O'Malley. Good luck with that."

The sun was beginning to set when Bob Burke drove into the CHC parking lot. From the number of empty parking spaces, most of their corporate staff had already left for the day. The medians were well landscaped, with equally spaced, round-topped pear trees that cast long shadows across the lot. He pulled into a dark space in one of them a few hundred feet from the building's revolving front door and waited. He had a clear view into the brightly lit front lobby and some of the individual offices. At the back of the lobby were second and third floor balconies and walkways, which connected the two wings. With the lobby's two-story floor-to-ceiling glass front wall, it was like looking into a large-screen television set.

As he watched, he saw a handful of casually dressed male and female staff members walk by carrying papers, interspersed with janitors pushing carts, carrying trash bags, and vacuuming. Other staff members headed for their cars, leaving a couple of bulky men inside in dark suits with two-way radios. Bob assumed they were private security guards. While everyone else appeared eager to be on their way home, the men in the dark suits looked anything but. They strolled around the floors slowly, without much of a purpose as they checked doors, hallways, and faces. Hired guns, he concluded. Most of the ones working security jobs like this were younger, usually ex-military, minimally trained, paid a nudge or two above minimum wage, and invariably dressed in gray slacks, white shirts, short hair, and blue blazers with some kind of crest or company logo on the breast pocket. However, these guys looked different. They appeared older, their clothes were a tad too gaudy and mismatched, and they neither moved nor walked as if they had much training at all, much less at the hands of their Uncle Sam.

On the first floor in the center of it all sat the diminutive figure of Linda Sylvester, hunkered down behind the relative safety of her tall, semicircular marble reception desk. Relative safety? Not in that building, Bob Burke thought. From her movements, she looked to be putting her things away and straightening her desk, getting ready to leave for the day. From the look on her face and the way her eyes darted nervously around the lobby, she appeared as unhappy as the night before. Clearly, something was bothering her, and Bob had a good idea what that was. She pulled on her jacket, clutched her purse to her chest, walked quickly to the back of the lobby, and turned to the left. As she did, Bob saw the muscular figure of Tony Scalese appear on the second floor balcony above her. He motioned and called down to her. he could not hear what Scalese said, but her head suddenly jerked to the right as she looked up at him. He couldn't hear what she said back to him either, but she didn't stop. She kept walking away, clutching her purse even tighter as Scalese leaned over the balcony, pointed a finger at her and said something else. Whatever it was, this one didn't go unanswered. She pointed a finger up at him, glared, and shouted back as she vanished down the side hallway and was gone.

Bob's present vantage point gave him a good view of the front lobby and door, but he knew the company "worker bees" would have been told to park in the rear, so he put the car in gear and circled the building to the left. Sure enough, by the time he turned the building's corner he saw Linda Sylvester hurrying out the side door and across the parking lot. As she approached the driver side of an old, dark-blue Toyota and pulled out her keys, he pulled in next to her and rolled down his window. Her reaction was immediate. Her head whipped around and her hand came out of her purse holding a small can of pepper spray, which she pointed at him.

"You keep away from me!" she shouted, terrified, as she extended her arm with the pepper spray toward his open car window.

"Whoa!" he answered as he raised both hands. "All I want is to talk for a minute."

"They told me not to talk to you," she said as she quickly looked around to see if anyone was watching. "They told all of us not to talk to anyone, and certainly not to you!"

"Good for them, I only want to ask you a couple questions about the woman I saw on the roof last night," he went on anyway. "Eleanor Purdue? Is that her name?"

"Oh, is that all? You want me to talk about Eleanor. Are you crazy?"

"No one's watching us," he tried to reassure her, concluding that if she hadn't sprayed him by now, she probably wouldn't, not as long as he stayed in his car and didn't make any sudden moves toward her.

"They're always watching. They have cameras everywhere now. Everywhere!" she answered, desperate, almost on the verge of tears. "They've been watching me, bugging my phones, my house, probably my car for all I know, and they've probably been watching you too. They watch anyone who is a threat to them."

"Let them, I'm not afraid of them, and you shouldn't be either. If you'll help me, we can put an end to all of this."

"You really are crazy; don't you realize who you're dealing with? Well, I do, and I can't afford any trouble, Mr...."

"Burke, Bob Burke, and I can protect you. We can go to the police, to the US Attorney."

"Don't drag me into this. I have a daughter and... Oh, leave me alone!"

"The woman in the white dress, Eleanor? She was a friend of yours, wasn't she? She was a good friend, and now she's missing." She stared at him, wide-eyed, her lower lip quivering. Clearly, the girl was on the verge of a breakdown. "Linda," he pressed. "I looked online, at the CHC website and I saw her picture. She is your head of accounting and finance. I don't know if you know this yet, but she was supposed to testify to a Grand Jury next week. That's why Greenway killed her."

"Nobody killed anyone." She quickly shook her head. "You made all that up. Eleanor is traveling, that's all. They told me she needed to meet with the auditors, and left early."

"Look at yourself," Burke answered. "You don't believe that any more than I do. She was up on the roof with Greenway as I said, and you know it."

"No, no, you're wrong. That can't be."

"No? Well, when she doesn't show up this week or next, and they tell you she quit and moved, it will be too late. Come with me and we'll both go to the police. I'll take you."

"The police? Out here? You've got to be kidding."

"Not Bentley, real police, like that Chicago cop I was with, or the FBI."

"Dr. Greenway told me you're making all that stuff up to ruin CHC. He told us his competitors are out to get him now, out to get all of us. And I've got a family, Mister Burke, I've got a daughter and I need this job."

Before she could say much more, a pair of Indian Hills patrol cars suddenly pulled up behind them, blocking him in. Burke quickly shoved one of his business card into her hand before either of the two policeman saw him, and whispered, "Call me, please!" For a moment, she stared down at the card lying in the palm of her hand as if it were a dead mouse, but she kept it; finally closing her fingers around it and shoving it in her pocket.

Chief Bentley climbed out of his big cruiser and walked toward him, while the burly young town patrolman he recognized from the night before scrambled out of the other car. The nameplate on his shirt read "B. J. Leonard." Bentley hitched up his heavy equipment belt over his gut and sauntered to the driver's side door of Burke's car, positioning himself between Burke and Linda Sylvester. Bobby Joe circled around to the passenger side and pointed a .38-caliber Colt revolver at him through the open window.

"All right, son," Bentley ordered. "Out of the car."

"And why would I want to do that? I haven't done anything wrong."

"You want to, because I told you to; and that's the only reason you need or I intend to give. Understood? There's been a rash of office burglaries out here. It's about dark, when they usually strike. Besides, I distinctly remember you bein' told to stay away from here. That makes it 'trespassin'," he added with a thin smile as the palm of his right hand moved from his belt buckle to his pistol butt. "Now, get out of that car."

Bob looked up at him, but realized there was no reason to give the fat cop or his trigger-happy pit bull an excuse, so he did what he was told. "Am I under arrest?" he asked.

"Well, since you asked, I believe you are," Bentley replied. "The last time you were here, it seems you didn't listen too well; so this time it might take a bit longer." Bentley turned him around and handcuffed him from behind, while Bobby Joe grinned at him and kept him covered with his long-barreled .38 Colt, holding it out in front of him in a classic two-handed shooting stance, knees bent and ever-so-serious.

Bob looked at him "Did your uncle give you a bullet for that thing, too?" he asked.

"The Chief ain't my uncle!" the young police officer glared at him.

"Best not sass Bobby Joe," Bentley warned Burke. "The boy just got back from Afghanistan, and he's got a mean streak in him like an itch he can't scratch."

"Afghanistan?" Bob repeated. "Well hot damn! What unit?"

"Wasn't you in the Air Force?" Bentley asked him. "At that Bagram place?"

"Doing what? Baggage handler?" Burke cocked his head and asked.

"No, I weren't no damned baggage handler!" Bobby Joe finally spoke up. "I was an Air Force cop… and then I did some construction."

"Ah, 'some construction?' " Burke nodded, appearing to think it over for a moment. "Let's see, I'll bet you were in Air Force Security and messed something up, probably a couple of times, at least. So Security kicked you out and they handed you a shovel. Yeah, that might leave a man with a 'mean streak,' but it was better than a court-martial, wasn't it?"

"That's none of your goddamn business! What the hell do you know, anyway?" Bobby Joe stepped closer and poked Bob in the stomach with the Colt.

"Be careful you don't get on Bobby Joe's bad side, now," Bentley warned.

"Oh, no, I sure wouldn't want to do that," Bob agreed. "But the next time he jabs me with that thing you better call for backup," he said as he turned and got in the rear seat of the Chief's car. That was when he saw Tony Scalese standing behind him, arms crossed over his chest, listening to the conversation and laughing.

"Some people don't listen, do they, Burke?" the big man said. "And it wasn't as if you weren't warned."

Bob smiled at Scalese. If his little trip tonight hadn't taught him anything else, it confirmed that Scalese was indeed Mafia and Bentley was in bed with them, right up to his four-star collar tabs. As the police cruiser pulled away, he looked back at the building and saw Lawrence Greenway standing in the side doorway. His eyes were focused on him much as they had been up on the roof the day before — cold, cruel, and analytical, as if he were studying a bug under a microscope.

After the two police cruisers left, Tony Scalese stepped over to Linda Sylvester's car. She started the engine, with every intention of driving away as fast as she could. "No, no, honey," he told her as he bent down, reached inside, and pulled the keys from the ignition. "You and me got some talkin' to do, before you go drivin' away."

"Let me go," she told him as she tried to get the keys away from him, but she would have an easier time if they were stuck in a vice.

"Cool your jets, little girl. I ain't like the Doc," he told her as he motioned toward Greenway standing in the building doorway. "I don't go where I ain't wanted, but we both know what he's like, don't we?" She looked up at him and then at Greenway and nodded, terrified. "So, if you don't want an extended stay on his couch some afternoon, you keep your big mouth shut. Stay away from the cops, stay away from the FBI, and stay away from that little prick Burke. He's gonna end up in more trouble than he knows what to do with, and you don't want to go down with him. You got that, honey?"

Linda Sylvester looked up into his dark, dead eyes and quickly nodded, terrified.

"Not good enough, Linda. I wanna hear you say it. I wanna hear you say, 'No, Tony, I don't want no problems like that.' "

"No, no, Tony, I," she managed to whisper, "I don't want no problems like that."

"Much better," he said as he dropped her keys in her lap. "I think we're finally makin' some progress. Now you get on home before the Doc comes over and decides to undo all the good work we've been doin' here."

Linda Sylvester didn't need to hear anything else. She was already spooked when she saw Greenway standing in the doorway, grinning at her. She jammed the key in the ignition, started her car, and drove it over the landscaped median and out of the parking lot as fast as it would go.

Scalese watched her drive away, and then turned and walked back to the rear door of the office building, where Greenway stood watching him.

"You let her go?" the Doctor asked. "I would have liked to talk to her."

"Yeah, I bet you would," Scalese chuckled. "But you've done enough of that crap lately. It's time you keep it in your pants for a while."

"Who are you to tell me what to do?" Greenway huffed indignantly.

"Ain't me," Scalese took a deep breath and straightened up to his full height, where he could intimidate even a taller man like Lawrence Greenway. "What I'm tellin' you is what Mr. D told me to tell you, *personally*, you got that?" Scalese poked him hard in the center of his chest with his index finger.

Greenway backed up a step and blinked, knowing he was way out of his league and way out of his weight class tonight. "Okay, okay, I get your point."

"Good, I hope so, because we don't want no more 'misunderstandings.' Pretty soon they get *real* messy, if you know what I mean."

"No, there won't be any misunderstandings, but what are we going to do about that troublemaker Burke? He saw me up on the roof last night. I know he talked to Travers, and now he's pressuring that damned receptionist. He's becoming a major pain in the ass. We need to shut him up, permanently!"

Scalese looked at him and smirked. "Permanently? You mean, like the way you got rid of that Purdue woman?"

"Yes! Before he brings us all down."

"The answer is no! I already talked the situation over with Mr. D. Things are too hot right now, and you need to learn to cool your jets, Doc. With that Grand Jury convening, Mr. D says, 'No more waves.' "

"No more waves? He saw me kill her, you dolt!"

Scalese stepped closer, well inside Greenway's space, and poked him in the chest again, much harder this time. "Dolt? You piece 'a shit! You callin' me a dolt?" he asked as he grabbed the doctor by the lapels on his expensive suit and turned him toward his beautiful blue glass office building. "Sounds to me like you're lettin' all this go to your head, *Larry*. If you're not careful, it can go away as fast as it came, and suck you right down the rabbit hole with it."

Greenway looked into Scalese's threatening, dark eyes, and felt his blood run cold. "Sure, Tony. Sure. I understand, I understand."

"Good. I talked to Bentley. He can get Burke locked up for thirty days easy, maybe more. Once he gets him inside that cracker box jail of his, him and that moron deputy can use some 'police magic' to make Mr. Burke go away for keeps. No muss, no fuss, only a little 'shot while attempting to escape.' All nice and legal, but it's gonna cost you twenty 'large' for me to get Bentley to fix all that, Doc. You understand me?"

"Twenty, sure, sure, Tony. Whatever it takes. I understand."

"See that you do. It's your last warning."

CHAPTER NINE

Chief Bentley personally walked Bob Burke up the front stairs and through the glass doors of the small but new Indian Hills Police Station. With a firm hand on Bob's elbow, he steered him through the lobby, past the Duty Sergeant's tall, imposing front desk, and into the rear service hallway, trailed all the while by the ever-eager Bobby Joe Leonard, his hand riding on his pistol butt like Wyatt Earp entering the O. K. Corral.

"Book him on 'Drunk and Disorderly,' Patrolman."

"I'm neither drunk nor disorderly," Burke countered.

"You are if I say you are, boy. Pretty soon, you'll learn that. And add 'Trespassin' and Resisting Arrest.' I'll think of a few more by mornin,' but that'll do for now."

When they reached the booking table, the Chief motioned for Bobby Joe to fingerprint Burke, which caused the fat patrolman to frown. With his hands still cuffed behind his back, Bob glanced at the equipment on the table. It was too clean and neatly arranged to have been used very often, if ever. That became obvious as he watched Bobby Joe pick up what appeared to be a fresh tube of "old-school" black ink and try to read the instructions. There were no digital fingerprinting pads or water-based ink in this jail like the Air Force used; no Sir, not while 4-Star Police Chief Cyrus T. Bentley was on the job. Unfortunately, that didn't help Bobby Joe much. First, his thick fingers couldn't uncap the tube. Then, when he did get it open, a thick gout of black ink squished out and got all over him. He wiped what he could on the glass inking plate and tried to wipe the rest off with a handful of paper towels, but that only spread the ink even further. He ended up with the black glop all over both hands and on the front of his shirt for his trouble. Finally, he grabbed the rubber roller and vigorously worked the ink back and forth on the glass plate to try to spread it out as best he could, grabbed a standard fingerprint ID card from the shelf above the table, and secured it in the cardholder getting his own fingerprints plus the excess ink smeared all over it.

Frustrated, Bobby Joe finally turned and faced Burke, frowning again, as if he knew there was something else he was supposed to do, but couldn't remember. "Well?" he asked.

"Well, what?" Bob answered.

"Well, gimme yer goddamned hand!"

"Can't." He shrugged.

"Wudjumean you cain't?" Bobby Joe pleaded, uncertain whether to cry or to shoot him.

Bob looked at him, leaned forward, and politely whispered, "You gotta take the handcuffs off first."

This got Bobby Joe even more flustered. He jerked Burke around sideways and began flipping through his fat key ring looking for the odd-shaped little one for the handcuffs. Burke said nothing. He didn't have to. He looked at Bentley and rolled his eyes. That was all it took.

Bentley, already embarrassed, snapped, "Jeezus Christ, Bobby Joe! I coulda fingerprinted the whole goddamned Purple Gang by now!"

That only made Bobby Joe angrier. He grabbed Burke's right hand, slapped it down on the inked glass, and slapped it on the fingerprint card, pressing hard, and aiming more for speed than artistry. Bob picked up a handful of paper towels and tried to wipe off the thick black ink. "Your sister's boy, right?" he said quietly to Bentley.

"Ah told you, he ain't my uncle!" Bobby Joe answered angrily.

Bentley said nothing. He picked up the fingerprint card and examined the gooey black smudges for legibility. "Nice," he commented. "Real nice." He turned toward Burke and looked down at him over the top of his glasses. "I don't suppose there's a bunch of 'Wants and Warrants' on you in the VICAP data base waitin' for me to run your prints against, is there, son?" Bentley asked as he tore the illegible card in two and dropped it in the trash.

"I doubt it, Chief," Burke said with a smile.

"Didn't think so."

"Then why are we doing this? Do Greenway and Tony Scalese have this much clout with you?"

"Oh, I wouldn't exactly put it that way," Bentley replied as he gave him a long, appraising look. "Let's say CHC is a big business in a little town, and you stuck your nose in places where it don't belong." With that, Bentley turned back to Bobby Joe and said, "Take the prisoner on back to his cell, Patrolman, *and I mean by the book*, you hear me! You screwed up enough for one day, and when I see this man in court tomorrow morning, he best look exactly like he does now — no scuffs, no bruises, and not one hair out of place. He's probably gonna be with us as the guest of the town for a good long while, more than enough for the two of you to get acquainted. You got that?"

"I'd like a phone," Bob told him. "I need to call my lawyer."

"Somehow, ah figured you'd say that," Bentley answered. "Bobby Joe here will take you to the phone so you can make your call, but it won't do you no good. The Mayor's the Town Court Hearing Officer, and he won't show up from his Kiwanis meeting until 9:30, maybe 10:00 o'clock tomorrow morning, dependin' on how he feels."

"So I get to sit back there all night?"

"Sit, lay down, or stand on your head, that's your choice; but you ain't *goin'* nowhere. If you want to pay your lawyer overtime, that's your choice too, but there ain't no sense him comin' around 'til at least 9:30 tomorrow."

Bob Burke spent that night in the Indian Hills jail, booked on the phony charges. There were four cells, and Burke was the only prisoner. From the looks of the place, he may have been the first prisoner, other than an occasional drunk driver, the high school seniors from nearby Elk Grove Village who got caught painting the water tower for Homecoming, or a burglar who drove up from the city and ran into a silent alarm he didn't know about. Still, when you add in the town's reputation as a speed trap on the two major state routes that ran through the area, Bentley's little operation was probably a major cash cow for the town treasury.

Chagrined and infinitely wiser by the time George Grierson was able to get in and see him shortly after 9:00 o'clock the next morning, the only good things Bob Burke could say about his stay was that the mattress was soft and the breakfast and coffee from the diner across the street were not half-bad. Fortunately, Bobby Joe's shift ended at midnight, and it was another of Chief Bentley's "nephews" who marched him from his cell in the new Town Jail to the equally new Town Hall next door. Obviously, times were good in Indian Hills, he observed, as he saw the new landscaping, streetlights, sidewalks, and generally spruced-up Main Street in daylight. Money must be pouring into the city coffers, and no self-respecting mayor or police chief was about to rock that boat. No, this is why they continued to be re-elected. Fraud? Dirty money? Organized Crime? The last thing any of the good citizens out here would question was the source. No one wanted to bite the hand that slipped it in their pockets.

Town court proceedings are about the lowest rung on any judicial ladder, and are supposed to deal exclusively with misdemeanors, such as speeding, drunk driving, zoning violations, littering, animal complaints and trespassing; most of which plead-out with a fine, but with no official record, they can usually do whatever they want. In fact, the Town

Council's meeting room doubled as the Court Room, and the Council's Conference Room was its Jury Room should that ever be needed. Today, it was not, so that was where the police officer delivered Burke to meet with George Grierson, his attorney.

Grierson sat behind his big open briefcase, thumbing through the charges as Bob took one of the chairs across from him. He looked up, and saw the rosy-cheeked police officer still standing in the doorway. "Mind if I have some time alone with my client, officer?"

"Your uncle said it was okay," Bob added with a smile.

"Oh, sorry, I forgot," he said as he quickly backed out of the room. "And he told me to tell you that the mayor will be here in a couple of minutes, so don't take too long."

"I'll try not to," Grierson replied deadpan as the young cop stepped out and closed the door behind him. Grierson turned his steely eyes on Bob and asked, "What's going on?"

"Hi, George, good to see you again, too."

"Drunk and disorderly, trespassing, refusal to obey a lawful order, and all the rest of this stuff? What the hell?"

"Never mind all that. Get me out of here."

"I will try my damnedest, but you don't make it easy."

"That stuff is all bogus."

"I have no doubt, but this is Indian Hills, Bob. In a town court, the hearing officer, as he's called, and the police chief can damn well do anything they want. You played some ball at West Point, so you know what 'home-court advantage' is, don't you? Well, the dumbass sitting up front in the black robe isn't really a judge and he's barely even a lawyer, but he can pretty much do anything he wants with you. They aren't even supposed to hear cases like this, but who's going to stop them? Do you understand?"

"I figured that out all by myself last night."

"Good. So, when we go in there, you shut up and let me do the talking — not that I haven't asked you to do that any number of times before, and not that you've ever listened to me before, but this time you damn well better. You got that?"

"Yeah, I think I do." Bob stared at him. "So, you're saying I'm screwed?"

"Oh, Indian Hills is the least of your problems. I hope we can plead this thing out. Decorated soldier, no record. Maybe we can get you off with some money, quite a bit, probably, some community service, an apology, and a look of sad contrition. Think you can do that?"

Grierson pulled another thick file folder from his briefcase. "Know what this is?" the lawyer asked as he held up the file for Bob to see.

"Don't tell me. Angie?" He shrugged without even looking.

"A 'Call for a Board Meeting.' Her lawyers must have been up all night working on it, because they even added your escapade over at Consolidated Health Care as one ground to have you removed. I got served at the crack of dawn this morning, and I'm sure they would've served you too if they knew where you were."

"I was hiding right here in plain sight." Bob smiled innocently.

"Yeah, well, they've dotted all the i's and crossed all the t's this time, and you're going to have to hold a Special Shareholders Meeting within 48 hours. There's no getting around it now, and you and I are gonna spend most of today figuring out how to play it."

"She told me yesterday she was going to do this, so I phoned the Pension Plan trustees and the banks. They were pretty noncommittal, so I suspect she already has them in her pocket."

"They wouldn't talk to me last night, either, but who knows?"

"True, but Angie knows how to count cards, and how to count votes. Ed taught her; so if she went this far, she thinks she has it wrapped up."

At 9:30 a.m., Bob Burke and George Grierson were sitting in the Indian Hills Town Council Meeting Room waiting at one of the side tables for Hizzoner the Hearing Officer to arrive. At 9:55 a.m., a side door near the front of the room finally opened, and a short, potbellied, half-bald "used car salesman" in an ill-fitting black robe entered and took the center black-leather chair on the tall dais at the front of the room. Right behind him came a buxom brunette in a tight dress carrying a steno pad, with three long yellow pencils stuck in her hair above her ear. Behind her came a man in a gray suit, Police Chief Bentley, and Bobby Joe Leonard. The woman took the chair at the far end of the dais and opened her steno pad. The three men continued on to the other table and took their seats. A nice, cozy relationship, Bob thought, but he kept his mouth shut, as he promised. He knew he was screwed regardless of what he thought or said.

The hearing officer began to fidget, moving things and looking around and under the dais. "Wilma?" he asked. "Where's that damned nameplate? And my gavel? I gotta have the goddamned gavel."

"Oh, the janitors must have put that stuff away again, Mayor," Wilma answered as she quickly got up and stepped over to where the magistrate was sitting. He pushed his chair back a foot or two as she bent down over him and began opening and closing drawers. Both of her hands were out of sight for a moment and Bob swore he saw him jump a few inches. "Here, I think I found them, Mayor," she grinned up at him.

"Yes! I do believe you did," he grinned back as she placed the nameplate down in front of him and they exchanged a quick glance as she scampered back to her seat. "I believe you did." He coughed, looked out at the nearly empty room, and dropped his gavel on the dais with several loud Bangs! Burke and Grierson both rose, as did the other three men.

"I am Mayor Hubert… uh, I mean *Hearing Officer* Hubert Bloomfield of the Indian Hills Town Court. For the record, Mr. David Schwartz, Town Counsel, Police Chief Cyrus T. Bentley and… Patrolman Third Class Bobby Joe Leonard of the Indian Hills Police Department are also in attendance. We are here this morning," he said as he looked down and shuffled through the papers. "Oh yes, here we are, Case #72 — drunk and disorderly, trespassing, disregarding a lawful order, resisting arrest, hindering a police officer in the furtherance of his duties, and a whole bunch of other things like that; alleged to been perpetrated within the boundaries of the Town of Indian Hills, Illinois, by one Robert Tyrone Burke of 847 Poplar Dr., Arlington Heights." Bloomfield droned on until he finally put the paper down and looked up at Burke, smiling like the cat that ate the canary. "That you, son?" Bloomfield asked, already thinking of how much money this little piece of business might bring into the city's coffers, and his.

"Your Honor," Grierson tried to interject, but Bloomfield cut him off with a disinterested wave of the gavel.

"Later, Counselor. I'm no 'Honor,' and this ain't a court, not a real one anyways, as we both know. Now, Mr. Burke, that's one hell of a lot of damned problems for one person to be creating here in our little town. What am I supposed to do with you?"

"Whatever you think is appropriate, Mr. Bloomfield. I realize I made a mistake last night and I may have said a few inappropriate things to the Chief, but I was on private property in a parking lot having an innocent conversation with a young lady. I think the rest of those items are a bit of an exaggeration," Burke answered as he looked over at Bentley.

"Mr. Bloomfield," Grierson dared to interrupt again, "in the interest of justice, I would like to point out that Mr. Burke…"

"I don't think I was talking to you yet, Counselor," Bloomfield snapped.

This time, Grierson ignored him and went on anyway, "As you may not be aware, Mr. Burke served two tours in Iraq and two more in Afghanistan in the armored cavalry, Army Rangers and Delta Force..."

"Now look here, Counselor..."

"...where he received the Distinguished Cross, three Silver Stars, two Bronze Stars, a Purple Heart with five Oak Leaf Clusters, a Legion of Merit, some Meritorious Service Medals, and... well, many more decorations which I shall not try to enumerate, before recently retiring as a Major." Grierson paused, but this time, the hearing officer did not interrupt him. "Mr. Burke has apologized and agrees to accept full responsibility for his actions," Grierson went on. "As we both know that Indian Hills has one of the largest VFW Posts in the northwest suburbs, with that beautiful new building over on Route 83. I was fortunate enough to be asked to speak there last summer, and I'm certain some of its members would take serious offense if it appeared a legitimate American war hero was not given appropriate consideration by its elected representatives."

At this point, Bloomfield's eyes slowly turned away from George Grierson to Bentley and Schwartz. His wrath followed, as he wondered what the hell they got him into this morning. Being mayor and the occasional hearing officer — a post he appointed himself to — of a small town with a fat, growing treasury like Indian Hills was a juicy plum for a semi-retired used car salesman with a 'mail-order' law degree from a 'paper mill' in Alabama, who owned a small lot at the corner of "Walk" and "Don't Walk" downtown. In addition to the multiple salaries he enjoyed from these two positions, he also received large stipends and expense accounts from serving on eight or ten outside boards and commissions that rarely met. No less important to him were the perks, the parties, the all-expense-paid junkets to the Super Bowl and World Series, Bears and Bulls season tickets, and the private hunting and deep-sea fishing charters sponsored by a few of the major corporations in town, including CHC... and of course there were his regular sessions with Wilma on Tuesday and Thursday afternoons. Yes, all things considered, Hubert Bloomfield greatly enjoyed being mayor. He had held the position for the past seven years, through two elections, and he was up for reelection again this fall.

Normally, the politics in a small town like Indian Hills never amounted to very much. The political party folks paraded around with

donkeys and elephants on their lapels, but that was for the state and
national elections. In the town and township races, the voters knew the
candidates, knew who they liked and did not like, and incumbents were
rarely opposed. Come Election Day, however, the Mayor knew full well
that the good citizens of Indian Hills would toss him or anyone else out
on his sorry ass if they thought he did something stupid or let the job go
to his head. That was why the last thing Hizzoner the Hearing Officer
needed that morning was a couple of dumb town cops and the town
lawyer shoving him into a very deep hole he would never climb out of
with the voters. Bloomfield remembered bellying up to the bar at the
VFW Post many a night, back slapping and buying drinks — and this
smartass Chicago lawyer had just nailed him right between his political
eyes. Those VFW boys vote, and the last thing Hubert Bloomfield ever
wanted to do was to rattle their cage.

Finally having collected his thoughts, he smiled and asked, "Is
that correct, Mr. Burke? What Mr. Grierson said, uh, does that pretty
much reflect your military record?"

Bob looked up and nodded, his dark, powerful eyes drilling holes
through him.

"Well, that sounds like an exemplary one to me," Bloomfield
went on. "Speaking for myself and the good citizens of Indian Hills, I do
want to sincerely thank you for your service," Bloomfield continued, his
mind racing. "And, uh, I appreciate your candor regarding the situation
last night and your willingness to accept responsibility. Therefore, I am
reducing these charges to one simple misdemeanor, charging you $500 in
court costs... no, let's make that $50, and the assumption that I shall
never see you in my court again. Wilma here will take care of the details,
Sir, and you are free to go."

Bloomfield slammed the gavel down on the desk and headed for
his office. "Chief! In my office... You too, Schwartz!" he shouted over
his shoulder. The Police Chief shoved Bobby Joe aside and hurried after
the mayor.

"Well, that was a lot easier than I expected, Bob," George
Grierson turned and whispered to Burke as he slipped his papers back in
his briefcase. "And I didn't even have to use the good stuff," he chuckled.

"You used enough," Bob answered as Chief Bentley turned and
looked back at him. His sneer was gone, replaced by something bordering
on wide-eyed fear. Bob nudged Grierson and said, "Let's get the hell out
of here, George."

It was shortly after 11:00 before Bob was able to pay his fine to the clerk and retrieve his automobile from the town impound lot. The "impound lot" consisted of three parking spaces on the rear side of the local Exxon service station. Apparently, it had the only tow truck in town, and the station happened to be owned by the Mayor Hearing Officer's cousin, Larry.

Thirty minutes later, Bob pushed through the door of the Toler TeleCom's office, feeling tired, unshaven, and stiff from a long night on a short jail cot. He took a quick right turn, hoping to get past Maryanne's desk without being noticed, knowing that was unlikely to happen; and it didn't. She gave him an appraising look over the top of her glasses and scanned him quickly from head to toe.

"Don't ask," he told her.

"I pretty much already know. The coffee's fresh, and I'll bring you a cup. I arranged the stuff on your desk in order of pain, and separated your phone messages into Critical, Dire, Life Threatening, and Telemarketers."

"Very funny, Maryanne," he said with a limp smile, as he walked into his office and closed the door behind him. All things considered, he knew he would have been better off if he went home and got some sleep before he tried to tackle the accumulated crap, but he couldn't do that. The business problems were mounting, and he needed a plan. Besides, he once spent five days and four nights straight chasing Taliban gunmen through the Afghan mountains without any sleep or hot food. True, he was a few years younger and in prime fighting shape then, but that was no reason to surrender to a touch of fatigue. No, like pain, being tired was a state of mind, he thought, as he flopped in his desk chair and looked at the stacks of paper. First things first, he thought. He picked up the first stack of pink telephone call slips and began to thumb through them. Most were from various local newspapers and several television stations that must have picked up his arrest on the local police blotter. Those, he immediately dropped into his trashcan, knowing the reporters had deadlines and would soon find something easier to cover.

Reluctantly, he turned his attention to the stack of correspondence and reports sitting in the middle of his desk. He pulled the top half dozen or so off the stack and began reading, when Maryanne buzzed him on the intercom and said, "Bob, you have a call on Line 1. The woman on the other end said she's from the US Attorney's Office. I assume it's the little weasel who stopped by yesterday morning, Mr. O'Malley."

"Probably so," he answered as he punched the button for Line 1, put O'Malley on speaker, and leaned back in his chair. "Bob Burke here."

"Mr. Burke, I understand you spent some time as the guest of that paragon of the local law enforcement community, Chief Bentley."

"Him, and Mayor or Hearing Officer Hubert Bloomfield, I could never quite get straight which, and the rest of the Indian Hills brain trust."

"Dirt balls through and through, and all on the payroll of your friends at CHC."

"I kinda figured that out all by myself."

"You're a smart guy, Bob, I expected no less."

"Look, Mr. O'Malley — if you don't mind my calling you Mr. O'Malley — I spent last night on a lumpy cot, I haven't had lunch, and I generally feel like hell. So, let's get this over; to what do I owe this pleasure?"

"I understand you talked to Linda Sylvester. What did she tell you?"

"Not much. She's got a daughter, and she's scared of Scalese and Greenway. They warned her about me and she thinks they're watching her and listening to everything she says. I tried to talk her into seeing you or the cops, but she doesn't trust anybody at this point."

"She's right to be scared of Scalese and Greenway."

"Yeah, but it's a lot more than that. She's really scared of Greenway."

"The gentleman is preceded by his reputation."

"I gathered that."

"What about Eleanor Purdue? Did she say anything about her?"

"No, she's still in total denial. She thinks Eleanor's on a business trip."

"Well, when her body finally shows up, like the others…"

"The others?"

"Remember the other photos I showed you, the ones you didn't recognize? As I said, the gentleman is preceded by his reputation. If I have it right, there have been three other women who disappeared before Eleanor Purdue, and there may be more. I've already interviewed most of the staff who work there, or at least the women under 40 whom I would have some plausible excuse to be interviewing. They're all scared, but the bodies of the missing women and any proof that could stand up in court are hard to come by with those guys."

"Well, I tried with her, like you asked me to."

"No, Bob," O'Malley laughed. "You went over there and talked to her for yourself, not because I asked you to."

He stared at the phone for a moment, knowing the bastard was right. "Maybe, but all it got me was a night in jail, and is probably costing me my company."

"Angie and the Special Board Meeting she's calling?"

"Are you bugging phones now, Peter?"

"Almost everyone's," he laughed. "But not yours. No need. I have a hotline from the County Recorder's office. My staff sees stuff before the ink is dry on their printer. Besides, I told you I have all that corporate business stuff covered. Play ball with me, and Summit Symbiotics will vanish with the morning fog. You'll have your company and the DOD contract."

"I don't know what else you think I can do?"

"Linda Sylvester — that's what I think you can do. Sweet-talk her, get in her pants, I really don't care which, so long as you get her to talk. She knows stuff. Then there's Greenway. You watched him kill that woman and that makes you a witness to capital murder. You've got him by the balls. All you have to do is give him a little squeeze, and he'll flip on the others."

"I've got *him* by the balls? You're out of your mind, O'Malley. Besides, I told you, I don't work that way."

"I hate to be corny, but it's my way or Angie and the highway. Take your pick. You can get your company back, have a fat contract, and put some really bad guys away, or lose it all and have the IRS make a hobby out of you. Think it over; I know you won't disappoint."

Burke was about to say something he knew he would regret, but he heard a click and realized that O'Malley hung up on him before he could. Figures.

Two hours later, Bob was only halfway through the stack of letters and reports when his office door opened and Charlie stuck his head inside. "Is this a good time, Boss?" he asked.

Bob looked down the doodles he drew on his yellow legal pad, and waved Charlie the rest of the way in. "There's no such thing. You come up with anything?"

"Not much that's any good," the fat man admitted as he took one of the chairs in front of Bob's desk and flipped through his notes. "Then again, I never did like this place."

"Good. Then you won't miss it."

As Charlie began talking, the intercom lit up and Marianne said,

"George Grierson's on the phone for you, Bob."

Charlie began to gather his papers and get up, but Burke motioned for him to stay where he was. "Speaking of outside business expenses," he said as he pressed the button for Line #1 and put it on speaker. "You got good news for us, George?" he asked.

"No, what I got was served with a Court Order, and I assume you'll be getting one shortly, too. Angie must have found a friendly judge, because he locked you out of the offices until the Board Meeting. She has her lawyers at Gordon and Kramer appointed Conservators, and they will take over tomorrow morning. Sorry."

Well, Burke thought as he hung up, reached into his desk, and pulled out the nearly empty bottle of Macallan. "Charlie, I'll be damned if I'm leaving this for her or the lawyers."

"Nope," Charlie said as he went for the glasses on the credenza. "When the going gets tough, the tough get drunk."

CHAPTER TEN

So far, the day had passed quietly, or so Linda Sylvester thought as she sat at her reception desk in the center of the CHC lobby. Her chair was on a raised platform, which in turn sat behind the tall, marble half-wall, putting her almost two feet above the lobby floor. Architects! It was as if she were working in her own private castle. The other girls would walk by and whisper, "Rapunzel, Rapunzel, let down your hair," to tease her. However, on a day like today, after a night like last night, being able to hide behind a thick wall had advantages.

Fortunately, Linda saw very little of Tony Scalese or Dr. Greenway all morning. More important, she saw nothing of the local police, the FBI, or *that* man Burke, which suited her perfectly fine. She didn't care to see any of them again, ever. Unfortunately, she saw nothing of Eleanor Purdue, either. Dr. Greenway had stopped by and told her Eleanor made a quick trip out of town to meet with the corporate auditors in New York, and she had said to tell her she would be gone for a few days. Funny, Eleanor said nothing to her about taking a trip, and that was unusual. Eleanor was ten years older than Linda, almost like an older sister. Despite the gap in their ages, she and Eleanor had become close friends over the past few months. If Eleanor decided to leave town, even for a few days, she would have asked Linda to check on her house, water her plants, and bring in the paper. She would have phoned, left a note or an email, or stopped by. She never would have left town without saying anything. That was not like Eleanor. So, was Greenway lying to her? It wouldn't be the first time. But why? Why would he make up a story like that?

Having been hired only four months before, Linda was still fairly new to CHC and to the job. Except for her friendship with Eleanor, she was already sorry she took it. The money was great, much better than her previous one, and she had a daughter to think of. Still, there was a creepy feel about the place. She saw it on the faces and in the eyes of the other women; CHC was not an office where you could relax. Most of the other employees were female, from 25 to 40 years old. That could be said about the previous two places she worked too, but it was different here. There was a tension right below the surface that was so strong she could feel it. The women were scared, especially the younger ones. At first, she thought it might be Tony Scalese, the muscle-bound head of security, or his hairy-knuckled guards. They were middle-aged Italians and most of them wore wedding rings. Scalese was a tough guy — big, muscular, and crude. Oddly enough though, as one of the other women whispered to her in the restroom, "Tony might break your arm, honey, but he'd never touch you... not like that."

Doctor Greenway, on the other hand, was different — smiling, polite, and impeccably dressed. It wasn't that Linda was a prude or hadn't been chased around a few offices by grabby young men who couldn't keep their hands off her. She'd been divorced for three years now. That was a long time. To be truthful, there were moments she wouldn't even mind it, depending on who was doing the chasing. With a five-year-old daughter, she learned the hard way that there were plenty of men around who she could hook up with for a one-night stand or even a long weekend; but that was as far as the commitment went with them. She was lonely, but not that lonely. Worse still, on several occasions in the past few weeks, she caught Doctor Greenway staring at her, and it creeped her out. He was more than twice her age, and there was something decidedly "off" about that man. He was tall, with long fingers, a thin, hungry smile, and hooded eyes that reminded her of a snake. After all, Linda had been around. She understood men and knew what they wanted, and that didn't bother her nearly as much as it used to. There were times when she wanted it too, but not with someone like Greenway. No, she did not like him and she did not trust him either. Two weeks ago over dinner and a big bottle of wine, Eleanor told her never to let him get her alone in his office. Eleanor did, and she learned to regret it. Linda pressed her for details, but she knew there were some things a woman wouldn't talk about, even with a friend, and that was good enough for her.

As the morning wore on, Linda still hadn't heard from her friend and she was getting scared. If Eleanor really did go out of town, as Greenway told her, she would have called by now. When that maniac from the airplane claimed he saw Greenway strangling a woman up on the roof, a woman in a white dress, and repeated it again last night, it struck a raw nerve. Eleanor wore a white dress yesterday. Tony Scalese might have tried to hush her up, but Linda had even complimented her on it when she walked in that morning. Did that man Burke see her somewhere else earlier in the day? Did he see someone else on another roof? Or was it really Eleanor he saw up on this one? Linda tried to block that from her mind. Whether he was drunk or crazy, that thought was too horrible to contemplate.

It was almost noon, more than twenty-four hours since she last saw Eleanor, and her friend was still missing. Linda looked into her lap and slowly opened her left hand. The sweaty, crumpled business card, which that man had thrust into her hand the night before, was still there. It read Robert Burke, President, Toler TeleCom. As the minutes slowly dragged by, he wasn't sounding nearly as drunk or crazy as he did yesterday. Maybe he really did see the unthinkable. All that Linda knew for certain was that she must find out what happened to Eleanor. She owed it to her friend.

Most of the employees in the building went out for lunch right at 12:00 noon, or they brown-bagged it in the break room at the far end of the first floor hall. Linda knew that would be her best chance, perhaps her only chance to get into Eleanor's office and see what she could learn. She asked Patsy Evans, one of the new girls in accounting, to cover the reception desk for a few minutes while she distributed some reports. To make it look legitimate, she grabbed two file folders and a half-dozen copies of the business magazines that routinely came to the office, and headed for the elevator, trying to walk slowly and keep her nerves under control.

Eleanor's office was on the third floor with most of the other managers and department heads. Hers was in the middle and Dr. Greenway's was around the bend at the far end. When the elevator door opened on three, she stuck her head out and looked to her left. Greenway's door was closed. Still, the mere thought of his door suddenly opening and of the doctor stepping out and seeing her at Eleanor's door froze Linda in her tracks. She stood halfway in and halfway out of the elevator, staring at Greenway's door, knowing she must do something, but she could not move. In all likelihood, Eleanor's door was locked, but she had given Linda a set of keys the week before. There was one to her office, one to her desk, and another one to her house. Linda didn't want to take them, but Eleanor had insisted. That was the night they met for dinner in one of the restaurant bars down the road from the office and had way too much wine. Eleanor put her hand on Linda's wrist and told her, "There's something you need to promise me, Linda. I know you're going to think this is crazy, but if anything ever happens to me, there's a small envelope inside a box of Cocoa Puffs in my pantry that…"

"Cocoa Puffs?" Linda giggled. Each of them consumed several drinks too many that night, and the image of Eleanor sitting at her breakfast table in her "jammies" leaning over a cereal bowl and reading the back of a box of kids cereal was too much. "You gotta be kidding."

"I know, I know. That's why I got them, because I knew I would never eat them. Now listen to me!" Eleanor closed her hand tightly around Linda's wrist. "There's a note inside the box, pushed down between the bag of cereal and the box itself. If anything happens to me, *anything*, you must go there, get the note, and do exactly what it says." Eleanor insisted, holding Linda's wrist in a death grip, begging. "Will you do that for me? Please?" Linda's giggle quickly faded when she saw the deadly serious expression on Eleanor's face. "Promise me you'll get that note and do exactly what it says."

"Okay, okay! I promise, relax," Linda finally answered. Crazy? Eleanor was right; Linda *did* think she was crazy.

"You can't say anything to anyone about this, especially to Greenway. He's... he's evil."

At the time, Linda didn't fully understand what Greenway had done to Eleanor, but she understood the terrified look in the other woman's eyes. "Sure, sure I'll get the envelope."

"And stay away from him. Whatever you do, don't let him get you alone."

"Okay, okay. Hey, you're hurting my wrist," she said and Eleanor quickly let go, embarrassed. "What's this all about?" Linda asked, but her friend refused to tell her any more. That was a week ago. Since then, everything Linda had learned made her more and more afraid.

As she looked out into the third floor hallway, she saw it was empty and knew she couldn't stay in the elevator any longer. With Eleanor's office key in her hand, she stepped quickly to the door, put the key in the lock, and slipped inside. The ceiling lights were off, but the curtains were open and the sun poured in through the window. She walked to Eleanor's desk and sat in Eleanor's chair. Linda had been in here many times before, and she knew Eleanor was anything but a neat freak. Today, however, there wasn't a single sheet of paper on her desktop, no sticky notes, no stacks of correspondence, nothing in her In or Out baskets, and nothing in her trashcan or on the credenza behind her desk, either. There was a small conference table in the office, with four chairs and a couch behind it, but there was nothing on any of them or the end tables, except for a few Annual Reports and business magazines.

She stopped to collect her thoughts, slowly looking around again. The company had been stressing document security for weeks.

Even so, this was not like Eleanor. Normally, her calendar and weekly planner lay open, next to her telephone. It was gone too. Eleanor used a small laptop computer and a "docking station" with a separate desktop monitor when she worked in the office. She took the laptop everywhere she went, so it was no surprise to find the dock empty, the laptop gone, and the monitor turned off. Still, there was a cold, empty feeling in here, as if someone had moved out and was never coming back.

None of the desk drawers were locked, which was odd. Looking more closely, she saw deep gouges in the wood above the locks. Someone had used a screwdriver or a knife to force the drawers open, and didn't care if anyone knew it. Linda opened the center drawer and took a quick look inside. It was completely empty — no paperclips, no pads of paper, no sticky notes, not even dust or lint. Nothing! There were three more drawers on the left side of the desk, and what looked like three on the right, but the drawer panels on that side were actually a door, which opened to reveal a pullout rack of hanging files. She grabbed the handle on the top drawer on the left side and pulled it open. That was where Eleanor kept makeup and personal articles. It was empty. The two drawers under it were also empty, as was the large pullout file rack on the other side. Turning around, the credenza's drawers also appeared to have been broken into, and they were completely empty, too. Now, Linda was truly afraid, but there was nothing to learn in here. Eleanor's office had been stripped bare.

She knew she'd been in here too long. Someone would surely be looking for her in the lobby by now and asking questions, so she rose, tiptoed to the office door, and listened. The hallway seemed quiet, so she slipped outside. She closed Eleanor's office door behind her, ducked into the fire stairwell at the end of the hall, and dashed down to the first floor. This situation was cascading from bad to worse, she realized, and she knew she had taken far too many risks already. She paused halfway down, dug into her purse for a pill bottle, fumbled with the cap, and picked out two Valium. Her mouth was dry, but she managed to swallow them, hoping she might actually make it through the rest of the day without falling apart.

When she got back to her desk, Patsy handed her a note and said, "Doctor Greenway called down for you a couple of minutes ago."

"Doctor…?" Linda felt the blood rush from her head and she began to stammer.

"Oh, don't worry, I told him you were on break, so he asked if you could stop up at his office when you got back. He didn't sound like it was a big deal."

"Doctor Greenway?"

"Yeah," she smiled. "He sounded okay about it, kind of friendly actually. You want me to watch the desk while you go up?"

Linda nodded nervously, knowing there was no choice. The girl was new. Maybe she didn't know, or hadn't heard yet. "Look," Linda turned and looked at her. "I'm going to run up there and see what he wants, but I'm going to tell him you and some of the other girls are waiting down here for me. So, if I'm not back in five minutes — five minutes — I want you to call up there and ask for me."

"Call up to Doctor Greenway's office?" The girl asked hesitantly.

"Yes, call up there in five minutes. Use the intercom. Say there's a package of checks down here that I have to sign for. Only me. Promise me you'll do that, Patsy."

Linda held the stack of magazines and file folders in her arms and clutched them to her chest as she turned and headed back to the elevator. She got inside and pushed the third floor button again, thinking how slow they move when you're in a hurry, and how fast they move when you don't want them to go at all. When the door opened on three, she turned left and walked slowly down the center of the hallway toward Greenway's office, her eyes moving left and right as she looked into the other offices she passed. It was still lunchtime. The doors were all closed and the lights inside were off, and she realized that she and Greenway were probably the only people up on the third floor right now. The door to his office stood open about six inches. Stepping forward, she peered around the edge of his door and saw him sitting at his desk as Eleanor's words rang in her ears, "Stay away from Greenway. Don't let him get you alone," but it was too late for that.

"Ah, Linda!" he looked up at her and smiled. "Come in and close the door, my dear. There are several things I need to discuss with you." She did what he said, closed the office door, and walked slowly forward, clutching the stack of magazines even tighter. "Oh, don't worry; I won't bite," he said as he rose and stepped around the front of his desk to meet her. The closer he got, the taller he seemed, as he looked down at her and grinned. She paused, unsure what to do.

"Here, come sit on the couch with me," he said as she felt his cold fingers on her elbow, steering her toward the large leather couch along the sidewall. He saw the stack of magazines and files she was clutching, almost like a shield, and said, "Oh, set those on the table, my dear." She did what he said, and sat on the end of the couch as far away from him as she could get. Unfortunately, that was no deterrent. He grinned and sat next to her, putting his arm over the rear cushion behind her and leaned in closer.

"Linda, I need to talk to you for a few minutes about Eleanor. I know the two of you were quite close. As I told you, she is out of town on a trip, but I've become concerned about her over the past few weeks," he said, looking deep into her eyes. "Eleanor is a very important member of my staff, as you are, but she seems to have become very tense, very nervous lately. I wonder if there are any changes going on in her personal life that you might be aware of? Has she said anything to you? Is there anything she's upset or worried about?"

"I, uh… No, nothing that I know of, Doctor Greenway."

"Nothing? Do you know if she has been talking to anyone outside the company? Has anybody been bothering her or upsetting her?" he asked, as his dark, hypnotic eyes bored into her. "By any chance, did Eleanor give you anything, perhaps some papers or reports she asked you to keep for her, or maybe a CD, a DVD, or a flash drive from her computer?"

"No, no, Doctor Greenway, nothing like that."

"You wouldn't be betraying a confidence if you told me, Linda," he said as he placed his hand on her knee and leaned even closer speaking to her in that soft, calm voice, his eyes drawing her in. "I'm only trying to help her, and to help *you*; but I need your cooperation, your *full* cooperation. After all, you have that lovely little daughter of yours, Emily, is that her name?"

"My daughter?" Linda reacted, getting flustered. Those eyes, that voice, his hand, and the Valium were all affecting her now, and she felt lightheaded. "What… What are you…?"

"And there's that new house you bought in Des Plaines last year, that little white Cape Cod," he went on, slowly rubbing her knee with his long, soft fingers. "I bet that house payment takes a bite out of things. How much is it, eight hundred and fifty a month? I'm sure that's quite a strain for young woman like you."

Her eyes went wide, suddenly terrified to realize how much he knew about her. She tried to push his hand away, but he leaned closer, his long fingers slipping down between her knees, rubbing the inside of her thigh, then higher, insisting, his face only inches from hers. "I can help you with that, Linda. Relax, problems like those are very easy to solve, Linda. You can have a great future here at CHC, if you only learn to cooperate with me, and relax."

"I… I don't know anything, Doctor Greenway. Please!" she said as she tried to push his hand away, feeling weak, but managing to get to her feet and stumble toward the door.

"Oh, I think you know *a lot* of things, Linda, and you *do* want to help me, don't you?" he answered as he quickly followed her. "You see, we have some files and reports missing."

"I don't know anything about that, Dr. Greenway," she said as she reached the door. Her hand found the doorknob, but he was on her before she could open it, engulfing her. He seemed like a large jungle cat, tall and powerful, as one hand closed over her mouth. There was something in it, a damp cloth. She took several deep breaths and suddenly felt very lightheaded. His other arm reached around her waist and she went limp. Almost effortlessly, he picked her up, carried her back to the couch, and bent her forward over the armrest. His left hand pressed her face into the soft leather cushion, while his right hand raised her dress over her back. He pressed his knee between her legs, separating them, ripped her panties down, and began to explore.

"I don't think you and I started off on the right foot, did we, Linda?" He leaned forward and spoke softly into her ear in that sleepy, dreamy voice, those long fingers rubbing ever so gently. She struggled, but her arms were limp. Her shoulders were pinned against the couch, and there was nothing she could do to stop him. She tried to scream, but her face was pressed deep into the cushion and all that came out was a muffled moan.

"That's better," he whispered softly into her ear. "I saw you sneaking out of Eleanor's office a few minutes ago," he said as he kept rubbing, beginning to probe with his long fingers.

"No, no, please," she managed to whisper, feeling so tired, so limp, as if she were caught in a dream.

"What were you doing in Eleanor's office, Linda?" he asked as he gently raised her head far enough for her to speak.

"Nothing, nothing!" she gasped. "I was delivering…"

"No, no, no, we both know that's a lie, now don't we?" he said as he pressed her face back into the cushion and began probing harder now with his fingers. "Did Eleanor leave something in there for you? Something you could use against us, against *me?* Last night, I saw you talking to that fellow Burke. I don't know what he promised you, or what you promised him — was it those papers that Eleanor took? I dislike disloyal employees, Linda. What do you think I should do when someone is disloyal to me?" he asked as his voice suddenly turned angry and he grabbed a handful of her hair, yanked on it and twisted her neck up. That snapped her wide awake so that she could see the cruel look in his eyes and realize what was happening and what he was doing to her was all too real.

"You were Eleanor's friend — her *only* friend, as far I can tell," he continued. "I figure you were her insurance policy. Is that what she talked you into becoming, Linda? Her insurance policy?"

"No, no, please, Dr. Greenway, I swear I haven't," she gasped, pleading with him.

"Linda, if you continue to lie to me, you leave me no choice but to discipline you; and that can be very unpleasant, for you anyway. Like any good employer, I always prefer to handle those tasks myself," he said as he pressed her face back into the cushion again and used his free hand to unbuckle his belt and let his pants drop to the floor. "What did Eleanor give you?"

He raised his shirt, looked down at her lovely, smooth skin, and smiled, feeling himself get hard. She was trembling now and he heard her sobbing into the cushion. "Eleanor took some company papers from us, maybe some reports, a data disk or a flash drive," he said as he stroked her with his hand, getting rougher and more demanding. She was helpless and completely at his mercy now, which was the way he loved it. "So tell me what Eleanor gave you," he asked as he leaned forward, his flesh against her flesh so she could feel him about to thrust himself into her.

"This is your last chance, Linda. I can tell you are wide awake now. To tell you the truth, some of the girls prefer a little hypnosis or a sniff of my 'joy juice' the first time, like I gave you. That way, they are never quite certain what happened, who said what, and what they might have done to encourage me. I'm sure you know what I mean. Personally, however, I prefer they be wide awake, as you are now, because I want you to be absolutely certain that it was rape."

As he spoke, a loud, grating voice called out to him from the intercom on his desk, breaking his concentration. "Doctor Greenway, is Linda Sylvester up there? Would you please tell her there is a special FedEx shipment down here that she has to sign for."

"You have to let me go!" She managed to twist her head far enough to get the words out. "You have to," she gasped. "They know

I'm up here, and those are checks I have to sign for. They're going to come up here looking for me any minute now."

He laughed and was about to thrust himself into her, but he suddenly stopped. Instead, he merely leaned against her, rubbing his bare skin against her as he pressed his face into the nape of her neck again. "You are a clever girl, Linda," he breathed heavily into her ear. "But do you really think your friends down there are going to come up here and break into *my* office to save you? Into *my office?* And if they do, who do you think they're going to believe?"

"Eleanor warned me about you. You killed her, didn't you?" she gasped.

"Ah, you've been talking to that fellow Burke. Yes, I killed her!" he suddenly pressed himself hard against her. "I killed her and I'll kill you too; but I'll do a lot of other things to you first, if you don't get me those papers!" Greenway let his words sink in. "Until you do, I own you, Linda; and I can do *anything* I want to you, because you are a thief, like Eleanor."

"Dr. Greenway? I really need to talk to Linda," the voice on the intercom spoke again

Finally, he backed away and released his grip on her neck. "You are involved in the theft of important corporate documents, and there's no one who can help you now — not the girls downstairs, not the police, not even your friend Robert Burke. No one!" he said as he pulled up his pants up and tucked in his shirt. "The next time I call you up here, plan on staying for a while and plan on being much more cooperative; that is, unless you want to find yourself in the unemployment line, or in jail, and your darling little daughter in the custody of Social Services."

"My daughter? You bastard!" she scrambled to her feet, pulled down her skirt, and tried desperately to straighten her clothes. "You…!" She wanted to scream something at him but she was too rattled to find the words.

"Believe me, Linda, that was nothing," he smiled. "No harm, no foul, as they say, simply a little *demonstration* of things to come, if you don't learn to cooperate."

"If you ever touch me again, or dare to touch my daughter, I'll kill you!"

"Really?" Greenway laughed at her and pointed down to her torn panties, hanging around one ankle, "Well, you might want to get rid of those first before you go back downstairs, killer."

"I'm calling the police!" She pulled them off and stumbled backward toward the door.

"Oh, be my guest," he laughed even harder as he pointed at the phone. "I have Chief Bentley on speed dial; so stop lying to me. As you should know by now, you are playing a very dangerous game with me, little girl. I want my papers back, and you are going to get them for me; because the next time we have one of our little chats…"

"There will never be a next time!" she seethed as she backed away.

"Oh, yes, there will, tomorrow afternoon, I think. Yes, I shall clear my schedule. Shall we say around 3:00? So plan to bring those papers and reports to me then, right here, in my office. I'll even open a nice bottle of wine for the occasion, as I did with Eleanor. Won't that be nice?"

"Nice…?" she sputtered. "I'm never coming back up here!"

"Oh, yes you will. Of course, if you'd prefer a little more privacy," he said as he belted his pants and grinned at her. "I suppose we could meet at your house in Des Plaines and have a 'play date' — you, me, and little Emily."

She turned and glared at him. "If you ever touch my daughter, I swear, I'll kill you!"

"Ah, we seem to have found a *hot button*, haven't we?" he laughed at her. "But if you don't like the prospect of being alone with me, then you *really* won't like spending a few nights with Chief Bentley in one of the cells in that new cracker box jail of his after I have you arrested as an accomplice to grand theft. I understand he and his boys can be quite rough on young women."

Linda's eyes went wide as she yanked the office door open and ran.

"Tomorrow, Linda, 3:00 p.m. tomorrow!" he called out as she ran into the hallway, slamming his office door behind her.

Red-faced, her hair and clothes in disarray, she was almost in tears when she reached the elevator and pushed the button. The twin stainless steel doors opened, but as she tried to step inside, she ran into Tony Scalese, who was coming out. Bumping into him was like bumping into a brick wall, and she let loose a small, panicked scream. She was already right on the edge of a breakdown, and quickly backed away, terrified, assuming Greenway sent for him. However, she could not have been more wrong.

Scalese paused. He looked at her and immediately noted her

mussed hair and twisted clothes. He saw Greenway's office door standing open at the end of the hall and frowned. Obviously, it did not take him long to figure out what had just transpired.

Linda swore she saw his eyes narrow as he mumbled, "Excuse me," sounding truly contrite. He stepped aside to let Linda enter the elevator, and then turned and marched toward Greenway's office.

Tony Scalese burst through Greenway's door, slammed it behind him, and felt his anger building to a towering rage. Greenway sat behind his desk and looked up at him with a contented smirk. Scalese saw the files and magazines scattered about the floor near the coffee table, and noticed that the cushions on the leather couch were out of place. He strode right up to the edge of Greenway's desk, leaned forward on both fists, and glared down at him.

"You don't seem to hear so well anymore, Doc. I told you if you didn't keep it in your pants, there'd be some serious repercussions. What? You think I was kidding?"

"Her? I caught her going through Eleanor Purdue's office."

"Purdue's office? So what! We went through the whole place — the desk, the credenza, even her computer. There ain't nothing in there, and you know it."

"But she didn't, Anthony," Greenway snapped back defiantly. "She was Eleanor's best friend, and she knows more than you think she does. I saw her talking to that fellow Burke last night, and was trying to find out what they were up to."

"Doc, that ain't what you were doin' here, and you know it."

"You're wrong," Greenway rose to the challenge. "She knows where Eleanor hid those reports; and she's going to get them for me."

"Really? How? Did you rape her like all the others?"

"No, no, not yet." He shook his head and smiled. "What you fail to understand is that certain forms of 'physical intimidation' can be highly useful in gaining a young woman's cooperation."

"Cooperation?"

"Yes, in her case, a small *demonstration* and the mere mention of her young daughter's name proved more than sufficient."

"Okay, what did she tell you?"

"Nothing yet, but tomorrow afternoon she will. She has far too much to lose now."

"You really are a son of a bitch, aren't you, Doc?"

Greenway looked up and sneered at the other man. "Anthony, I haven't come close to the *many* outrages you and the DiGrigorias have committed," he said. "Speaking of which, did Bentley get rid of that 'telephone man,' Burke, yet, as you told me he would?"

"No! I just got off the phone with that idiot," he said as he backed away, chagrined. "The judge let Burke walk, and Bentley says he may be a lot more difficult to get rid of than we thought."

"More difficult? Then stop giving me any more of your crap about what I do and how I do it!" Greenway jumped to his feet glared across at Scalese. "I shall take care of the lovely Ms. Sylvester any damned way I please, and I *will* get my missing documents back. *You* tell Bentley to do what we're paying him to do… unless you need me to do that, too?"

CHAPTER ELEVEN

When Bob and Angie Burke split eight months earlier, his friends referred to it as "the Big Bang," "the San Andreas Fault," or "the Eve of Destruction," subtle things like that. For his part, as things fell apart, Bob tried to take the high road, while Angie's idea of a road was the kind Sherman took through Georgia — burn everything and leave nothing behind but ashes. If she could not have it, no one would have it. That was Angie.

On the other hand, Bob was a realist. For him, all that remained was to acknowledge their situation with the "D" word, D-I-V-O-R-C-E, as the song went. Maybe it was the Army, but reality was simply part of his DNA. When it's over, it's over, and only the dumbass Marines fight battles they can't win. Not him. He and Angie argued enough, fought enough, and bled enough; they were well past any hope of reconciling. So why not part as friends? That was the only thing that made any sense to him, but Bob was a lot older than Angie was, and decades more mature.

In terms of money and property, he owned very little when he came into the marriage straight from the Army — a cheap apartment, a used Saturn, and maybe eight thousand dollars in the bank. He thought it only fair to leave the same way. However, the company stock was different. Ed Toler decided that Bob was the best choice to succeed him as President, and he gave him the job and controlling interest in the company. That was Ed's choice to make, and Bob felt obliged to honor that trust. The real estate and accumulated family wealth was different. The day he walked out, Bob handed Angie the keys to the big house in Winnetka and the condominiums in Vail, New York City, and downtown Chicago. Illinois divorce law aside, the real estate belonged to her father and mother, so Bob felt it should all go to her regardless. Fair was fair. She got the new, "polar bear" white Cadillac Escalade "war wagon," and he drove away from the big house in Winnetka in his "embarrassing" old Saturn, as she called it.

That was how he wanted the property settled; but his lawyer, George Grierson, could not disagree more. "Bob, you don't understand. That isn't how it works. If you give her all that stuff now, without even arguing, it comes off the table and then she'll get half of what's left, too."

"No, George, you're the one who doesn't understand. I don't want *any* of it and I never did. The truth is I should have stayed in the Army. I know that now, but Ed caught me in weak moment and I caved. Okay, that first year or so with Angie was really great, and the job was great, too. Ed would teach me stuff during the day, and Angie would turn me stupid all over again at night, but it was great. We were in love and I thought it would go on forever, until Ed got sick and went into the hospital, and that was the end of everything."

"It was for him, too."

"True, and for me and Angie. You see, she didn't give a damn about the houses or the cars, either. She thought it was all hers to begin with — and the company too. The truth is, I didn't want that either, but Ed made me swear I'd accept and honor his stock distribution plan. He insisted; he said he'd come back and haunt me if I didn't. He told her about it in the hospital, when the first set of tests came back bad. For 'Daddy Dearest' to do that to her... well, she blamed it all on me, of course, said I brainwashed him and that was the end of them and of us."

"I understand that, Bob, but the house and the condos are worth a lot of money, maybe more than the company when you net it all out. Can I at least talk to her about a trade, maybe some kind of a compromise?" Grierson suggested.

"George, you're missing the whole point. She thinks the houses and the condos always *were* hers, from day one. I can't trade them to her. If I did anything other than hand her the keys, she would have blown an even bigger fit. The problem is she thinks the company is hers too, by right. If I don't hand over *those* keys too, she's going to war. So give her the real estate, all of it. That's a sideshow. The real battle will be over the company."

That was why Angie ended up in the big houses with the expensive cars, and why Bob ended up in a modest two-bedroom rental townhouse in Arlington Heights with rented furniture and an old Saturn parked in the small attached garage out back.

It was already dark when Bob finally left the office, stopping home long enough to check the mail, see if there was anything on the answering machine, and change clothes. Normally, that would be followed by a hard martial arts workout at the gym, a 5-K run, some fruit and salad, and an early night's sleep. After six months of this Spartan regimen, he shed the excess "Angie" weight and his fat ass was almost back to fighting shape. He wasn't quite the "lean, mean war machine" of five years ago who could hump seventy-pound packs across the Hindu Kush all day long, but he was getting there. This Spartan regime, the modest townhouse, and occasional TV dinners didn't bother him in the slightest. He'd lived out of suitcases, Bachelor Officers' Quarters, cheap motels, tents, backpacks and occasionally on the hard, bare ground, so a ninety-nine-dollar mattress and Formica countertops were much more to his taste than the big house with all the marble in Winnetka.

He pulled a bottle of water and an apple out of the refrigerator and began to flip through the day's stack of junk mail when his phone rang. The display on the answering machine showed a number he didn't recognize, so he let it go to record.

He heard a young woman's hesitant voice say, "Mr. Burke, this is Linda Sylvester. I tried calling you before and... Look, I know it is late and I can call back, but I need to..."

He grabbed the receiver before she could hang up. "Linda, this is Bob Burke. Sorry about that, and I'm glad you called."

"I... I need to talk to you. Not like this though, not on the phone. I think they're..."

"I understand. Where are you?"

"Actually, I'm around the corner from your place at the pay phone in the lobby of the Marriott Courtyard, and I'm scared, Mr. Burke," he heard her sob. "I'm really scared."

"Wait right there. I'll pick you up at the back door in let's say... five minutes."

In the Federal Building downtown, US Attorney Peter O'Malley was signing the last of the correspondence on his desk when one of the intra-office phone lines buzzed. He pushed the button on his telephone and heard, "Mr. O'Malley, I'm glad I caught you. This is Stephens down in Audio Surveillance. I have something on the tap we installed on Subject Burke's home phone. There hasn't been much traffic on it, but you said to notify you as soon as..."

"Burke?" O'Malley suddenly sat forward and sounded very interested. "Good, good."

"It was a woman named Linda Sylvester," the technician continued.

"Sylvester? Excellent! I was hoping that might happen."

"The call only lasted twenty-three seconds. She said she did not wish to talk on the phone. She was scared; said it twice, and that's exactly the way she sounded. Anyway, the call came from a pay phone at the Marriott Courtyard in Arlington Heights. It must be close, because he said he'd meet her there in a couple of minutes. Then they hung up."

"Damn!" O'Malley exclaimed as he glanced at his watch. "It'll take an hour to get out there in this traffic. Keep it monitored, Stevens. At least we finally got something off that tap," O'Malley added as he ended the call. Linda Sylvester! It's about time, he smiled.

Bob Burke drove into the parking lot at Marriott Courtyard and pulled into a space near the rear door. Before he could turn the engine off, Linda Sylvester dashed out, opened his passenger side door, and jumped inside.

"Go! Go, please," she pleaded as she dropped down in the seat, keeping her head below the window level.

"Sure, sure," he answered as he backed out of the space and drove away. "Anywhere in particular you want to go?"

"No, just drive," she said as she raised her eyes over the back of the seat and looked behind them. "Is anyone following us?"

"Like Greenway or his pals?" he asked as he checked the car's mirrors. "Relax, I can protect you."

"No, you can't! I don't even know why I called you, except I'm terrified and there was nowhere else for me to turn." She looked up at him and pleaded. "Please, you've got to help me."

He looked over at her and saw she was trembling and on the verge of a breakdown. "Linda, have you eaten anything today?"

"No, there's no time, I have a babysitter with Emily."

"There's always time, you look like you're falling apart."

"Thanks! That's all I need," she said as she collapsed in the corner of the seat.

"I see a McDonalds up ahead. I'm going to hit the drive-thru," he said as he checked the rear view mirror. "There's no one following us, and you need food. While we are eating you can tell me all about it."

With a bag of sandwiches and two coffees in hand, he parked in the rear of the McDonalds lot in the shadows next to the dumpster. Five minutes later, between bites of a Big Mac and a handful of fries, she began to open up. "Eleanor is our CFO and Chief Accountant. I guess you already know that. She's older than I am and I'm new, but we are both single and we became friends. You know how it is in a small office. The other women are all married or teeny bops, and the handful of men are either gay or won't keep their hands off you. Eleanor's been with the company since CHC started down on the South Side. Greenway was

President and ran the clinics, and Eleanor kept the books. That was before Scalese and all of his creeps took over, she told me. Then, the business exploded, and they opened a lot of new clinics, the big new office building in Indian Hills, and other things."

"They 'took over?' "

"Oh, yeah. They run CHC now, not Greenway. I think Eleanor finally got fed up with all the crooked accounting and went to the cops with it. Maybe she went to Bentley, I don't know; but she dropped a few hints to me that she got herself into something very dangerous."

"I'd say so; Greenway killed her."

"I know that now. He told me he did, and he told me he'd kill me too."

"Greenway? He told you he killed her?" Bob asked, astonished. "When?"

"This afternoon," she said as she turned her face away, unable to look at him. "He told me he killed her to make a point, Mr. Burke!"

"To make a point? What kind of sick—"

"He was *demonstrating* that he can do anything he wants — to her, to me, to anyone — and get away with it. Anything!" He heard her sob.

He looked at her and began to understand. "What did he do to you?"

"Nothing! No, that's not true. Look, Mr. Burke, I don't even know you, and…"

"My name's Bob, and you can't keep this all bottled up inside, Linda. You need to talk to someone — your mother, your sister, a girlfriend, me, take your pick," he said as he turned her face toward him. "But since I'm here, close your eyes and start talking. Okay?"

She nodded, closed her eyes and turned away, and let the words spill out. "He got me up in his office this afternoon and almost raped me. He's so big and strong that I…"

"Almost? Well, that's a good thing," he tried to comfort her.

"Not really!" she said and quickly turned away. "He kind of hypnotized me, and then he drugged me with a cloth or something he held over my face. I felt strange, and it happened so fast. He grabbed me, bent me over his couch, and ripped my underwear off. I couldn't stop him, and… God! I was so scared, so vulnerable, so humiliated. He leaned against me and was about to… That was when one of the girls downstairs called for me on the intercom and he suddenly stopped. He… he let me go."

"He let you go?"

"Yes, he said this was a little *demonstration,* to make a point."

"A *demonstration?* I saw his eyes when his fingers were wrapped around Eleanor's throat up on the roof. That was no *demonstration.*"

"The whole thing was my own stupid fault. Eleanor warned me never to go up to his office alone. She told me... well, I think he did the same thing to her and a lot of others. Apparently, he wasn't quite as bad back when it started, but he got rougher and rougher until Eleanor told him to leave her alone. He didn't want to, but she threatened to talk to Scalese. He stayed away from her after that, but by then the office expanded and he could pick from dozens of younger women, as she said he did. I think that was when she went to the police. He's a sick pervert, but what he did to me wasn't sex, or even rough sex. It was a power game he was playing, trying to terrorize me, and it worked. Goddamn him, it worked."

"Only if you let it. But why did he suddenly pick on you? Was it because of last night?"

"Maybe. He told me Eleanor stole some things from the company — documents, reports, maybe a DVD or a flash drive. They must be important, and he thinks I know where they are."

"It wasn't Bentley Eleanor was talking to, it was the US Attorney."

"Oh, God! Greenway and now the US Attorney? I'm dead. I'm dead," she moaned and turned away, only to sit up and turn toward him again. "But how do you know that?"

"His name's Peter O'Malley. He came to see me this morning, to threaten me, and he was not very subtle about it. He has a Grand Jury looking into organized crime and Medicaid fraud, and his first target is CHC. Eleanor was secretly helping him, bringing him some reports and documents, probably the stuff Greenway is looking for. He must have found out what she was up to and it got her killed."

"I snuck into her office today. Her desk drawers were empty and everything was gone, her files, her computer, everything. They stripped it clean, but I do not think they found anything. If they did, Greenway wouldn't have come after me like that."

"He's desperate, so is O'Malley, and they have you and me sandwiched in the middle."

"Oh, my God." She slumped back in the seat and shook her head. "What am I going to do? Greenway threatened my job, my house, even my daughter, and he was about to rape me right there in his office, to prove he could do it and get away with it. He said he would keep doing it, keep violating me anytime he wants, until I get him those documents. And he knows there's *nothing* I can do about it."

"No, maybe you can't, but I can." Bob turned and looked at her, his eyes growing as cold and gray as a hard winter's day.

"You?" She looked over at him and opened her hand. Lying in her palm was his badly wrinkled, sweat-soaked business card. "But... you're what? A 'telephone guy?' That's what Scalese called you."

"Yeah, well, I do some of that too." He looked at the card and smiled.

"Scalese and his men are professional thugs. They'll kill you."

"Let me worry about them."

She frowned and said, "You really are crazy, you know."

"Maybe, maybe not." He shrugged, looking at her, waiting. "Well?" he finally asked.

"Well, what?"

"Well, do you have them — the documents, or whatever the hell it is they're looking for?"

"No! At least I don't think so. Oh, I don't know. A week ago, Eleanor and I went to a bar after work. It got pretty 'drunk out' that night. Anyway, she told me a lot about Greenway and CHC, and gave me a set of keys for her office and her house. She said she put something inside a box of Cocoa Puffs in her kitchen pantry, something important."

"A box of Cocoa Puffs?" He gave her an odd look, but that didn't stop her.

"I'm serious. She said it was a note, and she made me swear if anything ever happened to her, if she ever disappeared, or anything, I was to go get it and do whatever it said. She said something else, something about it being the key."

"The key?" Bob stared out the front windshield for a moment, thinking. "Then that's what we'll do. We'll go to Eleanor's and find out what's in that box of Cocoa Puffs."

"Are you sure? I didn't want to get you involved in this, but..."

"There was no one else you could call, right?"

"Makes me sound really pathetic, doesn't it? But I was too afraid to go over there alone."

"So you figured you'd call the 'telephone guy' and let him find out if there are any of Tony Scalese's goons waiting inside?"

"Well, yes, but I meant for us to go together."

"All right, when do you want to go?"

"I don't know," she answered, surprised by the question. "But it has to be before 3:00 o'clock tomorrow afternoon."

"Why? What happens then?"

"That's the deadline Greenway gave me — 3:00 o'clock tomorrow afternoon — or else he'll come looking for me and my daughter. So if this doesn't work, I'm on the road at 2:00," she said as she turned her face away. "God... I can still feel his hands, and his fingers all over me, and *him* pressed up against me. I get so sick every time I think about it, I told him I'd kill him if he ever touched me again — me or my daughter — and I meant it."

"It's not going to come to that, I promise. But do you have somewhere you can go?"

"Montana, New Mexico, Florida, I really don't care, so long as it's away from him."

"Then I guess we'd better make this work," he said as he started the car.

"Where are you going?"

"Eleanor's. I figure this is as good a time as any, isn't it? You can stay here, get yourself some more coffee, and relax. I'll go to her house and get whatever is in that box," he said as he held out his hand. "Give me the keys and tell me how to get there."

"I can't let you go there alone. It's too dangerous."

"Too dangerous? All right, then we'll both go."

"Well, do you have a gun or something?"

"A gun? No. The only thing a gun does is invite someone to shoot at you. Don't worry, though, I do have 'something.' If you come with me, however, you must promise to do exactly what I tell you to do, when I tell you. Exactly, agreed?" She started to say something until he put his finger on her lips and shook his head. "I mean it, no discussion and no questions."

Night fell on the north suburbs as they drove north on Route 53, got off on the Northwest Highway, and drove through Des Plaines, until they reached Mount Prospect, where Eleanor lived. Bob pulled over, disabled the interior dome light, and switched places with her so Linda could take the wheel. Before he got back in, however, he opened his trunk and dug through several boxes he kept back there. When he got in the passenger seat, he wore a black pullover sweater with big pockets on the front and soft-soled black running shoes. In his hand, he held a black knit ski mask and a pair of thin, black high-tech gloves.

"You're kidding, right? Are you some kind of a Ninja or something?"

"You've been watching too many movies," he chuckled. "Let's go."

Eleanor's house was on a cul-de-sac in a nice, tree-lined section of Mount Prospect. "What's her address?" he asked as he pulled out his smartphone.

"927 Asbury Circle. It's a nice two-story Dutch colonial, not too big, but cute."

"Cute, huh? I'm not sure my GPS app does 'cute,' " he said as he entered the address and began playing with the display, making it larger, and then smaller, until he memorized the surrounding streets. When they got within three blocks, he told her to make a series of turns, slowly circling Eleanor's street in an ever-tightening spiral. "Take the next right," he told her. "Go halfway up and park under the trees." When they got there, he turned to her and asked, "Okay, as we looped through her neighborhood, tell me what you saw."

"What I saw? Well, uh, trees, nice houses, some parked cars… it was pretty dark."

"It's not dark, there's a thin crescent moon — big difference."

"Really?" she said, obviously getting irritated.

"I'm serious. What else? Did you see anything unusual?"

"Like what?"

"Like the midnight-blue Lincoln Town Car parked one street over with a man slumped down in the front seat smoking a cigarette."

"Uh, no, I…"

"He's probably been sitting there all day."

"All day? How did you know that?"

"There were a half dozen cigarette butts in the street outside his window, and a City of Chicago registration sticker on the window. For future reference, we'll call him Bozo #1. All right, did you see the second car parked in the shadows inside her cul-de-sac? It was probably a Chrysler, with a man sitting inside that one too. He'll be Bozo #2."

"No, I… no. Who do you think they are? Greenway's men?"

"Greenway?" He chuckled again. "You may not think so, but Greenway's a lightweight. Those Gumbahs belong to Tony Scalese, or more correctly, to Salvatore DiGrigoria."

"You mean the Mafia?" her mouth fell open. "But why would they…?"

"Why? Because they own Greenway and CHC, and they're watching Eleanor's house, waiting for you, or for someone."

"But Greenway gave me until tomorrow afternoon."

"It's not his call, Linda. Scalese probably put them here this morning."

"You're saying if I had come here by myself... Oh my God!"

"I suspect you'd have ended up next to Eleanor, wherever that is." He looked over and saw the terrified expression on her face. "The two Bozos in the cars were easy to spot. There are probably more inside the house. They may take me a few minutes more, so relax."

"A few minutes? You can't go out there," she said, terrified. "When I asked you..."

"What can I say? I have a sudden craving for Cocoa Puffs," he grinned as he put the knit ski mask on and pulled it down. With eyeholes and a slit for his mouth, it covered his face.

"You really are crazy. I should never have dragged you into this, they'll..."

"You didn't drag me into anything; Greenway did when he strangled Eleanor Purdue up on that roof."

"But there's too many of them."

"Not when you take them down one at a time. Look, Linda, long before I went into high-tech telecommunication system design — not installing phones — I was involved in irregular warfare and counterterror operations in places a whole lot worse than Mount Prospect, Illinois. Believe me, *those* guys are the ones with the problem, not me." He looked at his watch. "I want you to drive away and stay away from here for thirty minutes, then come back around and pick me up here — thirty minutes, exactly. If I'm not here, drive away and come back ten minutes later. If I'm still not here, drive back to McDonalds and wait for me there. You got that?"

Her eyes went as round as silver dollars as he slipped out of the car and simply vanished into the shadows.

CHAPTER TWELVE

First things first, Bob Burke told himself as he vanished into the shadows like a supple black cat. First, he would check the perimeter of the house, and then go inside and retrieve the note in the pantry. After that, the games could begin. Approaching Eleanor's house from the rear, he passed between two occupied homes, avoiding the pools of light that fell onto the grass from lit windows, keeping low. He moved silently around the hedges and shrubs, quickly crossing another dark street and through more yards until he had a clear view of the rear of Eleanor Purdue's house. He was not afraid of the Mafia "soldiers" Tony Scalese probably left to watch the property, not after he saw the two Bozos sitting in the cars out on the street. Even if Scalese was smart and put still more eyes outside and inside the house, once Burke located them, he could take them out with minimal effort. The only things that concerned him were large, trained guard dogs and exotic electronic surveillance equipment or motion sensors he might not locate until it was too late. In a neighborhood like this, though, the dogs would likely be someone's house pet and the alarm systems came from Best Buy.

To Bob Burke, this was a recon mission, not a serious "Black Op." The men up ahead weren't battle-hardened Al Qaeda fanatics, Afghan mountain tribesmen, the Russian Alpha Group, or the Chinese PLA "Shadow" Special Ops troops, each of which he dealt with at one point or another during his career. Those missions were neither easy nor pretty. Tonight, the men he faced were third-generation arm-breakers from Cicero. They might think they were tough, but they were the ones who were out of their league. Whether there were only the two men inside the cars or a half-dozen more hiding in the house and around the neighborhood, they were about to learn why it didn't pay to eat too much pasta, smoke too many cigarettes, set up static, one-man observation posts in the front seats of big pimp-mobiles, or pick on a "phone guy."

The most common way to break into a house was through the front or back door. That was where burglars usually went, because most residential door locks came from Home Depot and could be jimmied with a credit card or a butter knife. All too often, however, they weren't locked to begin with, and burglars preferred simplicity. Eleanor's house was dark, with no lights on in any of the rooms or around the exterior, except for the dim glow of a television set on the rear screened-in porch. They're watching television? Amazing! It took him four minutes to circle the house and check the windows and doors for alarms and wires. Except for some third-rate commercial sensors on the windows, he found nothing serious. Circling around to the back again, he crept closer to the screened porch. From ten feet away, Bob smelled cigarette smoke wafting out through the porch screens and heard an old *Magnum P. I.* rerun playing softly on the television. It was another of Scalese's men, and he became Bozo #3.

Bob crept away and turned his attention to the basement crawl space. He pulled a folding tactical knife from his pocket and set to work on the wooden knockout panel. It took less than thirty seconds to cut the paint seal, loosen the panel, and slip inside. This was a fairly new house. As he expected, the floor of the crawl space was gravel covered with plastic sheets. He turned on a small, high-intensity penlight. Other than leftover insulation, paint cans, and wood trim, the crawl space was empty and there was an open access panel into the basement furnace room at the far end. Moving quickly and silently in a "duck walk," he crossed the crawl and dropped into the basement. Like the rest of the house, it was dark, with an empty, dead-air smell about it, so he headed for the stairs. One useful trick they taught him at an infiltration course many years before at Fort Benning was that new or old, bare or carpeted, a wooden staircase always squeaks. The only way to go up or down one without making any noise was to do it in slow motion, ever so gradually shifting your weight seamlessly, one pound at a time, as if making perfect Tai Chi movements. Slowly but silently, he moved up from one riser to the next until he found himself standing at the landing, listening at the door.

He pulled a small spray pen of WD-40 from his pocket and spritzed the hinges on the inside of the door, waiting a minute for the oil to penetrate before he silently eased the door open, crept into the kitchen, and paused to hear and smell. The sliding glass doors to the screened-in porch and deck were open, and he could see and smell the dim outline of Bozo #3 backlit by the TV set. He lay in a big recliner with his back to the kitchen, his feet propped on an ottoman, and a cigarette dangling from his left hand. A .45-caliber automatic pistol, a cheap Motorola two-way radio, and a cell phone lay on the end table next to him. Wedged in the chair with him was a large open bag of potato chips which he was noisily munching away on, watching the muted TV without a care in the world. Before he dealt with this clown, Bob turned, crept silently down the hall, and peeked into the dining room and living room. That was where he found Bozo #4 sleeping on his back on the couch. His shoes lay on the carpet next to him and his pistol lay on his big beer gut, rising and falling as he snored. How could incompetents like these two manage to live this long, he wondered.

He quietly checked the rest of the house but found no other gunmen lying around. Retracing his steps to the kitchen, he decided to take Bozo #3 off the board first, since he was awake. As Burke crept through the open doorway to the back porch, one of the floorboards creaked. "Eh! Dat you? I'm starved," the guy snorted with a mouthful of potato chips, turned his head, and looked back over his shoulder. "Want to order out for some pizza, or should…"

Good question, Bob thought as his hands and forearms slipped around the man's neck in a very effective chokehold that instantly silenced him and cut off the blood flow to his brain. Burke pulled back, squeezed hard, and Bozo #3 was quickly out cold. Bob could have as easily snapped the guy's neck or kept the hold on a while longer and killed him, but there was nothing personal in this, not yet, and killing them wasn't why he came. Instead, he rolled Bozo #3 out of his chair and onto the floor, cut off the cords from several of the horizontal blinds on the windows, stuffed the man's handkerchief into his mouth, and hogtied him with his feet and his hands drawn up behind his back. With that done, Bob shoved the .45 into his rear waistband and the man's wallet, radio, and cell phone into the deep pockets in his pullover sweater.

Bozo #4 proved even easier. Bob crept back into the living room, picked up the boxy, 9-millimeter Glock from where it lay on the goon's stomach, and pressed it against his forehead. "Eh, you wanna die?" Bob asked in his best Cicero accent. The clown must have been in a deep, slow-wave, Delta sleep cycle, because he woke with a start, eyes wide open. "Well, do you, punk?" Bob switched to Dirty Harry and pressed down on the Glock even harder. "Get on the floor, on your stomach, and put your hands behind your back. Now!"

He hogtied this one even faster than the last one, pulled off one of the man's socks, stuffed it in his mouth, and took his wallet. With both of the potential interruptions now out of play, he went back to the kitchen. Linda said the note was in a cereal box in the pantry. Inside, on the middle shelf, sat a giant-economy sized box of Cocoa Puffs. Eleanor was clever, he must admit. If you want to hide something, the best choice is to leave it in plain sight. Burke pulled the box down and examined both ends. The top was still sealed. Assuming there was something inside, Eleanor must have carefully re-glued the bottom. Turning it over, he separated the flaps, looked inside, and saw a small, 3"x5" envelope wedged between the plastic cereal bag and the box. He pulled it out, tucked it in his rear pants pocket unopened, and replaced the box of breakfast cereal on the shelf.

Before he left the kitchen, he pulled out the wallets he took from Bozos #3 and #4. Both were thick and well worn. He opened the first and flipped through the usual array of Visa, State Farm auto insurance, Knights of Columbus, AAA, Gold's Gym, and Sam's Club cards. How banal, he thought. There was also an Illinois driver's license in the name of Angelo Rocco, fifty-two years old, with a Mount Prospect address. They probably called him "Rocky Angels" or "the Big Angel," or some other Gumbah movie nickname, he thought. The contents of the second wallet appeared to be about the same, with a driver's license in the name of Stanley Hruska from Blue Island, Illinois, on the far southwest side. Hruska? A Blue Island Hunkie mixed in with all these Neapolitans and Sicilians? Dude, you really are lost, Bob thought. He pushed the two driver's licenses into his other rear pocket with the envelope. Bozos! He shook his head, knowing he pegged them spot on.

He returned to the living room, only to find Stanley had rolled onto his side and managed to wiggle halfway under the coffee table. "Where you going, Stanley?" Bob asked as he knelt next to him and rolled him back onto his stomach. He grabbed a handful of Hruska's thinning hair, pulled up on it, and turned Hruska's face toward him. "You're not trying to be a hero are you?" he asked. "I'm going outside, but I'll be back in thirty minutes. If you move so much as an inch from where you are right now, I'll get one of those dull kitchen knives and gut you like a Lake Michigan carp. You got that?" Hruska quickly nodded, so Bob let his head drop back onto the carpeted floor, nose first, with a loud "thunk!"

As he returned to the kitchen, he saw Bozo #3 was still out cold. No need to "duck walk" back through the crawl space, particularly since he was now carrying all their toys — a Glock 9-millimeter, a Colt .45, the two Motorola radios and cell phones, and their wallets. As he walked across the rear porch and out the back door into the backyard, he looked at his watch. Linda was due back in eleven minutes, which left him with a choice. He had what he came for, and in the process had fired two loud, embarrassing shots across Tony Scalese's bow. The smart play now was to return to the pickup point and wait for Linda. That might be the smart thing; but he was definitely on a roll and he hated to waste eleven minutes.

Keeping low, he worked his way through the landscaping and around the side of the house that backed up to Eleanor's lot. Parked in the shadow of a drooping maple tree was the Lincoln Town Car, with Bozo #2 slumped in the driver's seat. Approaching it from the rear, he could see the top half of the man's head through the window, a task made all the easier by the faint glow coming from the car's dashboard. Bob shook his head in disbelief. The fool must have the car radio on. He could keep the volume as low as he wanted, but the radio's LED control panel gave off a faint, green glow that was a dead giveaway, with "dead" being the operative word.

Bob crept along a hedge, out of sight in the Lincoln's passenger side blind spot until he reached the car. The driver's side window was down and the clown's elbow and forearm hung out as he smoked another cigarette. He listened for a moment and realized Bozo #2 had a Cubs game playing on the radio. A Cubs game? You gotta be kidding, Burke thought. Staying even lower, he crept along the rear of the car, turned the corner, and in two long strides reached the driver's window with Bozo #4's Glock in his hand. With a quick backhand blow, he nailed the driver in the temple with the pistol butt. He hoped the driver was recording the baseball game at home, because that was the last inning he was going to hear for a while. The man's eyes rolled up in his head and he was out cold.

Bob reached through the open window, pushed the button that opened the trunk, and dragged the clown around to the rear of the Lincoln. He propped him on the edge of the open trunk, tied his arms behind his back with his own belt, and grabbed his wallet, too. His driver's license was from New Jersey and the name read "Gino Santucci." Jersey? Bob Burke kept the license and the wallet, and gave the driver a gentle nudge, until he toppled backwards into the Lincoln's cavernous trunk. He gently lowered the trunk until he heard the lock click. In the front seat, he found an expensive 9-millimeter Sig Sauer P-226 semi-automatic pistol and another Motorola two-way radio on the center console. He added them to his collection and looked at his watch. There were two minutes left, more than enough time to make it back to the pickup point.

Bob knelt down in the deep shadow of a maple tree one street over. Less than a minute later, he saw Linda drive slowly around the corner in his Saturn. When she was 20 feet away, he stood up, pulled off the ski mask, and stepped into the street. As she pulled up next to him, he did not wait for the car's wheels to stop rolling before he climbed into the passenger seat and motioned for her to go.

"God, I've been so scared," Linda said, her knuckles white on the steering wheel.

"Everything's fine," he tried to reassure her. "Drive away, slow and easy."

"Was the envelope there? Did you get it? What did the note say?"

"I got it, but I didn't open it. I was a little busy. Besides, the note's to you, not to me," he said, as he dropped the ski mask, the gloves, the three semi-automatic pistols, two-way radios, and cell phones onto the floor of the back seat, keeping one of the radios in his lap.

Her eyes went wide. "Where did you get all that stuff?" she asked.

"I took them from three of Scalese's foot soldiers."

"There were three of them? Oh my God!"

"Actually there were four, but I ran out of time before I could get to the second car. It doesn't really matter, though. Those three are more than enough to send the message that needed to be sent to Tony Scalese and his boss."

"You mean you killed them?" she asked, suddenly terrified.

"No, no, I put a couple of dents in them and took their toys, but they'll be fine. I left them gagged and hog-tied back there, where their friends will find them. It shouldn't take much longer, before they are supposed to check in; then, it'll be like hitting a wasp's nest with a big stick. They'll come pouring out, angry and humiliated, trying to figure out who did this to them. They'll probably decide it's the competition or some other outfit, and that'll put them off-balance, which is exactly where I want them."

"Where you *want* them?" she repeated, stunned. "That's insane, Bob. What if they figure out it was you?"

"Me? I'm the 'telephone guy' and the last one they'd suspect. They'll be confused and looking over their shoulders for a few days, and the hotter and angrier they are, the dumber they'll get," he said as he pulled the envelope out of his hip pocket. "Here's Eleanor's note. Do you want to stop and read it?"

"No, I'm nervous enough driving. You read it."

He tore the envelope open and bent forward so he could read the note in the dim light from the dashboard. "Your friend, Eleanor, has tiny handwriting."

"What did she say?"

"Blah, blah, blah… Sorry to get you involved. I left a big envelope with spreadsheets that show CHC's real books… millions in Medicare and Medicaid fraud, falsified lab tests, even a report on the bad drugs they're making in India and selling all over Africa… Blah, blah,

blah… Ah, here's the good part. She hid all that stuff in her office, in a manila envelope, and she wants you to go in and get it."

"Her office? I looked there. So did Greenway. They tore it apart and stripped it bare."

"Apparently, none of you looked in the right place. She says she hid it in the ceiling, inside the air conditioning duct above the vent over her credenza. Clever woman." He sat back and nodded. "I'm sure they raised some of the acoustical tiles and looked up in the ceiling, but who would think of looking inside the duct? Okay, when do you want to go get it?"

"Go get it? Me? I can't go into that office again? I… I just can't, I…"

That was when the two-way radio in his lap finally sprang to life. The signal was weak and broken up by static but he heard, "Ay, Rocco, you're late. Where are you? I'm hungry and I gotta pee… Ay, Rocco?"

"That must be Bozo #1 in the Chrysler. It took him long enough, but now he's wondering where the others are." Bob picked up the radio and pushed the transmit button, coughing and speaking in his roughest New Jersey accent. "Ay! Hold it a freakin' minute, will yuz. Da boss is on the phone; I'll be dere," he growled, trying to fake it.

There was a long pause before Bozo #1 finally asked, "Rocco? Ay, who is dis?"

"He's takin' a freakin' nap, and it's none of your goddamn business. Now shut up and keep yer eyes on da street!" He expected to get more questions or an argument. When they didn't come, he figured Bozo #1 was onto him, and already running back to the house. He looked at his watch. "Any chance we can get in the building now?"

"No, they have magnetic locks on all the doors. The guards leave when the janitors are finished. That's when the alarms and motion sensors come on."

"Then it has to be first thing tomorrow. When do the doors open in the morning?"

"At 8:00 a.m., and there are usually a dozen early birds waiting at the door."

"Greenway or Scalese?"

"No, no, they never come in that early. A couple of Scalese's security guards will be around, but not him."

"Then that's when you'll have to do it, right at 8:00. Okay?" He looked at her as she closed her eyes and finally nodded. "There's no other choice, Linda. You should be in and get out in five minutes."

They drove on in silence until they reached the Marriott Courtyard. She drove around to the rear side of the motel, where she had left her own car. As Linda got out, Bob reached back and picked up the pistols, the Motorola radios, and the cell phones from the floor. He walked around to the rear of the car, popped the trunk, and tossed them inside.

"I'm giving all that stuff to Ernie Travers in the morning, along with the IDs on those three goons," he told her. "Maybe he can do something with them."

"You sure you don't want to keep any of it... like a gun?"

"No," he smiled. "They're of no use to me, and I don't want to give them or the police any excuse to shoot first. Look, there's a Bob Evans on Busse Road just north of Devon in Elk Grove Village. It's maybe three miles from the CHC building in Indian Hills. I'll be in the rear parking lot at 8:00 a.m. After you get the package from Eleanor's office, meet me there. We'll go through papers and figure out what to do next." She nodded woodenly, still very much afraid. "One other thing," he added. "Afterward, do you have anywhere you can go, you and your daughter? Family, friends? Some place they don't know about?"

"I'll have to think. I have an aunt in..."

"Don't tell me, it's better that I don't know. When you come here tomorrow morning, pack some clothes and things for you and Ellie; because you can't go home or back to the office until those guys are in jail. Oh, and give me your cell phone number," he asked.

She handed him her phone. "It's written on the back in magic marker," she said. "I can never remember, and... well, you know."

"Yeah, I think I do," he replied as he rolled his eyes and keyed her number into his phone. "There, I texted you with my number, in case you need to reach me. Remember, if they have your office and home phone bugged, they've probably got your cell phone covered, mine too. So keep it turned off unless there's an emergency. They can track you with it, so keep any calls short and cryptic."

He closed the car door and then looked back at her. "Don't worry. Greenway and the rest of them aren't half as smart as you think they are. They aren't looking for us; so, if we handle this right, by tomorrow night we'll be off somewhere having a beer and they'll be in the clink. Now get out of here and try to get some sleep. Tomorrow will be a big day."

CHAPTER THIRTEEN

Bob Burke was exhausted. After he dropped Linda off at the Marriott Courtyard, he went straight home and parked his Saturn in the one-car garage attached to the rear of his townhouse in Arlington Heights. The Saturn was an unobtrusive mid-range, mid-priced family car with none of the expensive extras, other than the first-rate CD player and sound system he added, which was probably worth more than the car now. He rarely listened to the car radio, but the CD player allowed him to get his daily fix of soft jazz from Miles Davis, Charlie Parker, Houston Person, and Sonny Criss, without whom he would be in a permanent funk. His modest apartment was much like the car. It came with cheap, disposable furniture, to which he'd added a large-screen HD TV in the living room, a very good Onkyo CD player, a set of Tyler Acoustics speakers, and two racks for his prized collection of modern jazz. Except for an occasional weekend football game, the TV proved a waste of money, because his schedule rarely allowed him time to watch much of anything that took three to four hours unless he recorded it and fast-forwarded through the commercials.

Other than the TV and audio system, the only other thing he put much money into was a state-of-the-art, integrated security system for his apartment. Having been on more than his share of radical Islamist hit lists, he knew that old enemies can be persistent. So, the day he moved in, he installed top quality wireless sensors on every door and window. He also installed motion detectors and miniature video and infrared cameras in the first floor rooms and the garage. With the help of some "black ops" pals at Fort Bragg, a couple of cases of beer, and some brats, he installed the system himself without getting permits or posting any of those cute little stickers on the doors or windows. No one knew the system was there, which was exactly how he wanted it. The door and window contacts and motion sensors were almost invisible, and the system control panel and video recorder were located high on the inside wall of his bedroom closet, behind a box. It was easily accessible for him, but the last place anyone else would think of looking to disable it. When he was away from home, if a sensor tripped, it would activate all the interior and exterior lights on the house, garage, and yard, and send an alarm to his cell phone. He knew from experience that bright lights were usually all it took to send an intruder running. On the other hand, when he was home, the sensors would only activate a series of small flashing lights, codes, and faint beeps on the phones in his living room and upstairs bedrooms. They wouldn't activate any of the inside or outside lights, but he could quickly stream a rotating set of camera feeds to his large-screen bedroom television. In that way, he could keep his options open, determine the extent of the threat, and decide which countermeasures to employ.

After locking the doors and keying the "home" code into the digital alarm switch, he went upstairs, dropped his wallet, cell phone, and car keys on his dresser, and crashed face down, spread-eagled in the middle of his king-size bed. He did not bother to take off his blue jeans or shoes, and immediately fell asleep. Sleep was rarely a problem for someone with his Special Ops background. He almost never had the luxury of a full night, so he learned to grab it in chunks whenever and wherever he could. That could be in a jungle rainstorm, a rock-strewn desert in Iraq, or on a freezing mountainside in Afghanistan. He employed a simple yoga self-hypnosis technique which focused his mind with slow, deep breathing. Whether he was standing, sitting, flying on an airplane, or lying in the mud, he could usually turn off his brain at will, but the quality and duration of that sleep was often beyond his control. That night was typical. He immediately fell asleep; but there were too many things poking, prodding, and pinching the edge of his consciousness, producing a shallow, listless sleep. That was why he snapped wide awake when he heard the first soft, insistent beeps coming from the house phone on the end table next to his bed.

He raised his head and turned on the bedroom TV. The security display showed 4:37 a.m. and he had an intruder in his garage. Someone had raised the overhead garage door, tripping the contacts and the motion sensors inside. He toggled the display to show all the camera feeds inside and outside the garage, both in video and infrared. Each had its uses, but the clarity and resolution of the infrared images left a lot to be desired. In both cases, however, the feeds from all the cameras went to a high-density DVD recorder in the system controller. Every six hours, those recorded images automatically uploaded and backed themselves up to his security account "on the cloud," where they were out of reach of anyone trying to erase them.

The overhead garage door faced the alley, not the house, but even with the infrared feed, he could make out the outline and green glow of two men standing at the rear of his Saturn behind its open trunk. He couldn't tell much else, like who they were or what they were doing, but they quickly closed the trunk, pulled the garage door down, and disappeared down the alley.

Without turning on any lights, he rolled off the bed and walked silently down the corridor to the townhouse's rear bedroom. Its double window faced the alley and garage. He had installed a set of two-inch-wide wooden, horizontal blinds, which he always left 80% closed. That kept the room shaded during the day, while giving him a narrow gap through which he could look down into the alley. While his own exterior lights were not on, there was a sodium vapor light on the telephone pole at the end of the alley. Normally, its eerie yellow bulb provided enough light to see what was going on in the alley and in his rear yard, but not tonight. Curiously, the light on the pole was out, and that immediately caught his attention. The sodium vapor light had been on when he pulled into the garage several hours before. Besides, those lights never wore out, and Bob didn't believe in coincidences.

He returned to the front bedroom and paused to look again at the display on the phone. The motion sensor in the garage had now reset to normal. The sensors on the door from the garage to the kitchen and the motion sensors inside the kitchen had not been triggered. Whoever it was had confined their activities to the garage and did not try to gain access to the house. Or that was what they wanted him to think.

Questions without answers were like fingernails down a blackboard to him, particularly when they involved personal threats. An intruder in his garage did not rise to the level of concern of an intruder in his townhouse or in his bedroom, so he did not go into an active personal defense mode. Still, his Saturn was parked there, and there was always the possibility of someone tampering with the car, rigging a bomb, or leaving some other present inside. Whichever, an intruder was an intruder, and they needed to be dealt with before they made it a habit. He was already dressed and had his shoes on, so he glided down the stairs to the first floor, looking left and right and checking out each room and closet as he went. None of the alarms or sensors inside the townhouse had been triggered, but that didn't mean the intruder wasn't as well trained and practiced as he was when it came to electronic security.

There were a dozen ways to play this. He could go directly into the garage from the kitchen. He could leave the house through the back door, cross the patio and rear yard, and enter the garage through its side "man door." Or he could go out the front door, loop around the neighborhood, and approach the garage through the alley from either end. He decided to go in through the kitchen, which would give him an opportunity to examine the car first. Adjacent to the sink was a drawer that held a six-cell police flashlight and a set of innocent-looking carving knives. The flashlight cast a long, narrow beam, and it was solid enough to double as a fighting club. As for the "carving knives," they had many other uses. He rarely cooked and almost never cut meat, so he left several of his favorite six-inch throwing knives in the drawer under the normal kitchen set. They had serrated blades and perfect points, fine edges, and perfect balance for stabbing, slicing, or throwing. In his hands, that was a lethal combination.

He unlocked the kitchen door and stepped into the garage, pausing to let his eyes, ears, and nose adjust to the space. The intruders had been standing by the car trunk, but he would clear the rest of the garage first. Dropping to his knees, he rolled onto his back and examined the underside of the car with the flashlight. There was nothing attached to the frame, the motor mount, transmission, or in the wheel wells. Methodically working his way back, he opened the side doors and looked under the seats, under the dashboard, and around the ignition and steering column. Nothing. Finally, he raised the front hood and looked around the engine, carburetor, and wiring. Still nothing. The overhead garage door wasn't open very long; so whatever they did, it had been quick and simple. He walked around the car and checked the tools and boxes sitting along the exterior walls. He looked in the corners of the garage, but nothing appeared moved out of place. Whatever it was they did, they got in, did what they came to do, and got out.

That only left the Saturn's trunk. The garage was small and the car was parked too close to the overhead door to allow him to open the trunk without first raising the door. That was a problem. He was already regretting having left the guns, two-way radios, and cell phones he took from Scalese's goons in there. He intended to deliver all that stuff to Ernie Travers later in the morning, but in hindsight, the smarter play would have been to dump it all down a storm sewer or toss them in the river. Too late now. He knew he needed to find out what they left. He walked back to the alarm system keypad at the garage's man door, entered the codes to raise the overhead door, and turned on the outside lights and cameras. As the garage door noisily ground its way up, he held the knife down the side of his leg, and waited. Rather than step directly into the alley, he gave it five minutes, opened the garage's man door instead, and stepped into the side yard. He looked into the alley through the gaps in the tall board fence, but still saw nothing, so he went back around through the garage and stepped out into the alley.

Whoever was out there, they were more patient than he was. The answer must be in the Saturn's trunk, so he turned and walked back to the rear of the car. He was about to pop open the trunk and see what they left inside, when he realized that in his haste he had left his car keys, his wallet and his cell phone upstairs on his bedroom dresser. No big deal, he thought as he walked around to the driver's side door, reached inside, and pushed the trunk release button. That was when all hell broke loose.

Three police cars came racing down the alley toward him, two from one end and one from the other. While their bright headlights partially blinded him, he could see that two were white and green police cars with low-slung red and blue light bars flashing on their roofs, their headlights on high beam, and their spotlights aimed at him. The other car appeared to be a black, unmarked sedan with a single red strobe light sitting on its dashboard.

The three cars screeched to a halt 20 feet away from him. Through the blinding lights, the clouds of dust, and the squeal of tires, someone with a bullhorn screamed at him, demanding he get on the ground, with his hands over his head. No doubt, that was his old friend Bobby Joe in one of the white police cruisers, and Chief Bentley in the other. They both got out with their guns drawn and pointed at him. Much to his surprise, he saw a reluctant Ernie Travers of the Chicago Police Department get out of the unmarked car. Unlike the other two, Travers had his hands on his hips and he kept his distance. He did not have his gun out or look very happy.

Bob dropped the kitchen knife and the flashlight, and raised his hands over his head; but that was as far as he went.

"Ah told you to get down on the ground!" Bobby Joe screamed as he stepped forward and pointed his long-barreled .38-caliber Police Special revolver at him.

"Take it easy," Bob told him. "That thing might be loaded."

"You bet your ass it's loaded! Look, Chief, the perp's got a knife!"

"It's from my kitchen, you moron, and I'm no perp! I came out here because someone broke into my garage," Bob snapped back.

"Well, that's mighty convenient," Bentley joined in.

"Yes, and this is Arlington Heights, not Indian Hills or Chicago," he countered as he looked at all three of them. "I know what these two are up to, Lieutenant, but why are you here? None of you have any jurisdiction."

"We do when we're in hot pursuit of a serial killer," Bobby Joe giggled.

"Now wait a minute," Travers said shaking his head. "You told me you had proof and you'd do this by the book, Chief."

"Oh, I am, Lieutenant. I surely am. We need to open this man's trunk."

"It's already open. You saw me open it as you drove up, and I was about to take a look myself," Bob told him. "My alarm system went off..."

"What alarm?" Bobby Joe frowned. "Ah didn't hear no alarm."

"Shut up and see what's in there," Bentley barked at him.

Bobby Joe eagerly stepped to the rear of the car and raised the trunk. Lying inside, they all saw the body of a woman wrapped in a plastic drop cloth. Travers picked up Burke's flashlight, turned it on high beam, and looked more closely. Through the multiple layers of twisted, clear plastic, he saw enough of her face to know it was Sabrina Fowler, the United Airlines flight attendant. She was naked, with a belt or piece of rope tied around her throat, and bruises all over her face.

"See, Ernie, I told you this guy was bent from day one. Didn't I?" Bentley beamed. "I'll bet he's the Northside rapist. Yes sir, that's who we caught here."

"The Northside what?" Bob turned and questioned.

"Oh, yeah, that's him all right," Bobby Joe giggled. "He already killed five women, not countin' this one, and I'll bet he killed that Purdue woman, too."

Travers stared at her body and then at Bob Burke, still not believing it. "I don't know, Chief," Travers said, looking suspicious. It was obvious someone had tipped Bentley about the body being here, unless he or Bobby Joe put her in the trunk. He wasn't buying it, and suspected Burke had been set up.

"Lots of luck finding my fingerprints on her, or on the plastic," Bob interjected.

"All that proves is you was probably wearing gloves," Bobby Joe quickly answered.

Bob looked at him and saw the thin, black leather gloves on Bobby Joe's hands. "You mean like those?"

"Never you mind what Bobby Joe's wearing. He's been with me," Bentley snapped and then turned toward Travers. "Ernie, your problem is you swallowed this man's story hook, line and sinker yesterday. You don't want to believe he did anything wrong."

"He was up in the airplane when the Purdue woman was killed."

"That's what *he* said happened. For all we know he could have murdered that Purdue woman the night before, got rid of her body, flown to Washington and back, and then made up that whole story about Doc Greenway on the CHC roof to send us on a wild goose chase," Bentley said, stepping closer, hands on hips and his beer gut out. "A clever bastard like him? I'll bet that's exactly what he done."

"That doesn't wash either." Travers shook his head. "That receptionist in the lobby, Linda Sylvester, she said she saw the Purdue woman that morning, in the office."

"Maybe she's in on it with him," Bobby Joe offered as he waved his Colt at the trunk. "That's the body of the stewardess what was with him, and it's his trunk, his car, and his garage. That's all we need to know, ain't it, Chief?"

Bentley smiled. "Bobby Joe isn't the brightest bulb in the pack, but I do believe he's got that right," he said, stepping even closer, going with the flow. "I figure Burke killed this one here, because she knew there never was anyone up on that roof. That's why he had to shut her up. Maybe the man's got some grudge against Dr. Greenway or CHC? I don't know. But I think he came out here to the garage because he was headin' out to dump her body, like he did with all those other women he killed. Unfortunately, we got here first, didn't we, Burke?"

Bob turned and looked at Travers. "You know this isn't right, Lieutenant. I don't know who killed her, but it wasn't me."

"Oh, no? Well, lookie here, Chief!" Bobby Joe crowed as he shoved Burke back with the barrel of his revolver and lifted a corner of the plastic sheet. "There's three handguns, some radios, cell phones, a black ski mask, a black sweater, and a pair of black gloves laying back here under her body. I suppose you need them tools to fix telephones, huh, boy?" he asked as he pushed him again in the stomach with the muzzle of his pistol.

Having put up with more bullshit than he felt like taking for one night, Bob's left arm swept down and pushed Bobby Joe's pistol aside. The fat police officer pulled the trigger and it went off with a loud Blang! He was surprised and seconds late as the bullet flew wide of the mark and struck the sidewall of the garage. In a lightning-fast Tai Chi move, Bob brought his right hand over, grabbed Bobby Joe's gun hand and twisted his arm clockwise. With little effort, he took the .38 from the fat patrolman's grip, while continuing the twisting motion, running Bobby Joe around in a small circle until a leg sweep sent him flying head over heels into Bentley and Ernie Travers like a bowling ball going for a 7-10 split.

The three policemen ended up in an awkward heap in the alley, with Bob Burke standing over them holding Bobby Joe's Colt revolver. "Don't move," Bob warned as he leaned forward and pointed the pistol back and forth between them. He learned a long time ago that nothing focuses the mind quicker than having the barrel of a handgun pointed at your nose.

"She was a nice girl, Bentley," Bob told him as he looked down at the police chief, his expression growing hard and ice cold. "And she didn't deserve to die like that — raped, beaten, and strangled. Is that your handiwork? How about you, Bobby Joe?" He poked the fat police officer in the gut with his own pistol. "Are you the one who did her?"

"No, man! I had nuthin' to do with that, I swear!"

"No? But you were already here, waiting for me to come out. You watched the ones who did put herand too much wine in there, didn't you? That's why you know there was no alarm."

"No, no, uh… The Chief got a call. He said he got a tip."

"Shut up, Bobby Joe!" Bentley banged him in the ribs with his elbow.

"Did the caller have an Italian accent? Or was it New Jersey?" Bob asked, not expecting an answer. Finally, he turned toward Travers. "I didn't ask for this, Ernie," he said as he bent down and quickly took Travers' pistol and Bentley's and tossed them into the car trunk with the body and the other guns and equipment. "This is a setup, and you know it. These two are either part of it or too damned stupid to understand."

"Oh, I know you didn't kill her or the other one, Bob," Travers answered, equally frustrated, "but you're digging yourself a deep hole here you're never gonna climb out of."

"Watch me, because I'm just getting started," Bob answered as he frisked them, patting down their pockets and tossing their two-way radios, wallets, badges, cell phones, Travers's and Bobby Joe's car keys, and even Bentley's wide-brimmed Smokey the Bear hat into the trunk of the Saturn. Both Bobby Joe and Bentley were carrying two sets of shiny, chrome-plated handcuffs in their patent leather police utility belts. They were intended purely for show, but not tonight. Bob then handcuffed Bobby Joe's left wrist to Bentley's left ankle, his right wrist to Travers's right ankle, Travers's left wrist to Bentley's right wrist in a daisy chain, using the last set to fasten them to the rear suspension of the Saturn. That should hold them, he thought.

"In a couple of hours, I'll have all the proof I need to lock Greenway, Scalese, and the rest of them up for a long time. You see, Eleanor Purdue stole a set of CHC's books — the real ones, which will show the phony Medicaid and Medicare billings, the crooked foreign sales, and the medical devices and the drugs nobody needed. They show all the kickbacks and payoffs, and I suspect Chief Bentley and the rest of the Indian Hills crowd are featured prominently on the list. Once I get that stuff to O'Malley, the State Police, or someone, I won't be the one in jail, they will," he said as he tossed the Colt into the trunk. "And here," he said as he reached into his hip pocket, pulled out the driver's licenses he had taken from the gunmen the night before, and held them up for Travers to see before he tossed them in the trunk, too. "Check those guys out. They're DiGrigoria gunmen who work for Tony Scalese and CHC as security guards. They were staking out Eleanor Purdue's house last night and I took the guns and all the rest of that stuff off them. I'm sure you'll find their prints all over Eleanor and Sabrina's houses, and all over the plastic and her body, too."

"You… 'took it off them?' " Travers asked, surprised, but not really.

"Like taking the pistol away from Bobby Joe, it wasn't all that hard."

"Okay, okay, I believe you, but don't do this, man," Travers warned. "Let me take you in. We'll do this thing together."

"It's not that I don't trust you, Ernie, but I'm more effective working alone. And don't worry, it isn't gonna take all that long." He looked down at Bentley, and added, "You know, I hate a crooked cop even more than I hate the men who did that." He motioned toward the trunk of his car. "They're sick animals who need to be put down, but you know better and you're going to pay for this."

"You can't touch me, boy!" The police chief glared back at him.

"I won't have to. As soon as your new pals decide you're their next liability, they won't keep you around very long. You'll get a love tap from a .22-caliber long in the back of the head. The *Chicago Tribune* says that's how Mr. D gets rid of 'loose ends,' followed by cement overshoes and a quick boat ride on Lake Michigan." Bobby Joe's eyes went wide as Bob looked over at him and laughed. "I'll bet your uncle didn't tell you about that last part, did he?"

Finally, Bob turned back to Ernie Travers. "Until now, this has been an interesting exercise in crime and petty corruption; but when they killed Sabrina like that and tried to pin it on me, they made it real personal, and they're going to regret that."

He walked to Bobby Joe's police cruiser and to Bentley's, turned off their lights, and grabbed the keys from the ignition. He threw them in the trunk of the Saturn with everything else, slammed it shut, and locked the Saturn's doors. Satisfied, he jumped into Ernie Travers's unmarked car, turned off the dashboard flasher, and drove away into the night.

Twenty minutes later, after one of Bob's neighbors finally called the Arlington Heights Police Department to complain about the bright lights, emergency flashers, and gunshot they heard in the alley, a half dozen Arlington Heights police cars descended on the scene with more flashing red and blue strobe lights, bright spots, and six officers with shotguns, helmets, and tactical vests. They quickly surrounded the three men lying handcuffed together in the alley outside the garage.

"You keep your big yap shut and let me do the talking." Bentley glared at Bobby Joe. "If you want a job tomorrow, you'll do what I say!"

There had been a bad stench emanating from Indian Hills for several years, and every other suburban police department knew it. When the Arlington Heights Shift Sergeant saw the two Indian Hills squad cars blocking the alley, and saw the three handcuffed police officers lying in front of the garage, including Indian Hills Police Chief Bentley himself and one of his patrolmen, it was far too good an opportunity to let pass. The last thing the Sergeant intended to do was set them free or cut Bentley any slack whatsoever. Despite the Chief's stream of pleas, threats, and curses, with no badge or ID visible, the Sergeant let them lie there until they had taken a full set of photographs from every angle possible.

"Sorry, Chief Bentley, this is a crime scene now, and you're part of it," the Shift Sergeant advised him. "We'll talk everything over after the forensics team is done, but not before." True to his word, almost a half hour later, after his own Chief and most of the other officers in his department had arrived and had ample opportunity to laugh at Bentley, take pictures of him on their cell phones, and even a few "Selfies," he finally unlocked the handcuffs and set the three police officers free.

The Arlington Heights Police Chief knew Ernie Travers and pulled him aside. While he sympathized with Ernie's plight, he shrugged and let him know that it was his misfortune to become "collateral damage," caught in the wrong place at the wrong time with the wrong people.

"Now wait a damned minute, boys," Bentley blustered and pleaded. "My keys, my gun, and all my other stuff are locked inside that trunk," he said, pointing at the Saturn.

When one of the Arlington Heights patrol officers finally pried the trunk open, his chief glanced inside and did a double-take when he saw the naked body of a dead woman wrapped in a plastic drop cloth. That was when all hell broke loose. The Chief pulled out his own pistol, trained it on Bentley, and ordered them all handcuffed again. When the crime techs finally arrived and lifted her out of the trunk, he saw the collection of semi-automatic handguns, portable radios, cell phones, car keys, a hat, and a ski mask, lying underneath her.

"That's your stuff in here? Is that what you said, Bentley? Well, I sure as hell don't know what's going on here," the Arlington Heights Chief said, "but none of you are going anywhere until we get this whole thing sorted out. Especially you!"

CHAPTER FOURTEEN

Over the next three hours, Indian Hills Police Chief Cyrus Bentley was photographed, fingerprinted, grilled by two Arlington Heights Detectives and a State Police Investigator, and thoroughly humiliated. He knew the surrounding jurisdictions had been gunning for him for years. He had handed them the perfect opportunity to stick it to him good, and that was exactly what they did. With no one to blame but himself and his sister's moron son, Bobby Joe, Bentley tried very hard to keep his famous temper under control. Largely, he succeeded. As long as the other police confined their games to grilling and insulting him, that was okay. It was the kind of payback crap he expected from his "Brothers of the Badge." However, if they actually tried to lock him up in the dungeons of the Cook County Jail or subject him to a strip search, a body cavity search, or something truly stupid, it would get very ugly very quickly. Fortunately for everyone, they knew there were limits to this little game of theirs.

Earlier that night, killing that flight attendant, Sabrina Fowler, and dumping her body in that little prick Burke's trunk was Tony Scalese's big idea. Bentley objected, because it was sucking him in much deeper than he ever intended to get, but Scalese made it clear that Bentley had no choice in the matter. It was almost midnight; Bentley was at home sitting in his big lounge chair in his boxer shorts, sleeveless undershirt, and Smokey the Bear hat. He was watching the end of a late football game with a beer in his hand, when Tony Scalese phoned and told him to meet him in the back of the deserted CHC parking lot. Pronto.

"Oh, come on now, Tony. Can't it wait until the morning?"

"Now, Bentley. And bring that idiot deputy with you."

"Oh, he ain't no Deputy, Tony, he's..." he started to explain, but the line went dead. Scalese had already hung up on him.

When he pulled into the parking lot at the CHC building with Bobby Joe's cruiser right behind him, he saw the big Italian was already there, leaning against the door of a midnight-blue Lincoln Town Car, waiting. Bentley parked next to him and immediately got out. Tony always drove that pale gold, "satin cashmere metallic" Lexus LS 460 of his, not a dumpy street car like that Lincoln. "Hey, Tony." Bentley smiled nervously as Bobby Joe joined him. "A little late for a house call, don't ya think?"

Scalese glared at them, and grunted. Clearly, he was in a bad mood as he reached inside the Town Car, popped the trunk, and motioned for them to take a look.

The Chief got out, followed closely by his fat "lapdog," Bobby Joe. They walked around to the rear of the Lincoln and Bentley glanced inside the trunk. "Oh, Jeezus Christ, Tony, Jeezus Christ!" he said as Bobby Joe leaned in, saw what was inside, and threw up all over Bentley's freshly polished patent leather shoes. The Chief leaned against the car and closed his eyes, but the image of that woman's naked, badly beaten body wrapped in a thin plastic drop cloth kept dancing around inside his head. The plastic drop cloth pressed against her swollen, bloody face. Her lifeless eyes were open, staring up at him, and Bentley knew right away it was the body of that airline flight attendant, the one he saw in the CHC lobby with Travers and that meddlesome little prick, Burke.

"I got a job for you, Chief. You too, dimwit." Scalese looked at them and smiled as he outlined his plan to get rid of their problem, for keeps this time. "My boys will put her body in his car trunk. You get that Chicago dick, Travers, and all three of you can find it there and arrest him. Maybe somebody saw something in his car. Or maybe you got a tip. Whatever, that Chicago cop is a real detective. Having him with you will give you some credibility, and even he can't deny it then."

Bentley shook his head, trying desperately to get out of the job, but Scalese reminded him of what Greenway said. "You're bought and paid for, Chief, and it's time you produce. We need to get rid of Burke, quickly and quietly, and arresting him for her murder is perfect," Scalese told him.

Bentley turned his head and glanced inside the trunk, then turned away and threw up again. "No, no, Tony, I can't..."

"Him or you. One of you is going to jail — you or Burke — take your freakin' pick."

Finally, at 6:50 a.m., the Arlington Heights police allowed Bentley to make a few phone calls. The first went to Tony Scalese's cell phone. When Scalese answered, it was obvious from his voice that Bentley woke the big Italian from a sound sleep and he was none too happy about it. However, Scalese was the one who had insisted he report in personally when the job was done, so Bentley gave him one. He tried to dance around the bad news, but Scalese was having none of it. When Bentley finally told him Burke had escaped, the conversation went downhill fast.

"You idiot! There were two of you, with guns, how could you let…"

"You're right, you're right, Tony. That was a screw-up, but that ain't why I called," Bentley interjected, cupping his hand around the phone and speaking in a whisper. "There's something else you need to know."

"What? Something worse than this?"

"You know, it could be. See, when *your* boys dumped that girl's body in Burke's trunk, it must have been pretty dark back there in that alley. They got in and out, but I'll bet they didn't waste much time looking around, did they?"

"Get to the goddamned point, Bentley!"

"Well, it's like this. When the Arlington Heights cops finally looked inside Burke's trunk, in addition to that stewardess' body, they found three handguns, some Motorola radios and cell phones, and the driver's licenses of three of your boys. All that stuff wuz *under* her body, which means it wuz in there first, *before* they put the body in, you understand what I'm sayin'? And I'll bet their fingerprints are all over that stuff… I thought you ought to know."

There was dead silence at the other end. Finally, Scalese said, "Bentley, three of my men got taken out last night over at that Purdue broad's house. We figured it was the Jamaicans, Mr. D's nephew, or maybe the Russians over in Buffalo Grove messin' with us. Now you're telling me it was that little telephone company prick, Burke, who done all that?"

"He took all three of 'em out?" Bentley asked, equally shocked. "You mean he killed 'em?"

"No, but he could have. We found them hogtied with their socks stuffed in their mouths. They never even knew what hit 'em… or who. And you're saying it was Burke?"

"Hey! He did the same thing to us. He took me down and Bobby Joe and that Chicago cop like we was nuthin', and Bobby Joe had the drop on him. The guy's quick, real quick."

"And you're a moron, Bentley."

"Maybe, but I ain't told you the worst part. He has Purdue's papers. That's what he told Travers anyway — the books, the reports, everything. So who the hell is this guy, Tony?"

"I don't know, and I don't care. Find him and kill him!" Scalese screamed.

"Me? You're the one with all the gunmen and the muscle."

"Don't go gettin' cute with me, Bentley. You're the cops and this is what we've been paying you for. Put out an 'armed and dangerous' bulletin. Say he was resisting arrest."

"Tony, half the cops in the area are already looking for him. It ain't gonna be easy."

"No? Well, if you can't do it and we have to take care of it ourselves, I guess we won't be needing you anymore, will we?"

"Oh, don't go getting all excited on me, Tony."

"Excited? I'll show you excited!"

"I didn't say I *can't* take care of it, but I saw what that fella can do. As I said, takin' him down ain't gonna be as easy as you seem to think. I'll get an APB out on the man, but you need to give me a little…" Bentley continued trying to explain, but he found himself talking into a dead phone. Scalese had hung up on him, again.

It was 7:25 a. m. when Angie received the first phone call that morning.

"Mrs. Burke, this is Sergeant Benson of the Winnetka Police Department. I want to let you know that we have dispatched two patrol cars to your house, so if you would…"

"To my house? she said with a yawn, irritated that anyone would dare wake her unless the house was burning down. "Why would you do that?"

"Well, we're concerned that your husband…"

"My husband? You mean Bobby?"

"I'm sorry, hasn't anyone from the Arlington Heights police called you yet?"

"Arlington Heights? What the hell are you…?"

"Gee, I apologize, Mrs. Burke, I assumed you knew. A warrant was issued thirty minutes ago for his arrest on two counts of murder, plus resisting arrest. He is armed and considered very dangerous. We're very concerned he might…"

"Bobby? You guys are something else," she laughed. "The last thing that man needs to be dangerous, is to be armed."

"Yes, well, uh, this is for *your* protection, and our officers will be there shortly. So, if you would let them in, they'll check out your house."

"Protect me? From him? That's ridiculous. I'm the last person he'd ever..."

"It's nice that you think that, but if you don't mind..."

"I do mind! You can send your men back to the donut shop, Sergeant. I'm in no danger, at least not from him. Trust me," she laughed and hung up.

The confident bravado Burke displayed to Travers and Bentley behind his garage faded with the morning sun. He knew he needed to move quickly and keep moving. Alone, cut off, and with his back to the wall, that was usually when he operated at his best; but this was suburban Chicago in the American Midwest, not a free fire zone in Iraq or Afghanistan. Fortunately, the law enforcement agencies were very fragmented in the suburbs. There were dozens of different departments in every city, town, township and county. Normally, they did not communicate with each other very much, but not this time. Thanks to Chief Bentley, they had labeled him a mass murderer and the infamous "Northside Rapist." To compound things further, Bob Burke was driving a stolen, unmarked police car; and he would soon be the subject of an intense, if slue-footed, manhunt. By midday, every police department within 100 miles would be gunning for him. As if they weren't enough, Greenway and Tony Scalese would have all their Gumbahs looking for him too, out to finish what they started.

Travers's unmarked car was an old Mercury sedan, painted black with black-wall tires. Bob shook his head. The downtown CPD motor pool probably dumped it on him because no one else wanted it. "Unmarked"? Who else but a cop with very bad taste would be caught dead driving something this ugly, he wondered. There was a multichannel police radio and a scanner mounted under the dash, and a silver whip antenna on the rear fender and a shorter one fastened to the roof. A heavy-duty screen separated the front seat from the back, and they had removed the door handles and lock buttons in the rear passenger compartment so the car could be used to transport prisoners. To top it off, there was a shotgun and rifle rack bolted, braced, and welded onto the island between the driver and passenger seats. The rack held a pump-action 20-gauge riot gun and an AR-15 automatic rifle. He rattled them. King Kong couldn't rip one of those suckers out of that rack, not that he wanted one, but it left the guns clearly visible from outside the car and that was one more dead giveaway.

Unfortunately, when that idiot Bobby Joe poked him with his pistol, Burke's temper got the best of him and his mind snapped into full tactical mode. Instead of thinking, he reacted; and now he was stuck with the consequences. He knew he had to talk to Ernie Travers and explain things, but not quite yet. Even if the Chicago Police detective really was straight and believed his story, Travers was a cop first. He would want Burke to surrender and be locked up until an official investigation could sort out the pieces and determine who was telling the truth and how much. Then, there was O'Malley to consider. The US Attorney was the real power player here, and he held all the trump cards. With all the Federal muscle he could command, O'Malley could turn CHC inside out provided Bob got him the proof he needed. Unfortunately, he didn't have it in his hands yet, and he wasn't certain he could trust O'Malley or anyone else within a hundred miles of Indian Hills even if he did. Hopefully, all those the papers, spreadsheets, and reports that Eleanor Purdue stole from CHC would become his "Get Out Of Jail Card" — his and Linda Sylvester's. If they were half as damning as Eleanor told her they were, those papers would put Bentley, Greenway, and Scalese in jail. First, however, Bob needed to get them in his hot little hands. Second, he needed to get Linda and her daughter out of harm's way.

As he continued to drive south and east, the sun was already well above the eastern horizon, and the morning rush hour traffic in full swing on the roads. It would be a half hour or more before Linda would be at the Bob Evans, and that was far too long for him to continue driving the unmarked police car without being spotted. He kept one eye on the road ahead, one eye on the rear view mirror and both ears glued to the police scanner, expecting that an APB would be broadcast soon. Scant minutes later, he heard the inevitable first call on the police radio net for all units to be on the watch for a black unmarked sedan. He was on Route 83, a major north-south boulevard west of O'Hare airport. Up ahead he saw the white and green sign for a large Holiday Inn Express. He drove into the parking lot and pulled around behind the building. Halfway back along the rear façade, he saw a six-foot-high wooden board fence that screened the motel's dumpsters from the hotel and the road. The parking spaces next to it were empty, so Bob backed the big car into one of them where it was hidden from view from the rest of the lot and from the motel's rear entrance.

Time to inventory his resources and consider his options, he thought. He left his apartment with nothing in his pockets — no money, no cell phone, no wallet, and no IDs. He wondered if Ernie Travers had left anything useful in the car. He bent over and looked under both of the front seats, but he found nothing except McDonalds wrappers and a few old rags.

The glove compartment was locked, but he found several keys on Ernie's key ring, which looked to be about the right size. The second one opened the lock, and he examined its contents. In addition to a half-dozen state, county, and township maps, he saw a plastic travel pack of Kleenex, a big bottle of Tylenol, and a thick business envelope. A big rubber band was wrapped around it, and on the outside was written, "Airport Softball League Trophies." He tore the flap open and saw a thick stack of $10 and $20 bills. Fanning the edges with his thumb he could see there was $400 or more inside. Ernie could call it whatever he wanted — petty cash, the office slush fund, or the football pool; but Bob could put it to much better use at the moment than the Chicago police. He stuffed the stack of bills in his jeans pocket, and looked through the rest of the small compartment, but found nothing else.

He got out and looked in the backseat, but there was nothing there that he could see. That left the trunk. He popped it open and looked inside. Not knowing what a cop should be carrying in his trunk put him at a significant disadvantage, he thought, as he poked around. He saw the usual array of tools, shovels, tire irons, and even a toolbox, but all it contained were some very ordinary looking hammers, pliers, wrenches, screwdrivers, electrical tape, and the like. There was a 2' x 2' fabricated metal box with two hasps and heavy-duty padlocks, and the word, "evidence" stenciled on the top. The padlocks were open. He looked inside, but it was empty. Figures, he thought. He also saw a pair of muddy baseball shoes, a baseball glove, some bats and balls, and a garment bag. Inside, he saw a baseball uniform, two dingy white dress shirts, a pair of "off the rack" gray slacks, and a cheap blue blazer on hangers. He looked at the labels, but he already knew Ernie was not his size. The tag on the jacket read 52 long. Underneath the garment bag, however, lay a badly wrinkled dark-blue Chicago Bears sweatshirt. He shook it out a few times and put it on. The sleeves were much too long; but if he pushed them up on his forearms, it would do. He also saw a Chicago Cubs baseball hat and put it on too. Checking himself out in the mirror, he didn't look half-bad.

He looked at his watch. Time to call Charlie. He would not have left for work yet, but by now he might be awake with his brain in at least first gear. After locking all the doors, he tossed the car keys in the trunk and slammed it shut. He pulled the hat down to shade his face, walked back to the rear entrance of the hotel, and stepped inside. He found himself in the rear corridor that led to the main lobby and the front desk from the parking lot. There was a security camera over the rear door and a second one pointed toward him from further up the corridor. Most of these chain business hotels offered a complimentary breakfast to their guests. From the sounds and smells, he could tell that was well underway. With the front desk and the service staff occupied cleaning tables, putting out food, and handling check-out, he figured no one would be monitoring the security cameras. Up ahead, he saw the sign for the men's restroom so he casually walked over and went inside. This was his first chance to see what he looked like since he left the alley behind his garage. He washed his hands and face and took a quick look in the mirror, but he saw no major issues. He needed a shave and some decent clothes, but this would do for the moment.

Across the corridor from the restrooms was a small alcove with a vending machine, trashcan, and a pay phone. He picked up the receiver, heard a dial tone, and smiled. In this cyber era when everyone over the age of four owned a cell phone or iPad, a pay phone, particularly one that worked, will soon become a quaint antique relegated to the Museum of Natural History downtown. He dialed Charlie's home phone number and waited.

On the fifth ring, the fat accountant answered. "Newcomb residence, may I help you?"

"I sure hope so, Charlie."

"Bob? Are you nuts?" Charlie was completely frazzled and began whispering.

"You can speak up. If someone's listening, whispering won't help."

"Jeez, Bob, the cops woke me up an hour ago. They handed me a search warrant and searched my house, my garage, my car... They think you killed Sabrina Fowler, the flight attendant! You gotta call George Grierson and turn yourself in, man; they're serious."

"I never touched her and you know it."

"I don't think that matters very much, Bob. They're gunning for you.

"It was Bentley, and his pals Greenway and Scalese who did it. They set me up. But for the benefit of all of you out there in 'Listening Land,' in a couple of hours I'll have their books and records, and enough proof to put them all away."

"In a couple of hours, you can be dead, too. Let me call George Grierson. Maybe he can convince them you panicked and ran. If you don't, it'll be open season on Burkes."

"All right, go ahead and call, Charlie. Tell him what I told you, that it was Bentley and that moron nephew of his, Bobby Joe. They're working for Scalese, and they set me up. Tell him that, and tell anyone else who will listen; but I'm not coming in. I've got a job to do."

On the fifth floor of the Federal Building downtown, an FBI audio technician saw the red audio sensor light up on one of his taps, indicating a conversation was taking place. It would immediately go to record without any intervention on his part, but to ensure that the sensor hadn't been tripped by some acoustical anomaly, he reached over, flipped that switch, and began listening. On his control panel were two narrow displays. The top one showed the acoustical profile of the incoming voice, while the lower one showed the profile of the voice on the receiving end. As both signals tracked along, his audio profile computers compared the voices to patterns already on file in the Bureau's database. Within five seconds, the name "Charles Newcomb" appeared in red under the bottom voice pattern. It took seven seconds more for the name "Robert Burke" to appear under the top one.

The sound technician picked up his phone and dialed the US Attorney's office upstairs. O'Malley wasn't in yet, which was none of the sound technician's concern. Burke's name was red flagged, at the top of the list, and any contact was to be immediately reported upstairs. He left a terse message with O'Malley's duty officer that a call came in to Charles Newcomb from Robert Burke, that it was being recorded, and he would courier an audio CD up to O'Malley's office in a few minutes for him to listen to. He then made a second copy of the conversation on a small cassette tape, tucked it in his jacket pocket, and headed down to the loading dock for a quick smoke and a quicker phone call.

After Bob hung up from his call to Charlie, he stood at the payphone thinking for another moment. There was a phone book chained to the shelf under the phone. Another relic of better times, he thought as he opened it, found a listing for the Security Office at O'Hare, and dropped another quarter into the phone.

When Travers' secretary answered, she said the Lieutenant was too busy to take any calls at the moment. "Oh, I'm sure he is," Bob replied. "Tell him it's Sam Somadafatch from the Indian Hills High School Band Boosters, and we'd love to have him be the Grand Marshal in our Homecoming Parade. I'm sure he'll want to talk to me."

Seconds later, an angry voice exploded in his ear. "Bentley, you asshole!"

"Ernie, Ernie, shame on you. Do you kiss your mother with that same mouth?"

"Burke? Is that you? Are you crazy?"

"You know, everybody keeps asking me that today, so maybe I am. Like I told you, I didn't kill that girl or do any of the rest of that stuff. It was Greenway, Scalese, and Bentley; and I can prove it. What I didn't tell you in the alley was that I added a state-of-the-art security system in my apartment, inside and out, that includes video and infrared cameras."

"You do? After you left, I searched the place with the Arlington Heights cops, and we sure didn't see cameras or anything."

"You wouldn't, Ernie. I've got high speed, miniature, embassy-level tech stuff that's 'way above your pay grade.' "

"Very funny, and I hear that a lot too, you cocky son-of-a-bitch."

"I have video of two of Scalese's men dumping her body in my trunk before any of you arrived. I didn't say anything because I didn't want them to tear my place apart or burn it down trying to find it."

Travers laughed. "A 'telephone guy,' huh? I knew you were a spook. The first time I saw that photograph from Afghanistan, I said… Anyway, can you get me that tape?"

"That's so 'old school,' Ernie. It's saved 'up in The Cloud,' where they can't get at it. As soon as I get my hands on a computer, I'm going to have some DOJ friends of mine run some face-recognition software on it and I'll email it and the results to you. And I'm not a spook, merely a hard-working, every-day grunt, but I do know a lot of people."

"I don't suppose I can talk you into coming in, can I?"

"Not a chance. These guys need to be put out of business, and that's exactly what I'm going to do. And by the way, I'm borrowing your softball league trophy fund."

"The 'trophy fund'? You found that? Not a problem, but you'd be doing me a favor if you found some way to wreck that damn car too. Then maybe they'll give me a new one."

CHAPTER FIFTEEN

At 7:58 a.m., Linda Sylvester sat in her six-year-old Toyota Corolla in the CHC Building parking lot, anxiously waiting for the stroke of 8:00 when the magnetic door locks would open and she could run inside and retrieve the package Eleanor left for her. She was terrified to be anywhere near the place, so she carefully picked a spot where she could see the building's rear door as well as the parking lot's front entrance in case she needed to run. To her shock, as she was about to get out of her car, she saw Dr. Greenway drive in and pull into his personal parking space near the building's revolving front door. Linda froze. No, not Greenway, she thought, and began to tremble. She ducked down in the seat, as low as she could go, and peeked out over the dashboard to watch him walk to the front door and use his executive key card to enter the building.

Greenway! She hadn't bargained for this. He shouldn't be here for another hour, she thought. His third floor office was down the hall and around the bend from Eleanor's, so maybe she could still pull it off if she didn't completely lose her nerve. She watched Greenway cross the lobby to the elevators and was about to open her car door, when to her horror she saw Tony Scalese's gold Lexus 460 tear into the parking lot. He was driving like a maniac, bouncing over the corner of a landscaped median, brakes squealing, as he skidded to a halt crosswise in one of the spaces next to Greenway's car. Scalese jumped out, leaving his car door hanging open, and ran up to the building's front door. He swiped his key card, yanked the heavy door open, and ran across the lobby toward the elevator just as the door closed behind Greenway. This was bad, she thought, really bad! She had hoped the building would be mostly empty, but to find both of them in the office this early? What choice did she have, though? She couldn't stay here, and she had to get that package in Eleanor's office. Bob was right. It was her only hope to get out of this mess.

Eight or ten other women were already standing around the rear employee door, sneaking that last cigarette before they went inside. Through the window, she saw one of the security guards coming down the hallway. He stopped to punch some numbers into the keypad near the door, pushed on the panic bar, and held the door open for the women to pass inside. Eleanor's office was at this end of the building, and there was a fire stairwell just inside the rear door, which went up to the third floor. From the way Scalese was acting, she figured he was following Greenway and would occupy him for a few minutes. Like it or not, this was the best chance she was going to get.

Linda jumped out of her car and ran up the sidewalk, clutching her oversized leather purse to her chest as she joined the end of the line entering the building. Brushing past the security guard, she turned, pushed through the fire door, entered the emergency stairwell, and ran up the three flights of stairs as fast as her feet would carry her. When she finally reached the third floor, she stopped and took several deep breaths to calm her nerves before she opened the door a crack; wide enough to allow her to peek down the hall. She looked in both directions, but especially toward Greenway's office. The corridor was empty and his door closed. Thank God, she thought. She listened and heard loud voices coming from his office. Greenway and Scalese were arguing. Praying that would occupy them for a few more minutes, she pulled the fire door open the rest of the way and scampered across the corridor on tiptoes. Eleanor's key was already in her hand. She slipped it in the lock and was inside the office before she dared to take another breath.

Linda didn't waste a second. She kicked off her shoes, hiked up her skirt, climbed onto the top of the credenza, and pushed the center acoustical ceiling tile aside. Standing on her toes, she stuck her head up into the plenum and looked around. The air duct and vent were next to her head less than a foot away. She reached up with both hands and got a firm grip on the duct, twisting and turning the bottom section until it separated from the vent. There! She almost shouted aloud as a thick, legal-sized, manila envelope slid out onto the ceiling tile next to her head. She grabbed it, lowered the tile back into place, and jumped off the desk onto the floor.

The manila envelope weighed several pounds. While she desperately wanted to stop and see what was inside, she was too terrified to try until she got somewhere safe. She jammed it inside her big leather purse, went back to the office door, and peeked out, praying the hallway would still be empty. It was. She opened the door further, crossed the hall as quickly and quietly as she could, and pushed through the stairwell door. Clutching her bag with one hand and the railing with the other, she raced down the bare metal stairs, flight after flight, desperate to get out of the building and back to her car. Finally, she reached the first floor landing, hit the panic bar with her forearm, and pushed through the emergency door into the first-floor corridor, only to run smack into Dr.

Greenway. He was twice her size but the force of the collision sent him sprawling. They landed on the hallway floor in a heap, arms and legs flying in every direction, with Linda on top, their faces only inches apart.

Stunned, he looked up and saw who it was. "Linda? My God! What…? What are you…? he began to ask, until he saw the large leather purse with the manila envelope sticking out and the panicked expression on her face. His eyes suddenly narrowed suspiciously. "What are you doing here? You never arrive this early, and what have you got in there?" He grabbed her arm and reached for the purse, but she would have none of it. She reached up with her right hand, her fingers extended like claws, and raked her fingernails down the left side of his face, digging four deep gouges down his cheek.

"Ahhhh!" he screamed and released her arm. As she rolled off him, he raised his hand to the side of his face and saw blood running down his fingertips. He flew into a towering rage. "You little bitch, I'll…" he said as he reached for her again, but by then she had managed to get to her feet. He grabbed her ankle and tried to pull her back down, so she swung the heavy leather bag around as hard as she could and caught him flush in the face. The blow stunned him and knocked him sideways. He toppled over as she turned and headed for the rear door as fast as her legs would carry her.

Tony Scalese had stopped by his own office to check his messages, and took the elevator down to the main lobby. He stood at the reception desk impatiently waiting for Greenway until he saw Linda Sylvester burst through the emergency stairwell door and knock Greenway flat. They struggled on the floor for a moment, before she broke free and dashed out the rear door. Scalese tried to follow, running down the corridor after her, but he was too slow and the distance too far to catch her. He had parked his car in front by the revolving door. She reached hers, got in, and fired up the engine before he could even reach the back door. Already winded, he stopped in the doorway and watched as she sped out of the parking lot. By the time he could hope to get back to his Lexus and give chase, she would be in the wind.

Frustrated, Scalese turned around and found Greenway sitting on the floor holding a handkerchief to the side of his face. The doctor pulled it away from his cheek and held it up to show Scalese the blood. "See this!" he screamed. "See what that little bitch did to me?"

Under the handkerchief, Scalese saw the four deep, bloody

furrows she dug down the side of Greenway's face and smiled. "Looks like one of your 'loose ends' grew claws, don't it, Doc? Your Mama ain't gonna like that very much, you know."

"I'll kill her, I swear I will," Greenway seethed.

Scalese looked down at him. "Really? Well, you gotta catch her first, and I think you're already in this shit way over your head."

"I can take care of it... and I can take care of her."

"Sure you can," Tony Scalese answered sarcastically. "And if you can't, Mr. D's gonna take care of you."

Bob Burke killed nearly a half-hour working his way from the Holiday Inn to the Bob Evans restaurant in Elk Grove Village where he agreed to meet Linda. As he left the Holiday Inn, he caught his reflection in the door glass and pulled the Cubs baseball hat even lower. As a disguise, it didn't help much, but it might be enough, he thought, as he walked across the parking lot toward the busy road beyond. He didn't want to arrive at the Bob Evans too early or too late, so he walked for several long stretches, took two buses, and even hitched a ride with a delivery truck. In doing so, he was able to loop his way around behind the Bob Evans, checking to see if there were any police cars or Lincoln Town Cars with hairy-knuckled Italians inside waiting for him. The traffic in the area was growing thicker by the minute but he saw nothing suspicious or anything to indicate that their meeting place was already under surveillance.

By 8:10 a.m., he was famished, and the smells wafting out of the back door of the restaurant were too good to pass up. One thing the infantry teaches even the newest recruit is to grab food and sleep wherever and whenever you can, because you never know when those opportunities will come again. He went inside, took a seat in a back booth, and ordered the biggest steak and egg breakfast on the menu, with grits, a side of biscuits and country gravy, and a pot of coffee. He smiled and asked the waitress to make it as quick as possible because he had an airplane flight to catch. Cholesterol? No doubt about it, but under the circumstances, he should live so long.

One other thing the Army taught him, particularly when bullets were flying, was the ability to "inhale" even a large meal in sixty seconds or less. However, the Bob Evans breakfast looked considerably better than your average mess hall food or, God forbid, a quick MRE, so he relaxed and allowed himself a few leisurely moments to actually taste the food. An MRE consisted of freeze-dried field rations in a plastic bag which someone with a sick sense of humor labeled "Meal, Ready-to-Eat," or MRE, which grunts everywhere loved to hate. He mopped up the last of the real, Bob Evans gravy with his biscuit as he saw Linda's Toyota drive past and turn in. She headed straight for the rear parking lot, and he knew she would be in full panic mode if she didn't find him waiting where they agreed to meet. He dropped twenty dollars from Ernie's envelope on the table and hurried to the rear exit.

When he got there, he saw Linda parking her Toyota in the rear row. Her head pivoted left and right as her eyes searched desperately for him. Her hands were wrapped around the steering wheel in a white-knuckled "death grip," and as soon as she saw him, he saw her heave a sigh of relief. He walked to her driver's side door and motioned for her to move over to the passenger side. As she did, she picked up the heavy leather shoulder bag lying there and clutched it to her chest. The top was open and he saw a thick manila envelope sticking out.

"So it really was there?" he asked, holding out his hand.

"Now?" she asked nervously. "You want to stop and look at this stuff now?"

"Why not?" he asked as he looked casually around the crowded parking lot. "We're as safe here as we'll be anyplace else. So relax."

"Relax? Greenway was there. That son-of-a-bitch! I ran down the fire stairs, flew through the door into the first floor corridor, and ran right into him. And I mean I *ran* right into him. I knocked him flat! Scalese was there too, back in the lobby, so I took off. God, I never thought my fat butt could run that fast," she said, her voice animated and excited.

"I thought you said they didn't come in that early."

"They never do. Something must be going on, probably you. But I got him good!" She held up her right hand, extending her fingernails for him to see. "Right down his cheek, and then I decked him with my purse. Do you have any idea…" she began to say, and then stopped. "No, you couldn't, and I must be crazy to be doing this, much less sitting here in a Bob Evans parking lot of all places, trying to act normal, as if nothing's going on, as if nothing's wrong," she said, looking as if she was about to have a nervous breakdown then and there.

"Linda, like I said, relax. Take a couple of deep breaths. Go ahead," he told her. She looked across at him, reluctant at first, until she finally did — one, two, then a few more and she could feel the world around her begin to slow down. "I'm not going to let them get their hands on you ever again — Scalese or Greenway," he tried to reassure her as he laid a reassuring hand on hers. "Trust me."

"Trust you? Bob, I haven't trusted a guy since sixth grade."

"Good!" he laughed. "Keep telling yourself that, and you just might make it.

She started to pull her hand away, but then stopped, looked across at him, and began to tremble. "Oh, hell!" she said. He held his arms out and finally, reluctantly, she fell against his chest. "Oh, hell," she repeated and then lay there crying for a few minutes until it stopped and she slowly sat up. "Thank you," she said in a barely audible whisper. "I needed that."

"You earned it. Now, when was the last time you ate anything?"

"Eat? I don't know, yesterday morning, I guess. But we don't have time."

"Yes we do. Bring your stuff, we're going inside."

"Bob, I couldn't eat a thing, really."

"Stop arguing. It's time to refuel. You're not doing anybody any good in the condition you are in," he said as he got out of the car and motioned for her to follow. She began to argue again, but then stopped, opened the car door, and did what he said. He led her back through the restaurant's rear door to his original booth and made her sit. The waitress had not even cleared his dishes yet, but he caught her eye and motioned for her to come over again.

"Sorry, but I thought you left," she said, confused.

"Nah, I'm back again for round two," he smiled and turned to Linda. "What do you like? Eggs and ham? Oatmeal? Pancakes?"

"God," she said as she turned her face away and shook her head. "I was thinking more of a dry English muffin."

"Linda, we're safe here, and you need to eat — no caffeine — but you need real food."

"Okay, okay, pancakes, then." She bristled and told the waitress, "Some of those cinnamon chip ones you guys make. They're my daughter's favorite. Oh, my God, my daughter," she said, as she ran her fingers through her hair and looked as if she was coming apart all over again. "What am I doing here, Bob?"

"She's fine," he smiled at the waitress. "Borderline diabetic, you know. She gets this way when her blood sugar gets a little low. So bring her a large orange juice too, and bring me some more coffee, and another order of those biscuits and gravy."

The waitress gave them both an odd look. "Sure, orange juice, coffee, the biscuits and gravy, and the cinnamon pancakes," she said, as she scurried away, looking concerned.

"Relax, Linda. Your daughter's safe and so are you. Besides, Scalese and Greenway are the ones with the big problem now."

"Big problem? *They've* got a big problem?"

"Yeah, they've got me."

She stared at him for a moment in disbelief. "You really are nuts. Don't you know who those guys are, what they do to people?"

"Sure I do, but they don't know who I am, or what I can do to people when I want to," he answered quietly. "Men like Scalese, Greenway, and Bentley are bullies. They think they're the only tough guys out there, that they can do what they've always done and get away with it, and that they get to define the rules of engagement. It's classic. Take me. They tower over me, see the name Toler TeleCom, and think I'm some kind of 'telephone guy,' who came in to install their phones. Right?" he asked and saw her trying not to smile. "They're civilians. They have no concept of war and don't know any better. Nobody here does, except for Ernie Travers. He was in the Army, and I think he understands."

At the front of the restaurant, he saw the waitress talking to a young man in a white shirt and tie, who also turned and looked back at them. He must be the manager, Burke thought, not wanting to create any more attention. Could they have gotten his face on TV this quickly? He doubted it. "So relax," he told her, "everything's under control."

"Under control, huh," she said as she gave Bob a long, skeptical look in return, taking the time to study him for a moment. Who was he, she wondered, still trying to figure him out. The Army, she thought dismissively. He looked more like the Salvation Army. He was of average height and weight and looked to be in good shape, cute, but not exactly bulging with muscles. As she focused in and looked at him more closely, she saw a thin, jagged scar above his left eyebrow, two shorter ones on his right cheek and another on his chin. She had two older brothers and she could recognize a broken nose when she saw one, but what did that add up to? Maybe he was right. Maybe they were all underestimating him.

That was when the waitress arrived with her breakfast and orange juice, giving them both a series of odd looks as she set the plates down.

"I brought you some extra cinnamon chips," the waitress said. "You looked like you could use 'em."

Linda smiled as she sniffed her platter, poured the rest of the cinnamon chips on top of the cinnamon pancakes, and dove in. She paused to drink half the orange juice, and then attacked the rest. "You were right." She finally came up for air. "I can't believe how hungry I am."

"Hey! I know these things."

As she chewed, she leaned forward and whispered, "All right you aren't the 'telephone guy.' You were in the Army, but so was my brother. I think he said he drove a truck in Iraq. He came home with all sorts of 'war stories,' but he doesn't disappear into the night in a ski mask, unarmed, and come back carrying a bunch of guns and radios he took off a gang of thugs. Who are you? And don't give me any of that 'If I told you, I'd have to kill you' kind of stuff."

He smiled. "Nothing quite that dramatic. Let's say I did a lot of different things in a lot of different places. I've dealt with guys a lot tougher than Tony Scalese and his pals, and I'm still walking around on the top of the grass while most of them aren't. So trust me, no one's going to touch you again."

"That's nice." She looked across at him and smiled. "Maybe you even mean it; but why do you care? And not only about me, but about all this stuff."

He paused and thought it over for a minute. "I guess it started when I saw Greenway's face when his fingers were wrapped around your friend Eleanor's throat up on that roof. It was the sheer arrogance of it all. Then last night, they murdered that flight attendant, Sabrina Fowler, and put her body in my trunk..."

"Murdered? In your...? What?" Linda exclaimed with a mouth full of pancake.

"Yeah, I didn't have a chance to tell you how I spent my night. You remember the United Airlines flight attendant who was in the lobby with us? Well, I must have gotten too close and rubbed a raw nerve, or maybe it was payback for what I did at Eleanor's, but they killed her and let Bentley arrange to find her body in the trunk of my car last night."

"Oh, my God! And you got away?"

"I'm here, aren't I? Let's say they made this thing *real* personal; and if they thought I was getting too close before, they haven't seen anything yet."

"You, against them? I don't think so, Bob," she replied. She'd been around, and she thought she had a well-tuned "bullshit meter." However, as she sat there studying his face, whether he was right, wrong, or totally nuts, she saw he meant every word of it. As improbable as that might sound, she began to believe him. "This has been a nightmare. I thought I would wake up, but it isn't a dream is it? It's real."

"Yes. Eleanor was a very brave woman to try to take them on alone, and so are you."

"Not me, her, and it cost her her life. That's why I can't let her down."

Bob took the manila envelope from her bag and placed it in his lap, where it was out of sight below the table. He opened the flap and poked around inside, pulling out each print out and report far enough to read their covers. "There's a report here on foreign drug sales in India," he said, "and several African countries, some lab test reports, some stuff from the CDC, and a lot of spreadsheets."

"Eleanor told me a few things about those foreign operations. The FDA requires that any pills that don't pass their quality inspections be destroyed, but Greenway began repackaging them under another label and selling them overseas, mostly in Third World countries."

"He's a real sweetheart, isn't he?"

"Well, some of the problems with the pills — colors, lettering, that kind of thing — they were merely cosmetic. You might even give him the benefit of the doubt on those, but most of it was bad batches, spoiled lots, and screwed-up ingredients that could make the medicines totally ineffective or harm people. That Third World production is a 'charity' thing. It gets hefty US Government grants, subsidies, and tax write-offs. Most of it is cost-plus, so Greenway told her to expense all sorts of other unrelated expenses to those jobs. I guess you can call it 'quadruple-dipping.' It was substandard production to begin with. Then, they charged costs from a lot of other operations to that account to pad the net. The rejected pills were supposed to be destroyed, but CHC used them to fill the contracts to Third World countries, and then sold the good stuff from the subsidized projects on the open market. They made millions and millions, and that's only from the foreign drug production, which is only a small part of their total business."

He looked inside the manila envelope again. "Yeah, the rest looks like it's along the same lines — lab reports, foreign market surveys, UN and CDC letters, things like that. But there's a flash drive down at the bottom. You know anything about that?"

Linda frowned. "Eleanor ran accounting. She could have copied some of the financial reports onto it."

He picked up the flash drive and read the label. "Thirty-two gigabytes? Linda, she could have downloaded their entire corporate database onto one of those. No wonder Greenway was after her."

"That might explain it," Linda managed to say through a mouthful of gooey pancake. "Greenway and Scalese have been behaving strangely the last couple of weeks, very nervous, very short-tempered."

"I'll bet they got a tip someone was talking to the Feds, so they went on a witch-hunt."

"Eleanor knew she was at the top of their list, and she was terrified about it, terrified they would figure out it was her. Then she got that subpoena, and she and Greenway argued about it for days. He didn't want her to go, but even our lawyers told him there was no choice. That was when things got really ugly. Greenway's a control freak and Scalese is even worse. There was no telling what Eleanor might say behind closed doors, and they don't trust anyone."

"Sally Bats does, as long as he can see them from his office window."

"Sally Bats?" She looked puzzled and asked, "Who's that?"

"You don't know who 'Sally Bats' is? Old Sal DiGrigoria?"

"You mean Mister DiGrigoria?" She sounded surprised. "Tony brought him by last month. He's a cute old man, very formal, very polite. He went around and introduced himself to everyone in the office, and I mean everyone. He shook hands and made little bows to all the women. Tony warned us to be sure to call him 'Mister DiGrigoria,' and nothing else."

"Not 'Don Salvatore'? You didn't have to kiss his ring?" he asked. She paused in mid-fork, puzzled, so he explained, "Sally Bats is one of your 'cute old guy's' nicknames. In his younger days, he used a Louisville Slugger to settle disagreements. Now that he's the Mafia boss of the North Side, he lets his thugs like Tony Scalese do his 'wet work.' His office is up in Evanston. From his fourth floor window, he can keep an eye on people he doesn't like or doesn't trust. They're about a half a mile out in the lake with their ankles chained to a couple of cinder blocks." He shrugged. "Hey, I'm quoting *The Chicago Tribune*. That's what they say."

"You're scaring me, Bob." She stopped eating and put the fork down.

"On purpose, because I want you to understand who these people are."

"But I have a daughter, and I'm alone. That's why I have to be done with all this, Bob, done with him, and done with CHC."

"That would be nice, but I'm not sure they're done with you."

"But why?" She leaned forward and put her hand on his, pleading. "You have the envelope, the reports and that flash drive. Can't you give it to police or the Feds?"

"Absolutely, but to whom?" he replied. "I don't trust any of them. Oh, I trust Ernie Travers, but I'm not so sure about anyone else above him in the Chicago Police Department. O'Malley? Who knows? Before I go talking to any of them, I want to know who CHC is paying off, whose names are in their books. To do that, I need a computer," he said as he looked around the restaurant and then down at her plate. "If you're finished, we should get out of here."

"Finished?" she said as she looked down and saw that her plate looked scrubbed clean. "Yeah, I guess I am," she said with an embarrassed smile.

"I don't like the way that manager behind the cash register keeps looking at us."

"Too bad for him," she smiled. "But you were right. I needed that."

"You were dehydrated, low blood sugar, and in need of some serious carb loadings. Add in no sleep, stress, getting yourself badly scared a couple of times, and..."

"What? Are you a shrink now, or a doctor?"

"No, I'm an old infantryman. They train us to spot all that stuff."

Now, she was really staring at him. "Bob, they were only cinnamon pancakes."

"I could say the same about the steak and eggs. Let's get out of here."

"You mean, before I eat anything else and put on a quick five pounds? Good idea."

"Trust me, it won't show."

"Well, thank you." She beamed. "I try — and I've reached the age when I really do have to try — but hanging around all day with six-year-old kids, middle-aged women who don't care, and a bunch of thugs and perverts, it's nice to get feedback from an actual adult male."

"You know I didn't mean anything by that."

"No, you probably didn't; but to be perfectly honest, Bob, I don't care if you did. You seem like a nice guy, and I'm afraid I've reached *that* age too."

"I understand, and I guess I've reached that age too. After the last couple of days, we're both emotional. It's natural."

"Maybe, but after everything that's happened the last couple of days, I'm finally beginning to understand you, a little anyway." She started to say more, but then turned her face away in embarrassment.

"Oh, let's get out of here before I say something stupid and *really* embarrass myself."

He smiled as he dropped another $20 on the table and they headed for the back door.

CHAPTER SIXTEEN

The skirmish in the alley in Arlington Heights, the resulting arrest warrants, and the manhunt for Bob were all that Angie Burke required to shift her corporate takeover machinery into high gear. With the help of a friendly circuit court judge, who was a former senior partner at Gordon and Kramer, she stormed through the front door of Toler TeleCom at 9:30 a.m. with a confident smile and a freshly signed court order in her hot little hand. In her wake followed four pinstriped, Gucci-shoed, briefcase-toting Associates from Gordon and Kramer and a half dozen beefy, uniformed, gun-toting, private security guards she had hired.

Margie Thomas was Toler TeleCom's receptionist and one of the first people Ed Toler hired when he opened the office. In addition to being his eyes and ears, Margie was the corporate "gatekeeper" and pit bull he placed in the lobby to screen phone calls and prevent unauthorized visitors and salespeople from bothering the company staff or himself. Over the years, there wasn't much she hadn't seen or done, including being tasked with the planning for Angie's "surprise" fourteenth birthday party. Angie hated everything about it, and she and Margie hadn't gotten along since. Angie screamed that the cake wasn't big enough, that the hotel wasn't elaborate enough, that the horse her father gave her wasn't pretty enough, and finally, that the rock band was not nearly as "hot" as the one Jennifer Gollancz's Dad got for her party the month before. For her part, Margie considered Angie a spoiled brat, and wasn't afraid to let her, her father, or anyone else within earshot know. For the next decade, Angie missed no opportunity to pay her back.

That morning, when Angie and her entourage blew through the front doors of the office, Margie opened her mouth and began to say something, but quickly realized it was hopeless. Ed was gone, Bob was missing, and Margie recognized a pack of braying lawyers when she saw one.

"Good morning, Mrs. Burke," she offered with a polite nod.

"Margie," Angie replied pleasantly enough, just waiting for an excuse. When one didn't come, she swept around the reception desk and through the frosted glass doors without breaking stride. The business office consisted of neat rows of five-foot-high cubicles arranged along several horizontal and vertical aisles. The people who "officed" there called it "the bull pen." In addition to the small cubicles, there were glass-walled individual offices along the floor's outer windows for the managers and department heads. Angie walked to the center of the room where the two main aisles crossed, and stopped. Hands on hips, she slowly turned around to survey her new empire. This morning, the bull pen was filled with the usual noisy din of a busy office — the clicking of keyboards, the chattering of printers, and buzz of worker bees talking and laughing with each other over the partitions or on the phone. How nice, Angie thought as she put two fingers in the corners of her mouth and let loose with a nerve-shattering whistle, loud enough to summon a New York City cab in rush hour. In addition to her taste for expensive, single malt scotch, the loud, two-finger whistle was one of the few things her father taught her that stuck. It was a guaranteed showstopper.

Every head turned and the room fell silent. She stood on her toes and extended herself to full height, raised her arm, and waved the court order high over her head. "Yo, everybody! Stop what you are doing, and I mean now!" she screamed as her eyes swept across the top of the cubicles. Between the loud whistle and her commanding voice, every conversation on the floor suddenly stopped. Heads popped up over the walls of the cubicles like gophers coming up for a quick look on a hot summer day, and every one of them turned her way to see what was going on. Eyes went wide as they saw it was the dreaded Angie, and a collective groan and a half-dozen loud obscenities quickly passed through the room.

"Nice, real nice, people!" she responded as her eyes turned hard and angry. "Well, get this! I'm holding a Court Order. Those of you who can read the itty-bitty lawyer language will see that it says I'm now in charge of Toler TeleCom — *ME*! Angelina TOLER and no one else." She did a slow 360 to study their shocked faces. "After you morons digest that little tidbit, I suggest you get back to doing whatever the hell it was you were doing before I came in. While you are busily working away, these nice gentlemen in the dark suits will come around, department by department, cubicle by cubicle, and meet with you. They have a list we put together this morning that says which of you still have a job here and which of you don't. In a few cases, I'll be calling on you *personally* to give you the big news. Most of you know who you are, so you can save both of us some time and start clearing out your desks. And if there's anyone else who can't accept the prospect of daily contact with my delightful, radiant personality — well, you can get the hell out too!"

Angie walked over and slapped the Court Order down on the closest desk, and glared around the office again. "Oh, one other thing," she said. "For those of you who *will* be departing, don't try to take anything with you except your lunch money. These nice young men from Ambrose Security will be checking *everything* that goes out the door, including you; and I'm told they love body cavity searches. So have a nice day, or what's left of it."

Angie motioned for one of the larger security guards to follow her as she turned away and marched through the office, up one aisle and down the other, pointing at people, saying, "You, get out! You too, out! Oh, yeah, you can get out too. Now!" and began quickly terminating everyone and anyone who she knew was loyal to Bob or who gave her a problem. Having dealt with the petty offenders in the cubicles in less than ten minutes, she slowed her pace and began to circle the managers' offices around the perimeter with a maniacal grin. After years of slights and perceived insults, she intended to enjoy every minute of this. Slowly, she strode down the outside row, skipping most of them and going directly to Charlie Newcomb's office. He sat at his desk watching the show and shaking his head as she stepped in.

"Angie, you're certifiably nuts."

"Be that as it may, are you gonna stay and help me or are you leaving too?"

"Me? Work for you? I don't see how that could work for very long," he said with a sad smile. "Besides, why would you even want me? We both know you're going to do whatever you want, and you aren't going to listen to a damned thing anyone has to say, much less me. So what would be the point?"

"The point, Charlie? The point is you think I'm an idiot, and usually I am, but even I must admit that you're very good at what you do. You're right, though. I *am* going to do whatever I want, as much as I want, anytime I want; and I'm probably *not* going to listen to a damned thing you say. Even still, I might want to get your thoughts on something from time to time, so who knows? Maybe I *will* listen to you, and you can't turn down a challenge like that."

"Oh, yes, I can; because you enjoy pulling the wings off butterflies and torturing puppies, and you always have. Since Bob isn't here for you to kick around, you need a proxy — a dumb schlub like me — and I'm not getting paid half enough money to put up with it, or with you."

"Charlie, Charlie." She smiled and shook her head. "Whatever did I do to give you such a low opinion of me?"

"Angie," he smiled back at her, "that would take more time than…"

She threw up her hands. "Well, you can't blame a girl for trying, can you? Okay, what did Bobby tell you when he called you this morning?"

"Bobby? Why would he call me?"

"Don't get cute with me, Charlie. He's going to need help to get out of this — a boatload of help — and I figure you're about the last friend he's got."

"You're wrong, Angie. He's got a lot more friends than you think he does, a whole army of them," he said as he picked up his briefcase and began to stuff some papers into it.

"Oh, no, you don't!" she snapped. "As you'll soon learn, I have a team of shiny new bean counters that'll be here by noon, and everything in this office stays right where it is — pens, papers, cell phone, keys, files, laptops, briefcases, everything — except your fat ass."

He smiled as he put the briefcase back on the floor, stood up, and walked out the door. "Have it your way, Angie."

"I always do, Charlie," she called out after him. "I thought you'd have learned that by now." He strode away down the main aisle and she quickly walked around to the other side of his desk. Since Charlie was so interested in taking the briefcase, she picked it up, opened it, and poked around inside. After that, she went through his desk drawers, still having no idea what she was looking for even if she did find something. Still, for years, Charlie had treated her as if she were a nitwit, and getting this first taste of raw revenge left her with a growing appetite for more. One down and a whole lot more to go, she thought with a self-satisfied smile, as she took a last look around his office. All in all, not a bad way to start a day.

By lunchtime, Angie had finished her stroll through the managerial and executive offices, having sent a half-dozen more people packing, and she felt even better. Most of the ones she fired were the new hires Bob brought in after her father died. Since then, she rarely went into the office, and barely knew most of the company staff. Whether they were competent or not, they were Bobby's people, and there were more useful things Angie could to do with her time than sort out loyalties and reeducate disgruntled employees. With this morning's preliminaries completed, she turned and approached her father's old corner office. The President's Office! That was the big prize. Sitting outside the door at her own large desk was Maryanne Simpson, her father's and Bob's long time Executive Secretary and Administrative Assistant, and Angie's stern and unofficial "aunt." From the expression on Maryanne's face, she did not approve of Angie's antics this morning, not that she ever did.

"Well?" Angie asked as she stopped short of the desk, arms crossed in front of her chest, glaring down at the older woman.

"Well, what, *Mrs. Burke?*" came the polite and proper reply.

"Mrs. Burke? When did we become *that* formal, Maryanne?"

"Oh, I suspect it was this morning."

"Ah, you noticed I was making a few changes."

"Yes, and I think someone is very full of herself, if I may be so bold as to say," she turned away and muttered.

"Maryanne, you can stay or you can go, it's entirely up to you; but don't start being a smartass and think you have a free ride."

"I work at the pleasure of whoever occupies the corner office. My job is to make theirs easier, so I'm afraid it is entirely up to you."

The two women glared at each other for a moment, locked and loaded, until Angie turned away toward the President's office. "All right, but there is something you can do for me," she said as she noticed "Robert T. Burke, President" painted in black letters on the door. "Get a painter out here and change the name on *my* door… and I want the lettering in gold. That will make it look more… permanent, don't you think?"

She continued into the office and closed the door behind her. Bobby had occupied it for the better part of two years, not that anyone could tell. It looked almost exactly as her father left it. Despite her incessant needling and prodding, Bobby never did any redecorating or even replaced the furniture. It was as if the room had fallen into a time warp. Other than carpet cleaning and vacuuming, each piece of furniture sat where her father originally placed it years before. Well, she thought, there's a new Sheriff in town and that's gonna change. She looked around at the PR photographs and 'Chamber of Commerce' plaques hanging on the walls; at the pads of paper, stapler, and pen and paper clip holders lying on the credenza; and at the standard array of business books and telephone directories in the bookcase. This was supposed to be the president's office of a moderate-sized corporation, yet it looked as if it was on a weekly rental and Bobby did not have the time or inclination to change it.

The only personal touches she had added, over Bob's strenuous objections, were the two Army photographs on the wall and a beautiful, silver-framed photograph on the credenza of Bob stuffing cake into Angie's mouth at the wedding. It made her pause. Who were those people, she wondered? They were smiling, attractive, and obviously very much in love, at least back then. She turned and looked at the two Army photographs on the wall, the one from Iraq and the one from Afghanistan. Bobby was laughing and grinning in the middle of those two god-awful, rock-strewn, Middle Eastern deserts, having the time of his life. She walked back to the credenza and picked up the wedding photograph, turned, and compared the expression on Bob's face with the ones in his two Army photographs on the wall. Where did he look happiest, she asked herself. For sure, it wasn't the wedding photo, she quickly concluded. That was why she came to hate the other two. They were a constant reminder to her that she was only second-best. She understood it the minute she hung them on the wall; and despite his denials, he knew it too. Angie let loose an anguished, frustrated scream, and sent the wedding picture crashing into the sidewall.

If it was an unhappy morning in the offices of Toler TeleCom in Schaumburg, things were no happier in the offices of Federated Environmental Services in Evanston, some 15 miles to the east. While Schaumburg was the glitzy new retail and high tech center of the northwest suburbs, located at the junction of the region's two major interstate highways west of O'Hare Airport, Evanston would always be the stolid dowager queen of the north side, located on Lake Michigan at the end of the scenic north Outer Drive. Evanston featured big oak and elm trees, old brick homes, and the lovely campus of Northwestern University. As with the rest of Chicago's older, "inner ring" suburbs, Evanston had been in slow decline for decades. It now featured patches of deteriorating buildings, gangs, a thriving drug trade, and rising street crime. This was not true everywhere in the city, however. The area on both sides of Sheridan Road along the lake shore between the sprawling Northwestern campus and the north branch of the Chicago River was still relatively prosperous and problem free. Another area with virtually no crime, for those who cared to closely examine the statistics, was a two- or three-block strip on either side of Green Bay Road to the west of City Hall. While it might be politically correct to attribute the absence of drugs and street crime there to its proximity to the municipal buildings and Police Headquarters, those on the other side of the law knew full well that this "no-fire zone" had much more to do with a very ordinary four-story red brick office building at its center.

The sole tenant in this building was Federated Environmental

Services, one of central Evanston's oldest and most stable businesses since 1959. It now employed 75 full-time people in the building, plus another 400 or so in its trash and recycling trucks and in its trash and recycling centers throughout the northwest suburbs. Those numbers only counted the people on the official FES payroll, however, and did not include a much larger number employed in numerous illegal operations on the city's North and West Side, from downtown Chicago to Aurora in the west and to the Wisconsin state line in the north. Those activities included bookies, wire rooms, meth labs, houses of prostitution, card rooms, heroin and cocaine-cutting parlors, a small army of wholesale and retail distributors on the streets, and a hard-core cadre of "made-men."

FES was a privately held corporation and a wholly owned subsidiary of Federated Investments, which was in turn owned by Federated Industries, a privately held Delaware corporation, owned by Diamond Tropics in the Cayman Islands, owned by S-D Investimenti in Naples, Italy. While "environmental services" cover a wide range of activities, Federated's main business was trash hauling and recycling. It was now the almost exclusive player in the northwest suburbs of Chicago, with virtually every restaurant, hotel, residential complex, and large or small business under contract. Their corporate offices in Evanston were a throwback to the 1960s and a comfortable, quiet, perfect fit for the small city. Their trucks were always clean and well maintained. Their "field" personnel were always in uniform, clean, polite, and among the best paid in northern Illinois, and loyal members of Teamsters Local #485. Federated Investments was co-located with FES and had still broader interests to include some of the best-managed restaurants, busiest car dealerships, concrete and asphalt plants, and, more recently, neighborhood clinics and health care. The walls of its lobby were covered with plaques, photographs, and awards from every city, town, and Chamber of Commerce in the northwest suburbs, showing smiling mayors shaking hands with FES's Chairman and founder, Mr. Salvatore DiGrigoria. The ultimate irony was that "Sally Bats" was now making far more money from his far-flung legal businesses than he ever did from the rackets.

"Mister DiGrigoria" as he was invariably called by his employees and the sycophants and back slappers standing with him in the photographs, was a short, stocky, block of a man with muscular shoulders and forearms, a large head with thinning black hair, and a pencil-thin mustache. Some of the people who met him thought he resembled a wine barrel on legs, but they usually kept observations like that to themselves.

Mr. D could crack walnuts with his bare hands, and you wouldn't want to aggravate him when he was shaking one of yours in his. Unlike many of his business associates, especially those from the New York and New Jersey families, he was quiet, polite, and soft-spoken, unless prodded. He didn't start out as a street thug, thief, or killer. He grew up in "da garbage business," not "the environmental business," "the sanitation business," or "the trash business," and was never embarrassed to admit it.

Over the years, Salvatore rose through the ranks of power and influence in the Chicago mob. As he did, he grew to detest those Mafia movie names and ancient Sicilian titles such as "the Don," "Capo," "Consigliere," and all the rest, and insisted upon being called, "Mister DiGrigoria." This wasn't some uppity affectation on his part. When asked where he came from, he would always say he was born and raised on Maxwell Street. When asked what he did, he would always and proudly state that he was a "garbage man and a card-carrying member of Teamsters Local #485."

He began working on the garbage trucks for his uncle Luigi, or "Louie Griggs" as he was called. Salvatore mostly worked the garbage routes on the tough West Side of Chicago, standing on the rear bumper of the moving truck, hanging on with his left arm, while grabbing and lifting trash cans with his right, over and over again, all day long. It gave him a powerful right arm and a unique perspective on life. When Uncle Luigi died, Salvatore's older brother Pietro, or "Petey D," took over the South Side territory, while his younger brother, Enzo, who everyone called "Da Kid" for lack of anything more original, took over Milwaukee and southern Wisconsin down to the Illinois State Line. The territory between, from Wisconsin down to Madison Street in Chicago, the unofficial 38th Parallel or DMZ between the North and South Side interests in the city, became Salvatore's and his alone.

The office staff on Green Bay Road in Evanston worshiped Mister DiGrigoria. Most had worked for him for decades, and he knew their birthdays, their spouse's names, their children's names, and even the names of their grandchildren. He was very paternalistic toward all of them, which was how he believed any employer should act. If there was an illness in anyone's family or a personal problem, Mister DiGrigoria seemed to know it as soon as they did, and expected to be informed if they or anyone in their family needed help. He believed in the old-fashioned virtues of honesty and loyalty to one's employer. "If a man puts bread on your table, dat's da least you owe him." Disloyalty, dishonesty, embezzlement, and petty theft never happened in his office, and no one who worked there would ever think of talking to a reporter, a cop, or a lawyer. They knew better.

As the office staff got up in years, they appreciated the personal safety and lack of crime in the area around the building, day or night. While the building and adjacent parking lot featured lights, security cameras, and its own private security guards, not to mention frequent visits by the company's own "field personnel," it was said that the primary deterrent to street crime was an incident that occurred some 35 years earlier. As the story goes, Mister DiGrigoria happened upon four young men who were breaking into a car and trying to assault one of the company's young female employees in the company's rear lot. The four thugs were half DiGrigoria's age, two were high school football players from the West Side of Chicago, and they all carried knives or clubs. Twenty minutes later, when the police arrived, the old man exhibited a few minor cuts and bruises, but one of the thugs was dead and the other three required ambulances, major surgery, and lengthy hospital stays prior to prison, which none of them survived. Simply put, Mister DiGrigoria was a very moral man who did not appreciate criminals, unless they worked for him, of course.

It was late morning. Salvatore DiGrigoria sat behind his large, oak desk in his fourth-floor corner office. His shoes were off and he dug his stocking feet in the thick, plush carpet, as was his habit. He grew up in a one-room, cold-water basement flat with bare, cold, linoleum floors off Maxwell Street on the city's tough West Side. There were times when young Salvatore didn't have shoes, much less socks or a carpet, so wiggling his toes in his very own plush carpet became one of his delicious little pleasures. While he put extra money in this top-of-the-line carpet, his desk, the overstuffed leather desk chair, the two armchairs in front of the desk, and even the leather couch along the sidewall were discount-store ordinary. Like him, the office was working-man solid, neither large nor ostentatious, and the furniture was meant to last. There was no computer on his desk, because Salvatore would not know how to turn one on, much less how to use it if he did have one. Instead, he used a yellow legal pad, a neat stack of orders and sales receipts, a half-dozen freshly sharpened #3 pencils, a 1940s-era "hand crank" adding machine, and an old-school, green canvas-backed ledger book sitting on the desk in front of him.

It wasn't that Federated Environmental Services didn't have

computers. Most were located in the accounting department on the second floor. They were used for the myriad of legitimate businesses owned by FES and federated investments, but the reports they produced were solely for the benefit of the IRS, state regulators, and nosy state and Federal prosecutors, or "Dem pricks!" as Salvatore called them. The only "books" that really mattered in his business were the green, canvas ledger books sitting on his desk, where he wrote in a neat, abbreviated, colloquial Italian dialect that could only be understood in a handful of very small villages in the hills above Naples, Italy, taught to him by his sainted grandmother. In truth, Salvatore didn't need the ledger books either. As Uncle Luigi preached to him many times, "Keep da good stuff up here, in your freakin' head, boy." Luigi "made his bones" as a young foot soldier in the Capone mob in the late 1920s. As the old man often reminded his young nephew, "When dem Federal pricks finally nailed 'Big Al,' it weren't for no murder, no bootlegging, or da 'rackets,' it was for income taxes, for goddamn income taxes! Remember dat, Sal. Paper'll come back around and bite you on da ass; so, don't make it easy for dem!"

It wasn't that Salvatore didn't believe in modern business practices, but he believed much more in security. No one — no vendor, no repairman, no plumber, no electrician, nobody — got past the lobby unless he was cleared by his guys and accompanied by one of them the entire time. They swept the offices and phones daily for bugs, and not only the crawling kind. Recently, he installed a new high-tech "white noise" jamming and acoustic system which rendered directional microphones, other listening devices, and even cell phones useless and sent the neighborhood dogs running. His office used "old school" dial phones. There were no fax machines, only one closely-monitored copier, no internet, no computer network, no e-mail, no scanners, and no recording devices, anywhere. Cell phones? "If I don't freakin' need one, nobody freakin' needs one" was his simple reply. Even with all these precautions and the high-tech security, inside the office he spoke in guarded phrases when he spoke at all.

Mister DiGrigoria was in the process of posting the week's receipts from the card rooms, whorehouses, loan sharking, street crews and bookies in a series of cryptic, handwritten notations in his newest ledger book. When he was finished, he would place it on top of a stack of 37 similar ledger books, one for each year he ran the business. Other than seventy or eighty thousand dollars in "petty cash" to be used for city permits, minor purchases, and bribes destined for the pockets of various local cops and inspectors, all that was in the safe was the cash and the ledger books. They were the only reason he owned the safe to begin with. It was a huge, double-walled Yale model which he had inherited from his uncle Luigi. Standing six feet high and four feet wide, it weighed over six hundred pounds empty, requiring special floor bracing, a crane, and a small army of movers to get it up to the fourth floor to begin with. It was specially built for Luigi, who added one additional number to the combination, making it very difficult to crack. The safe's interior walls were also reinforced, and the amount of Nitro it would take to blow the door open would bring half the building down. As his uncle Luigi said proudly, "Now, dat's a safe!"

      Salvatore was finishing his last series of meticulous entries in the ledger when his spinster older sister and longtime secretary Gabriela buzzed him on the intercom and told him that Tony Scalese would like to see him. Secretaries, lawyers, accountants, underlings, and even hit men might come and go, but as Uncle Luigi often said, "blood is forever." When he was doing the books, Salvatore's office door was always closed and locked, the window shades pulled down, and an Italian opera playing on his old Victrola phonograph, so Tony could wait. Gabriela knew Salvatore would unlock the door when he was ready and not a minute sooner. He took one last look at the entries and numbers, put the ledger book back in the safe at the top of the stack, closed the door, locked it, and spun the dial. He dropped the service order forms and receipts into an industrial-strength paper shredder, which sat in the corner and turned the paper into a fine dust. Back at his desk, he put on his shoes and suit jacket and straightened his tie. Only then did he walk over, open the door, and motion for Tony to come in.

      After both men settled in their chairs, Tony Scalese got right to the point. "This 'thing' is startin' to spin out of control, Mr. D, and I don't like it."

      "Yeah, me neither. Too bad, but it happens," the old man replied cautiously, as was his habit. "We made good money wit dem pills and dat clinic 'thing;' but nuthin's forever in dis business, Anthony. Besides, you and me, we got bigger fish to fry."

      "You think it's time to shut it down?"

      "I think it's drawin' too much attention now, like from dat prick O'Malley I keep seein' flappin' his mouth on TV. Pretty soon, somebody'll start talkin,' then it's film at 6:00."

"Yes, sir, I couldn't agree more."

"Good. I see a lotta freakin' loose ends over dere, like dat guy from the airplane."

"Yeah, him and *his* big mouth need to disappear... permanently."

"Yeah. He ain't da only one, but you better make him da first."

"We're lookin' for him, but he took off. He's been a little hard to find."

DiGrigoria shrugged. "So I hear. Why don't you squeeze his wife, or dat bean counter? They're always the first ones to squeal. But stay away from dat Chicago cop. We don't need dat kinda trouble, but somebody knows where he is. And after you do him, shut all da rest of it down, all of it. Dat Fed rat bastard O'Malley's gettin' too damned close."

"The doctor, too?"

"Especially dat prick! He's a freakin' pre-vert. He ain't got no respect for women, and you know what I think of pre-verts, Anthony. Worse, he's reckless. Shut it down and get rid of him. Da big money's all been made, anyway. All dat's left now is peanuts. Roll da cash and da bank accounts offshore to da Caymans. And get rid of dat dumb ass Bentley, too. You can never trust a crooked cop. Remember dat. Dey ain't got no loyalty, and dey ain't got no ethics."

"Yeah, he'd be the first one to flip on us."

"Dat's da problem with loose ends, kid," DiGrigoria said as he leaned across the desk and glared at his young protégé with the hardest, coldest eyes he had ever seen. "You gotta snip 'em off, before somebody snips *you* off. So, get your boat out. I want dem pricks out dere where I can see 'em, if you know what I mean."

Scalese swallowed hard. He knew exactly what the old man meant.

CHAPTER SEVENTEEN

As they began to exit through the rear door of the Bob Evans restaurant, Bob paused, held out his right arm, and blocked Linda's way. "Wait a minute, let me look outside first," he said as he opened the door to the parking lot. He made a quick tactical scan of the area from left to right, his training taking over as his eyes searched the parked cars and open spaces for any potential threat or anomaly.

"No problem, simply checking," he told her, trying to sound casual, but he could see she wasn't convinced. "We can go."

He opened the door for her, but as she passed by, she wrapped herself around his right arm. "I thought we should pretend we're a couple. You know, camouflage and all," she said with a nervous smile.

"Uh, wait a minute," he said as he pulled his arm away.

"Oh, God, forget I did that, Bob. Sometimes I can be so stupid," she said as she quickly let go and backed away, embarrassed.

"No, no, it's not that," he countered as he stepped around to the other side of her and held out his left arm. "Here, take this one. I'd rather keep my right hand free, in case... well, you know," he said, leaning in closer to explain. "In case there's someone out there we'd rather not bump into."

She stared at him deadpan for a moment. "Boy, I've heard of some lame excuses in my day," she said as she suddenly smiled and wrapped herself around his left arm this time, pressing into him with her small, firm breasts and squeezing tight.

"You're right," he smiled. "It is pretty good camouflage."

She looked up at him for a second, and then finally said, "This has been such an insane, terrifying couple of days. All you've done is try to help me, and I've acted like such a jerk not believing you and not trusting you."

"After what you've been through, I understand," he said as they walked out the door and headed toward her car. Unfortunately, they were so busy talking, and smiling, and touching, that they did not notice two men come out of the restaurant behind them.

"All right, Mister, that's far enough!" Bob heard and turned his head far around to see it was the manager of the Bob Evans and an overweight, baby-faced private security guard. They stood in the doorway behind him, not ten feet away. The early morning sun was reflecting off the manager's thick glasses as he held up the morning's newspaper and showed it to Burke. The security guard carried an old 38-caliber Smith and Wesson Model 10 police revolver in a holster on his hip. Wide-eyed, he pulled it out and pointed it at Bob. The guard's hand shook, and it was obvious the kid was in uncharted territory now.

"Whoa!" Bob answered as he turned and saw the gun. "Be careful with that thing."

"No, you be careful, Mister... Burke!" the manager said as he pointed at the newspaper. "That's right, we know who you are," he added as he pointed to Bob's picture on the front page, below the headline, which read, "Manhunt on in Suburbs."

"Oh, not that thing again!" Bob quickly countered as he raised his hands in frustration, shook his head, and laughed. "Once they print that kind of stuff, there isn't a damned thing you can do about it," he laughed as he began walking toward them, keeping himself between Linda and the revolver.

"That's close enough, Sir!" the security guard warned in a high-pitched voice as he raised the revolver higher and his hand started to shake even more.

"That photograph — it's not me. They got them reversed. I'm a soccer coach and they were doing a story on our team, but they ran my photo with that man's story, and his photo with mine. They apologized, but as you can imagine, that's all I heard around the office this morning," Bob added as he read the fat security guard's nametag and kept walking toward them. "Look at the photo, Leonard," he said as he pointed at the newspaper. Like a lemming, Leonard turned his head and looked, which was when Bob snatched the pistol out of his grip. Bob's hands moved so fast, he could have been catching flies. He grabbed the pistol with his left hand, his palm holding the hammer back, and twisted, while his right hand grabbed Leonard's forearm. Bob pressed his thumb into a nerve in Leonard's elbow and he pulled the pistol from the guard's limp hand before Leonard even knew it was gone.

The guard's jaw dropped as he looked down at his empty hand, and then up at Bob.

"I told you to be careful with this thing, Leonard," Bob said as he glanced around the lot. "These old Smith and Weson .38s don't have a safety, you know. You might've actually hurt somebody. Now come on, both of you," he told them, casually waving the revolver toward the dumpster enclosure twenty feet away along the rear of the building. He walked them to it, opened the gate and shooed them inside.

"Can I shoot these two?" Linda asked. "You shot the last ones."

"Well," Bob paused for a moment, looking at the two men and then at her as if he were deciding. "Nah, I don't think that'll be necessary; do you, guys?" he asked as he bent down and opened the pockets on Leonard's patent leather security guard equipment belt. He pulled out two speed loaders and tossed them into the dumpster. "No handcuffs? Figures," he grumbled, but he did find a handful of plastic Kwik-Cuff zip ties, the latest in "cop toys," and pulled them out. "Sit down, both of you." He motioned toward the dirty concrete pad next to the dumpster. "You weren't in the Air Force, were you, Leonard?" Bob asked, but the guard quickly shook his head no. "Just curious, because I think I met your twin brother."

He used the zip ties to secure their wrists, and then one man's hand to the other man's ankle, as he did with Bentley, Bobby Joe, and Ernie Travers the night before, finally tying them to the thick steel handle on the dumpster. "If I were you, Leonard, I'd find a new line of work, maybe the Post Office, because you're going to get yourself hurt doing this stuff."

"Okay, let's go," he turned and said to Linda as he threw the .38-caliber revolver into the dumpster, too.

"You're not going to get away with this, Mister!" The restaurant manager glowered at him, red-faced.

Bob looked down at his nametag. "George? Sure I am. Look, I figure you worked your way up through the 'Bob Evans' ranks out here in the burbs, and they finally gave you your very own store, right?" he asked the manager, who reluctantly nodded. "Well, think about it, George. No shots were fired, no one got hurt, and you get to brag to your bosses back in Ohio how you and Leonard *saved* the restaurant. You got a vicious murderer and his psycho girlfriend out of your store, into the parking lot and away from all your good paying customers; and you saved the cash register, to boot. Dude, if you play that right, it should be all over the papers this afternoon, maybe even make the national news. You two will be heroes back in Ohio, so it sounds to me this was one hell of a great morning for you."

As the light bulb slowly came on behind the manager's thick glasses, Bob added, "Better still, your little Bob Evans here is going to become a local tourist attraction. You can put a shiny brass plate on that booth that says, 'The Bonnie and Clyde Breakfast Booth,' and people will line up to take 'selfies' sitting in *our* booth eating a plate of your biscuits and gravy. God, the promotional opportunities are endless!" He let that sink in for a moment, and added, "Unfortunately, I didn't do any of that stuff they're talking about in the newspaper. That will all be cleared up in three or four days, so you'll want to get your story out today and milk it for all it's worth before that happens."

"You gonna leave us tied up here like this?" the manager squawked.

"Oh, shut up George," Leonard told him. "How do you want him to leave us?"

"Leonard's right, George, it could be a whole lot worse. So sit there and behave. I'm sure someone will be out here looking for you in short order. Meanwhile, y'all have a nice day."

Bob led Linda out of the dumpster enclosure and closed the gate behind them. "That should hold them for a while. Let's get out of here," he said as he continued to scan the lot until they reached her car.

"The 'Bonnie and Clyde' booth? Not bad, for a 'telephone guy.' "

"Oh, that was nothing. When you asked if you could be the one to shoot those two, I thought Leonard was gonna wet his pants right there."

"That was kind of mean of me, wasn't it?" She tried not to laugh too loud. When they reached her car, he drove out of the parking lot, wound his way back to Mannheim Road, and headed north again. "Look, Bob, we have the reports and that flash drive Eleanor left. If we need a computer to open it, why can't we just go buy one?"

"I'd rather try my friend Charlie first. He's my head of Finance and Accounting, and the closest thing to a computer whiz I know. Even if she encrypted the flash drive, he has software that can pop anything open in two seconds flat. That's why I need to call him and find out if he's learned anything," Bob told her as he looked out the driver's side window and saw they were passing a long line of motels and fast food restaurants. "I'm sure there must be a pay phone in one of these motel lobbies. It won't take very long."

"Here." She reached into her purse and pulled out her cell phone. "Use mine."

"No, no," he smiled. "By now they'll be looking for you too, and a cell phone is too easy to track. It would leave an electronic trail from me right back to you."

"They?" she asked.

"At a minimum, the Feds; and I don't want you any more involved than you already are."

"Somehow I don't think that matters anymore," she smiled sadly.

"Scalese and his pals are probably looking for you now too, but I doubt they have the in-house technology. My guess is they pay off some people at the phone company or even the FBI to get whatever they want. In any event, don't use the cell phone and we should pull the battery," he told her as he held out his hand for her phone. "They can track you through the GPS."

"I can do it!" she said, beginning to show her irritation and frustration. "If you have a six-year-old daughter, you learn how to take apart a cell phone, put in a Walmart battery, pull the SIM card, or disable it when the kids decide they don't like your rules."

"A six-year-old with a cell phone?"

"Hey, don't give me any of that. Do you have any kids?" She turned and glared at him. "No, I didn't think so. With a six-year-old, some days, you just do what you gotta do to get by," she said as she opened the back of the phone, pulled out the battery, and snapped the case shut.

"Point taken, and you're right; I apologize. It really is none of my business," he said as he looked over and saw her staring at him with a strange expression on her face. "What?" he asked getting confused trying to keep up with her.

"Well, for a Neanderthal, you're a very polite one."

"A Neanderthal?"

"The term covers a lot of territory, but it's what I'd call any guy who obviously spent most of his developing years running around the woods with a bunch of other guys shooting things and blowing stuff up, without a gentle female touch to grind down the sharp edges."

"Grind down?"

"Don't get smart! That's pretty much you, isn't it?"

"Oh, I think I'm a bit more complicated than that," he answered sheepishly.

"I'm sure you are, but now my daughter and I are very much your business, Robert Burke, whether you want us or not. After all, you're the one who gave me the courage to stand up to them, and I owe you big time."

"Oh, I think you had the courage all along," he said as he pulled into the parking lot of a Sheraton Inn, drove around to the back door, and parked her Toyota behind the hotel dumpster.

"I didn't think I'd have to make it up to you this quick, but behind the dumpster? Classy guys go in and get a room," she said with a droll expression.

He turned and looked at her, equally droll. "As truly enjoyable as I'm sure that prospect would be, I only stopped here to make a phone call."

"So a room's out of the question?" He gave her a look, so she added, "Just kidding."

"I'm sure you are, but rolling stones gather no bullets. Wait here, and behave. I'll only be a couple of minutes," he said as he got out of the car and looked around the parking lot.

"Do you want me to hit the horn if I see anything?"

"No, get down on the seat or on the floor and stay there. I'll take care of the rest."

"You'll take care of the rest? Why does that not surprise me," she muttered, but he was already gone.

He entered the motel through its rear service door and walked down the corridor toward the lobby. Near the swimming pool he saw a pay phone. He tried Charlie's cell phone number. The call immediately rolled to his voicemail, so Burke hung up. That was odd he thought. The fat accountant never went anywhere without his cell phone. It was never out of his reach. He called Charlie's direct-dial office number, but got the same result — no Charlie, only a recording. Finally, reluctantly, Bob tried Toler TeleCom's main number. He did not really want to talk to Margie or any of the staff, but there was no choice. To his surprise, a new receptionist answered. She sounded young and overly confident, like a certain almost ex-wife he knew. When he asked her to connect him to Charlie Newcomb, all the woman would say was, "I'm sorry, but Mr. Newcomb is no longer with the company."

"Then, can you connect me to Maryanne's extension?" he asked.

"I'm sorry, but Maryanne is tied up in meetings with the President."

"The President?"

"Yes, Mrs. Burke," she gushed.

"What about Margie, is she there?"

"She's been reassigned to purchasing. Would you like to leave her or Maryanne a message?"

"No, thanks, I'll call back," he said and quickly hung up. Bob was surprised, but with a clearer idea what was going on back there. He turned and walked down the hallway toward the rear door, head bowed, deep in thought. He expected Angie to do something like this, but the speed of her attack was a surprise. While he might be an expert in military tactics and strategy, he felt like a novice in these business battles. Angie "stole a march on him," as one of his West Point professors described it, much as Albert Sidney Johnston did to Ulysses Grant at

Shiloh. Grant ended up winning the battle and the war, but it became a bloody affair. Angie swung into action while he was eating biscuits and gravy at a Bob Evans. It was time he got his head out of his ass and caught up.

Lawrence Greenway spent the past half hour in the rest room applying cold water and a pile of paper towels to the side of his face to get the gouges in his cheek to stop bleeding, and to wash the worst of the stains from his suit jacket. Fortunately, the suit was dark, and the spots barely visible. He wished he could say the same about the side of his face. It was red and burning hot, with deep, suppurating wounds. Finally, he returned to the relative safety of his office, threw his suit coat over a side chair to dry, and collapsed in his desk chair when Tony Scalese burst in on him. Greenway looked up and shook his head. "Anthony, I am not a 'morning person.' And this morning? Well, it hasn't been much fun, so leave me alone."

Scalese ignored the complaints. "Shut up, Doc, and listen to this," the big Italian said as he walked up to Greenway's desk, pulled out a hand-held voice recorder, and turned it on. "One of Mr. D's lawyers has an FBI lab guy on the pad. I recorded this as he played it to me over the phone. The sound ain't very good, but you'll get the drift."

As soon as the recording started, Greenway recognized Burke's voice as he talked to his friend Charlie about grabbing the CHC books and records. "That stupid Bentley!" Greenway flared. "I thought you said he was taking care of this fellow Burke."

Scalese snorted. "Our turn. Looks like you and me gotta take care of this crap ourselves."

Greenway sat back in his chair and thought about it for a moment. "I have an idea, Anthony. Let's split up. I'll go visit that receptionist, Sylvester, and find out what she knows, while you track down his accountant friend. How does that sound?"

Scalese leaned forward and put both of his meaty fists on the doctor's desk as his eyes grew dark and angry. Greenway quickly backed away.

"All right, all right, Anthony. I suppose we should *both* visit Mr. Newcomb. Perhaps with the proper motivation, we can persuade him to tell us where we can find his meddlesome friend."

"That's better, *Larry*. Meet me downstairs in my car in two minutes, and bring that little medical bag of yours. No tellin' when somebody might need a doctor."

CHAPTER EIGHTEEN

It was late morning. Angie continued to plow through the Toler TeleCom books, financial statements, and official filings, trying to make some sense out of them. On paper, she had majored in business at Northern Illinois, but that was to placate her father. Her interests ran more to fraternity parties, beer, spring break in Cancun, and the football team. When it came to a serious financial statement, a tax or SEC filing, cost accounting, or extended depreciation schedules, her father could pound it into her head as long as he wanted, but it remained Greek to her. Besides, what difference did it make? If she had an accounting question, she'd *call one of the goddamned accountants!* Unfortunately, she never expected to fire the lot of them in a fit of spite, and have to figure it out for herself. Oops!

She stared at the stack of books and papers strewn about the desk and lying in a half-dozen piles at her feet, frustrated, and certain that Charlie Newcomb did this to her intentionally. That fat bastard. He knew their days were numbered and that she'd be taking over, so he made everything twice as complicated, to make her feel stupid. She turned and looked at the clock on the credenza. It was 11:21 a.m. Before Bob came around, she was "lending a hand" in the PR department, as her father called it. She would usually roll into the office around 9:30 and be gone by 11:00 for a tennis lesson or a quick nine holes of golf. After a massage and a late lunch at the club, she'd return to the building around 3:00 for an hour or so. Try as she might, it was hard to get too serious about anything after a couple of spectacular martinis. Yeah, she thought, Charlie did this to her intentionally.

Sitting in Bob's big desk chair, she looked down at her legs. She hitched up her skirt and studied her thighs. She slapped them a couple of times, stood up, and squeezed her buns, hard. God, it was worse than she thought. The ten pounds were heading toward fifteen, not down to five. She could *feel* them hanging on her like giant globs of cellulite, while she sat here and looked at… numbers! Instead of beating a tennis ball around the court or working it off in the gym and getting her fat ass back to her wedding day weight, here she sat in this office behind a desk pretending to understand accounting, sales, and corporate finance reports. For how long? A week? A month? A year! How could she be this stupid!

Fortunately, there was a knock on her office door to snap her out of her temporary depression. Maryanne stuck her head inside and said,

"There's a Mr. O'Malley out here to see you. He doesn't have an appointment but…"

"I know who he is," Angie answered glumly. "Send him in."

US Attorney Peter O'Malley entered, briefcase in hand, and took one of the two chairs opposite her desk without waiting for an invitation. "How nice to see you again, Mrs. Burke."

"Nice, but not nearly as exciting a view, is it Peter?"

"No, but your circumstances seem to have dramatically improved since yesterday, haven't they? You looked very good relaxing at the pool, but you look even better here behind your husband's desk. Imagine! And here I heard you didn't care much for business."

"Oh, I don't," she laughed. "In fact, I can't stand it. Accounting puts me to sleep. I tried sales, but I can't lie well enough to be good at that. All the technical telecommunications stuff? It gives me a head-splitting migraine. Let's face it, I'm not cut out for business; but I know it. If I could, I'd sell this place today, take the money, and sip martinis on the beach; but now I can't even do that. Losing that DOD contract destroyed our valuation multiples, and I might actually have to start working."

"So, that's all it would take to make you happy? Getting the DOD contract back?"

"Well, that's not the *only* thing, Peter," she answered with a sexy smile. "But it might be a good start."

"You know, that contract is a lot like your Court Order, *Angie*. Neither of them is worth the paper it's written on, and I should know. I write them. I can make them appear or disappear as fast as you can snap your fingers; and I can do the same for your husband's murder charges, if I want to."

"Imagine that?" she replied. "The local TV news channel says that half the cops in northeast Illinois are after him for murder."

"Murder is a very serious offense."

"Oh, very serious, *Peter*," she murmured as she leaned closer. "Now, I'm not a lawyer, but I was under the impression that *murder* was a state offense, not a Federal one?"

"Oh, maybe yes, maybe no. It all depends how motivated I am."

"Wow! You mean a US Attorney can actually make a state murder charge go away?" she asked as she snapped her fingers, "like that?"

"I can make a lot of things happen, Mrs. Burke. I can make your husband's problems go away, or I can drop him in a deep dark hole that he'll never climb back out of."

"And all you need is the proper motivation? How delicious."

O'Malley smiled back at her. "A woman after my own heart."

"Me? Oh, I'm not after anyone's heart, *Peter.* I want that damned DOD contract and I want Bob Burke in jail and out of my hair long enough for me to unload this place."

O'Malley rested his chin on his fingertips and looked perplexed. "But if I lock him up, what incentive would he have to testify against Greenway for me?"

"I can usually get Bobby to do a lot of things he'd rather not do. All I have to do is call on his sense of morality and civic duty. Trust me; I can get him to testify. Once he does, all you have to do is find some reason to void your little agreement with him and lock him up again."

"And I would want to do that, because…"

"Because you'd have Greenway and that guy DiGrigoria you're salivating over, you'd have a new multiple-murder conviction on Bobby that you can hold press conferences over and brag about to the voters, and — dare I say it — you'd have little old me. I assure you I can be very motivating and very, very appreciative."

"Very, very?" O'Malley smiled. "And you're really worth all that trouble?"

"Oh you have no idea! I know ways to *appreciate* a man you've never even dreamed of."

"As lovely as that sounds, and so that there is no misunderstanding here; when I convene that Grand Jury, I must have your husband in there testifying against Greenway, giving the jurors a lurid, bloodcurdling image of what he saw take place on that rooftop. And if you can arrange for his pal Charlie to provide supporting testimony, that would be even better."

"I think I can do that, Peter, because I have some unique 'leverage' of my own, and I can be very persuasive. But remember what the deal is — Bobby and Charlie testify, I get the DOD contract, and Bobby goes away for a long, long time."

"And I get?"

"Why, little old me, of course, and won't that be fun," she said with a wicked smile.

Bob Burke came out through the rear door of the motel and hurried back to Linda's Toyota. From the expression on his face, she could see there were problems.

"All right, what's wrong?" she asked.

"Well, tracking down Charlie might take a tad more time than I expected, and things have gotten more complicated back in the office, too," he said as he put the car in gear and drove back to Route 83, turned north, and headed for the Toll Road.

"More complicated? For you? That's hard to imagine."

"You'd think so, but my darling soon-to-be ex-wife Angie got a court order giving her custody of my company. I expected that, but not this quickly. Apparently, she blew in this morning, took over, and fired Charlie and a whole lot of the others."

"Uh, 'your darling *soon-to-be*-ex-wife?' " she turned and asked. "I see you're wearing a ring and I hate to be nosy, but what's that supposed to mean? Yes, no, maybe?"

"It means exactly what I said. Our marriage was on life support, then it cratered when her father left me in charge of the company instead of her. She took it *very* personally. She refused to give me a divorce, and now it's turned into a major business brawl over who's going to run Toler TeleCom. If you add that to my other 'legal difficulties,' she's kicking my butt; hopefully not for much longer, but whenever it does end, it's not going to end pretty."

"But it's over now, I mean between the two of you?"

"Oh, yeah, it's been over. Sooner or later, she'll get bored sticking pins in me and she'll calm down. We'll set the business battle aside and get the divorce papers signed, and she'll take a bunch of money and go off and pout with her tennis pro for a while."

"Her tennis pro?"

"Or her golf pro, one of her lawyers, or anyone else she thinks might hurt me. Angie believes in thermonuclear war, fighting 'til the death, and taking no prisoners."

"What a cupcake! And it really is finished, between the two of you? Because I don't..."

"Relax. It was over a long time ago."

"I shouldn't have asked," she turned away, suddenly embarrassed. "It's none of my business."

"Like your daughter is none of mine? I think we're both well past that now, aren't we? Or, at least I hope we are."

She stared at him for a moment and nodded. "I hope so too, but I guess we'll have to see, won't we?" she added. "So what's the plan? Where are we going?"

"We still need a computer, but that's gonna have to wait. We need to get rid of this car."

"*My* car? I beg your pardon," she said. "I kind of like it, and it's mine."

"It would only be temporary. The car and those license plates are too hot. That's why we need to get a new one."

"You mean rent one or something?" she asked.

"No, that would create a new paper trail. Besides, all the rental car companies require credit cards, and I don't have any of mine or my IDs. They're in my wallet, sitting on the end table back in my apartment. I suppose I could go back there and try to grab them after it gets dark, but the cops probably bagged and tagged all my stuff a long time ago."

"No, no, my nerves couldn't take you breaking in somewhere again. I have a couple of credit cards. Can't you use one of them?"

"They'll have a security block on mine and probably on yours too, by now. Besides, I wasn't thinking of 'renting' a car, Linda, I was thinking of 'borrowing' one, maybe from the long-term lot out at O'Hare. The odds are that no one would even miss it for a few days, maybe more."

"Borrow? How quaint. You mean steal one, don't you?"

"Tomatoes, to-mah-toes, but 'steal' sounds a bit harsh, don't you think?" he smiled.

"Bob, where I grew up in Detroit, most of the guys had Grand Theft Auto in their resumes by eighth grade," she laughed. "One thing, though, my daughter gets out of school at 3:30. I need to be there to pick her up, and then I'm taking her to my sister's in Prospect Heights. I don't want her anywhere near this stuff."

"Good idea," he nodded. "After we switch cars, we'll swing by Charlie's house, and then go pick up Ellie," Bob told her as he reached inside the brown manila envelope, pulled out the flash drive Eleanor had left, and held it up. "Getting in this thing would be a piece of cake if I was at the office or could get to my own machine at home. I could pop it open like a beer can, but I guess those are both out."

"I have a computer at my house, and it's a lot closer," she offered.

"No, the cops will be watching my apartment and after what you said you did to Greenway's face, Scalese's people will be watching your house too; so those are out. Besides, the flash drive is probably encrypted and Charlie has all kinds of software."

"You don't think they'll be watching him too?"

"I don't know. I guess that depends on how many men they've

got; but one way or the other, we need to find out. We have the reports and if the stuff on the flash drive ties it together, that will help our bargaining position with O'Malley and the local cops," he added.

"Do you think it's enough to put Greenway and the rest of them in jail?"

"Do you think Eleanor would have risked her life for anything less?"

Linda thought about it for a moment. "No, she was brave; but she wasn't stupid."

"That's why we need Charlie's computer. But we need to change cars first, then we'll figure out how to crack the flash drive."

Whether or not Tony Scalese agreed with Mister DiGrigoria, he was the Boss, and Tony always did what the old man told him to do. Driving west on Golf Road and then south on Route 53 toward the CHC offices in Indian Hills, the midday traffic was as thick as usual, but Tony didn't mind. It gave him time to think.

The old man put him in charge of Greenway's lucrative healthcare scams four years ago for one simple reason. Scalese was smarter than all of DiGrigoria's other underbosses put together. He knew how to make money, lots of money, and everyone knew it. Someday, if things broke right, Tony Scalese expected to be Salvatore's successor; but that would require the old man's blessing and a lot more. He would also need the agreement of Salvatore's older brother Pietro on the South Side and his younger brother Enzo up in southern Wisconsin. Get their agreement or take them out, one or the other, and everyone knew that too. It was the way it was in their "business." He would also need at least the tacit approval of the heads of the families in New York. They would expect two things in return: a somewhat peaceful transition and a bigger piece of the Chicago action.

Salvatore had three daughters and no sons, and women were never part of the "family" equation. They had been married off to various minor lieutenants and "made-men" in the organization. While they and their husbands received a modicum of respect and reasonable income, they were no threat or competition. Pietro, on the other hand, had two sons — a Neapolitan curse if there ever was one. He was eight years older than Salvatore, and aging badly. Even if he lived a few years longer, he was not likely to put up much of a fight with Tony Scalese over the North Side succession. The focus of the two brothers would be to solidify their own positions in their father's South Side territory and fight each other off, not on expanding into their uncle's North Side territory. By the time they tried, Tony Scalese would already have them locked out.

Then there was Enzo. He was Salvatore's and Pietro's much younger brother, and the most hotheaded. He made no secret of his long-standing belief that he was the heir apparent with a God-given natural right to take over both of his older brothers' territories and consolidate the entire Chicagoland operation under one supreme boss when they died. That was why Scalese and Pietro's two sons would face an immediate challenge from their dear 'Uncle Enzo,' long before they faced challenges from each other. Unfortunately for Enzo, that was easier said than done. He was called "the Kid," and not in a friendly way, by his brothers and their underbosses; and that did not bode well.

By its nature, change is abhorrent to any bureaucracy. The underbosses and lieutenants on both the North and South Sides were not about to welcome a new boss whom they did not know and did not know how he might affect them or their turf. Further, either of the two Chicago territories dwarfed whatever money, organization, and prestige Enzo could command in Milwaukee and southern Wisconsin. True, he was a DiGrigoria, and blood always counted; but what counted far more was the ability to make money, a lot of money, for those above you and below you. That was where Tony Scalese excelled. Whether Enzo, Pietro, or his two sons liked it or not, that was why Tony Scalese would eventually end up running the entire Chicago region, not them, provided he kept Salvatore DiGrigoria happy, stayed out of jail, and managed to live that long. But above all that, Tony Scalese wanted it. He was smarter and more vicious than the three of them put together; and he wanted it all. Three Neapolitan pissants who happened to have the *proper* last name were not about to stop him.

Unlike your average Mafioso, not only could Tony Scalese read, he was an avid reader ever since he was a child. In particular, he enjoyed history. He read everything he could get his hands on from Medieval European, Japanese, Chinese, and Italian history about the political intrigues and empire building of various kings, princes, and even popes. He read and reread Machiavelli, Sun Tzu, and *The Godfather* so many times that his copies were dog-eared. That was why Tony made it a point to remain friends with Pietro to protect his flank. When Pietro passed on, which wouldn't be long now, Tony would build a strategic alliance with one of his two sons, presumably the weaker one. With "Crazy Enzo," as he called him, Tony had made soft forays into his Milwaukee empire, making friends with several of his underbosses. Above all else, he kept in close contact with the New York and New Jersey Dons, anticipating the day that Salvatore finally passed on.

Until then, Tony knew his priorities. It was time to make the CHC operation disappear and snip off all those loose ends, "without leaving a ripple in the water," to quote an old Italian saying. To do that, the meddlesome "telephone guy," as Salvatore called him, also needed to disappear. Unlike Salvatore, however, he was beginning to suspect that Burke did not have much to do with telephones, and he might not be all that easy to make go away.

CHAPTER NINETEEN

As they continued east on the I-90 Toll Road past O'Hare Airport, Bob drove Linda's Toyota through a spaghetti bowl of interchanges that took them onto Higgins Road and then Zemke Road, which ended at the massive O'Hare Economy Parking Lot F. All the way along this tortuous path, he kept an eye on the rear view mirror and the traffic behind them.

"I think we're clean," he told her. "I don't see anyone following us."

"How could they? I'm lost; why wouldn't they be?"

"Oh, it's not that bad," he laughed as they pulled up to one of the automated ticket kiosks at the entrance to Parking Lot F.

"Sheesh! Nine bucks a day?" she said as she read the rates posted in large letters on the front of the machine. "I don't fly much, but that's ridiculous."

"That's for the cheap seats in the Economy Lot. If you prefer the close-in convenience of the big parking ramp, it's sixty bucks a day."

"Must be nice to travel on an expense account," she said, as he pulled the ticket from the machine.

"Maybe, but I won't pay that much either, even if it is a business trip — twenty-five dollars one-way to check a suitcase, big fees to change or cancel a reservation, heck, they're even starting to charge for carry-ons. The nickel and diming has gotten ridiculous."

"If it's a business trip, it's not your money."

"The company's money *is* my money, Linda. I own twenty-six percent of it, or I do until Angie gets finished with me. And if it makes you happy, I usually park right here in the F Lot or get dropped off at the terminal."

"All right, all right, I'm sorry. You are a true 'man of the people,' " she laughed at him.

"It's not that. My dad was a hard-core, card-carrying AFL-CIO union member. He hated big business and bosses and foremen, and all that stuff. However, the one thing he did drill into my pointed little head that stuck is to try to do the right thing, especially when it comes to other people's money. Whether it's the Army or a business I may own part of, you don't spend what you don't need to spend."

"Wow! They sure don't look at it that way at CHC. Greenway doesn't," she said as she looked out over a sea of parked cars. "What now?"

"Now, we pick out a car. I'll start going up and down the rows. When we find what I'm looking for, we'll find a space and park."

"All right," she said as they began traversing the center of the lot. "What's your preference in stolen cars today, Mister Burke? Feel a little racy?" she asked as she wiggled her eyebrows and gave a passable Groucho Marx impersonation. "I see a Volvo over there with your name on it. On the other hand, how about a sleek, two-door Mercedes? That should be what you need to outrun those Lincoln Town Cars. Better still, I see a huge Ford Expedition SUV, if you'd prefer to play Demolition Derby with them."

"No, we need something old and nondescript, something no one will pay any attention to."

"By no one, you mean the cops? There! I see a dusty, dark-green Toyota two rows back that looks like it hasn't moved in weeks. I know how to drive one of those. What do you think?"

"Close, but not quite," he said as he turned, came back down the next aisle, and saw she was right about the dust. "Look for a domestic car, maybe eight to ten years old, preferably a Ford if we can find one. They're the easiest to hot wire, and they don't have any of those new remote control door locks."

"That sounds like the voice of misspent youth." She looked at him suspiciously. "Am I to assume you've done this before?"

"A few times, but overseas, not here in the States, and it wasn't all that long ago," he answered. "We might hope to find one that the owner didn't bother to lock. You'd be surprised how often that happens."

"An old, beat-up Ford? Why would they lock it to begin with? They probably left it here with the key in the ignition, hoping it would get stolen."

"No, not at these rates. Nowadays, if you want something to 'get stolen' out here in the 'burbs,' drive it back into Maywood, Cicero, or the near West Side and leave it. They'll have it stripped for parts in thirty minutes, flat," he laughed. "And you don't have to pay them nine bucks an hour for the opportunity." He turned his head from side to side and continued to look up and down the aisle. "I'd like to find one with some dust on it to show it isn't an overnight trip, but not too much. That might mean the owners are due back soon."

"What about that one," she said as she pointed to an old maroon Ford Taurus, with sufficient dents and rust spots to make him smile.

"Good call. Looks like an '03 or '04, and that should be perfect.

It's less obvious than the imports, and I won't need a computer to get into the ignition," he said as he pulled the Toyota into an empty space three cars down and they both got out.

"So, you're an expert on old cars too?"

"Oh, not really," he laughed, "but I used to own an '04 Taurus like this one — briefly, I might add — because it got stolen from my driveway before the ink was dry on the insurance policy. That's how I learned how easy a Ford was to steal. One of the local cops showed me how to do it, and then I got a graduate degree in most of the major civilian felonies in the classes the Army put us through at Fort Bragg during my Special Ops training and Camp Perry for a couple of CIA things."

"A couple of CIA 'things?' " she frowned as he parked and they both got out.

"Charm school, you know. Do you have a phillips screwdriver in your glove compartment?"

"What's a phillips?"

"Never mind," he said as he shook his head, reached into his pocket, pulled out a quarter, and handed it to her. "While I'm getting the car door open and getting it started, I want you to take off the front and back license plates, and then find two other cars in the next row. Find ones a little bit apart, not sitting right next to each other. If they're parked head-in, take off the front plates. If they're backed in, grab the rear ones. We'll replace them with your two and the two from the Taurus, and put two of theirs on your Toyota."

"But they won't match."

"Doesn't matter. No one looks at both the front and the back plates on a car, not even the cops. They only look at one, unless it's a full-blown arrest, in which case it won't matter at all."

"Now, that really is sneaky, Bob. Did the Army teach you all that stuff, or the CIA?"

"Actually, I'm thinking it was an Elmore Leonard novel or an old episode of MacGyver; I can't remember which. Now get moving. This may be Chicago, but the airport security guards do occasionally drive by, even here."

As he expected, one of the Taurus' rear doors was unlocked. He opened the others and quickly went to work on the wiring harness in the car's steering column, until he heard her call out to him, "This isn't doing much for my fingernails, you know. Damn, there goes another."

"It's an occupational hazard."

"Maybe yours, but my occupation is *not* car thief; and I don't think I'd make a very good one, even if I were… Did you learn this stuff overseas, or wherever you were stealing cars or doing whatever it was you were doing?"

"Me? I was defending truth, justice, and the American way of life, of course."

"You and Superman?"

"No, not really. I can't fly," he smiled as he heard the solenoid click a few times before the starter turned over and the engine finally fired.

"Tell me something," he heard her suspicious voice call out to him from the next row. "This business with those guys at Eleanor's house last night, you seemed to handle them rather easily."

"They told you I was some kind of telephone guy, didn't they?" He smiled. "Toler TeleCom designs and builds highly sophisticated, highly secret telecommunications software and hardware for the Defense Department. We don't install phones."

"I'm so glad to hear that," came her sarcastic reply, "because I don't see much future in stealing cars or installing telephones. Still, that doesn't explain what you did to the men at Eleanor's house. They work for Tony, and I know who they were. They are *big,* with muscles on top of their muscles, and I've seen them push people around."

"I guess they pushed on the wrong one this time," he shrugged and set to work taking the front and back plates off the Taurus. "Linda, I spent some time in the Army, quite a bit of time, actually; and I wasn't a supply clerk. I picked up a few tricks here and there…"

"A few tricks? Bob, you're a pretty average-looking guy…"

"Gee, thanks."

"That's not what I meant. They were twice your size…"

"Size has nothing to do with it."

"That's what all the guys say… sorry."

"In that, it doesn't," he looked over at her, exasperated. "Neither do muscles from Gold's Gym… are you done with the license plates yet?"

"Almost, I'm putting the last one on, but don't change the subject. I'm not done with you."

"We'll have plenty of time later. I have the car running and the plates are off this one. Bring me the last two and recheck your own car. Make sure you don't leave anything in the trunk or the glove compartment, then let's get out of here."

"Are you sure my car will be safe here? Eventually, I'm going to want it back, you know."

"Linda, who's going to steal a car from a lot where they'd have to pay these rates to get it through the gate? If they do, they're going to pick a Mercedes or a Lexus, not an old Toyota."

"Except for 'professionals' like you, who pick an even older Taurus."

With the ignition wires tucked above the steering column, he looked at his watch and said, "It's 12:45 now. That should give us enough time for me to get to Charlie's, and I have a couple of other things to do before we swing by the school and pick up your daughter. Hop in, I'll drive."

Bob followed the Exit signs back through the parking lot to the entrance on Zemke Road. Business must hit a low around noon, because only one of the six cashier booths was open, and their Taurus was the third car in line. He pulled up to the open window, handed Linda's ticket to the bored, middle-aged woman sitting inside, and smiled at her. She inserted it into her ticket reader, stared out at him over the top of the pink, oyster-shell sunglasses that sat down on the tip of her nose, and said, "You only been here twenty minutes, hon, that ain't very long."

"Our flight got cancelled, you know how it goes," he said innocently.

"Guess I do, but that'll be five bucks anyway."

"Five bucks? Sheesh, that's a rip," Linda said from the far side of the seat as she reached into her wallet, found a five-dollar bill, and reached across Bob to hand it to the cashier.

"It sure is," the cashier commiserated as she reached her arm out and patted the price list on the side of the booth. "The mayor says he needs the money."

"Told you that himself, I bet."

"He did indeed!" she laughed. "Old Rahm parks here hisself and he told me last week."

"He's parking that big black limo in the Economy Lot now?"

"And he told me to tell you to have an exceptionally good day!"

"But five bucks lighter."

"You got it, hon!" he heard the attendant cackle as he drove away and headed back west toward Schaumburg.

"Sneaky, very sneaky, indeed," Linda smiled as she sat back in the seat and tried to relax as he backtracked, went on and off a series of interchanges, and finally got on I-90, the Northwest Toll Road. "I give, you've got me all turned around," she said. "Where are we going now?"

"Out of curiosity, I want to drive past my office."

"You aren't going inside, are you? That doesn't sound very smart."

"All I want to do is take a quick look from the outside. Maybe I can see in some of the windows, look around the parking lot, and get a feel for what's going on inside. With all my contacts gone I feel completely cut off."

When they finally merged into the "through" lanes and headed west, she turned her head away and looked out the window. "Uh, look, Bob, not to keep flogging a dead horse about this 'darling soon-to-be ex-wife' stuff, but since we are getting to know each other a little, if your marriage is dead as a doornail, why are you still wearing the wedding ring? I took mine off the day I threw *him* out. You have no idea how good that made a 'sweet young thing' like me feel."

"A sweet young thing like you?"

"Don't get smart!"

"You mean this?" he asked as he held his hand up in the air and looked at the ring. "To tell you the truth, I almost forgot I was still wearing it, but you're right."

"It's hard to miss, and you need to make up your mind; because that's something I don't do." He was about to ask her what that meant, when she added, "You know exactly what I mean; I don't get involved with married men or men who can't decide if they're married."

"I didn't know we were getting involved." He tried not to grin even more.

"We're not! Now stop that! I have a couple of firm rules, and 'unmarried-married guys' like you are right at the top of the list," she said, but that only made her more flustered. "Don't take that wrong, I said it… in case, for some completely inexplicable reason, we ever…"

"I completely understand. Technically, I'm still married; but it's long over and we're well on our way to a divorce."

"Well on our way? You know how many times I've heard that one?"

"Not from me."

"Look, you know what a girl's like when she doesn't get her daily fix of gossip. Come on, you can trust me. Tell me what happened."

"Is this where I'm supposed to say, I haven't trusted anybody since sixth grade?"

She covered her eyes. "Did I really say that?"

"I may never forget."

"I'm sure you won't."

"All right, all right, you know that old Johnny Cash song? How's it go? 'We got married in a fever, hotter than a pepper sprout…' "

"Yeah, I ate one of those, too."

"Not like this one!"

"All right, but how did you two…"

"How does anybody? I can't explain it. The first year or two were fantastic, until her father got sick and he left the company to me, of all people."

"Well, I never ate anything like that."

"I doubt anybody has, but she couldn't handle it and the marriage crashed. So what happened to yours?"

"Well, nothing nearly that interesting. My husband decided the eighteen-year-old interns in his office were a lot more fun than I was."

"I guess that happens too."

"Not to me it doesn't. I threw him out, filed the papers, and never looked back.

"And you have a daughter…"

"Ellie," she beamed. "She's six years old, and she's my life."

"That's nice. I like kids, but Army Special Ops and family life usually make a bad fit. Besides, Angie hated kids, and frankly I never really gave it much thought."

They cast furtive glances at each other across the front seat and he could see how nervous she was. Finally, she turned away and closed her eyes. "All right, let me get this all out. I'm twenty-nine years old, married for three years and divorced for five more. When this thing is over, maybe you'd let me cook you dinner or buy you a drink or something. You seem like a nice man, and… well, I thought I'd better say it while I have the chance."

"That would be very nice. I'd like that."

"You would?" she opened one eye and looked at him. "And you really *are* getting a divorce? Not that I mean anything by that, but I'm not stupid."

"Yes, I am really getting a divorce. Here, you don't believe me?" he asked as he managed to pull the wedding ring off, rolled the window down, and tossed it out.

"Whoa!" She sat back, wide-eyed. "I didn't mean for you to do something like that."

"Maybe you didn't, but you have no idea how good it felt."

Bob got off I-90 at I-290 near the big Woodfield Shopping Center and headed down the side roads toward the Toler TeleCom building.

"I still don't think this is very smart," she told him.

"All I'm doing is sizing up the opposition, doing a little recon."

"And if they catch us?"

"Why would they? No one will recognize the car, the license plates, or us if you scooch down a bit," he said as he drove in through the rear parking lot entrance and slowly circled the building. It was midday, but there were far fewer cars in the lot than he expected to see. It looked like Angie's house cleaning was in full swing. He pulled in and parked near the building's left front corner under a large tree with a clear view of the lobby and the Toler TeleCom offices.

Looking into the lobby, he saw a woman he didn't recognize sitting at the front desk, and two men in blue blazers walking around inside. Private security, no doubt. At least these guys were younger, with buzz cuts and matching blue blazers with logos on the breast pockets. They were definitely a cut above Scalese's men at CHC. It looked like Angie was pulling out the stops to protect her little empire.

"Let's go," he told Linda as he backed up and slowly drove out of the parking lot. "I've seen enough."

He drove down the road and headed back north toward the Kennedy Expressway, until he saw a Shell gas station with a pay phone on the sidewall near the restrooms.

"If you're getting gas, I'm hitting the little girl's room," Linda told him.

"Why do women always say that? The 'little girl's' room?"

"All right, I'm going to the almost-middle-aged woman's room and take a pee. Is that better?"

"I guess that does lack the 'cutesy' charm. Anyway, while you're doing that, I'm going to make a couple of phone calls."

"Who are you going to aggravate this time?"

"No one, I hope. I'm trying Charlie's number again. After that, I should probably check in with George Grierson, my lawyer."

"Your lawyer? It's a little late for that, don't you think?"

"I'm sure that's exactly what he's going to say, but I should probably check in anyway."

She left him at the phone booth and stepped into the nearby Women's Restroom. "Guard the door, D'Artagnan, and kill anyone who follows," she said as she closed the door behind her.

"Don't tell me you've been reading Dumas?"

"Me? No, Ellie is," she called to him over the transom. "She's into the Three Musketeers and runs around the house with a toy sword and a towel tied around her neck."

"Nice to see she's reading," he said as he dropped some coins in the phone.

"You got that. The girl is *not* going to grow up like her mother."

Bob knew there was no sense in calling Charlie's office number. If Angie did fire him, Charlie would be long gone by now. He tried Charlie's cell phone, but the call rolled over to voice mail, as it did the last time he tried. He tried Charlie's house, figuring he'd be home by now, but the call went to his answering machine like the others. Finally, he dialed George Grierson's number. His secretary said he was tied up in meetings all afternoon, but as soon as Burke gave her his name, it was amazing how fast she tracked George down and how fast the lawyer got on the line.

"Are you nuts, Bob?" the otherwise mild-mannered lawyer came on the line, shouting.

"Everybody keeps asking me that today, but I'm fine, George. How are you doing?"

"Very funny, very funny. Nothing ever seems to worry you, but this time it should. They're looking for you everywhere — the FBI, the US Attorney, the Chicago cops, and half the police departments in the north suburbs. You gotta turn yourself in and let me see what I can work out, Bob."

"Relax, they're a long way from catching me."

"Yeah? What they're going to do is shoot you on sight, and there isn't a damned thing I can do about it."

"That's fine. Here's what I want you to do, George. Call Peter O'Malley for me."

"The US Attorney? You've been talking to *him*? I guess that's great news."

"Maybe. Tell him I have Eleanor Purdue's files — reports on their foreign manufacturing, the scams, the spreadsheets, who's on the pad, and all the other stuff she put together on Greenway and CHC for his Grand Jury. Most of it is on a 32-gig flash drive. If he wants it, he needs to call off the dogs, all of them. I'm still putting the last few pieces of it together, and if I get shot by some overeager cop before I do, well... tell him I'll turn everything over to him later tonight or first thing in the morning. You two can work out the details. But if he wants it, I want a complete walk for me and Linda Sylvester."

"How nice that you remembered little old me," she said as she came out of the restroom, snuggled up next to him, and wrapped herself around his arm again. "No prison time? You know, men have used a lot of different pickup lines on me, but that's a first. How sweet."

"Who's that?" Grierson asked, still flustered.

"The aforesaid mentioned, Ms. Sylvester. Say 'Hi' to George, Linda."

"Hi George. It sounds like Bob keeps you busy."

"You have no idea. But Bob, are you sure O'Malley is going to know what I'm talking about, when I phone him?"

"Oh yeah, he'll know, George. Look, I gotta go."

Linda leaned in. "He usually says, 'Rolling stones gather no bullets.' "

"Ignore that woman. I'll talk to you later," Bob said as he hung up.

He turned toward her, their faces only inches apart. "He might be my lawyer, but I would rather he not know everything I'm up to."

"We aren't up to anything yet, but you owe me, big time, and now I have a witness," she smiled demurely up at him. "Shall we go?" she asked.

"Yeah, let's go see if Charlie's home and I can borrow his computer."

CHAPTER TWENTY

Charlie lived in a modest, Dutch colonial on the fringe of
Wheeling, Illinois. He was in a newer area of town where the houses and
lots were bigger, but the subdivision was laid out across hundreds of
acres of former cornfield. The resulting developments lacked the mature
trees, vegetation or any semblance of character to be found in the rest of
Wheeling and the older communities to the south, such as Arlington
Heights, Des Plaines, or Winnetka, much less Evanston. Bob approached
Wheeling from the south on Route 53, turned east on Dundee Road, and
then passed through a series of larger subdivisions. As he neared
Charlie's area, he made a series of slow, circling passes around his
neighborhood, coming closer each time, but always staying a block or
two away from Charlie's house.

"Bogie at 10 o'clock," Linda said, nodding toward a Village of
Wheeling police car parked on a side street, and she ducked down on the
seat.

" 'Bogie?' You're trying way too hard," Bob laughed as he drove
by, but the police car did not move.

"Must be on a donut break. Or maybe they're not expecting us."

"What they're probably expecting is a Toyota with a couple
inside," he said as he turned and drove up Charlie's street.

"We're a couple now?"

"Don't let the camouflage go to your head," he told her as he
drove around the neighborhood. The street appeared empty and there
were no suspicious cars parked on either side. Nonetheless, he passed
Charlie's house at a conservative twenty miles per hour. "The Dutch
colonial with the green shutters on the right, that's his."

"There's no way you can go in there in broad daylight, Bob."

"You watched me operate once, and suddenly you're the expert?"

"That is not like Eleanor's house. There are no trees or bushes for
you to hide in, and it's *broad daylight*. Besides, I didn't watch you. I sat
in the car driving around in circles, terrified, praying you'd come back."

"This isn't any more or any less dangerous than Eleanor's, it's just
different and requires a different approach, that's all" he answered as he
turned the corner and drove down the street to the rear of Charlie's.
Halfway down, he saw a dark, late-model Buick parked against the curb
with two men sitting inside. "As we drive past, see if you can get a look
at them," he told her.

"Want me to smile, too?"

"If you want to. I'll have my face turned the other way. As we get close, if they look like a couple of beefy, middle-aged Italians in cheap sports coats, like the clowns who work for Tony Scalese, I want you to turn away too, so they can't see your face, either."

As they passed the Buick, she said, "No, I've never seen them before. They look younger and much better dressed, in suits, with short haircuts. So I smiled."

"I'm sure it made their day, but from your description they must be Feds."

"Sheesh, that's even worse. What're you gonna do now?"

"The address of the house we passed is 239 Yarborough. Remember that."

"Aye, aye, Captain. Why?"

"You'll see," he told her as he drove out of the subdivision and back onto West Dundee Road where he soon saw a 7-11, pulled in, and parked. They walked inside. Near the cash registers, he saw a pay phone hanging on the wall and walked over to it.

"Pay phones are beginning to have some real advantages over cell phones," she said as she snuggled closer.

"I'm sure they do. What I want you to do is Dial 911." She held out her hand for a quarter, but he said, "It's a free call. Sound flustered and worried. Tell them you live at 239 Yarborough Street and say there's a dark Buick parked in front of your house with two men sitting in it. Say one of them has a gun out, some kind of pistol. They've been sitting there for an hour now, and you're getting very worried. Say you have kids and you'd like the police to come by and check them out."

"And if they ask for my name?"

"Tell them you don't want to get that involved, but the Buick is sitting in front of 239 Yarborough. They can't miss it."

"You're being very sneaky again."

"Hopefully, the Wheeling Police don't talk to their neighbors, and certainly not to the State cops or to the Feds, and they'll send that squad car we saw sitting around the corner to check it out, probably with some backup."

"And what exactly is that supposed to accomplish for us?"

"Well, with the police focusing over on Yarborough, you're going to drop me off in front of Charlie's house. I'm going to walk up his front sidewalk and through his front door, and none of them will ever be the wiser."

"I don't know," she said as she scrunched up her nose and shook her head. "I'm not sure that's going to work out here."

"Why?" he looked over at her

"Well, this is the gun-toting, white, Republican part of Cook County up here; as opposed to the gun-toting, black, Democratic big city part down there," she said as she threw a thumb over her shoulder. "I don't think some story about a guy sitting in a car with a gun is going to get them too excited."

"You got a better idea?"

"Maybe," she said with an impish smile as she punched the numbers 911 into the phone, and waited until the operator answered.

"Oh my God!" she said breathlessly. "Is this the police? Look, there's a car sitting in front of my house with two men inside, and... well, I don't know how to put this, but they're exposing themselves, and my kids... Look! It's a dark car, a Buick, I think, and it's parked at 239 Yarborough. They've got dark suits on and they both look really creepy, especially the way they keep looking at the neighborhood kids... No, no, I'd rather you don't have my name, not with my kids involved.... Uh, oh, I can only see one of their heads above the dashboard now. You've got to send some police cars over here, before more kids come by," she added and then hung up and turned toward Burke with a big grin on her face. "You don't think that was too over the top, do you?" she asked.

He looked back at her, opened his mouth and began to speak, but then stopped, not knowing what to say. "So they think you're only a receptionist."

"Yeah, well, I do some of that too," she smiled.

"Let's get back over to Charlie's. I have a sneaking suspicion that half the cops in northeast Illinois are about to descend on Yarborough Street, and I want to get there before they shut the whole neighborhood down."

"All right, but once you get in the house, how are you going to get out?"

"All I need is a couple of minutes, and they can't have that mess on Yarborough sorted out that quickly. I'm coming back out Charlie's front door the same way I went in, taking a right on the sidewalk and walking down the street until you come around and pick me up."

"That's pathetic. They spend all that money sending you to government sneaky schools and you're going to walk in and out the front door?"

"With any luck at all, yes. Now let's go."

As he expected, the Village of Wheeling police car at the corner was gone, and they could see sets of flashing lights through the trees and back yards one block over. She stopped in front of Charlie's house. Bob got out of the Taurus and slipped on a thin pair of latex gloves as he walked up the path to the front porch as Linda drove away. Charlie bought the house the year before, and the lock on the front door was a run-of-the-mill, builder-quality, Kwikset model. Bob told him after he moved in to replace that crap with some quality locks and deadbolts, reinforce the doorframes, and put in a good alarm system on the doors and windows, but those were some of the many things the overweight bean counter never got around to doing. In a way, though, that was a good thing, because they wouldn't begin to slow down anyone with Bob's training. His lock picks were in in his hands before he reached the door. He slipped them in the lock and opened it in about three seconds. As he did, his trained eye immediately saw other faint scratches around the keyhole. They could come from many sources — from the initial construction and installation through an intruder's fumbling hands. Still, they put him on edge. Without looking back, he opened the heavy door and slipped inside.

He stepped silently into the entry hall and then stopped, listening intently. During his twelve years in the infantry and Special Ops, Bob saw more than his share of dead men, both friend and foe. He knew what it looked like, knew what it smelled like, and all too often knew what it felt like. When he came upon it, it rarely came as a surprise. He stepped through Charlie's front door and paused. The foyer and living room appeared perfectly normal to the untrained eye, but each of his senses screamed a warning. Something was not right in here, he realized, as he stepped away from the door, dropped into a defensive crouch, and waited. First, the house was deathly quiet, too quiet; and second, there was no cat. They say that pets and their owners often begin to resemble each other. Charlie and his old Persian cat were no exceptions. She was a white, very overweight, and very nosy Persian. Bob had visited the house often enough to know it was impossible to set foot inside without hearing the distinctive clatter of cat claws on the hardwood floor as the ever-suspicious feline would run out to see who was invading her empire. No cat meant big problems.

The house plan was simple, with a large living room, dining room, office and kitchen on the first floor, a central staircase, three bedrooms up, and a largely unfinished basement down. That was one of the many improvements that Charlie kept telling him he would get around to someday. Bob didn't believe in collecting "things" and had never "nested" anywhere for more than six months at a time until he met Ed and Angie Toler, as his sparsely furnished apartment in Arlington Heights more than attested; so he could only look at Charlie and laugh. Now, however, he wasn't laughing.

He advanced slowly down the entry hall with his back to the outside wall. Room by room he cleared the first floor. Charlie never was much of a housekeeper, but someone had trashed the living room and the office. This wasn't a home invasion or burglary. It was a messy, destructive search by people who didn't care what they broke and may not have even known what they were looking for. Still, Bob didn't see anything alarming until he reached the kitchen, where he saw a lump of bloody white fur lying in the far corner. It was the cat. Someone shot her, and she was dead. What had been a cautious, combat-ready look in his eyes suddenly turned ice-cold, as if an arctic wind had blown through the house. He understood killing when it was necessary, and had done plenty of that himself. What he could not tolerate was needless, stupid cruelty. He went to the knife rack near the stove and pulled out two carving knives from a German cutlery set that Charlie had won in a raffle. One knife was eight inches long and the other six inches long. They were heavy, solid, well balanced, and razor-sharp, and he hoped he would find an excuse to use them. He retraced his steps to the stairs, crept silently up to the second floor. One of the bedrooms was empty and one held three useless, complicated, and largely unused pieces of exercise equipment that Charlie had seen on TV, and had to have. The master bedroom and its closets had been ransacked like the first floor rooms, but that was all he found.

That only left the basement. He quickly retraced his steps to the kitchen, as the old warning bells began to clang louder and louder in the back of his head and his combat instincts took over. He opened the basement door and immediately sensed that all-too-familiar smell of death hanging in the air. It wasn't something you can readily describe to the uninitiated, but to an infantryman or perhaps a homicide detective, you knew it when you stumbled onto it. The basement ceiling lights were on. Bending low, he dropped to the floor and edged far enough down the stairs to see into the basement.

There was no need to be quiet, and there was no need for the knives. The basement was empty, except for Charlie. He sat upright, naked, tied to an old kitchen chair in the center of the room. Even from halfway down the stairs, it didn't take a practiced eye to see that he was very much dead. Bob got to his feet, descended the stairs, and quickly walked the perimeter of the basement, but there was no one else there, only the body of an old friend. Charlie was tied tightly to the chair with what looked like electrical wire, which they must have found down here or ripped from the ceiling. He'd been beaten, burned, and tortured. No doubt, he struggled, because the wire cut deep into the ample fat and soft tissue on his arms, chest, and legs.

When normal people stumble upon an awful scene like that, they would feel their heart pounding in their chest, hear a ringing in their ears, and probably find that big Bob Evans breakfast rising in their throat. Not him. If a doctor was there with him at that moment and hooked him up to a blood pressure cuff and a heart rate monitor, he'd barely find an uptick in the readings. The Army and the CIA had trained those normal human reactions out of him years before. Still, he was not a machine, far from it. What all that "wet" work and training did was to focus that fear, revulsion, and anger into a cold energy.

He stepped closer and examined the body. Unfortunately, he had seen too many similar scenes during his years in Iraq and Afghanistan. Usually it was locals — Sunnis doing it to Shia, Shia doing it to Sunnis, or Al Qaeda, drug lords, or one tribe doing it to another, not that the reason mattered much. The result was always the same. From the bruises and burn marks on Charlie's face and the small pools of blood on the floor, they went at him for quite a while down here and the fat bean counter died hard. What did they think Charlie knew? What were they after? Bob knew that answer the moment he stepped inside the house — they were after him and the game had changed once more. First, it was Eleanor Purdue. That angered him, but he didn't know her. Once he met Greenway and Scalese, Bob wanted simple justice for her. Then came Sabrina Fowler, and his reaction shifted to anger and a grim determination to see that the arrogant perpetrators of a crime like that were punished. Now, after what they did to Charlie, it became intensely personal. He wanted justice and punishment, but his desire turned much darker. They had declared war on him and his, and they were about to get one back the likes of which they had never seen. He would decide the rules of engagement, not them. He would define the battlefield. It would be Burke's war. He'd have his vengeance, he'd give no quarter, and he'd take no prisoners.

About ten feet from the body, he saw a puddle of vomit on the bare concrete. It was too far away to be from Charlie. Perhaps things went too far and one of them discovered a conscience? He found that hard to believe, but there was nothing more he could learn here. He reached out and touched the back of his hand to Charlie's chest. The basement was cool, and so was Charlie — cool, but not cold. Most of the streaks of blood on him were dry, but the larger pools on the floor were not, which meant he was killed less than an hour ago.

With knives at the ready again, Bob climbed back to the first floor and went into Charlie's small rear office, located off the kitchen. It had been ransacked worse than the living room or the upstairs bedroom. They had pulled the books out of the built-in bookcases and tossed the files from the drawers in his desk and file cabinet all over the floor. A thick, random layer of books, paper, pens, and other office paraphernalia covered the carpet. He stepped into the room, pushing the books and papers aside with his toes so as not to step on a sheet of paper. The men who did this were not so careful. He saw several large footprints in what appeared to be dried blood on several sheets of white copier paper. He placed his own foot next to one of them. He wore a size ten, but the shoe print from the other man was much larger, at least a size twelve or thirteen, and it showed a deep, one-inch long nick on the left side of the heel. Bozos, he thought. Whether they didn't know or didn't care, a distinctive shoe print like that could be as good as a fingerprint. However, since they owned half the cops in Cook County and hired the best lawyers in town, they probably figured they'd never go down for "nuttin."

From the randomness and the completeness of the destruction, it appeared they tossed the room for the sake of tossing it. Even if they didn't know what they were looking for, they were determined to make it appear they were thorough. Bob knew if he went back to his own apartment in Arlington Heights, it would look about like this too. So would Eleanor Purdue's by now, and Linda Sylvester's too. They were looking for whatever Eleanor Purdue took with her, but they didn't know exactly what that was. Being low-tech thugs, they expected it to be paper, which was why they tossed the place out of frustration. They didn't understand computers, so their medieval Sicilian predilection was to smash all the office equipment, as if they were killing the malevolent little Jinni inside. They threw his printer on the floor, dropped his desk monitor, and ripped the modem from the wall. Not having found Eleanor's papers in his files, they vented their remaining energy on his new HP Envy desktop computer. It had been repeatedly dropped, kicked, stomped on, and shot. They got those Jinni real good, Bob thought as he continued to look around.

He remembered Charlie also owned a small, older model ASUS

notebook computer, which he used on business trips such as the one they took to Washington. Burke didn't immediately see it in the rubble, giving him at least a short burst of hope, until he saw its small black carry-case lying in the corner with a bullet hole in the center. He bent down, picked it up, and unzipped it. Pulling the small computer out, he saw they had shot it, dead center, but if the bullet missed the hard drive, he might be able to move it to another machine and there could yet be hope.

He looked at his watch, gave the room a last, quick look, and then headed for the rear kitchen door. Time to get moving, he realized. He had touched nothing inside, and unlike Tony Scalese's Bozos, he left no footprints. True to his "Ghost" *nom de guerre*, he would come and go, leaving no trace behind. With the knives in one hand, the blades pressed against his forearm, and the computer case dangling from the other, he used his handkerchief to cover the knob again, opened the rear door and gave the back yard a quick scan as he slipped outside. It was empty. Through the gaps between the houses behind Charlie's, he saw the flashing lights from at least a half dozen police cars. He figured the entire Wheeling Police Department must be back there, checking out the two perverts in the Buick. Good, that meant there would be none around to watch the rest of the neighborhood. He walked across the rear yard and around the side of Charlie's house as casually as he could.

Tony Scalese parked his LS 460 Lexus in his usual space at the rear of the CHC parking lot. His foray out to Wheeling with Greenway and two of his men to "visit" Burke's accountant had not been a success. Killing him didn't bother Tony Scalese in the slightest. It was not being able to make the stubborn bastard talk and not finding anything useful in his house that left the big Italian seething with anger. He should have let Greenway use his drugs on him, but the Doc got sick watching his boys work on the fat man. Scalese in turn became impatient, lost his temper, and hit him hard one too many times. Now he had nothing. Well, it was that stubborn accountant's own fault. All he needed to do was tell them where they could find Burke. Now, Scalese must try some other approaches. He would find that "telephone company" bastard. It might take a bit longer now, but when he did, he would kill him the same way he killed his friend — with his bare hands, and he would enjoy every minute of it.

Scalese entered the building quietly through the back door and walked down the long hallway past the employee lounge to the lobby. It was already 11:30. Normally, the lounge was full of laughter and chatter from the early lunch crowd, but not today. The building was surprisingly quiet, as if a tense pall had fallen over the place. "And not a mouse to be heard," he thought to himself as he smiled at several of the worker bees taking an early lunch in the lounge. They smiled back, politely enough, but quickly turned away. Scalese understood exactly what that meant. They all knew Purdue was missing and that Sylvester was now missing too. The office jungle drums would have picked that up a long time ago, and now they were all scared.

When he reached the lobby, he saw a new girl sitting at the receptionist desk. She must be the one from accounting. She was young and cute, definitely Greenway's type. Seeing her sitting there reminded him of another problem he must take care of — Linda Sylvester. From her dust-up with Greenway in the hall this morning, apparently she had thrown her lot in with that little prick Burke. That made her one more problem he could lay at Greenway's feet.

First things first, however, he decided as he took the elevator up to the third floor and turned right toward the Doc's office. He didn't bother to ask the receptionist whether he was in, because Scalese didn't care. Greenway's car wasn't parked out front, but if he was in, he would soon wish he wasn't. The arrogant doctor showed no hesitance to rape and strangle women, but he couldn't watch a man take a good, old-fashioned beating. Greenway had run up the basement stairs and disappeared, just when Scalese might have used him and his bag of drugs. That left Scalese angry at both Greenway and the bean counter, which became a lethal combination.

Well, the doctor's absence would give Scalese the opportunity to take a long look around inside his office. Scalese turned the doorknob and walked in without knocking. As he expected, Greenway was out. No doubt, he remembered some Chamber of Commerce or Kiwanis luncheon he just had to be at, and was hobnobbing with the local gentry, letting himself be seen. Or, Greenway could have driven into the city and was making a nuisance of himself in one of CHC's clinics or warehouse operations down there, trying to corner another young girl in the stockroom. That pompous ass actually believed that his sexual antics were no one's business but his own, and that was an immense miscalculation on his part. Old Sal went to Mass every afternoon and considered himself a moral man. Like most of the senior Mafiosi he had committed every crime listed in the State and Federal Statutes, but those were 'business.' They were never personal. In his day, he had mistresses and frequented prostitutes. That was simply "men being men, with willing women" in the finest Italian tradition. However, sex crimes like rape, sexual blackmail, and any other form of forced, non-consensual or non-compensated sex was an "infamia," an evil act that ranked right up there next to child abuse; and it would soon earn Greenway a quick trip to Hell..

Scalese looked at Greenway's ridiculously large desk and the oversized credenza sitting behind it under the window. "You can tell a lot about a man by looking at what he leaves out on his desk," someone once told him. Tony agreed, but you could tell even more by seeing what he was hiding inside. He sat in Greenway's large, black-leather chair and looked around, but saw nothing of interest lying on top of the desk. However, there were three drawers on the left side, a thin drawer in the middle, and a cabinet door on the right, which he assumed held vertical files. All were locked. Reaching into his jacket pocket, Scalese pulled out his 9-inch stiletto, opened the blade, and worked it into the gap between the top of the left drawer in the desk. He worked it back and forth until the lock snapped open. Rummaging through the drawer, he found an untidy collection of office supplies, a calendar that was largely blank, and a stack of pornographic magazines, which seemed to run toward S and M, leather, and the very kinky. Disgusted, he turned his attention to the two drawers beneath it. The top one held pens, pills, note pads, and nothing of interest. When he opened the thin, center drawer, however, he saw a small .32-caliber Mauser automatic pistol lying in the clutter. Scalese pulled out his handkerchief, carefully picked up the Mauser without touching it, and slipped it in his jacket pocket, thinking the small 'pimp' gun could be useful later.

Scalese quickly went through the remaining desk drawers, broke the lock on the file cabinet, and went through the credenza behind the desk as well, but found nothing of any particular use. He shoved the drawers closed halfheartedly, not really caring whether Greenway knew someone had rummaged through his desk or not. Satisfied, he left the office and walked back to his own office at the other end of the hall with a thin, fresh smile on his lips.

CHAPTER TWENTY-ONE

Bob Burke took a half-dozen steps into the front yard and realized trouble had arrived. The old Ford Taurus sat at the curb on the other side of the street, engine running, with Linda inside. Instead of circling the block, she must have stopped and decided to wait for him to come out. That was when a dark-blue Lincoln Town Car pulled in behind her. She should have tromped on the accelerator and driven away right then, but maybe she was watching the house and didn't see them. Now it was too late. The Lincoln's front doors hung open, its trunk was up, and two large Gumbahs in cheap suits stood next to the driver's side door of the Taurus, guns drawn, daring her to try. Their backs were to him, their attention focused on her and the car, but he immediately knew they were Tony Scalese's men. One of them was rattling the driver's door, trying to pull it open, while his pal worked on the rear door. They were shouting at her and she was shouting back. Despite the panicked expression on her face, they hadn't succeeded yet. All four doors were locked, but that wouldn't keep them out much longer.

That was all Bob needed to see. To him, there was one basic rule of fighting — there were no rules — and at that moment, he burned to give them a little payback. That meant hit first, hit hard, and end it before the other fellow even realized he was in a fight. That was particularly true when there were two of them, each of whom was bigger than him by five or six inches and at least fifty pounds. Unfortunately for them, they were so intent on getting into the Taurus, that they had no idea what was about to hit them.

"Hey guys," Bob said in his friendliest voice as he stepped up behind them. They stood shoulder to shoulder at the side of the car, which worked to his advantage. The one on the left, trying to get in the driver's door, wore a thick bandage on the side of his head. He was Bozo #2, whom Bob had surprised as he sat in his big Lincoln outside Eleanor Purdue's house listening to a Cubs game the night before. It was dark and he only saw the gunman from the side, but that was enough. Bob never forgot a face.

"Well, hot damn! Gino Santucci, is that really you?" The Gumbah's head suddenly snapped around as he realized someone was behind him, talking to him. "By the way, how's the lump on the side of your head?" he went on, all the while shifting his weight onto his left leg. "Man, I'll bet that sucker hurt."

Santucci was angry at being interrupted while he tried to get this stupid woman out of her car, and wanted to lash out. Slowly, however, the dim light bulb came on in his pea brain and he recognized the man standing behind him. "You! It's you, you son-of-a-bitch!" The big Italian roared and continued turning the rest of the way around. He held a SIG Sauer 9-millimeter pistol in his right hand; but before he could get it halfway up, Bob snapped a powerful karate kick into Santucci's left knee — in and sharply downward. Normally, a kick like that would knock a man down, but delivered by a master black-belt it tore all the cartilage and tendons and caved in his knee like a stick of dry kindling. Santucci dropped the gun, grabbed his leg with both hands, and crumpled to the asphalt screaming and writhing in pain.

"There! Now you won't have to worry so much about that headache, Gino," Burke said. He didn't recognize the new Gumbah with him, but that didn't matter. He pivoted and jammed the knuckles of his left hand into the man's lower back with a short, straight, shot that went in below his ribs, straight into the kidney. It made no difference how big the guy was. A punch like that could paralyze an eight-hundred-pound gorilla, and it drained all the fight out of this one before it even started. Burke then wound up and kicked him hard in the groin. That did it. The gunman grabbed his crotch and toppled over onto the pavement next to Santucci.

Bob bent down, picked up both of their handguns, and tucked them in his belt. "Gino, I see you bought another SIG. I'll bet that cost you a few bucks. Me, I'll shoot about anything, but this SIG will be a nice addition to my growing collection. By the way, what size shoe do you wear?" he asked as he bent over and picked up Santucci's foot, the one attached to the now ruined knee and took a closer look. "Looks like a size nine, maybe a nine-and-a-half, like mine."

"Ah! Ah!" Gino screamed. "Yeah, yeah, a nine-and-a-half. Ah, Christ, you bastard!"

Bob dropped Gino's foot and turned toward the other Gumbah. As he did, he saw the top half of Linda's face, inches away, looking out at him through the Taurus's side window, wide-eyed and terrified. Good, he thought. That was just how he wanted her. Bob turned back and continued with the other man, kicking him in the ribs with the toe of his shoe. "A Glock? You cheap bastard," he said as he pulled the wallet from the man's pants. The name on his driver's license read Peter Fabiano with a Chicago address. He tucked the pistols into the small of his back and looked down at Fabiano's right foot. "You know, Gino, Peter's shoe looks like a twelve to me. Does it look like a twelve to you? And look at this deep cut here on the heel," he said, as he picked up Fabiano's foot with both hands and twisted it sharply a half-turn to the right. "It looks just like the footprint inside, imagine that."

Fabiano screamed and almost levitated off the pile, so Burke continue his experiment by immediately twisting his foot sharply back a half-turn to the left until he crashed back down on top of Gino Santucci with most of the tendons in his ankle and knee torn up.

"Peter, you left a bloody footprints inside my friend's house. You two tortured him and killed him, and now you won't be leaving footprints much of anywhere for a while." Finally, he looked back at their big Lincoln. "Why's the trunk open, Gino? Was that for me or Linda?"

"No, man, for nobody, I swear," Santucci pleaded.

Burke bent down, grabbed Fabiano by his right foot again and dragged him back to the rear of the Lincoln, ignoring his screaming and moaning. He picked up the much bigger man with a two-handed grip on his belt and tossed him inside. Returning to the Taurus, he picked up Gino Santucci and did the same, dropping him inside the Lincoln's trunk on top of Fabiano.

Finally satisfied, he bent down over the two big men and pulled out Fabiano's Glock. "By the way, are you the two guys who did the flight attendant yesterday?" Both men were moaning and appeared to be in equal pain. They were trying to ignore him, so he pressed down hard on Santucci's knee and whacked Fabiano on the ankle. "Was there an answer in there?" he demanded to know. "Are you the guys who did the flight attendant, or not?"

"No, not me, not me, I swear," Santucci begged. "It was him, him and Rocco."

"My old pal Angelo Rocco from Eleanor Purdue's house?"

"Yeah, yeah, him, and Fabiano here, too. They're the ones who did her."

"You lying sack 'a shit!" Fabiano roared. "You wuz dere too. You took your turn."

"Confession is good for the soul, Peter. You should discuss that with your priest, when he comes to visit you in the hospital," Bob said as he lined up the 9-millimeter Glock and shot Fabiano in his good knee. "Same for you, Gino," he said as he turned and shot him in his good knee too. "My Irish forebears in Belfast, who were a lot tougher than you two clowns, call that 'kneecapping.' It hurts like hell, doesn't it, and you'll never ever walk right again, but you'll remember. Normally I don't do things like that, but after what you did to Sabrina and now to my friend Charlie, you're lucky I don't pop you both in the head."

"That wasn't us," Gino moaned. "We wuz dere, but we didn't kill him. I swear."

"No? Then who did? The Easter Bunny?" he glared and pressed the gun barrel against Gino's other knee. "Who! You want another one? Maybe the knee and then the elbow next"

"No! It was Tony. The guy wouldn't talk and he lost his temper."

"When they question your sorry asses in the hospital, make sure they know it was me, especially Scalese and DiGrigoria. Make sure they know. Rocco, too. Tell them I'm coming for them, all of them."

"Yeah, yeah, I'll tell them, you son of a bitch! Don't worry, I'll tell them."

"Good. And tell Tony he wanted a war, and now he's got one. However, if I were you, I wouldn't let them discharge you from the hospital too soon. Enjoy it, the clean bed and the food, because I suspect Mr. D's already got a spot picked out for you two out in the lake."

With that, he slammed the trunk, satisfied they would be out of commission for the duration. He stood and looked around at the nearby houses, not surprised that you could take down two big men at midday in the middle of a suburban street and shoot them twice, without a ripple. Hubby was probably off at work downtown, and the princess was at the club, having lunch or a round of golf, or shopping. He walked back to the Taurus with the two pistols and Charlie's notebook computer, the one with the bullet hole, and looked in at Linda through the driver's side window. She still looked terrified as he smiled and asked, "Are you okay?"

"Am I okay? Am I okay!" she answered. "I know those two, Bob. They work for Tony Scalese and they were after us, weren't they?"

"Yes, but they didn't appear to have learned much from last night's lesson, so they can spend the next six months on disability. Anyway, that's two down."

"Two down? You're not planning on…"

"Yes, I am. I found Charlie's body inside. He's dead. They tortured him and Scalese beat him to death. They left those two behind to see if we showed up. They told me they were the ones who raped and murdered Sabrina Fowler last night, and I'm sure they planned to do the same thing to you, so they're damned lucky that's all I did to them." Her jaw dropped, so he figured she needed the full shock treatment. "It's a war now, Linda. The cops can't stop them, so I will. I'm going to kill them, all of them. Don't worry. I'll make sure you and your daughter are clear of here before I get started. Are you okay?" he asked again. "Okay enough to drive, anyway?"

She pushed the button and opened the driver's side door. "I'd rather you do," she said. "I don't think I can."

"I really need you to try. I'm driving their car, so follow me."

"Their car? What are you…?"

"Follow me. I have a delivery to make. It won't take long, I promise. Then we'll go get Emily."

"Those guys scared the hell out of me… and so did you, Bob," she quickly added.

"That's a good place for you to be. It focuses the mind. Sit there for a couple of minutes more and try to relax. I'm running back inside. I need to make a phone call."

"Make a… are you crazy? The police are…"

"They're busy over on the next street. I'm calling O'Malley."

Back inside, he went to the extension phone in Charlie's living room. He put his handkerchief over the receiver and picked up, so as not to leave any fingerprints. He got a dial tone, surprising given all the other destruction in the house. He pulled a badly wrinkled business card from his pants pocket and used his fingernail on the touch pad to dial the US Attorney's number.

"I'd like to speak to Mr. O'Malley, please… I'm sure he is, but if you tell him Bob Burke is on the line, I think he'll find the time… Have you got that, the rest of you listening out there in audio-land?"

It took O'Malley less than a minute to get on the line. Frankly, Bob was surprised it took the US Attorney that long. "Mr. Burke, I can't tell you how glad I am you called."

"Surprised Sal DiGrigoria's people haven't gotten me yet?"

"Something like that. I suppose I can't talk you into coming in, before they do?"

"They won't, but that's not what I'm calling you about."

"Where are you?"

"At my friend Charlie Newcomb's house in Wheeling, as your audio guys sitting on the phone tap will tell you; but don't bother scrambling the cars, I'll be long gone before they get here. I found two of DiGrigoria's gunmen waiting for us. I also found my friend and VP of Finance Charlie Newcomb in the basement tied to a kitchen chair, dead.

He was tortured and Tony Scalese beat him to death."

"And you know this… how?"

"Confession is good for the soul. They told me."

"Confession's good for…" O'Malley chuckled. "You really are a piece of work, Burke."

"In about an hour, if you have your people check the trauma centers around Indian Hills, they'll find Gino Santucci and Peter Fabiano in admissions."

"Santucci and Fabiano? I'm familiar with the names."

"I thought you might be. You'll find Charlie's blood on the bottom of Fabiano's shoe and his footprints in Charlie's office, and I'm sure you'll find their fingerprints all over the place. They also raped and murdered Sabrina Fowler last night. Angelo Rocco was in on it, too. So, why haven't you gone after them yet, O'Malley? Greenway, Scalese, DiGrigoria —you should have enough *without* Eleanor Purdue's books and reports. Why haven't you gone after them?"

"Why?" the US Attorney laughed. "You ever go big game hunting, Major?"

"Only for the 'most dangerous game' as they call it — for men."

"Me too. And when I do, I don't intend to merely 'hit' them; I go for the kill. That's what I'm going to do with DiGrigoria and all the rest of them, but I need Eleanor's papers and the CHC books to do that. Your lawyer told me you have them. You do, don't you? At least tell me that much."

"I do. Reports and spreadsheets, and when I pop open her flash drive…"

"She left a flash drive? Jesus Christ, those things can hold…"

"Yeah, they do. But when I do get it open, am I going to find your name in there on the 'pad' along with Bentley and all the rest of the cops around here?"

The question caused O'Malley to pause. "Bob, we gotta trust each other. If we don't, if you don't get me that stuff, they win. We can crack that flash drive right here in our FBI tech lab, so come on in. Please. You're no good to me dead."

"Don't worry, when I finish decrypting it, I'll send you a copy, unless your name really is in there. If it is, then the whole thing goes to *The Tribune*, and 'God can sort the pieces out.' And by the way, I think my lawyer told you to call off the manhunt, didn't he?"

"Well, yes, he did, but there's…"

"No 'buts.' If I see another FBI car or a stakeout at one of our houses, you'll never see those books. I'll mail it all to *The Trib* and you can read about them in the papers. Make up your mind, Pete. Until then, Ciao."

On the street again, Bob waved to Linda as he ran past the Taurus. "Follow me," he said as he headed for the Lincoln Town Car, closed the passenger door, and jumped in the driver's seat. He drove out of the subdivision, turned on the main road, and headed back toward Indian Hills. The big Lincoln drove like a Greyhound bus compared to Linda's Toyota, his own Saturn, or even Ernie Travers' police cruiser. Too bad it isn't January, he thought. With all that extra weight riding in the trunk, when it comes to keeping traction on an icy road or plowing through the drifting snow in Chicago, having two fat Gumbahs in your trunk would be much better than a load of sand bags.

When he reached the Consolidated Health Care building, he drove halfway around the landscaped island turnaround, and stopped in front of the revolving door. Pausing for a quick look at the lobby, he threw the gearshift into park and got out of the car. Except for a new face behind the big reception desk, the lobby and the second-floor walkway were empty. Glancing back into the rearview mirror, he saw that Linda Sylvester had followed him up the main drive in the old Taurus, but she had stopped in the entry road a hundred feet further back. He hadn't told her where he was going, for good reason. Even from this distance, he saw her eyes go wide as she shook her head and her lips formed a panicky, unspoken, "No!" He ignored her, took the keys from the Lincoln's ignition, and headed for the building's front door. As he did, he turned back, smiled, and raised his index finger. "One minute," he called out as he reached the building's revolving door. Whether she heard him or not, she understood the message and didn't like it one bit.

Bob pushed through the revolving doors and walked confidently across the spotless travertine lobby floor to the raised reception desk, where Linda formerly sat. A young, attractive brunette, perhaps in her early twenties, sat smiling and studying him as he approached.

"Hi," he smiled back and dropped the keys for the big Lincoln on the marble counter in front of her. "Is Tony in?"

"Mr. Scalese?" she asked pleasantly enough. "Do you have an appointment?"

"No, but I don't really think I need one. Is he in?"

"I can find out. Who may I say is asking?"

"Bob Burke. No, on second thought, don't bother him. Tell him I left his car outside in the turnaround with a package for him in the trunk. He'll understand. Here are the keys," he said as he slid them toward her. "And thanks a bunch. Your name is?"

"Patsy," she smiled. "Patsy Evans."

"Patsy," he said as he leaned closer to her. "You know who Dr. Greenway is, don't you?"

"Of course." She smiled again. "Why?"

"Why? Because you look like a nice kid. Don't ever let him get you alone in his office, or anywhere else, because he rapes and murders young women like you," Burke said as he watched her smile begin to wilt at the corners. "If you don't believe me, ask some of the older women the next time you're on break. They know all about him, which is why they were so happy to see you sitting down here. Greenway likes them young, like you; but he'll settle for one of them in a pinch."

Her mouth dropped open. As he turned and began to walk away, he looked up and saw Tony Scalese appear on the second-floor landing. At 6'3" and 240 pounds, dressed in dark gray slacks, a silk sharkskin sports coat, and an open-collared royal blue shirt with gold chains around his neck, the big Italian thug was hard to miss. Apparently, Scalese had just left his office and was walking toward the elevator when he glanced down into the first floor lobby below. Scalese's eyes narrowed to two cold, angry slits. "Burke, you son of a bitch!" he shouted as he stepped to the railing and pointed down at him. For an instant, the big man looked as if he might jump over it and come after him, until he realized that the twenty-foot drop would probably break his legs, if it didn't kill him.

"Hey! Good to see you again, Tony." He looked up and gave Scalese a big smile and a wave. "As I was telling Patsy here, I left your Lincoln in the turnaround — the one Gino and Pete were driving. She has the keys, but I wouldn't wait too long if I were you. That stuff in the trunk will start smelling real soon."

"The stuff in the...? You son of a bitch!"

"That makes five."

"Five? What the hell are you...?"

"The truth is, I'm not sure how you want to count them, since I nailed Gino twice. And what about Bentley and Bobby Joe? I don't know how you want to count those two, either."

"How I want to...?" Scalese said as his grip tightened on the railing and his knuckles turned white. "You're a dead man, Burke."

"Seriously, Tony. Is that the best you got? With the first three guys you left at Eleanor Purdue's house, all I did was give them a few dents and try to embarrass them, hoping you might get the message; but you didn't get it, did you? Instead, you told them to rape and murder Sabrina Fowler," he said as his eyes narrowed, colder and hungrier than Scalese's. "And then I found the present you left in the basement of my friend Charlie's house up in Wheeling, so I left two for you in the Lincoln's trunk. Charlie was a nice guy — a bean counter and a 'civilian.' He didn't understand evil people like you, but I do. I've been fighting men like you my entire career, which makes me your worst nightmare. You're a dead man walking, Tony — you, DiGrigoria, and all the other street clowns you send after me."

"There won't be any 'others,' Burke. I'm going to do you myself!"

"God, I hope so, because I'll be waiting. No more 'mister nice guy.'"

"You got a big mouth for such a little guy."

"Yeah I do, and I back it up. The law may not be able to touch you, Greenway, and DiGrigoria but I can."

"Oh, really?" Scalese looked down at him and sneered.

"Count on it," Burke answered as he formed his right hand into a pistol and pretended to 'shoot' him. "Bang, you're dead," he said, then turned and walked away. When Burke reached the revolving door, he paused and looked back up. Scalese's ever-confident sneer was already melting. It was obvious the big man wasn't accustomed to anyone talking to him like this, but before Scalese could pull out a real pistol, which Bob knew he would be carrying, he slipped through the revolving door and strode away down the sidewalk. Fortunately, Linda was waiting and watching the show from the front seat of the stolen car. She raced up and stopped only long enough for him to open the passenger side door and jump inside, before she tromped on the accelerator. The Taurus sped away down the business's entry drive and onto the road beyond, leaving a puffy black cloud of exhaust in her wake.

"I can't believe you did that. I can't believe you did that," she kept repeating until they reached the main road, as if she was in a daze. "Scalese? You're crazy to bait him like that. Do you have any idea how dangerous he and those other men are?"

"Of course I do."

"Then why provoke him like that?"

"Because that's exactly the way I want him — angry, off-balance, and out to get me in the worst way."

"But he'll kill you, and then he'll kill me"

"Oh, he intended to kill both of us a long time ago, or at least he was going to try. This way, when he does come after us again, he'll be angry, seeing red, and that's when he's going to make even more mistakes than he already has."

"But..."

"No 'buts.' "

Bob looked at his watch. "We said we'd get your daughter next. Do you want to pull her out of school now?"

"No, no, that would cause too many questions, and I don't want to scare her. I thought I'd pick her up when they line up to board the busses, so we should wait," she told him as she looked at the notebook computer case on the floor. "You found that at Charlie's? It looks broken."

"Sort of. One of Scalese's morons put a bullet through it," he told her as he held it up, put his index finger through the hole, and wiggled it at her.

She shook her head and gave him a curious look. "Seriously? Do you really think you can make that thing work?"

"What? You don't think I can?" he asked her straight-faced. "Actually, I'm sure this one is toast, but if they missed the hard drive, I might be able to re-install it in another machine and use Charlie's software to crack that flash drive Eleanor left."

"Then, why don't we go to Best Buy now and buy one? There's a store in Woodfield."

"With what? We'd need $1,000 or maybe $2,000 to buy a decent laptop. The wallets I took off of Scalese's two gunmen were pretty thin, and neither you nor I have that kind of cash handy right now."

"We don't need cash, I still have the CHC Visa Card that Eleanor got for me. I use it to charge office supplies at Best Buy, Staples, Office Max, and a bunch of other places. Of course, it has a five-thousand-dollar limit."

"Five thousand? You're kidding?"

"Not at all, and I can see no reason why Dr. Greenway shouldn't pick up the tab, do you?"

"Won't they call and verify a credit card charge like that?"

"CHC is a bunch of crooks, but they aren't stupid. There is an approved signatory list, and my name is on it. I have the corporate credit card and corporate ID, and the Purchasing Protocol that Eleanor set up with all of the vendors requires them to email her within 24 hours on any charge over fifty dollars. I'm sure that's exactly what they'll do, but I don't think she's going to be around to read it do you? And after 24 hours, I doubt you're going to care anyway."

"A computer would be great, but the flash drive is probably encrypted. You knew Eleanor. How sophisticated was she when it came to data protection? Do you know of any particular software she might have used? Or passwords she liked?"

"Me? As the Army people in the movies say, that's way above my pay grade."

"Charlie's got the best encryption and decryption software on the market, so if we can make his hard drive work, there's no problem. If not, there's a ton of other programs on line I can download and try."

Linda looked at her watch. "You said that laptop is an Asus. After we run over to Best Buy, we can swing back and pick up Ellie in Des Plaines."

CHAPTER TWENTY-TWO

Lawrence Greenway tried without much success to relax on the overstuffed leather couch in his office. He flipped nervously through the pages of the new issue of *Health and Medicine Magazine* with one hand, while swirling two fingers of his favorite Makers Mark bourbon in a hand-cut crystal tumbler with the other. This was his third drink and he was still unable to forget that horrid trip to the house in Wheeling. Damn that Scalese! Greenway knew his thugs were animals, but he couldn't believe what he saw Tony do. He beat that man to death with his bare fists. Worse, the big bastard made Greenway stand there and watch, until the doctor turned away and vomited. That was all he could take. He ran up the stairs, out of the house, and drove back here to the office, to his sanctuary.

Things weren't supposed to be this way. His expensive suit jacket lay in a heap on the floor. His usually perfectly knotted silk tie hung askew, his crisp white shirt was sweaty and badly wrinkled, and his freshly polished black leather dress shoes showed bits and pieces of his breakfast. From his fifty-dollar haircut to his capped teeth and impeccably tailored suits, since he moved up to the suburbs, Dr. Lawrence Greenway, M.D., took intense pride in looking like one of those Hollywood plastic surgeons who get their studio portrait shots on the cover of *GQ*. Looking around his expensively furnished office and out the window across the panorama of the north suburbs, he couldn't help remembering that first rat-infested clinic of his at 63rd and Cottage Grove. It was in the heart of "gangland" on Chicago's infamous South Side, complete with break-ins, muggings on the sidewalk, and paying "protection" by patching up bullet and knife wounds without asking any questions. They say poverty builds character, but that was usually said by people who had never experienced it "up close and personal." No, he left "Larry Greenway" behind on Cottage Grove Avenue, and he hated that name now. Rich was much more fun than poor and he would never go back to that dreary life again.

Still, as he scanned through the pages of the glossy medical magazine and saw the feature story on "Top Doctors" of Chicagoland, he was more than a little peeved. He had paid a lot of money — or, to be accurate, CHC paid a lot of money — to have their PR flacks get him recognized by his professional peers. He sponsored elaborate receptions at the state and area AMA conventions and large booths at the tradeshows; took out pricy ads in the glitzier industry magazines; and bought so many lunches with top regional AMA and HHS staff that his extensive wardrobe of custom-tailored suits were beginning to feel snug. Despite these efforts, the city's AMA crowd continued to snub him, all because of his "alleged" and completely unproven ties to the DiGrigoria Mob and those nasty whispers about his sexual improprieties. As if any of *them* were perfect, or produced one-tenth of the good work he did on the mean streets of the city's South and West Sides. What was a man to do, he wondered.

He placed the heavy tumbler on the wide leather arm of the sofa, and ran his fingers lightly across the soft leather before he brought his hand up to his nose, closed his eyes, and sniffed his fingers. The hand-tooled leather did a marvelous job of trapping all the smells, the memories, and the excitement of the many things that occurred on this couch over the past year. Perhaps it was only his vivid imagination, but he got hard thinking about them. Yes, after a horrid afternoon such as this, perhaps it was time he held another "counseling session" up here with one of the younger, female staff members.

Greenway looked at his watch. Linda Sylvester was due in his office at 3 o'clock. He was becoming both impatient and randy, convinced she would show with the documents Eleanor Purdue stole. That would prove to Tony Scalese and the rest of those animals that *his* methods of persuasion could be far more effective with the women than theirs, and ever so much more fun. He *knew* she was coming, because she wanted him. So did all the others. He knew what these thirty-ish suburban women were like, lying in the bathtub after the kids were in bed, with candles, a cheap romance novel, and a vibrator. Sylvester had been single long enough now. Her marriage may not have worked out, but she was a woman with needs. She would make a fine replacement for Eleanor Purdue, because a man who wanted her and took her hard was exactly what she dreamed of at night. She might have screamed and scratched his face this morning, but that was merely a sign of her passion, part of the little "game" they like to play to make it seem more exciting. Yes, she wanted him and he would have seduced her long ago, were it not for that meddlesome twerp, Burke.

He looked at his watch again. She should be here any minute now.

Greenway leaned back into the soft cushions, raised the tumbler, and let the last of his bourbon roll down his throat. The more he thought about Sylvester, however, he must admit she was getting a touch old and haggard for his tastes. So was Eleanor Purdue, but she had had her moments right here on this couch. Still, one of the younger ones would be much more tantalizing. What was that nosy new girl's name? Patsy Evans? Yes, that was it he remembered and smiled. She was much more to his taste — younger, buxom, slightly plump, with the kind of soft, well-rounded bottom he loved to bump up against. She would do very nicely! He closed his eyes and imagined Patsy up here with him this afternoon, her bare bottom bent over the arm of his couch, waiting for him, wanting him.

However, Greenway forced himself to admit that it must be business before pleasure. Scalese had become a major annoyance. Someday soon, Greenway must rid himself of the loud, crude, Italian, but he must do it in a way that Salvatore DiGrigoria wouldn't come after him. But why should he? His boys say the old man stays up all night watching Marcus Welby reruns on cable TV, sitting in his recliner in his stocking feet. So a dapper middle-aged doctor with graying hair should be the last one he'd suspect.

Know thy enemy, went the old adage, and Greenway had done his research. Sal DiGrigoria was a dinosaur and Tony Scalese was an arrogant psychopath. Neither man was as smart as he thought he was. Perhaps he could arrange things to let the police do the heavy lifting by planting some evidence that would point toward the big Italian. If he was arrested and facing jail time, Tony would be a dangerous liability to Salvatore DiGrigoria. The old man would figure Tony might roll on him, and Sal would dump him in the lake without giving it a second thought. Yes, perhaps he could plant drugs in Tony's car, or do something with that signature 9-inch stiletto knife he was so proud of. If Greenway had his choice, however, he would prefer killing the big bastard himself. Scalese usually parked in the rear lot. It was dark back there, and he could walk up to him in the parking lot and put a couple of bullets in the back of his head with his .32-caliber Mauser automatic. Tony's guard would be down and he would never expect that Greenway was capable of doing such a thing. Yes, two small-caliber bullets to the back of the head would make it look like a mob hit, and be the perfect solution.

Greenway went to his desk and opened the center drawer where he kept the Mauser under some papers, but it wasn't there. He went through the drawer again, all the way to the bottom, and then through the other drawers, but it wasn't there either. As he did, he saw scratches and chips around the locks and realized the drawers had been forced open. He sat back in his chair and wondered who would dare come in here and do such a thing. He wondered, but he already knew the answer. It was Tony.

But why? The inescapable conclusion was that Scalese was planning some moves on his own, which meant Greenway couldn't wait to strike first.

That was when his meditations were disturbed by the sound of loud, heavy footsteps coming down the corridor toward his office. His office door suddenly flew open and crashed into the sidewall. Unfortunately, instead of the lovely Linda Sylvester arriving early for her reluctant rendezvous, it was Tony Scalese who stormed in. One look at the big Italian told Greenway the lovely Mrs. Sylvester was not coming.

"Where the hell did you go," Scalese yelled at him. "I needed you."

"Hardly! The only thing you needed in that basement was a mortician, and that is *not* in my job description." The two men glared at each other with angry unyielding expressions. Finally, Greenway sat back in his chair and looked up at the big man with a thin, plastic smile. "Anthony, Anthony," Greenway said in a condescending tone and shook his head. "You really do need to learn how to knock."

Scalese stopped halfway across the floor and glared down at him. "Greenway, we've got big problems. Get your head out of your ass before it ends up there permanently."

"All right, what did you do now?"

"It isn't me! It's that son-of-a-bitch Burke, who *you* brought into this thing, because you couldn't keep it in your pants and went after that Purdue woman up on the roof. Remember?"

"There was nothing *sexual* about that. I caught her rifling through my desk, as it appears someone else has now been doing," he said as he glared across at Scalese. "As I told you before, Eleanor gave me no choice. Besides, you disposed of her body, and Bentley's task was to 'dispose' of our little 'telephone repairman,' wasn't it?"

"You moron! Last night, your 'telephone repairman' took out three of my men who were watching Purdue's house and they never even knew he was there. All he did was tie them up, take their wallets and guns, and make them look stupid."

"Not a terribly difficult thing to do, from the sound of it."

"Well, a little while ago, that little son-of-a-bitch pulls up in front of the building here, driving Gino Santucci's Lincoln Town Car. You remember Gino, don't you, from our trip to Wheeling?"

"One of those knuckle-dragging thugs who was with you in that basement, wasn't he?"

"One of my... you dumbass! They're what keep you sitting here."

"And your point is?"

"Gino was in the Lincoln's trunk. So was Peter Fabiano. It seems the 'telephone guy,' as you called him, isn't playing games anymore. They're both on their way to the hospital with gunshots and badly broken legs. Now, who the hell is that guy?"

"How am I supposed to know? Why don't you go ask your boss? Isn't 'Old Sal' the one with all the contacts?"

"We did," Scalese shot back angrily. "Burke was in the Army before he went to work for this Toler outfit, but beyond that, nobody's heard of him — State, City, County, not even the goddamned FBI. We checked with all our sources and they come up with nothing. Nothing! His freakin' Army records are all classified."

"Hardly my department then, is it?"

"It is now, *Larry*. You and I are going to find out who the hell he is."

"Me? He's a security problem. That is *your* department, Anthony, and *you're* supposed to deal with those kinds of 'loose ends,' as I recall, not I."

"Yeah? Well, let me clue you in, *Doc!*" Scalese said as he bent over the couch and poked Greenway in the chest with his index finger. "Has it ever occurred to you that you and I are the ones who are becoming the 'loose ends?' Mr. D don't like screw-ups, mistakes, or freakin' *'loose* ends.' What he usually does is *snip* 'em off, so that nothing ever blows back on him. You understand what I'm tellin' you?"

"Yes, but I did nothing wrong."

"No? You started this thing, you damned fool. You're the one who caught Burke's attention, and if *we* don't put an end to him, *Mr. D's* gonna to put an end to *us*. Now get up off your dead ass. I want you to track down Burke's wife and pay her a little visit. Getting women to cooperate with you is something you're supposed to be good at, isn't it, *Larry?*"

"Well, I can't disagree with you there, *Anthony*, but I don't even know the woman."

"And fortunately, she doesn't know you. I don't care how, just do it."

"All right, all right, I'll try my 'charm' on her."

"Good, and while you're doing that, I'm going to apply some serious *leverage* to our missing receptionist, Linda Sylvester. It looks like she threw in with Burke."

"Linda did?" Greenway answered. "Oh, how disappointing."

"Yes, she was driving the other car when Burke dropped off the Lincoln."

"Then, it would appear she won't be making our 3 o'clock *play date*."

"Your what?" Scalese glared at Greenway. "No! She won't. So get your ass up and track down Burke's wife. I want you to find out where he is, and what makes him tick."

"His wife?" Greenway thought it over for a moment as a sly grin crossed his lips. "Well, Anthony, if you insist."

It took Bob and Linda twenty minutes to drive to the Best Buy store on the perimeter of Woodfield Mall. It stocked all the items he needed to crack Eleanor Purdue's flash drive, with the exception of some exotic software he hoped to find on Charlie's hard drive, if he could get it to work, or online if he couldn't. Bob walked quickly through the aisles, while Linda pushed the shopping cart and tried to keep up.

He grabbed an updated version of Charlie's Asus notebook computer — one without a bullet hole — a portable printer, a set of screwdrivers, some accounting software, a wireless Wi-Fi adapter, two flash drives to make additional back-up copies, and two burner cell phones. As they stood in the checkout line, Linda waited quietly with her CHC credit card, while the cashier rang up each item and Bob stacked the boxes back in the cart. The total came to slightly over $1,500 dollars, but Linda was right. In the end, all that Best Buy required was an ID check. When she showed the cashier her driver's license and corporate ID card, the charges flew through with no delay.

"Do you think we should send Dr. Greenway a Thank You card?" Bob asked.

"You can kick him in the nuts as far as I'm concerned," came her quick reply. "In fact, I hope you do, and hard!"

"Sheesh. 'Hell hath no fury,'… but I get the general idea," he chuckled.

Tony Scalese stormed back out of Greenway's office, feeling as if the walls were closing in on him for the first time in his life. He was a gritty street fighter, but this bastard Burke was proving to be far more formidable than he expected, and his options were narrowing. Rather than wait for the elevator, he ran downstairs to the first floor reception desk, shoved a startled Patsy Evans aside, and pawed through the drawers, looking for any personal items that Sylvester might have left behind. In the bottom drawer, he found make-up, a Kleenex box, a paper bag with a clean blouse and underwear, a pile of newspaper coupons, some fashion and travel magazines, and a long row of pill bottles — the type of things he'd expect to find in a woman's desk.

"Is this crap yours or hers?" he asked brusquely.

"Those are Linda's things, but I don't think you should..."

"Shut up!" he snapped as he picked up the pill bottles and quickly read the labels. There were the common over-the-counter medications like Tylenol, Midol, Motrin, antihistamines, and cough and cold stuff, but he saw prescription bottles of Xanax, Paxil, and Imitrex as well. Being in the "drug" business himself, Scalese knew his pharmacology. Those were the heavy-duty stuff for anxiety and migraines. Working here with Larry Greenway ready to pounce on her at any moment, he could hardly blame the woman.

When he pulled open the other drawers and began pawing through them as well, Patsy Evans finally objected. "Hey! Some of that's my stuff, you have no right..."

"Yes I do. And if you don't like it, go upstairs and take it up with Doc Greenway. I'm sure he'd love for you to tell him all about it," he grinned at her, and she shrank away.

Unfortunately, there was nothing else to be found in the desk drawers other than some pay stubs, company annual reports, marketing material, pens, staplers, Post-it notes, and other routine secretarial supplies. Frustrated, he stood up, getting angrier by the second, as he scanned the desktop one last time. There! Sitting right in front of him the entire time, was a framed photograph of a cute, young, dark-haired girl, maybe five or six years old.

"Is that yours?" he said as he pointed at the photograph.

"Mine? Oh, no, that's Linda's daughter, Ellie," Patsy replied, shaking her head.

That was when he remembered Linda Sylvester had a daughter! Scalese smiled, realizing he had found his leverage on Sylvester, and through her, on Burke.

He turned and ran up the emergency stairs to the second floor, where the Human Resources Department was located. Their department receptionist looked up and began to say something to him until she saw the expression on his face and quickly turned back to her computer screen. He blew past her desk and strode on to the closed door marked

"Henrietta Jacobs — Manager." Without knocking, Scalese opened the door and walked in, closing it behind him. Jacobs was a thin, attractive, black woman in her mid-forties. She sat behind her desk talking on the telephone as he burst in. She was in midsentence when he walked up to her desk, took the phone from her hand, and hung it up. Stunned, she stared up at him, open-mouthed, as if an avalanche had fallen on her, not knowing what to say. He leaned forward and placed both of his big paws on her desk, intentionally towering over her and intimidating her.

"Mr. Scalese, that was…"

"I don't care. Get me Linda Sylvester's Personnel File," he ordered, watching her eyes grow wide as she tried not to lose it. "Now!"

"Her Personnel File? You know that's confidential. I'm not allowed to…"

"Henrietta," he glared down at her. "Do you like working here? Because I don't give a rat's ass about rules, privacy laws, or much of anything right now. I'm Chief of Security, this is a security matter, and I'll give you one minute to get me that file. If you don't, I'll have someone else get it, or I'll get it myself; but then I won't need you any more, will I?"

She blinked once, twice, and then quickly rose to her feet. She walked across the room to a bank of file cabinets, opened one of the middle drawers, and pulled out a thin green file folder. "Here," she said as she placed the folder on the desk. "But this is highly…"

Scalese dismissed her comment with a wave of his hand, and didn't wait. He opened Sylvester's folder and began to paw through the sheets until he found the sheet of paper he was looking for — her Personal Data Sheet. "You can type, can't you?"

"Me? Well, yes, I…" she said, beginning to look even more worried

"Good. Get out a sheet of CHC letterhead stationery, the good stuff, and type what I tell you." Jacobs quickly placed a sheet of embossed company letterhead stationery in the paper drawer of her printer and sat down at her desk behind her computer keyboard. He scanned the form and saw that Linda Sylvester was divorced, with a daughter named Ellie enrolled in Warren Heights Middle School in Des Plaines, and she had been given sole custody.

"Address the letter to… Doris Falconi, Principal, Warren Heights Elementary School, Des Plaines, Illinois. Here's the address," he said as he leaned over and showed her the form.

Realizing there was no choice, Lawrence Greenway finally extricated himself from his soft leather couch, pulled on his suit jacket, straightened his tie and attempted to make himself look as presentable as possible under the circumstances. As he left his office and headed for the elevator, he passed Tony Scalese's office and saw the door stood half-open and that Scalese was not there. He stuck his head inside and saw Scalese's god-awful sharkskin sports coat hanging carelessly over one of the chairs. Greenway stuck his head back out in the hall and listened intently for a second or two. He heard nothing, so he quickly stepped over to the chair, picked up Scalese's coat, and felt the pockets. In the right front jacket pocket, he found his signature stiletto switchblade knife. Using his handkerchief, Greenway pulled the stiletto from Scalese's jacket pocket and dropped it in his own, quickly re-hanging the jacket over the chair.

He turned and quickly walked out of the office and down the hallway to the fire stairs, and he began to smile. "Two can play this little game, Anthony. Yes, two can play, and we'll see how *you* like it."

CHAPTER TWENTY-THREE

Warren Heights Elementary School was located in an older, wooded section of Des Plaines, not more than a twenty-minute drive from Indian Hills in midafternoon traffic. Tony Scalese parked his "satin cashmere metallic" pale gold LS 460 Lexus in one of the visitor's spaces behind the school. The car was new, and he loved it the moment he drove it off the dealer's lot. Sweet! The deal was even sweeter, because one of Salvatore DiGrigoria's shell companies owned the dealership and wrote the Lexus off as "stolen off the lot." They then billed their insurance company and Scalese hadn't paid a dime. He thought it was a classy ride nonetheless. It came with so many bells and whistles that even after three weeks he kept the Owner's Manual open on the passenger seat. The car's color was freakin' *gold!* The pompous faggot of a sales manager who sold it to him called it "satin cashmere metallic," making Scalese want to puke. Hopefully, none of "the boys" heard that. Oddly enough, after a few weeks the name grew on him. What he liked most about the car, however, was that it wasn't a Lincoln, a big Continental, a Cadillac stretch limo, or anything else that screamed "Big Freakin' Wop-Mobile." Sitting behind the wheel, it made him look and feel like a successful businessman, which was exactly how he pictured himself.

As Scalese drove past the school and into the parking lot, his head swiveled back and forth looking for cop cars or that old beat-up Taurus he saw Linda Sylvester driving as they sped away from the CHC building a little while ago; but he saw nothing. There was a long line of bright yellow school buses snaking through the parking lot and down one of the side streets, queued and ready for the flood of kids about to pour through the school's side doors. He looked at his watch. It was 3:15 p.m. School wasn't out until 3:30, so even if Sylvester and Burke were coming to pick up her daughter they wouldn't show this early.

Satisfied, Scalese got out of his car, straightened his jacket, and walked quickly and confidently toward the school's back door. Stepping inside, he found himself in an "air lock" between the outer door and a secure, steel-clad inner door. To one side was a thick glass window, which looked into the school office, a small counter, a buzzer, and an intercom, just like the afterhours window at the bank. A harried, middle-aged secretary stood on the other side, head down, thumbing through a stack of papers.

He stepped up to the window and pressed the bell. "Pardon me."

Scalese smiled as he asked, "Is Principal Falconi around?"

"Honey, this isn't really the best time..." The secretary finally looked up over the top rim of her glasses and saw a handsome, 6'4", 240-pound block of Italian granite towering over her. "Oh, sorry," she said, flustered. "I thought you were..."

"That's okay, Jenny, I'll take it," a tall, thin older woman in a business suit said as she stepped up to the counter next to the secretary. "I'm Doris Falconi. You are...?"

"Scalese, Anthony Scalese," he smiled as he handed her his business card. "I know you're busy, so I'll be brief. I'm Director of Security for Consolidated Health Care, where Linda Sylvester works. I believe her daughter, Ellie, is one of your students," he said as he pulled a cream-colored business envelope from his jacket pocket. "A little while ago, Linda was subpoenaed to testify later today in front of a Federal Grand Jury regarding a former employer. She's not in any trouble, but she won't be home when Ellie gets off the bus. Our President, Dr. Greenway, assured Linda that we'd pick Ellie up and bring her back to the office until she returns later. This letter should explain everything to your satisfaction." Scalese said as he handed her the envelope.

The Principal opened it, looked at the typed letter on heavy, embossed CHC stationary, and began to read:

> Ms. Doris Falconi, Principal
> Warren Heights Elementary School
> 713 West Central Ave.
> Des Plaines, Illinois 60016
>
> Dear Mrs. Falconi:
>
> Unfortunately, I've been called away on official business and won't be home to meet Ellie when she gets off the bus. I know this is a bit unusual and he is not on my signature list, but please allow Tony Scalese, our Director of Security, to pick Ellie up this afternoon.
> > Thanks for everything,
> > Linda Sylvester

"As she says, we know this is a little unusual..."

"Oh, these days, nothing's all that unusual, Mr. Scalese," the Principal replied as she handed him back his cards and kept the letter. "The letter and signature appear in order, so if you'll wait a minute, I'll have Ellie brought out to you when the bell rings and the kids line up for the buses."

"Here, keep my card, too. You never know who might ask," he told her.

As he waited, he looked through the glass into the school office and the hallway beyond. He was surprised at how clean, bright, and quiet the hallways seemed. Admittedly, his experience with public schools was limited, but this wasn't how he remembered Hancock Elementary School in Cicero, at least not while he was a student there. Whether class was in session there or not, his school was a chaotic place — harsh, noisy, and dimly lit, with worn linoleum tile floors, institutional green walls, fights in the hallways, clouds of cigarette smoke billowing out of the open restrooms, and bad food in the cafeteria. He smiled as he looked around at the well-lit, pastel colors and brightly carpeted hallways here.

Behind him in the air lock sat a handsome, early-American maple bench, which looked as if it just came from an Ethan Allen showroom. Des Plaines was obviously much farther away from Cicero than he could ever have imagined. He took a seat on the bench near the door and waited, drumming his fingers on its turned-wood arm. They had a much more solid, functional bench in the principal's office at Hancock, as he remembered. He was sent there so often that his mother thought they'd give it to him as a graduation present.

Finally, the bell rang for the end of the class, and the once-quiet hallways on the other side of the security door outside instantly turned into bedlam with running feet and young children's voices everywhere. Two minutes later, a teacher pushed a small, six-year-old girl with bobbed hair and a pink Cinderella backpack through the door.

"You're picking up Ellie Sylvester?" she asked. "Okay, well, I gotta run," and disappeared as quickly as she came.

The little girl looked up at Scalese, studying him suspiciously, as only a small child can. She barely came up to his waist. "You know, you have your mother's eyes," he couldn't stop himself from saying as he reached his hand out to her. The little girl looked up at him for a long moment, studying him and thinking it over. Smart girl, he thought. You can fool an adult woman and you can fool a cop or a judge, but you can't fool a little kid. They can see right through you. Finally, she took his hand and they walked out the door into the parking lot.

Scalese smiled. Yep, Des Plaines sure enough was a long way from Cicero; but in Hancock School, they weren't stupid enough to let a Mafia hit man walk into a public school and walk out hand in hand with a six-year-old girl. Then again, in Cicero they saw a few more of them.

Outside and a half-block down the busy street, Bob Burke and Linda Sylvester sat in the front seat of the stolen Taurus. They were slumped down, their eyes at dashboard level, watching the long line of school buses waiting along the side of the elementary school.

"Her bus is usually the tenth one back," Linda told him. "They line the kids up inside and the teachers bring them out by class and bus route."

"You sure you can handle this by yourself?"

"I've picked her up like this a half-dozen times. That's what they're all doing," she pointed toward a cluster of women standing on the sidewalk where the kids pass by. "With young children, things always come up at the last minute, so don't worry. The teachers know me, and getting her shouldn't be a problem," Linda said as she got out of the car and slowly walked to where the other mothers waited.

Maybe so, he thought, as his eyes continued to scan the street and the rear view mirror, but he saw nothing out of the ordinary. Even from a half-block away, he saw lines of happy kids come out, one after another, and quickly board the buses. Two buses would leave and another two would pull up, ready for the next group of kids. Every now and then, one of the waiting mothers would intercept one of the kids, give a few hugs and waves, and walk away toward the parked cars. Gradually, the crowd of women thinned until Linda was left standing there alone. Finally, when the last two buses pulled up and began loading, she walked over to one of the teachers and began talking. Bob sat up as he saw the conversation became more and more animated. Linda's hands went to her waist, her arms began to wave about, and from her expression he could tell something was very wrong. Her meeting with the teacher ended, Linda turned, ran up the sidewalk to the front door of the school, and dashed inside.

To Bob's consternation, she did not look his way or give any hint as to what was going on. Then again, the more he thought about it, he was probably the last thing on her mind at that moment. He debated what to do, whether to continue to wait or get out and follow her into the school. The latter was what he preferred, but with his face spread across the front pages of all the daily newspapers and on the TV news shows that morning, he couldn't take the chance. Finally, he gave her one more minute. When she did not immediately reappear, his left hand went to the door handle and he was about to get out and follow her inside when he heard the Taurus' rear passenger-side door open. The old instincts immediately took over. His head snapped around, his left hand closed into a fist, and he was leaning forward, about to cold-cock whoever it was who came in, when he heard a familiar voice call to him from the back seat.

"Whoa! Stand down, Major. I'm one of the good guys, remember?" It was Chicago Police Lieutenant Ernie Travers holding up both hands in mock surrender as he squeezed his long legs into the rear seat and closed the door.

"You sure about that, Ernie?" Bob asked as he stopped his arm a few inches from the big cop's head. "This isn't a good time to screw with me."

"Yeah, I can see that; and you can see my hands are empty. No gun."

"I already did, but you didn't bring any friends, did you? Like the SWAT team or some shooters up on the roofs?"

"Even if I did, those guys couldn't hit their own asses with a shotgun. But no, I'm alone; and I came here to help." Bob looked back at him, even more skeptical. "Look, I know you didn't kill the Fowler girl or any of the others," Ernie continued. "I know that, and I know Greenway's people and that idiot Bentley set you up."

"I appreciate the vote of confidence, but you've got no jurisdiction here. Half the cops and all the crooks in Chicago are looking for me now. If you hang around with me, you're only gonna get yourself in trouble."

"Give me a little credit. I've been talking to the State Police's Organized Crime Task Force, and even to the FBI. They'd be moving on this right now, if you come up with some proof or anything to back up your story."

"Oh, I have plenty of that, and I'll be turning it over to them as soon as I can go through it and figure out who I can trust and who I can't."

"You trust me don't you?"

Bob studied him for a moment. "I think so, Ernie, despite the fact you're Chicago PD; but that doesn't mean I don't want to go through those files first," he answered as he turned his head and looked back at the front door of the school. Finally, he saw Linda come out the front door and head his way, running. "But how the hell did you find me here, anyway?"

"You? What did your men call you? The 'Ghost?' I didn't even try; I tracked her," he said as he pointed through the window at Linda. "A young mother with a six-year-old working for a bunch of scum balls isn't all that hard to figure out."

"Yeah, well, let's hope you're the only one," he added as Linda opened the passenger side car door and got halfway into the front seat when she saw Ernie sitting in the back and froze. Her eyes went wide and Bob saw her begin to tremble. "He's okay, Linda, come on. Where's Ellie?"

"Tony Scalese has her," Linda managed to say as she handed Tony Scalese's crumpled business card to Burke, turned, and fell into the front seat, crying. "That son-of-a-bitch... that son-of-a-bitch," she kept mumbling, over-and-over. "How could I be this stupid?"

Bob handed it back to Travers. "Don't worry," he told her as he put a comforting hand on her shoulder. "I'll get her back."

"He won't hurt her, Linda. He's not crazy," Travers added.

"I told you not to antagonize him!" she said as she shoved Burke's hand away. "I told you! Now look what happened."

"Do you want me to put out an APB on him?" Travers asked.

Bob sat back in the seat and looked out the window for a moment. "No, not yet. Besides, he probably has more cops on his side than you do. No, let's see what he wants," he said as he started the car and drove away, making a U-turn and heading back toward the Interstate.

"Where are we going!" Linda demanded to know.

"To call Scalese. It's me he wants, not you or Ellie."

"No! He wants those damned files!" she snapped. "God, I should've left that stuff up in the ceiling and stayed the hell out of this. I'm so stupid," she moaned. "He has Ellie; give them to him!"

"Those files are our only leverage, Linda. Without them..."

"Bob's right," Travers told her. "Once he has those papers, he'll kill you two and Ellie — hell, he'll probably kill me too — and you know it."

Linda turned away, sobbing. "I should've never gotten involved in this."

"I'll get her back, Linda. I promise," Bob told her, and then turned toward Travers, his eyes locking on the big Chicago cop. "They aren't going to kill anybody, Ernie. I'm going to kill them first — Scalese,

Greenway, DiGrigoria, all of them."

Travers stared at him for a moment. "You really are crazy aren't you?"

"No, I'm the sanest man you ever met. Give me your cell phone for a minute," he said and held out his hand. Travers shook his head, but he pulled out his old Motorola flip phone and handed it over. Burke opened the top and began punching a series of numbers into the touch pad from memory. After the eighth ring, the other phone went to voice mail and they could all hear the loud recorded message, "Ace Storm Door and Window, Ace speakin'. I'm out. Leave a message."

"Storm doors? You've got to be kidding me," Linda told him, not at all amused.

"That's a little Army humor. Don't worry. The only thing Ace knows about doors or windows is a hundred different ways to break them." When he heard the beep, he said into the phone, "This is the Ghost. Give me a call at this number. I could use a little help."

"One of your Army pals?" Travers asked.

"A lot more than that," Bob Burke answered with a thin smile.

Five minutes later, the cell phone rang. "Sorry I took so long, Major, but I was giving a class and I didn't recognize the number. What's up? Things getting a bit crusty in the private sector?"

"You have no idea, Ace. What's your Twenty?"

"Bragg."

"What about the other guys?"

"Vinnie's here with me. Chester's over at Benning and Lonzo's back 'in country.' "

"It's 16:40 your time. Can you guys get up here to Chicago tonight? Say by 21:30?"

"I'll call them as soon as I get off. Can't see why not."

"Great. Spend whatever you need, it's on my dime; and bring Nancy and any other toys and tactical gear you can get your hands on. My plan is to set up at 22:00, run the Op around 23:00, and have you fly back out in three hours or so, with as little ground time as possible."

"Yes, Sir! I'll book a charter flight over at Windimere. They have a G-5 available over there, and we can stop by Benning to pick up Chester."

"He's good with C-4 and getting in things, as I recall. Have him bring five or six ounces from the training supply room and some detonators."

"This is sounding like fun, Sir! Mind telling me what we'll be up against?"

"A dozen fat Italians who really pissed me off, maybe a dozen more."

"Hardly seems like a fair fight."

"I don't want it to be. Think street punks with handguns. I doubt any of them have any tactical training. But so you understand, I'm not planning on taking any prisoners."

"That won't offend anyone's 'tender sensibilities' down here. By the way, there's a couple of other guys from the old unit stationed here now. You remember Koz and The Batman? They'd never talk to me again if they miss out on a party like this. Mind if I bring them along?"

"As long as they understand it's a private contract with me, very wet, and they'll have no official sanction. None."

"Fighting for 'truth, justice, and the American way of life,' again?" Ace laughed.

"You got it. There's a private airport up here near Mount Prospect that I've flown in and out of a couple of times. It should work for what we need. Call me when you have an ETA."

"Roger that... and we'll all be proud to kick some ass with you again, Sir."

Burke rang off and stared at the phone as his smile slowly faded.

"Nancy?" Linda asked. "They're bringing a woman with them? I could use the company... not that you aren't good company, but... well, you know what I mean."

"No apologies necessary, but this 'Nancy' isn't a woman. She's an M-110 sniper rifle. It's like hurricanes, we usually name our most lethal weapons after women."

"Well, with the way the Army's been going, I suppose it could have been 'Bruce.' "

When Tony Scalese parked his Lexus in the rear lot of the CHC office building. He walked around the car, opened the passenger side door, and held out his hand to Ellie. The little girl looked at this huge man standing next to her, and then up at the building. She was still unsure, but he smiled down at her and she finally put her small hand in his and got out of the car. She barely came up to his waist and they made a very odd-looking pair as they walked up the sidewalk and into the building.

Funny, Tony Scalese thought as he looked down at her. He kind of liked the little kid and liked walking with her like this. When all this shit was over and his other problems with the DiGrigorias solved, maybe it was time to start a family of his own.

Inside, he saw Patsy Evans sitting at the reception desk. She turned at the sound of footsteps and smiled when she saw them walking toward her. "Isn't that Linda's daughter, Ellie?" she asked, surprised to see them together.

"Has Dr. Greenway gotten back yet?" Scalese asked her.

"No, I haven't seen him. Hi, Ellie," Patsy looked down at the little girl and smiled. "Are you visiting us this afternoon?"

"Her mother's going to be tied up for quite some time talking to the police about this Burke business, and I'm in a bind. You look like you're good with kids."

"Well, I don't know about that, but I have three younger sisters."

"That'll do. Look, I'm taking her up to Greenway's office. It's nice and comfortable, with that couch and all." Scalese saw her expression change the instant he mentioned Greenway, his office, and the couch; and knew he had another problem that he needed to solve, permanently.

"Don't worry about Greenway. When he comes back, he'll be going right back out. So will I. What I'd like you to do is to go up there and babysit Ellie for me, maybe 'til midnight, maybe longer."

"That late? Gee, I don't know if I can do that, Mister Scalese. I've got..."

"You'd be doing Linda and me a real big favor, Patsy. I'll pay you triple time, you can have the rest of the week off, and I'll throw in a couple extra hundred. How's that sound?"

"That's more than generous, but Dr. Greenway's office?"

"Don't worry about him. I'll have three or four of my security guards here all night. I'll have one of them sit outside his door the whole time. You remember Freddie Fortuno? He's a nice guy and he'll look out for you. Okay?" Finally, Patsy smiled and nodded. "Good," he said as he glanced at his watch. "There's a big Walmart down the street. Why don't you run over there and buy some kid stuff — coloring books, maybe a doll, some toys, board games, and some drinks and snacks. Get some books and magazines for yourself, whatever you want. You can even take my car. It's parked right outside."

He pulled out his money clip and dropped two one-hundred-dollar bills on her desk. "Here, and you keep the change," he told her, and then added another one. "Here's some extra, in case you need to order some pizzas or anything later. I'll take her up to Greenway's office until you get back. Call up to Personnel and tell them to send somebody down here to cover the front desk. They don't do a damn thing up there anyway."

Ellie looked up at him, and frowned. "My mother says not to use bad words."

Patsy laughed and Scalese actually felt embarrassed for the first time in a very long time. "Your mother's right Ellie. My bad." He looked back at Patsy and said, "Have them forward my calls to Greenway's office."

Bob Burke opened Ernie Travers's cell phone again and dialed another number. Three rings later, a young woman answered, "Consolidated Health Care, how may I help you?" He recognized the voice of Patsy Evans, and put the call on speaker.

"I thought I told you to get out of there and find another job, Patsy?"

"Mr. Burke?" she whispered into the handset. "You know I can't talk to you."

"Okay, look, you haven't seen Tony Scalese and a little girl around there in the last few minutes, have you?"

"I… you're going to get me in a lot of trouble."

"It's a simple question, Patsy. Did you see Tony with a little girl?"

"Yes, yes, a couple of minutes ago. It was Linda's daughter, Ellie. He asked me if I would babysit this evening. He said Linda was tied up with the police. Is something wrong?"

"No, no, nothing's wrong, and I'm really glad to hear you will be with Ellie. Stay with her, and don't let her out of your sight."

"You're scaring me again. I've only been here two days, and I hate this place already."

Linda tried to grab the telephone out of Bob's grasp, but he held her back and covered the mouthpiece. "No," he told Linda. "If you talk to her, you'll scare her off. You need her to stay there with Ellie."

"Oh God," Linda turned away toward the other corner and began to cry.

"What's wrong?" Patsy asked.

"Nothing," Bob answered. "Everything's fine, you take care of Ellie. And if you would, connect me with Tony Scalese." She put him on hold and after fifteen long seconds of "elevator music," he heard the big Italian's confident voice at the other end of the phone.

"Hey! Is that you, Sport?" the big Italian laughed. "I thought you'd be calling."

"Picking on little girls now, Tony? Shame on you."

"Well, you didn't give me much choice. I want the stuff your girlfriend took from the office. Give it to me, and you can have the kid back."

"Linda wants to talk to her daughter."

"What? You don't think I have her? She's sitting here on Greenway's floor decorating one of our Annual Reports with a Magic Marker. But if Linda wants to talk to her, that's fine. Here, Ellie," he said as he handed the phone to the little girl. "Say hi, to your mother."

Bob handed Linda the cell phone and they heard a little girl's voice through the cell phone's speaker, "Hi, Mom."

"Are you okay, honey?" Linda asked between sobs.

"Yeah, I'm fine. I'm sitting here coloring, like Uncle Tony said. Then Patsy's coming up and we're going to play some games," Ellie said until Scalese took the phone away.

"There, satisfied? She's a cute kid and like she said, your pal Patsy's coming up here to take care of her. She'll be fine, unless you torque me off, Linda," he told her.

Somehow, Bob managed to pull the cell phone out of Linda's hand. "Okay, Tony, when and where?"

"How about right here, the CHC building, say 9 o'clock tonight after the hired help has gone."

"I don't think so. I'm not going anywhere near that place again."

"You want the little girl back?"

"You want the files?"

"Look Burke, I ain't screwing around."

"Neither am I. If we're going to do this, it's going to be a neutral site where everybody gets to walk away. Let's try the picnic pavilion in the Parker Woods Forest Preserve. It's east of O'Hare, not far from Indian Hills. You know where that is?"

"A picnic area?" Scalese snorted. "No, but I'll find it."

"Good, you guys come in through the North lot and we'll come in through the South. In the middle of the woods is a big picnic area, with tables and some barbecue grills. We'll meet there, in the pavilion."

"The picnic area in Parker Woods?" Scalese stopped and Bob could almost hear him thinking. "Okay, if that's what you want, smart guy, Parker Woods it is."

"And let's make it 11 o'clock. That'll give us a little more privacy."

He heard Scalese laugh. "You want 'privacy?' You got it," he said as he hung up.

"11 o'clock? What are you going to do?" Linda turned and asked in near panic.

"I'm going to get your daughter back," Bob answered her.

"Taking them on like this is stupid," Travers told him. "You don't know those guys."

"Yes I do, but they don't know me."

Linda turned to Travers and said, "You can't let him do this. They'll kill him."

"Bob, let me get some help," the Police Lieutenant said. "I can call in the State Police SWAT team, or even Chicago's. We can have the whole place locked down."

"Don't worry, Ernie. I'll have all the help I need. And I'll get her back," he turned and said to Linda Sylvester. "Trust me, I'll get her back."

Tony Scalese sat in Greenway's third floor office, in Greenway's desk chair, at Greenway's desk watching Ellie Sylvester. She was lying on an expensive Oriental carpet in front of Greenway's leather couch coloring in one of the CHC corporate Annual Reports with a set of magic markers as Lawrence Greenway walked in. He looked down at her, up at Scalese, and then back down at the little girl. "Is that Sylvester's daughter?" he demanded to know. "Are you out of your mind? What do you think you're doing, bringing her here of all places?"

"What am I doing? Your job. And I thought we agreed you were going out to track down Burke's wife and see what you can learn about him. What are you doing back here?"

"I did 'track her down' as you call it, Anthony. I went to their offices, but she's gone for the day. She lives up in Winnetka, so I'm going to pay her an impromptu visit in a few minutes. After our earlier escapades in Mount Prospect, I decided I needed a clean shirt. After all, a gentleman should be properly dressed when he calls on a lady, wouldn't you agree?"

"A gentleman? You? Don't make me laugh, Doc. You find out what she knows, and I don't care how you do it."

"What's the hurry? Is something going on that you haven't told me about?"

"I'm meeting Burke tonight at 11:00 p.m. We're swapping the girl for Purdue's files."

"Burke? You're meeting with him? Then why should I go chasing around…?"

"Because I told you to, Doc. He's a sneaky son-of-a-bitch and I…"

Ellie looked up at him again and frowned. "My mother said that's another bad word."

"I'm sure she did, honey," Scalese looked down at her with an embarrassed smile again. "You go back to your coloring and Uncle Tony will try not to talk like that anymore. Anyway," he turned back toward Greenway, "I'm meeting him in one of the Forest Preserve parks, in the picnic area over in Parker Woods."

"In the woods, at night? You? Surely you jest," Greenway scoffed at the idea.

"Don't worry, I won't be alone. And don't press your luck, Doc. We really don't need you anymore. Never did. So do what I told you. Go find Burke's wife and see what you can find out about him. I hear he was in the Army. Find out what he did and how he thinks," he said as he glared across at Greenway and watched him wilt under the heat.

Greenway coughed and looked away. "All right, but what about the little girl? You can't leave her up here alone, you know."

"With you around? For once in your life, I think you're right. That new girl in accounting is coming up here to babysit her as soon as we leave."

"Patsy Evans? Oh, how yummy. You have given me a delicious incentive to hurry back, Anthony," Greenway said with a thin crocodile smile.

"Not so quick, Doc. One of my guys, Freddie, is going to be sitting right outside that door with a loaded 9-mil and orders to shoot you in the ass if you touch either one of them before I get back," Scalese said as he pointed his finger at him. "You got that?"

"Me? Anthony, how could you possibly think…?"

"And if he doesn't, I will!" Scalese's angry eyes locked on Greenway's. "But I'll tell you what, Doc. Once this business is over, you can have Patsy as a special present from me; but not one minute sooner, you got that?"

CHAPTER TWENTY-FOUR

Lawrence Greenway drove his midnight-blue Mercedes SLK55 AMG roadster between the decorative fieldstone pillars and up the curving driveway at 242 Stanley Court in Winnetka. The car was the most expensive and powerful sports model Mercedes built, and the "Lunar Blue" color complemented his usual choice in suits. With a 416 horsepower V-8 engine, the lovely beast provided ridiculous overkill on the Chicago expressways, especially during rush hour, when everything slowed to a crawl. However, he loved the thrill of knowing the power was there if he wanted it; and he could take it out on the back roads of Kane County and blow out the pipes, his and the car's. It cost almost $125,000 with all the optional toys he added, more than he made his first three years out of Med School combined, so why did he buy it? Why? Because he could. Greenway smiled to himself every time he thought about it. Because he could!

He drove slowly around the beautifully landscaped turnaround, and parked in front of a large, impeccably designed English Tudor home, where he and the car could not be seen from the street. Looking up, he admired the house's steep, slate tile roofs, leaded glass windows, exposed half-timber on the second floor, and the massive front entry. Pure class, he thought, and precisely the type of home he wanted for himself. The Mercedes was his latest personal upgrade, and a magnificent house like this would be the next. He'd call it 'Lawrence 3.0;' and he wondered if the house might be coming on the market anytime soon. It just might, he grinned.

Parked ahead of him in the curved driveway was a huge, white, Cadillac Escalade war wagon. From his research, he knew it belonged to Angie Burke, which meant the "mistress of the house" must be home. When he got out of his Mercedes, he picked up his black leather "doctor's bag," and strode confidently up the semicircular granite stairs. The front door stood nine feet tall and was made of stout antique timbers, with a large, brass lion's head doorknocker in the center. Amazing, he thought, as he raised the lion by its chin and let it drop onto its brass baseplate with a loud, echoing Boom! Greenway put his hand on the door and grinned as he felt the old wood vibrate. He was about to do it again when the door opened and a short, fat, Hispanic housemaid looked up at him. She wore a gray and white uniform and her raven hair was braided into a bun at the back of her head. "May I help you, Señor?"

"My name is Greenway, Dr. Lawrence Greenway, and I'm here to see Mrs. Burke." He smiled and tried to walk past her, but the maid shifted to her right and blocked his way.

"Do you have an appointment, Señor?" she asked sternly.

"No, but if you mention my name, I'm confident she'll see me."

"And I am confident she will not!" the maid retorted.

"I am her doctor," he said as he showed her the black leather bag. "She called and said it was important, so if you don't mind," he pushed past her, "is she upstairs?"

"No, no, Señor, out by the pool, but you cannot…"

Greenway didn't wait for her to finish her protest. He strode into the foyer, through the kitchen, and out the open French doors to the large patio deck and pool, where he saw a very attractive blonde woman lying on her stomach on a recliner in the sun, buck-naked. Greenway's eyes immediately went to her scrumptiously shaped rear end, but he saw enough of her face to know who she was. As he approached her chair, she raised her head, put on her large, black sunglasses, and paused to look him over from head to foot.

By this time, the maid caught up. "I am so sorry, Mee-sus Burke, but he…"

"That's all right, Consuelo, toss me my towel." The maid hurried over with it and tried to cover her up, but Angie took it from her and stood up without evidencing the slightest concern regarding how much of her gorgeous body she revealed. Very slowly, she wrapped the towel around herself and sat back down on the chair, watching Greenway's eyes the entire time.

"You must excuse me for barging in on you unannounced," he said, pretending not to have noticed she was naked.

"He said he was your doctor!" Consuelo said angrily.

Greenway held up his small black medical bag and gave her his best smile. "I must apologize, Mrs. Burke, this usually gets me in everywhere."

"I'm afraid it's not going to get you in *everywhere*," Angie shot back in amusement.

"I'm Doctor Greenway, Doctor Lawrence Greenway," he smiled at her and pulled down on his French cuffs. "I'm the President of Consolidated Health Care."

"Gee, a doctor who makes house calls," she laughed at him. "And here I'm not due for a *physical* for another four months… doctor."

"Oh, it's nothing like that, my dear," he laughed along with her.

"I didn't expect it would be, and I know who you are, *Doctor* Greenway." She turned toward the still flustered maid and said, "Consuelo, why don't you bring us two of those marvelous Texas Teas you make… Like the ones you made a few days ago, *por favor*."

"Si, Señora," the maid replied in a huff and scurried back to the kitchen.

"So what brings you up to Winnetka, doctor? Sightseeing?" she asked as she straightened the towel again and motioned for him to take the lounge chair across from her.

"No, not that there aren't some wonderful things to see up here."

"Okay, cut the crap, *Larry*. What do you want? Or did you come here to get me angry, like you did my husband?"

"Heavens no, my dear; and what an unfortunate misunderstanding that entire situation is turning out to be. It has been so sad and disruptive for everyone, you included, and I want to personally apologize for whatever small role I might have played in creating these problems to begin with."

"How nice of you," Angie replied. She might be a lazy and indifferently educated young woman with a large ego and lightning quick temper, but she did inherit a finely tuned "Bullshit Meter" from her father, as he called it. Every time Greenway opened his mouth, the needle went off the dial.

"Yes, so unfortunate. When I met your husband, he looked like an ordinary enough fellow. I think he said he was in the Army, although I must say, he isn't exactly what I would have expected in a military type. He mentioned he was in 'communications,' and I assumed that meant he was some kind of a telephone installer or a cell phone nerd, or something."

That cracked Angie up. "Bobby? A phone installer? A cell phone *nerd*? You have no idea how funny that is. I've heard him called a lot of things, but never a *nerd*."

"Please call me Lawrence, Angie. Obviously, your husband is a fascinating young man."

"Husband? He's my soon-to-be-*ex-husband*, *Lawrence*, and that can't happen soon enough; not that it's any of your goddamned business."

"You know, I could not agree more. That's what makes this entire affair and his delusion that I go around murdering women, so very unfortunate."

"Oh, so, now he's delusional?" she cackled. "What a morning!"

"Well, perhaps I can help. I'm a doctor, and an MD. I spent the past fifteen years bringing comprehensive medical care to the slums of Chicago's South Side. I saved hundreds and hundreds of lives down there. I thought perhaps if we worked together we could find an appropriate place where Robert could receive some suitable professional care."

"You want me to help you put him in the nut house?" she looked at him, astonished.

"I wouldn't put it that way, but I would like to understand the young man better."

"Bobby? What you see, is what you get. But 'be advised,' as his guys used to say, you're making the mistake of your life if you keep pissing him off."

"Oh, I am not afraid for my own safety, Angie. I have more than enough people protecting me now."

"You really think so?" she smiled at him, clearly amused.

"Well, yes, but the young man does need help. He is disrupting my business, and I understand he's been causing you a lot of problems, too. So if you can help us find him…"

"Doctor, if half a dozen suburban police departments, the Chicago cops, the FBI, and the US Attorney's office can't find him, what makes you think I know where he is?"

"The US Attorney? You know you can't trust politicians, Angie. All Peter O'Malley cares about is Peter O'Malley."

"I'm shocked. I can't trust a politician? What about a doctor?" she asked as she slowly re-crossed her legs, letting the towel ride up, mocking him. "Why don't you tell me what really happened up on that roof, *Larry*? My bet is you strangled that woman, Bobby saw you, and now you want me to help you find him, so you can shut him up."

"Nothing happened up there!" he snapped, seeing he was getting nowhere with her and turning angry. "I'm asking you for your help, nice and friendly, for the last time."

"Is that a promise?" she laughed at him again.

"Where is he? Where can we find him?"

"Larry, as the ancient Greeks used to say, 'Be careful what you wish for.' "

Greenway glared at her for a moment and then softened his expression. "You are right, of course, but may I use your restroom? I'm afraid I drank far too much coffee at lunch."

"There's one off the kitchen. Consuelo will show you."

Greenway got to his feet, and retraced his steps through the

French doors, where the maid was placing two tall crystal glasses on a silver tray, which already held a large frosty pitcher and ice. Her back was to him as he reached into his pocket and pulled on a pair of latex surgical rubber gloves, but she must have heard his soft footsteps coming up behind her. As she turned her head to look, he placed one of his large hands on the back of her head and grabbed her chin with the other, giving them both a quick twist. With the leverage his long arms and height provided; he snapped her neck like a dry chicken bone, and she collapsed on the floor at his feet. The crystal tumblers, pitcher, and tray fell on top of her with a loud Clang! and Crash!

Greenway turned and quickly walked back out the patio doors to the deck.

"What was that?" Angie asked, suddenly concerned.

"Oh, nothing, I think Consuelo dropped the tray," Greenway smiled as he returned to his chair and opened his black-leather bag.

"Consuelo?" Angie called out as she swung her legs over the side of the chair and began to stand up.

"Oh, don't go, Angie," Greenway grinned as he shoved her back down. He swung his long leg over the lounge chair, straddled her, and grabbed her by the throat with his gloved left hand. With his right hand, he snapped open Tony Scalese's 9-inch stiletto, and pressed it against her throat. "Our little conversation is beginning to get interesting," he said with a thin, sadistic smile. "In a little while, I think you'll warm to the subject, and warm to me. Meanwhile, let's talk about your husband a bit more. Where did you say I could find him?"

As they reached the Interstate, Ernie Travers's cell phone rang. He pulled it from his jacket pocket, looked at the display, and frowned. "You might want to hear this," he motioned to Bob as he put the cell phone on speaker. "Travers," he mumbled indifferently.

"Lieutenant, this is Peter O'Malley. I've been calling your office all…"

"I haven't been there, Mister O'Malley. There's been a sharp increase in thefts in the baggage area, so I've been out and about inspecting and inventorying."

"Really? I left four messages on your office phone and talked to your secretary. She doesn't seem to have a clue where you are."

Travers paused. "That's what she's supposed to say. What can I do for you?"

"Are you aware of what happened this morning?"

"Regarding something at the airport?"

"No, regarding your friend, Burke."

"That's not my case, he's not my friend, and I'm busy. What else can I do for you?"

"He phoned me this morning. He has the reports and things that Eleanor Purdue was to turn over to me, and I've got to have that stuff. Look, I know you two talked."

"I haven't the slightest idea what you're talking about, Mister O'Malley."

"Someone tortured and murdered his friend Charlie Newcomb. Burke thinks it was Tony Scalese's men. He also thinks they killed Eleanor Purdue and that flight attendant, Sabrina Fowler. At last count, he's put two of them in the hospital, and he told me he's just getting started. We need to find him and get him off the street before they do."

"We?" Travers chuckled. "Well, for starters, I'd be a little more worried about them than I would be about him, if I were you. But as I said, it's not my case. If you want him to come in, offer him a deal and give him full immunity," he said as he looked up at Burke and smiled.

"You know I can't do that!"

"Why not? The charges against him are bogus and you know it. He didn't kill those women. All you have to do is decline to prosecute. Happens every day."

"The newspapers would eat me alive."

"Really? When he releases all those records, you'll have no choice anyway. The smart play for you is to get ahead of all that and make it look like it was your idea. The longer you wait, the worse you're going to look. But hey, I gotta run, Mister O'Malley. My bowling league's in a roll-off tonight, and you know how cranky they get when the high-pin guy's late. Ciao," Travers said as he rang off and looked over at Burke with a contented smile.

"Your bowling league?" Burke laughed. "The high-pin guy?"

"What was I supposed to say? God, I hate those guys."

"Which 'guys?' The Feds? Sleazy politicians in general? Or only the Irish? Look," Bob said as he drove east and got on the I-90 expressway, checking his rearview mirrors as he did. "Ernie, we have over four hours before my guys arrive and we need to take a shot at that flash drive. Before we went to the school, Linda and I bought some computer equipment from Best Buy, and we have what's left of Charlie's laptop. What we need is a place where we can set it all up and see if we can make it work."

Looking out the window, Linda saw the long line of motels down Mannheim Road. "Why don't we find a motel room? They usually have Internet."

"Better still, how about my office?" Travers asked. Bob appeared skeptical, so the big Chicago cop went on, "No, think about it, it's the perfect choice. My office staff leaves for the day at 4:00, so it's empty. I have a couple of big, fast laser jets that'll bang out those documents as fast as you need them. I also have Xerox machines, fax machines, phones, a couple of other computers, and about anything else you might want. Best of all, we'll have complete privacy in a secure area surrounded by chain-link fences and protected by the TSA. How can you beat that?"

"Sounds like a plan to me," Linda added, and Bob agreed.

Travers's key card opened the rear Security Gate at O'Hare. They parked behind Ernie Travers's office, and went inside. In short order, they had the boxes unpacked, the flash drive inserted in one of the computers, and a pot of coffee brewing. Bob immediately set to work on the new Asus notebook, while Ernie tried to open the case on Charlie's older one with the through-and-through bullet hole. It looked like a simple enough task, but there were a dozen tiny screws securing the back panel to the case. Ernie volunteered to take them on with the little phillips screwdriver Bob bought. However, after trying to loosen three of them, he handed the phillips to Linda. "Not with these meat hooks," he told her, holding up his big hands. "You work the screws; I'll go down to the food court and get us some stuff to eat. Looks like we may be here a while."

"Where is he?" Greenway asked Angie again, even more demanding this time.

"How the hell would I know?" she shouted up at him.

"I'm not going to ask you again," he threatened, tightening his grip on her throat.

"You bastard, get your hands off me!" she said as she hit him in the face with a balled fist. "You're a goddamned maniac!" Her punch was surprisingly hard and caught him flush on his cheekbone where Linda Sylvester's deep gouges had barely begun to heal.

"Ah!" he screamed and hit her hard with a monstrous backhand. "You're hiding him, aren't you? Is he in here in the house or in some other place you own?"

The long fingers of his left hand tightened around her throat and he dragged her off the chair and onto the deck. Her towel fell away as she struggled, thrashing from side to side, leaving her naked as he sat on her, straddling her, and holding her down. "Tell me, you stupid bitch," he screamed into her face and brought the knife against her throat again. "Didn't you believe what your husband told you about me; what might happen to you if you cross me?"

"We never talked about you, you asshole!" She reached out with both hands this time, fingernails extended like a large cat, going for his eyes. Unfortunately for her, he saw it coming and pushed down hard on her throat, cutting off the air to her lungs. His arm was much longer than hers, and the best her deadly, perfectly manicured fingernails could do was to grab his coat sleeve.

"You see, Angie, I've done this before — many, many times before — and I enjoy it!" He said as he squeezed even harder and watched her face grow red and her eyes bulge out. "Last chance. Where can I find him?" he asked as he released some of the pressure on her throat, enough for her to take in a small, desperate breath and cough.

"Screw you, asshole!" she coughed and gasped. "Screw you!"

Greenway snapped. Looking down into her eyes and seeing the anger and hatred behind them, he felt himself getting a powerful erection and squeezed even harder, completely cutting off her air. Her face turned beet red this time. She turned and twisted, her naked body writhing beneath him, which excited him even more. As she began to lose consciousness and her eyes closed, he slowly drew Tony Scalese's stiletto across the side of her neck. With surgical precision, it neatly severed her carotid artery. Her eyes shot open and Greenway quickly pulled his hands away as her blood squirted sideways across the pool deck, narrowly missing him. As he sat on her naked body and watched her bleed out beneath him, feeling the life flow out of her, he had an orgasm. It was his usual reaction in times like these, but this one was stronger and more vivid.

Greenway looked down into her lifeless eyes and whispered, "Thank you, Angie." Finally, he rolled off her, got back up on shaky legs and dropped the stiletto next to her body. Before he left, he stepped over to the pool, stuck his hands into the water, carefully washed her blood off his surgical gloves, and dropped them into his medical bag. Nicely done, he thought. There was nothing here to link him to her murder. But Tony Scalese? That's his knife and those are his fingerprints all over it. Tony Scalese the North Side Rapist? Who would have guessed?

Greenway returned to his car, drove slowly down the driveway, and turned left at the street. At the next major intersection, he saw a combination Shell gas station and McDonalds restaurant. He parked his Mercedes in the side lot and walked inside. He saw a pay phone hanging on the rear wall between the two stores. The restaurant was crowded with high school kids, and no one was going to notice one more adult. He picked up the receiver and dialed 911.

An emergency operator answered after a few rings. Greenway placed his handkerchief over the mouthpiece and hurriedly told her, "My name's Samuel Jamison with FedEx. I was making a delivery at 242 Stanley Court in Winnetka. The front door was hanging wide open, so I knocked and called out 'FedEx' a couple of times. I finally stepped inside a little bit and called out again, but that was when I saw those bodies. There's a woman lying in the kitchen and another one out in back by the pool. She's been cut up, somethin' bad."

"Are you at the scene, Mister Jamison?" the operator asked.

"Hell no, lady, I got my ass out of there."

"I'm dispatching a patrol car right now, but I'd like you to go back and..."

"Me? I didn't see nuthin' else, and there ain't no way you're talkin' me into goin' back there."

Greenway hung up, casually wiped down the telephone handset with his handkerchief, and walked away smiling. That should stir things up, he thought.

CHAPTER TWENTY-FIVE

Tony Scalese sat in his office, waiting. He hated waiting, so he spent the time cleaning and reloading his pistols — a Glock, a Beretta, and his old standby, a Colt M-1911 — plus his favorite sawed-off shotgun. It was only 7:30 p.m. The guns were oiled and reassembled now and lay on the desk in front of him in a neat row. He had cleaned every piece and part there was to clean, and all he could do now was sit and wait for the rest of his crew to arrive. Ten of his men were already there. Three were "regular" hourly security guards, who would be staying to watch the building. The others were from various "crews" down in the city. They were hanging around downstairs smoking and drinking coffee in the employee lounge, playing gin and pinochle, or studying tomorrow's Racing Form for nearby Arlington Park. He had another ten to twelve men coming up later — all that firepower against one ex-Army "telephone company" creep and a goddamned receptionist? Even if Burke did call in a few friends to help, maybe some duck hunters, maybe a "moke" with a deer rifle, or maybe even a few of his old Army buddies; it would be a slaughter. He and his crew would kill them all. After that, he would kill Sylvester, Bentley, Greenway, and all the rest of them. Tonight he would snip off all those *loose ends*, as Mr. D ordered. He'd snip them all.

He leaned back in his desk chair, spun it around, and looked out through the third floor window into the dark night. His office faced west. Until the first day he worked out here in the "burbs," he would never have believed there could be so many trees in the world. There must be millions of them. From the occasional twinkle of lights, he knew there were thousands of houses out there too, hundreds of stores, gas stations, and McDonalds restaurants; but the trees were much taller and hid most of them. Their crowns were all you could see as far as the horizon. Scalese grew up on the near North Side where trees were spindly little things. As a kid, he believed they kept them around for the dogs, so they'd have something to pee on. He was a city boy, and still found all that green out there a bit disconcerting.

When he first saw the CHC building, he figured he would take an office facing the city. From the third floor, you could see downtown on a clear day, with the Hancock and Sears towers, the Prudential building, and all the rest. That was what he told his pals back in the city, that his new office looked out at "Big John" Hancock. That was something they would understand and envy, but he lied. He passed on Big John and took an office facing west, where he looked at the pretty sunsets and all those goddamned trees. He loved the sunsets and at times, he even liked the trees. If he was honest with himself, however, the scale of it all was beginning to creep him out. He remembered that *Lord of the Rings* movie, where the trees got up and started going after that wizard in the white robe. There was something primordial about that, something a city kid like him didn't "get," and didn't want to.

Last month, Scalese tried to meet the trees halfway. He went out and drove around the back roads for a couple of hours. He even visited some of the County Forest Preserves, but he still didn't "get" it. What did that Aussie guy in the movies, that Crocodile Dundee, call it? "The Great Outback?" All those trees — or were they woods or forests? To Tony, they were just a waste of good lumber, construction sites, union jobs, kickbacks, paving contracts, pension plan loans, permits, bribes, and escrow scams. Yeah, the more he thought about it, no matter how many gunmen he brought with him, he was nuts to tell that moke Burke he'd meet him in the woods, especially at night.

Looking out his office window, the sun had long set on what had been a tiring day — too long and too tiring, he thought. 11:00 p.m. He should have never given that prick Burke that much time. Scalese had the kid and Burke had a panicked mother to deal with. That should have sealed the deal and let him put an end to this business hours earlier.

That was when one of his men, Jimmy DiCiccio, knocked on the frame of his door and said, "Boss, dat local cop Bentley's downstairs. He says he needs to talk to you."

"Tell him there's too many ears around here. I'll meet him over at that big white water tank of his in ten minutes," Scalese answered as he used his handkerchief to pull Greenway's little .32-caliber Mauser "pimp gun" from his pocket and check the magazine. "Tell him I have a present for him from Mr. D, something *special*. And tell him he should bring that fat turd of a nephew of his, Bobby Joe, with him, too."

Scalese got to his feet and picked up his favorite .45-caliber Colt automatic off his desk. After checking that magazine too, he jacked a round "up-the-pipe" and tucked it behind his belt in the small of his back. He opened his bottom desk drawer and pulled out a wrinkled, brown paper lunch sack. Inside were a dozen small plastic envelopes containing rock crystals of crack cocaine. Good, he smiled; as he rolled the sack closed and brought it along. He picked up his sharkskin blazer from the chair where he had tossed it, pulled it on, and headed for the door until he felt his cell phone vibrating in his pants pocket. He paused and pulled it out. Odd, he thought as he looked at the small screen and saw a phone number he did not recognize. Odder still, because only a handful of people knew this very private cell phone number.

"Yeah," he said as he answered the call.

"This is your friend downtown," he heard, and immediately recognized US Attorney Peter O'Malley's voice. "Go out and find a pay phone, and call me back. We need to talk."

"This phone's clean."

"Anthony, it's time you learned that *nothing's* clean. So stop arguing and do what I told you. It's important," O'Malley said as he rang off. Scalese stared at the phone, growing angrier by the moment. O'Malley! He was another one of those loose ends the big Italian couldn't wait to snip off.

There was a Pizza Hut three blocks away, which he and his crew frequented, and he knew he could always use their phone. When he got there, he gave the manager a fierce glare and took their delivery phone from his hand. He dialed the number and said, "It's me," getting increasingly tired of being told what to do by anyone. Hopefully, that would all soon end.

O'Malley began without any pleasantries "I talked to *that* guy a little while ago. Despite your best efforts, it seems he got his hands on those CHC reports."

"So what, that bitch Purdue is dead and nobody can prove a goddamned thing."

"He also claims he has a flash drive that she left. He says it has all of your books and financial reports, the '*real*' ones. He thinks it has the list of all the people you guys are paying off. He hasn't been able to get it open yet, but we both know whose name he'll find prominently displayed in there, don't we?"

"Ah, he's blowin' smoke up your ass, O'Malley. Old Sal's the only one with the '*real*' books, and he keeps 'em locked in that big damned safe of his up in Evanston."

"Maybe, but I'm taking the version of the *real* ones that you gave me to the Grand Jury. If Burke suddenly shows up with a different set of *real* ones that implicate you *and me*, my campaign will go down in flames before it even gets started, and you'll lose all that money you spent trying to elect a *friendly* new Governor."

"Then you won't need to worry, will you? Neither will I, because old Sal will plant the both of us out in Lake Michigan five minutes after the *Tribune* lands on his front doorstep with a story like that. But it ain't ever gonna happen, because that little prick Burke and his reports and spreadsheets ain't gonna survive the night. Neither are Greenway, Bentley, Linda Sylvester, or anyone else who knows anything about any of this."

"Be careful, Tony. That guy Burke is dangerous."

"So am I. Look, we got the computers from Purdue's office and from her house, and we got Sylvester's, we got Burke's, and we even got his friend's up in Wheeling. We busted 'em all into a million little pieces, so how…"

"None of that matters. The documents are on a little flash drive; and one way or another, he'll get it open," O'Malley warned. "You know what he had the balls to ask me? He asked if he'll find *my* name in there, so maybe he already knows."

"You think he's bluffin'?"

"How should I know? But if he didn't have something on us, something big, don't you think he'd have cut and run a long time ago?"

"Maybe, but it doesn't matter. We're takin' care of him tonight. He's a dead man."

"Good, because my Grand Jury meets next week, and this thing's starting to unravel."

"Not unless you let it, and I'm paying you a lot of goddamned money to make sure it doesn't do that, *Governor*. Two weeks ago, I gave you enough *stuff* on old Sal, to put him, his brothers, and his nephews in the Federal pen for a long time, plus a dozen other wise guys who ticked me off. So, what are you waiting for? Get it done!"

There was a small, gravel parking lot at the base of the Indian Hills water tank. When Scalese turned in off the main road, he immediately saw he chose his spot well. A tall, ragged, hedge surrounded the small service lot, and there were four ground-mounted floodlights illuminating the big water tank, but leaving the parking lot below in deep shadow. Police cars tend to put a chill on late-night romance and the drug trade, so the only cars in the small lot were the two white and green Indian Hills police cruisers — Bentley's and Bobby Joe's. They were parked side by side facing the water tank, so Scalese pulled in behind them, blocking them in. He pulled on a pair of paper-thin, Italian leather driving gloves, pulled Greenway's little Mauser from his jacket pocket, and dropped it in the brown paper sack with the cocaine. When he got out of the car, he took the sack and left the engine running.

He walked around the rear of the Lexus and then between the two police cars, stopping next to Chief Bentley's open window. The two cops must have been talking as Scalese walked up. Bobby Joe sat on the hood of his car with his feet dangling over the side, looking like a fat, grinning toad; while Bentley sat inside his car smoking a cigarette, his seat tilted back as if it were his personal recliner on wheels.

As Scalese stopped next to him, Bentley looked up and saw the gloves. "A little hot for them things tonight, ain't it, Tony?"

"I like to wear them when I'm driving. Lets me pretend it's a sports car," he answered. "So, what's so goddamned important that you had to see me tonight, Chief?" he asked as he leaned through the window and gave Bentley his best crocodile smile.

"Plenty. Look, I don't know if you heard about Burke's wife, yet..."

"Burke's wife? Heard what?"

"Seems she got herself killed this afternoon."

"Seriously kilt," Bobby Joe chortled. "Somebody broke in her house up in Win-net-ka. They found her out back by the swimming pool, naked as a jaybird with her throat slit. Found her maid too, lyin' in the kitchen with her neck broke."

Scalese frowned, not liking what he heard. "Okay, thanks for letting me know." he said as he straightened up and put his hand in the paper sack.

"Yeah, well, that ain't the half of it," Bentley sat up, thinking Scalese was leaving. "Seems they found a knife layin' next to her body, a 9-inch Italian–made stiletto. Now, I hate to bring this up, Tony, but every cop in town knows you favor a knife like that, so this business is gettin' a whole lot more complicated than I bargained for."

"A stiletto?" Scalese's hand patted his inside jacket pocket, but he felt nothing. His knife was gone. "Greenway," he whispered to himself as his eyes narrowed and his anger built into a towering rage. "That son of a bitch!" Unfortunately, that worthless doctor wasn't there to be on the receiving end of the big Mafia hit man's anger, but these two hick cops were.

"Yeah, and I think it's high time you and I sat down and discussed our 'financial arrangement.' " Bentley continued, with a new tone of confidence.

Scalese stared in at him again, "When?" he asked.

"When? Well, I guess now's as good a time as any."

"No, you moron! When was she killed?"

"Burke's wife? I heard a couple of hours ago, maybe three, but they ain't finished their investigation. It came out over the regional alert system earlier, so I… Now wait just a damned minute, boy! Who the hell you callin' a moron?" Bentley bristled.

"You!" Scalese reached inside the paper sack and found the grip on Greenway's .32-caliber Mauser. In one smooth motion, he pulled it out and extended his arm toward Bobby Joe. The fat cop sat on the car hood with a dumb grin until he saw the small German pistol in Scalese's hand, and frowned. Some people are too terminally stupid to waste air on, Scalese concluded, especially a very dumb cop. He pulled the trigger three times and put a nice, tight shot grouping into the center of Bobby Joe's face.

They call a .32 a "pimp gun" for good reason. The small bullet it fired wasn't good for much except disciplining a whore by shooting her in the butt when she got out of line, or for scaring away a troublesome John. However, in Scalese's experience, a .32 or even a .22 was more than adequate to kill someone if you shoot them in the head at point-blank range. A big .45-caliber slug from his Colt would blow half the man's head off and pass right on through. A .32, on the other hand, makes a little hole on its way in and rattles around inside for a while, turning the brain to mush. It's a lot less messy, but the vic ends up just as dead. In Bobby Joe's case, he toppled over backward onto the car hood.

The Police Chief's jaw dropped as he saw Bobby Joe's body spread-eagled there like an overstuffed hood ornament. Scalese didn't wait. He turned around and pressed the muzzle of the Mauser into Bentley's left ear. The chief turned and looked up into the coldest pair of eyes he would ever see as Scalese pulled the trigger, twice. Bentley's head snapped to the right and his body collapsed sideways across the car seat. Scalese extended his arm and shot him once more in the head for spite. By the time he turned back around, Bobby Joe had rolled off the hood and lay on the gravel staring up at him, quietly blowing bubbles. Scalese was surprised at how little noise even six gunshots from a little .32 made, not nearly enough to be heard over the roar of traffic on the nearby road. He tossed the Mauser onto the ground next to Bobby Joe's police cruiser. There would still be plenty of Greenway's fingerprints on the pistol and the shell casings inside. Serves him right, Scalese thought, but it wouldn't begin to even the scales with the arrogant doctor.

Scalese reached into the brown paper bag and pulled out a dozen of the small, clear plastic envelopes that contained the yellow-brown "rocks" of crack cocaine. He bent down, picked up Bobby Joe's hand, and pressed several of the envelopes against his fingertips and thumb before he dropped them on the ground around him. He reached inside Bentley's car, grabbed his hand, and did the same for four or five more of the plastic envelopes. He dropped two of them into Bentley's lap and dropped the rest and the empty sack on to the floor of Bentley's car, where he knew the police Crime Techs would have no trouble finding them later.

Finally, Scalese stood up and looked around. All in all, not a bad night's work, he reflected. He had snipped off two of Mr. D's loose ends, permanently — Bentley and Bobby Joe — and soon he would add Greenway to the list. He walked back to the Lexus with a broad smile on his face, and drove away.

While Linda removed the small screws on the back panels on both of the notebook computers, Bob tried the flash drive in one of Travers' desktop PCs. He inserted it into one of the USB ports, but when he clicked on the drive, a screen came up asking for a user password. That was what he expected would happen; so he tried some of the other automatic Windows features, and finally "Run," "Search," and "Internet Explorer," so that he could at least find a "File Directory," all to no avail. The same screen requiring a user password came up each time. Frustrated, he sat back and wished Charlie were here. Bob knew a few rudimentary computer tricks, but Charlie was the Grand Master. In his absence, Bob hoped the decryption software on Charlie's hard drive could be made to do the job. Even though his notebook had a neat, three-quarter inch hole through its center, if the bullet missed the hard drive, it might still be usable in another machine. Sure enough, after Linda removed the last screw, he pried the case open, and saw that while there was a hole through the motherboard, the keyboard, the screen, and numerous circuits, the bullet had missed the hard drive, barely.

"Linda, while I'm switching out the hard drives, get me the cable to one of Ernie's printers and make sure it has plenty of paper."

From that point, the work began to move quickly. He switched the drives, closed the case with all those little screws, and powered the new one up. Like Frankenstein's monster with its new brain, the new Asus booted up thinking it was Charlie's old machine. "It's alive!" Bob cried out, imitating Colin Clive's exultant voice in the old 1931 movie. Unfortunately, when he tried the flash drive, he received the same response he got on the desktop, asking for a user password. He sat at the computer for a few minutes more, trying all the usual ones like "Password," "123456," "abcdef," and a few others, to no avail.

Frustrated, he leaned back in his chair and looked at Linda. "Before I start banging away with some of Charlie's decryption routines, did Eleanor give any hints about a password?"

"No, and I don't know much about computers."

"But she did, and she must've said something."

"I didn't think to ask," she shrugged helplessly.

He stared at her. "When she gave you the keys and told you about the cereal box with the note inside, what did she say? What were her exact words?"

"Well, she gave me the keys to her house and office and told me there was an envelope in the Cocoa Puffs box in her pantry, and something about it was the key."

Bob sat back and thought for a moment. "She didn't have any kids did she?"

"No, only Ellie and me."

"And she said, 'it was the key,' " he repeated and suddenly turned back to the keyboard. "Wait a minute. Sometimes things need to smack you right in the face before you see them. She meant the *password key*," he said as he typed in 'Cocoa Puffs' and hit Enter. The screen suddenly changed and a file directory opened up. "I'll bet the farm that Cocoa Puffs is Ellie's favorite breakfast cereal, isn't it?'

Linda's mouth dropped open as she stared at him. "God, I feel so stupid."

"Don't. Eleanor was very clever, that's all," he told her as he looked at his watch. It was already 9:15 and time was running out. The directory of the documents in the files was long. Most of them contained CHC in the title or related to the medical services company in one way or another. Some appeared to be monthly Excel spreadsheets and financial reports dating back over the past twelve months. There were also Word memos and letters with titles or names and dates, as well as copies of scanned documents that looked very much like monthly statements and records of deposits in banks, mostly foreign banks.

That was when Ernie Travers came back carrying several bags of food and drink. "You got it open?" he asked.

"He did it, not me," Linda laughed as they dove into the burgers and fries.

"There's a ton of stuff on this flash drive, way too much for us to go through right now," Bob said as he pulled it out of the Asus notebook computer, plugged it into Ernie's secretary's machine, and used the password to reopen the files. "Linda, this one is already connected to Ernie's printer. I want to get a good cross-section, enough to scare the hell out of Scalese's people; so go through the directory and pick out anything that sounds good, but isn't too big, particularly if it has a recent date — financial reports, spreadsheets, bank statements, and any correspondence that sounds incriminating. Print them out. Time's short, and I have to find some terrain maps before my guys get here. There's some good sites online, and…"

"Man, I've got a ton of that stuff right here, like aerial photos of the area and USGS maps," Travers interjected. "We need it in case of a crash or a ground search or anything like that."

"You have USGS maps?" Bob beamed. "I'm in Infantry heaven! Show me the Quad Sheets with Parker Woods Forest Preserve on them."

Travers went to his storage room, which held a large horizontal-drawer file cabinet with two dozen wide, flat drawers. They held aerial photos, maps, and blueprints of the airport. He opened one of the lower drawers, thumbed through the sheets and pulled out three green-toned, multicolored USGS maps covering the area east of O'Hare. Ernie laid them on his conference table and they saw that Parker Woods slopped over onto two of them. "Here," he said as he pointed to the center of the park. "But why'd you tell Scalese you'd meet him in the picnic area?"

"One of our vendors held a company picnic there last summer, and I saw most of it."

"And an old infantryman never forgets a good piece of ground, does he?" Ernie asked, but Bob just smiled. "Actually, it's a pretty smart choice. If they come in from the north lot, like you told them to do, and we come in from the south…"

"Ernie," he smiled. "I told him a lot of things, but one thing's for certain. He isn't going to do what he said, and neither am I." That was when Bob's cell phone rang. When he pulled it out of his pocket and looked at the display, he saw an incoming call from area code 910. "Excuse me for a minute, Ernie, but it's my favorite storm door and window company in North Carolina… "Hey, Ace," he answered.

"Reporting in as ordered, Sir. We should be wheels down and 'ready to rumble' in… forty-eight minutes."

"Roger that. See you then," Bob replied as he rang off.

While he was on the phone, Ernie Travers stepped across the room and scanned the accumulated messages on his teletype machine. He tore off two of them, read them more closely, and walked back to where Bob was standing. "There's something else I need to show you, Bob," Travers said as he handed him one of the pages, his expression turning serious. "This came across the Metro police wire while I was out. There's no easy way to put this, but this report says your wife's dead."

Bob read it and paused a moment to absorb what it said.

"The Winnetka police found her by her swimming pool earlier this evening, murdered," Travers continued. "They've got your name linked to it, of course, with an APB out, but you were with me the whole time. If we live through this business tonight, I can clear that up. It appears there was a fight and someone cut her throat."

"You missed the interesting part," Bob said. "They found an Italian stiletto lying next to her. Isn't that what Tony Scalese likes to use?"

Travers nodded. "Yeah, that's his 'rep,' but I'm having a hard time believing he'd be stupid enough to leave his own knife behind like that."

"Unless he's sending me a message," Bob said as he turned and looked at the other man. "You're probably wondering why I'm not more emotional about this. Well, truth is Angie and I started breaking up a long time ago. Not that it matters, but I'm not the type to get angry or emotional about much of anything. Instead, I'm the kind who gets even. So, whether it was Scalese, Greenway, Bentley, or one of their other pals, tonight's going to be payback."

"That's the other thing," Travers said as he held up the other piece of paper. "Bentley and his 'nephew' Bobby Joe were found shot to death in the parking lot next to the Indian Hills water tank a little while ago — small caliber, three head shots each, execution style."

"I suppose they'll try to pin those on me too?"

"Probably," Travers shrugged. "But anyone with a brain in his head knows that's how Salvatore DiGrigoria and his brothers terminate an employee."

CHAPTER TWENTY-SIX

The private airfield was located twelve miles north of O'Hare Airport, outside the small town of Mount Prospect, Illinois. In rush hour, even that short distance could take thirty minutes to drive. At 9:50 p.m., the short convoy of two of Ernie Travers's black, oversized Chevy Suburbans, complete with low-profile, red-white-and-blue light bars, trailed by an old, rusty Ford Taurus, took less than half that time. Ernie Travers and Bob Burke drove the two SUVs, while Linda tried to keep up in the aging Taurus. The airfield was located in what used to be cornfields to the west of Mount Prospect decades before. Since then, the small towns had grown and closed in around it. For a private airport, it was surprisingly modern and busy, even that late at night, due to its ease of access to major expressways and the growing Northwest suburbs. It was home to many corporate jets, private charter companies, privately owned propeller planes and helicopters, fractional ownership airplanes, flight schools, police and rescue helicopters, sightseeing companies, and even the traffic-copters for three local radio stations.

The terminal and service facility normally closed to the public at 9:30 p.m., but Ernie Travers's CPD detective badge and O'Hare report credentials allowed them inside the terminal. From the loudspeaker in the lounge, they soon heard the conversation between a Gulfstream G-5 private charter from Windimere, North Carolina and the tower. The G-5 was on final approach. With the distinctive upward flip of its wing tips and sleek, needle nose, it was the current undisputed king of civil aviation. Fast, efficient, and economical, it could carry sixteen passengers up to 6,300 miles at 600 miles per hour. In less than a minute, the G-5 touched down on the runway, slowed, and taxied to the transient parking spaces located to the left of the terminal. The pilot turned its nose so the small jet faced back toward the runway and powered the engines down.

With Ernie Travers' badge, they received permission to drive the two Chevy Suburbans through the airport security gate in order to park next to the airplane and unload. By the time they returned to the SUVs, drove them around to the airplane and parked, the pilot had blocked the G-5's wheels, opened the passenger door, and pulled down the exit stairs. Five men emerged from the airplane and stood on the tarmac, stretching and laughing. Two of them displayed beards and shoulder-length hair, one wore a ponytail and a droopy handlebar mustache, and neither of the other two had anything even close to a military haircut. Their clothes were a random collection of blue jeans, nylon windbreakers, sweatshirts, sunglasses and baseball hats. What they had in common, however, was that they all appeared to be around thirty years old, were in excellent physical condition, wore beige "desert" combat boots, and had 'that' look.

Linda frowned as she walked over to Bob. "You said these guys are Army?" she asked skeptically, folding her arms across her chest. "Whose army?"

He smiled too, as the co-pilot opened the G-5's cargo hold and the passengers formed a chain to unload a half dozen metal packing crates and a number of large, nylon carry bags from the airplane, and throw them in the back of the two SUVs. One of the passengers left the others and walked up to Bob Burke. He appeared a little stockier and a little older than the others, wearing a Washington Redskins baseball hat above a long, tightly braided ponytail. "Reporting as ordered, Sir," he saluted and broke into a toothy grin. The two men greeted each other with muscular, shoulder-grabbing, backslapping, man-hugs.

"Ace, it's been too damn long," Bob began.

"Since that fiasco you called a wedding."

"Fiasco? That was only the beginning."

"Like they always say, 'If the Army wanted you to have a wife...' "

"...'they'd have issued me one.' Anyway, tell the pilot and co-pilot to stay here. You should be back in three, maybe three and a half hours, probably with a few more passengers, but we'll give them a call. Then, it'll be wheels up in ten minutes."

"Roger that. I'll tell them," Ace said as he walked back to the airplane.

When Ace returned, the others gathered around for introductions. "Okay, Major, what's the Op? Who do you want killed?" one of them grinned as he gave Bob a bear hug bigger than Ace did, lifting him off the ground. "God, I miss the old days."

"Guys," Bob began. "This is Ernie Travers. He might look like an offensive tackle with the Bears, but he's a Chicago Police detective who runs security at O'Hare."

"The police?" Vinnie laughed. "When I saw those big, black SUVs with the light bars, I wondered whether we were being arrested by the FBI or getting a Secret Service escort."

"Don't worry, he's on our side. And this is Linda Sylvester. The guys we're going after tonight kidnapped her daughter, so she's on our side too." He turned back to the five soldiers and said, "Ernie and Linda, meet Ace, Vinnie, Chester, Koz, and the Batman. As unusual as they may look, they are some of the top 'operators' in the business," he said as he looked at his watch. "We need to be in position in less than an hour, we have an operations plan and some maps to go over, and we need to gear up, fast."

"The airport supervisor said we can use his conference room, Bob," Ace told him.

"Bob? Bob? Who the hell is Bob?" Chester asked. "Oh, you mean Casper the Ghost?"

"The clock's running, guys, show me what you brought," Bob told them.

Ace led them around the back of the two SUVs, pointing at the metal cases and canvas bags. "First, not knowing how big the party was, I grabbed a dozen of those nifty British SAS radios we started using, the ones with the earbuds and cheek mikes, which I've preset to a secure tactical net."

"Can anyone else listen in?" Ernie Travers asked.

"No one this side of the NSA, and I'm not even sure about them," Ace answered. "These are very low-power on a highly restricted tactical band, and the range isn't more than a mile or two. That's a long answer for, 'not very damn likely.' As for weapons, again, I guessed what you might want, so I grabbed a half-dozen Berettas with noise suppressors, two of your favorite M-110 sniper rifles, four of the new SCAR Mk 17 assault rifles with infrared night vision scopes and noise suppressors, and one of the ever-popular Benelli M-4 automatic 12-gauge shotguns. No noise suppressor there, but I also grabbed some night vision goggles, the latest 'covert' tactical body armor, some tactical knives, four 'ghillie' suits…"

"What's a ghillie suit?" Linda asked.

"A huge camouflage suit that can even make someone my size disappear," Travers said.

Ace looked at him for a moment. "Well, almost anyone, but I also brought dark coveralls a couple of 'poncho liners,' lots of ammo, web belts and tactical harnesses, some small packs, canteens, two fully loaded Medic field packs, and… oh, and the Semtex and detonators you told Chester you wanted, and… Well, I guess that's about everything."

"Automatic rifles and Semtex? Christ," Travers laughed. "Is any of this stuff legal?"

"Every damned piece. And I signed for all of it," Ace answered.

"So I need to get this stuff back, or I won't have much of a payday next week."

"We'll try, except for the bullets," Bob told him. "One other thing: everybody wears the body armor, everybody! No exceptions, not even you, Vinny. The new stuff is thin and lightweight, and you guys need to report back to Bragg in the same condition you left. Got that? Now, let's go inside and I'll show you the map and the plan. As I told Ace, we're up against at least a dozen Gumbahs…"

"Gumbahs?" the Batman asked. "Let's see, we've taken on Pashtuns, Tajiks, Uzbeks, Chechens, Sunnis, Kurds, and I don't know how many other tribes. What's a Gumbah?"

"The Mafia, from the DiGrigoria crime family here in Chicago," he said as he laid several maps on the table in the small airport conference room. The others gathered around as he began pointing out locations on the map. "Anyway, Scalese and his people are supposed to be coming in from the North parking lot, we're supposed to be coming in from the South one, and meet them in the picnic area in the middle, where we'll exchange Linda's daughter for some documents."

"Ain't nobody gonna do what they said they're gonna do, are they?" Koz asked.

"That's a good assumption. There's eight of us, so we'll deploy in four two-man fire teams. Ernie, you come with me and take one of the ghillie suits. You're too big to hide behind a tree. We'll set up in the woods between the picnic area and the North lot. Koz, take one of the M-110s. You and Batman find a good firing position along the east edge of the North parking lot, where you can cover it and the trailheads there. Chester, you take the other M-110 and do the same on the edge of the South lot. Find a spot on the edge of the woods where you can cover the vehicles, the south trailhead, and the parking lot entrance. Linda will go with you, and I want the two of you in ghillie suits as well, since you'll be by yourselves down there. Linda, if there are problems, curl up in a ball and don't move. You'll be invisible in that thing. Take one of the night vision goggles and you can spot for Chester. Sooner or later, they'll make a play for our SUVs. When they do, Chester, take them out."

"But won't they be bringing Ellie to the picnic area?" Linda asked. "I want…"

"I doubt Scalese will take her there. He isn't planning to exchange anything; so if he brings Ellie here at all, she'll stay inside one of their cars in the North lot. Frankly, that's where she'll be safest anyway," he said, thinking that was the last place he wanted her to be. Linda looked at him, and it was clear she didn't like the idea. "Don't worry," he added. "I'll get her back, Linda." He turned toward the others and added, "That's the mission. Everybody got that?"

"Isolate, rescue, and destroy?" Koz asked nonchalantly.

"Yes, but before you do, we need to know if they have Ellie in one of the vehicles. Be prepared to take out their personnel who come in on foot, on my command. Otherwise, everyone stay crusty, observe and report. Ernie and I will take up a position northeast of the picnic area, where we can cover it and the trails coming in from the North lot. Ace, you and Vinnie do the same on the south side, where you can move north and support us, or go back south to support Chester, depending on how Scalese positions his men. Questions?" he asked as he looked around from face to face.

"Who's this Scalese?" Koz asked.

"Tony Scalese. He's an underboss in the DiGrigoria crime family, a big guy with weight lifter shoulders and a bigger mouth, and I'm told he likes to use a knife."

"Then, I expect you'll be taking one of ours?" Vinnie smiled.

"I expect I just might," Burke smiled back.

"For the record, are there any Rules of Engagement?" Ace asked.

"What I expect to find out there tonight are middle-aged city hoods wearing street shoes and sports coats, armed mostly with semi-automatic handguns and shotguns, maybe a few automatic rifles, and commercial two-way radios. I expect them to come walking up the trails with big flashlights, swatting mosquitoes, stumbling over tree roots, and getting whacked by branches." Bob paused to look around the table and saw his men smiling and shaking their heads. "I know, I know, it hardly seems fair, does it? You'll know them when you see them. When you do, put them down, hard, and with 'extreme prejudice.' Head shots, if you can. They wanted a war, and they're about to get one."

Vinnie turned toward Ernie Travers. "You got any problem with that, Mr. Chicago Police Detective?" He asked. "You *do* understand what he's telling us to do, don't you?"

"Oh, yeah, I understand," Travers answered. "I'm fine with it, and I suspect the brass downtown will be fine with it too, except the ones on their payroll."

"God, don't you love a Chicago cop?" Koz laughed.

"This one happens to be an MP Full Colonel, in the Reserves anyway. Back in the day, he ran some of the POW stockades behind us in Iraq, so he understands what we do. I'm sure Scalese is bringing his whole crew tonight. He thinks it's only Linda and me, maybe a few friends and crazies, and he's out to send a message. Unfortunately, for him, he doesn't know about you guys."

"I doubt he knows about you either, but we'll be sure to send flowers," the Batman said.

"Don't get cocky. We could still be outnumbered two or even three to one in places. They're out to kill us, and they've shown no hesitancy to do exactly that so far. Tonight, however, we have them on *our* ground, in *our* kind of war, and we're going to kill them first, kill all of them. If anybody has any problem with that, stay here with the airplane."

"Negatory, Sir, we're all in," came the unanimous reply.

"Good, and I don't expect them to have any night vision gear or any trained shooters. That's *our* game, not theirs, and they're going to pay for it."

"What about their command-and-control?" Chester asked.

"Scalese will be 100% in charge of his people, and I doubt he's very good at sharing or delegating. So far, all I've seen are cheap, commercial, Motorola 'walkie-talkie' radios, and no night vision optics. Once we take out their communications, they'll be like a bunch of overweight Boy Scouts stumbling around in the woods, blind and lost."

"That should be no problem, Sir. I brought one of our tactical jamming units," Chester piped up. "I'll scan the commercial channels. When I pick them up, we can shut down their radios and cell phones. They'll suddenly find no bars."

"Perfect. Nothing like finding yourself in the deep, dark woods with a dead radio to shake up a city boy. Look, guys," he concluded, his eyes moving from face to face. "Don't underestimate them. They've already killed three people, plus my wife…"

"Angie?" Linda asked in shock. "My God, they killed Angie?"

"Jeez, why didn't you say something?" Vinnie asked.

"Now we understand," Ace said with a solemn nod to the others. "You can count on us."

"We'll talk about that later. Our primary objective tonight is to get Linda's daughter back safe and sound, put them all down, and have no casualties on our end. They'll be easy to spot. Keep your cover, be aware 360, and stay in contact. There's no reason to get up close and personal with them. We'll take them all out in the woods, in the dark, or in the parking lots with the long guns. That's my plan. If you see anyone else out there, especially a cop, that's a fight we don't want. Report and back away. Anyone else you bump into who is carrying a gun, put them down hard. In the end, none of them are leaving here alive. On a personal point though, Scalese is mine. Everybody got that?"

At 10:55 p.m., the Parker Woods Forest Preserve North parking lot was empty. It sat at the end of a long, curved service road. There was a chain stretching across the entrance, padlocked to two stout, concrete posts, both of which bore large red-and-white signs that said "No Entry after Dark." The parking lot formed a gentle arc along with the tree line, thirty feet away. It was freshly paved and striped, and featured a string of tall, sodium vapor streetlights. Even though the park itself was closed, the lights remained on all night. They did a fine job of illuminating the paved parking areas, but the eerie, yellow-white cones of light they cast ended at the tree line. Beyond that, the dense woods lay in complete darkness.

Traffic on the surrounding roads was light at that hour. A small convoy of two Lincoln Town Cars, a Continental, and a Mercedes, led by Tony Scalese's pale gold Lexus turned off Route 53 at the Irving Park Road interchange and headed east. Scalese drove and Jimmy DiCiccio sat in the front passenger seat next to his boss, with his own .357-Magnum Colt Python revolver and Scalese's prized Lupara double-barreled sawed-off shotgun lying in his lap. It was handmade in Sicily and measured only eighteen inches long. Tony's Uncle brought it back with him from the Old Country. The Lupara had been the weapon of choice for close-in killing and settling grudges in the hills above Palermo, Messina, and Catania for more than a century.

In the back seat of the Lexus sat a very unhappy Lawrence Greenway, a thoroughly terrified Patsy Evans, and Linda Sylvester's daughter Ellie. Patsy had her arms wrapped around the little girl, holding her close and as far away from Greenway as she could. Scalese glanced in his rear view mirror and saw Greenway staring out his window, chin up, detached, and pretending not to care. That was fine with him, Scalese decided. He spent most of the late afternoon on the telephone calling in various crews of "made men" from Salvatore DiGrigoria's organization, exercising IOUs, making promises, and renting a few others, and the five cars carried eighteen of the best gunmen in Chicago. Nine, plus him and Jimmy DiCiccio, were headed for the North lot, while seven more headed for the South lot. Scalese smiled. All were stone-cold killers, and that smartass little prick Burke would never know what hit him. Tonight, the "telephone guy" would find out what it felt like to go to war against a freakin' *real* army.

When they neared the North entrance to the Parker Woods Forest Preserve, Scalese slowed and reached for the Motorola Talkabout two-way radio sitting on the console between his seat and DiCiccio's. He keyed the mic and called one of his Lieutenants, Eddie Fanucci, three cars back. "Yo, Eddie, it's me. You keep drivin' east and circle around to the South lot, like I showed you on the map. Junior, you follow him. You other two morons follow me," he said as he turned off into the North lot service road. He heard a string of, "Gotcha, Tony," and, "Yeah, okay," as the two cars continued east. "You got ten minutes to get your asses down there and get in position," Scalese added. "Then we all move in."

"Yeah," "Right," "Got it," and "Okay," he heard back and smiled to himself, thinking, "This is gonna be good!"

Bob Burke and Ernie Travers lay in the woods near the northeast corner of the picnic area, less than two hundred yards from the North parking lot and one hundred feet from the picnic pavilion. They were nestled in the bushes between the two winding, gravel trails that came in from the North lot. Bob had an unobstructed view of both trails and the woods beyond, while Ernie faced the other way, watching the raised, white-painted pavilion and the open area around it. Underneath the thick ghillie suit, Travers looked like another bump on the forest floor, while Burke lay under one of the camouflage poncho liners. In the dark forest, one of Scalese's men could've stepped on either of them and still not known they were there. Travers wore night vision goggles, and they all had body armor and a tactical harness loaded with ammunition, water, and a Beretta with silencer. Bob carried one of the new SCAR assault rifles with a night vision scope and noise suppressor. Travers said he was not very good with a rifle, so he chose the Benelli shotgun. "Being an old Chicago cop, you can't beat a 12-gauge for crowd control, can you?" he said as he loaded shells into the receiver, and finally jacked one into the chamber. "The Chicago Police Department — bringing you peaceful conventions since 1968."

They lay there for ten minutes, until Bob Burke heard Chester's first report on the tactical radio net.

"Ghost, Chester, I'm picking up chatter on one of the commercial bands. I make it five, I say again, five units, using first names like Eddie, Tony, and Junior. They aren't using anything close to proper 'radio telephone procedure;' so they aren't cops, fire, or the Feds."

"10-4, sounds like our guys."

"They're dividing their force. I say again, dividing. Sounds like two cars are headed around to the south lot, while the base group of two or three is coming in as you expected."

"Ghost, to ya'll. Everyone copy that? Looks like they split their forces. That's their first mistake, over."

"Ghost, Koz. Now wait a damn minute, ain't that what Bobby Lee done at Chancellorsville, and that sure weren't no mistake."

"That guy ain't Bobby Lee," Vinnie broke in.

"When did you start to read?" Bob laughed. "Ace, you and Vinnie drop back and support Chester on his left. When they leave their vehicles, give me a head count. When they're halfway to the SUVs, we'll cut their communications and neutralize. Then fall back here."

"Roger that."

When Tony Scalese found the North parking lot entry road blocked by a heavy chain hanging between two solid-looking concrete posts and a sign that read, "No Entry — Park Closed," he simply ignored them. He bounced his Lexus over the curb, through the grass, and around the right-side post. The other two cars followed as he returned to the service drive and continued into the empty North lot. He parked the Lexus in front of a sign, which read, "Picnic Pavilion" with an arrow pointing toward the first trail. The other two cars pulled in next to him. Their doors opened and his men got out, laughing and stretching. Most carried one or two large handguns, but one of his men had an AR-15 semi-automatic rifle balanced casually across his shoulders, while two others carried sawed-off shotguns, like their boss.

Johnny G. pulled his pants up over his ample gut and shouted toward the woods, "Okay, you assholes, come out, come out, wherever you are!"

"Yeah, Tony, where are these stiffs?" another man joined in as he checked the load in his big, chrome-plated, "Dirty Harry" .44-caliber automatic. "I got a pinochle game to get back to."

Dressed in suits or sports coats and slacks, they all wore white or pastel-colored dress shirts open at the neck, with chains and gold "bling" hanging around their necks, and leather street shoes. The clothes were more appropriate for a Saturday night at the Italian-American Bocce Club in Cicero, than a walk in the woods, as they would soon find out.

Scalese opened his car door and joined them. As he did, he heard

Greenway open his rear door too. Scalese's head snapped around. "You ain't goin' nowhere, Doc," he told him. "You're stayin' right here, all three of you; and Jimmy's stayin' here with you."

"Anthony, why did you bring me along, if you had no intention of allowing me to help?" Greenway asked indignantly as he swatted a mosquito. "I have better things to do with my time."

"No you don't. When I'm done with your friend Burke, you and I have some unfinished business, *Larry*," Scalese told him as he reached inside his jacket pocket and pulled out a stiletto knife, watching Greenway's eyes as he flicked the blade open and held it up. As the light from the lamppost reflected off its razor-sharp edge, the doctor blinked, obviously surprised to see a stiletto in Scalese's hand. "What?" the big Italian asked him. "You thought the one you used on Burke's wife was the only one I owned? As you can see, that one has a beautiful sister."

"Tony, I don't know what you think…" Greenway began to stutter.

"Shut up! So it's 'Tony,' now, and, 'what I think?' You can get back in the car and 'think' for a while; 'cause when I get back, I'm going to use it to cut you up for fish bait, Doc."

Scalese turned toward Jimmy DiCiccio. "You stay here and watch them, Jimmy. Nobody leaves 'til I get back. Nobody."

"You got it, Boss," DiCiccio replied as he held up his .357-Magnum Colt Python revolver and motioned casually for Greenway to get back inside and close the door.

Deep in the woods between the trails, Bob Burke and Ernie Travers lay hidden, waiting.

"I haven't dressed up like this since the Advanced Course at Fort Gordon," Travers whispered.

"Bet you never wanted to, either," Bob answered as his radio earbud came alive.

"Ghost, Koz. I have three cars in the North lot — a Lexus, a Lincoln, and a Continental — and I count twelve, I say again, twelve Gumbahs getting out of the three cars. It looks like two are staying with the Lexus, one inside and one standing guard outside, but the other ten are walking toward the trailheads. The one in the lead looks big, and he has one of those Motorola walkie-talkie things. I suspect he's your man, Scalese."

"Roger that. Any sign of the little girl?"

"Negative, but I see a couple more heads in the back seat of the Lexus."

"10-4. Keep me advised. Ghost out."

The men in Scalese's other two cars slowly gathered around in a small circle, waiting impatiently for him until he walked over. "Jeez, Tony," one of them said, shifting nervously from foot to foot. "I hope this don't take too long, I really gotta pee."

"Keep your big yap shut, and spread out," Scalese snapped with cold, humorless eyes as he realized they continued to call him "Tony" and it was beginning to chafe. Well, in a few weeks it would be Boss, or even Mr. S. "Alright, those two paths lead to the picnic area. Johnny G, you take your five down that trail over there. The rest follow me. We'll meet at the Pavilion. Oh, one last thing, if you melon heads look around, you don't see Gino Santucci or Peter Fabiano here, do you?" he paused as he looked around from face to face. "They're in the hospital, both of 'em. That bastard Burke put 'em there. He busted 'em up, good, so don't think this is gonna be easy. But when we find him, nobody touches him. He's mine!"

With his Lupara dangling in his right hand and the Motorola two-way radio in the left, Scalese turned and set off through the ankle-high grass toward the trailhead with five men following him. The other group veered off through the parking lot toward the second trailhead one hundred yards further to the east. There were large signs at each trailhead with arrows that pointed toward the 'Picnic Area.' When he reached the edge of the woods, Scalese signaled both groups to stop. He picked up the Motorola, keyed the mic, and asked, "Eddie, you guys ready?"

"Yeah, Tony, we're at the entrance to the South lot. I see two big Ford Explorers parked in there. What you want us to do?"

"Take 'em out, and anybody else who's down there. That's what I'm payin' you assholes for. Now, go!" Scalese ordered as he lowered the radio and signaled for both of his groups to start walking down the two trails.

His earbud whispered to Bob Burke again. "Ghost, Chester. South lot, I have two incoming cars. They stopped at the entrance, but now they're heading for the SUVs."

"Chester, Ace here. I'm tracking them too. When they stop and get out, I'll take the group in the lead car. You take the rear car. We'll start on the edges and meet in the middle."

"Ace, Chester. Roger that. Age before beauty, I'll wait for you to engage."

"Chester and Ace, figure four Gumbahs per car. Once they're on foot and closing on the SUVs, Chester, you commence action by jamming their radios, then you both fire at will. We'll wait on your command, and then open fire up here too. Got that Koz?"

"Roger that. I'll take out the guard on Chester's command, and then engage anyone else in the parking lot."

"Linda, Ghost. You stay behind Chester. He's the best shot in the unit. Ghost out."

It had rained earlier that evening. The grass around the parking lots and the thick bed of plants and mulch covering the forest floor were still wet, but the trails themselves consisted of a thick layer of coarse gravel. When heavy men in leather-soled street shoes walked on it, the gravel crunched beneath their shoes.

"Goddamn, Tony, these are the new shoes I got in Naples last year," one of his men said as he hung back in the thick, wet grass complaining. "I didn't know we wuz goin' on no freakin' nature hike."

"Yeah, and these are my good pants. I didn't expect to be doing this shit, either," another voice further back said.

The others broke into a burst of confident laughter, but Scalese didn't find it amusing. "Shudup and do what I told ya!" he turned and snarled angrily at both of them.

Several of the others stopped at the dark wood line and squinted, trying to see into the dense underbrush. "Wuddaya think's in there?" one of them asked. "You think there's any snakes or bears or other shit?"

Scalese opened the breech of his sawed-off shotgun, saw that both chambers were loaded, and snapped it shut loudly. "If I hear any more crap out of youse, I'll shove this Lupara up your asses and pull the trigger, then you won't need to worry about no snakes! Now move!"

Bob's earbud came alive again, with "Ghost, Koz. My kid's Cub Scout Den's more organized than these idiots, and they make a lot less noise. I count ten, I say again ten, coming your way in groups of five each down the two trails. Trust me, you'll hear them."

"10-4."

"You want us to redeploy and come in behind?"

"Negative. Stay where you are. I want to draw them all the way in. You two take out the guard. When we engage here, I'll take down the ones I see, and the rest should go running back to their cars. If I'm right, you'll have a 'target-rich environment' very shortly."

"That's why we came. 10-4, Koz out."

CHAPTER TWENTY-SEVEN

"We screwed around here long enough," Scalese snapped at the four men behind him. "Let's go," he pointed toward the path with his Lupara and marched confidently into the dark woods. The others quickly followed, trying to keep up as their leather-soled shoes slipped on the wet grass and gravel. Confidence is a fickle thing, however. The pale-yellow glow from the sodium vapor streetlights ended at the tree line, making the woods beyond seem even darker and more menacing, the closer they got.

Scalese's feet understood, even if he didn't. The moment he entered the woods, his steps became halting, until the feet stopped moving altogether. It was as if the dark, damp trees were sucking the willpower out of him. His eyes had not yet adjusted to the dark, and the best he could see were the dim shapes of nearby trees and bushes, while a warm, musty dampness wrapped around him like an old, wet blanket. The four men behind him seemed to have the same problem. When Scalese stopped walking with no warning, they piled into him and each other as if they were in a Three Stooges short.

"Jeezus, ain't nobody got a freakin' flashlight," one of the men behind him grumbled.

"Shut up!" Scalese growled angrily. "And spread out, like I told you morons. Ain't you ever seen no war movies? You never want to bunch up. So get your fat asses off the trail."

"Christ, Tony, it's all mud and crap out there, and I can't see a damned thing."

"And who's da moron, anyway?" a muffled voice asked. "We didn't pick a freakin' place like dis for no meet."

"Shut up and do what I tell ya!" Scalese ordered as he set off down the path again, his men cussing as they crashed through the underbrush behind him.

"Chester, Ace here," Bob Burke heard. "I have a gaggle of Gumbahs in the South lot. They're out of their cars and all bunched up like the Iraqi National Guard on field maneuvers. I count eight men on foot approaching our SUVs."

"Roger that. Prepare to engage on my mark. The group up here is bumbling and stumbling through the woods and finally coming in sight. Am acquiring targets..."

"**Yo, Tony,**" Scalese heard over his Motorola radio. "It's Eddie down in the South lot. We got a big problem, here. These two black SUVs belong to the goddamn Chicago cops."

"The Chicago cops?" Scalese asked, suddenly concerned.

"Yeah, the license plates, the lettering on the sides, even the light bars on top — it's the goddamn CPD. Maybe it's their Tactical Unit. You didn't say nuttin' about us shootin' it out wit no cops. My cousin Rico's wit dem."

"Wait a minute, let me think," Scalese slowed down again. "You sure?"

"No question. But dere ain't nobody here. Wuddaya want me to do?"

Through the pale-green glow of the night vision scope of his own SCAR Mk 17 assault rifle, Bob watched the surprisingly clear shapes of five men emerge through the trees and tall bushes on each side of the trail. In the lead came the broad shoulders of Tony Scalese himself. As much as he'd love to put him down first, the underboss could wait.

"This is Ghost, pick your targets," he whispered calmly into his chin mic as he placed the crosshairs on the head of the Gumbah who appeared to be farthest away to the left. "Chester, how we doing down there?"

"This is about as good as it gets," Chester answered. "They suddenly stopped short of the SUVs. Looks like one of them's talking on the radio."

"Roger. On my mark, jam their radio and phones… Five, four, three, two, one, now!"

Scalese raised his two-way radio and was about to reply to Eddie Fanucci's question, when a loud squeal suddenly hit his ear. "Ah! Goddamn!" Scalese growled. "Eddie, what the…"

In the South lot, Fanucci experienced the same problem. With his radio to his ear, the blast of static cut into his head like a migraine. "Christ!" he exclaimed as he dropped the radio on the asphalt, where it broke into a dozen pieces.

Bob Burke calmly pulled the trigger and watched the impact of the 7.62-millimeter NATO round through his scope. This rifle was a new model he hadn't fired before; nor did he have the opportunity to 'zero' this specific one. As a result, the bullet struck perhaps an inch high and right of where he aimed, not that he would complain about a near-perfect shot under the circumstances. After all, a headshot was a headshot, and the target dropped like an overweight sack of potatoes on the forest floor, dead. The new SCAR featured very little recoil and deadly accuracy. With its noise suppressor, it was unlikely that at this distance anyone standing ten or even five feet away from his target would understand what they heard, unless the barrel was pointed directly at them, in which case what they heard wouldn't matter. Bob quickly traversed the rifle barrel and found his next target.

Jimmy DiCiccio leaned back against the right front fender of Tony's Lexus and paused to look up at the stars. The two groups of "family" gunmen were gone now, having disappeared down the trails into the dark Forest Preserve. That was fine with Jimmy, and good riddance. He was painfully overdue for a left hip replacement, and entirely too old to play hide-and-seek in the woods chasing an ex-soldier and one of the girls from the office. He had seen Linda Sylvester at the front desk often enough to know she seemed like a nice kid. So did the one in the backseat of the Lexus with the little girl. Every now and then, DiCiccio turned his head and glared at the doctor. DiCiccio kept his Colt Python revolver out, making sure the 'Doc' saw it too. DiCiccio had also worked security in the CHC building off and on, and he had heard the stories. He was a good Catholic. If it were his decision, he'd march that evil prick Greenway into the trees, cap one behind his ear, and never shed a tear. He did that to plenty of other guys for Old Sal, but the truth was there was already too much blood on Jimmy's hands. He respected Mr. D, but they were both getting a little old for this stuff. He didn't think much of Tony Scalese, however. If Tony ended up in charge... well, then it would be time for Jimmy to dust off those retirement brochures for Miami Beach and say goodbye to the Chicago winters.

He pulled a pack of cigarettes from his jacket pocket, bent down, and lit one with his old Zippo lighter. He took a deep drag and was actually beginning to enjoy the crickets and the other earthy sounds of the forest, when a 7.62-millimeter rifle bullet hit him in the cheek and blew on through, splattering his brains, blood, and half his head across the front windshield of the Lexus.

Inside the car, Patsy Evans screamed and covered Ellie's eyes, and Lawrence Greenway's mouth dropped open. He was a doctor and had personally covered the late-night shift in his inner city clinics on many occasions. The sight of blood and gore like this, even a lot of it, didn't usually bother him. However, the shock of seeing old Jimmy's blood and brains suddenly running down the Lexus's front windshield was a "game changer" for him, as they say.

"Ghost, Koz. The guard's down. Want us to take the car?"

"Not yet. The others will be coming back and you need to re-target to the trailheads. After you knock them down, have the Batman take the Lexus while you provide cover. Copy?"

"Roger."

"Ghost, Ace. One down and two to go on my side."

"Ghost, Chester. Two down and two to go on mine, but the rest took cover behind the SUVs with Ace's leftovers." Keeping his own quick body count, that meant six down and twelve to go, including Scalese.

"Chester, Ace. They won't stay there long. I have a good angle. I'll see if I can skip a couple of rounds underneath and flush them out."

"Go for it, but don't hit the SUVs. We'll need them."

As he talked, Burke put the crosshairs of his rifle on another head, aiming slightly lower and left, and pulled the trigger. The result was the same. The second Gumbah toppled over backwards into the bushes with a loud grunt. Both of the gunmen he put down had been walking behind Scalese. As he watched, the big Italian continued to try to fix his radio, oblivious to what was going on around him, or that two of his men behind him were now down. He finally screamed at the radio, and threw it against a tree in frustration.

As Bob turned his aim on one of the two men still standing behind Scalese, two loud Booms went off behind him as Ernie Travers opened up on the other trail with his Benelli 12-gauge shotgun.

"Jeez, Ernie!" Bob turned his head away and complained, as the shotgun blasts broke his concentration and sent his rifle shot high and wide. Out of the corner of his eye, however, he saw two dark shapes go down from Travers' buckshot. That made eight, he figured, but the advantage of surprise went down with them.

"Yeah, but even I can't miss with this thing. Damn, this is fun,

Bob!" Travers laughed.

Through the scope, he watched as Scalese and his two remaining street thugs tried to squeeze behind some of the thicker tree trunks. In a dense forest like this, sound ricochets. They twisted and turned, but could not tell where the gunshots were coming from. To make matters worse, they could now hear a fusillade of gunfire coming from the South parking lot — unsilenced, large-caliber pistols from the sound of it, which meant his crew.

When one of the Gumbahs behind Scalese peeked around the trunk of a thick oak, Burke took him out with another clean head shot. The man toppled over backward, landing spread-eagled on the ground near Tony's feet.

Scalese twisted around and looked back up the trail, convinced that the gunshot must have come from the parking lot behind him. Confused, he pulled his cell phone from his pocket, turned it on, and looked at the display, but there was nothing there — no bars, no apps, no nothing, only a blank screen. He was stunned. Even the goddamned cell phone was working against him now. In a fit of rage, he smashed it against a tree with a loud "crunch."

Finally, he turned toward his last remaining gunman. "Corso," he called out sharply. "This way, come on! We gotta get to that picnic area and find some cover, quick."

"Like hell, I ain't goin' nowhere," Corso answered. He was lying flat on the wet, muddy ground, looking around at the growing collection of bodies near him, as he crawled behind the biggest tree he could find. "You and your freakin' big ideas, Tony!"

"Well, we can't stay here. I think they're shooting at us from the parking lot. Maybe we can work our way south and meet up with Eddie Fanucci and his boys."

Scalese tried to look through the dark shadows to the other trail, where he expected to see his second team coming in from the North lot. "Johnny!" he shouted and waited for a reply that never came. "Johnny G., you over there?"

Finally, a familiar voice called back to him. "He's down, Tony. It was that freakin' shotgun." Scalese knew that was one of Johnny G's crew talking. "And he's hit bad," the man shouted out. "Christ, he's bleedin' like a stuck pig. That bastard Greenway's a doc, ain't he? He still back in your Lexus? Well, we're gonna drag Johnny and Petey back there."

"No, no! You need to keep heading for the picnic area… You'll pay for this, you rats, the both 'a youse," Scalese barked, but they weren't listening to him any longer. "Corso! Come on, let's go."

"Not me, Tony. Those guys are right. I'm goin' back to the car with them."

"You son of a bitch," Scalese screamed. As Bob watched through his night vision scope, Corso crawled away through the brush, trying to find the trail that led back to the parking lot. Bob took aim, but before he could shoot, Scalese stepped from behind his tree, took two steps toward his own man, and fired both barrels of the sawed-off shotgun into Corso at point-blank range. The flaming-red blast from the 12-gauge Lupara bounced Corso off the ground and almost cut him in half.

Well, Bob thought as he watched Corso's lifeless body lying in the bushes, that makes eleven down and seven to go — the two heading back up the trail here, the four pinned down behind the SUVs in the South lot, and Tony Scalese.

"Koz, Ghost," he called, knowing he should warn the team covering the North lot. "Two Gumbahs are retreating back up the trail toward you."

"Copy that."

"Ghost, Ace here. We put a couple of rounds under the car and they took off like quail flushed from a Nebraska cornfield. Chester and I dropped two of them, but the last two got away. We might have winged one, but as far as I can see, they're still runnin' up the entry road beyond the streetlights. Do you want us to go after them?"

"Negative. Let 'em go. They aren't worth the risk, and I don't care if someone makes it back to tell the tale. Chester, disable their two cars, then you and Linda go back to the SUVs and get ready to leave. Ace, you and Vinnie come back up to the campground, south side, ASAP."

"Roger that."

Now, it was Big Tony S's turn, Bob decided.

The evening had not exactly gone the way Tony Scalese planned, he thought, as he bent down behind a tree and reloaded the Lupara. He brought eighteen men with him. As best he could tell, over half of them were already down, maybe all of them; and he didn't have a clue what hit them. No, that wasn't true. It was that bastard Burke, the little "telephone" twerp. Other than those two shotgun blasts and a lot of moans and groans, he hadn't seen or heard a goddamned thing. Were they using silencers? That had to be it. Even so, who could make those kind of shots at night, out in the woods? Nobody he knew. The bastard wasn't human. As for Eddie Fanucci and his boys in the south lot? With their radios out, who knew? Scalese was completely in the dark, literally and figuratively now. All the boys he brought with him were "made men," tough street soldiers whom he had begged and borrowed from one DiGrigoria crew or another. Most of them were now dead or running back to the cars, and the entire operation had blown up in his face. There would be hell to pay in the morning. When Mr. D called him on the carpet to answer for all of this, Tony knew who the last casualty would be. It would be him.

Scalese knew he should never have taken out his frustrations on Louie Corso, but the dumb bastard wouldn't follow orders. The truth was, if Scalese could have hit those other two with the Lupara or the Colt .45, he would have done that too. Unfortunately, by the time he reloaded the shotgun, those cowards were long gone, disappearing up the trail and leaving him alone in these wet, stinking, goddamned woods.

"Ghost, Koz. We put down the two coming back to the North lot from the trailhead dragging two other guys. While we were doing that, somebody got out of the back seat of that Lexus, got in the front, and is driving away. You want me to stop them, over?"

Bob thought about it for a brief second and answered, "No. Cease Fire. The girl might be in the car, and I can't take that chance. Let them go."

Scalese figured his best shot was to work his way down to the South parking lot. He bent over as low as he could and crept slowly through the trees, hoping he might be able to sneak away and find Fanucci's boys. Unfortunately, the farther he went into the woods, the underbrush and the trees only got thicker and thicker, snagging his new sharkskin sports jacket and scratching his face. He tried to bull his through the bushes; but he was making more noise than a rampaging moose in heat, so he stopped. His mind immediately conjured up that scene in *Lord of the Rings* again, when the trees came alive and closed in on the evil, white-robed wizard, and a shiver ran down his back. That had to be it, he thought. It was the goddamned trees! They were creeping him out again.

Every twenty feet or so, he stopped and listened intently for any sound, but all he heard were the goddamn crickets and the mosquitoes buzzing around his ears. Off to his right, through a gap in the trees, he finally saw the grassy picnic area in the pale, white light of a quarter moon, so he set off in that direction. Maybe he could work his way around the edge and find the path to the South lot. Yeah, that could work. His luck might've run bad, but that didn't mean Eddie Fanucci and his crew weren't down there waiting for him at that very minute. Then, he'd get them organized and come back up here. Yeah! He still had his Lupara, his Colt .45, and his stiletto, and there would be payback. Nobody could do this to Tony Scalese and live to get away with it, especially not that little prick Burke.

He finally reached the edge of the picnic area and looked at it through the trees. He saw a tall, white pavilion standing in the center, with picnic tables scattered around it under the maple and pine trees that dotted the open area, casting deep shadows in the moonlight. The pavilion itself had a steep cedar shingle roof, a tall cupola, and a raised, wooden dance floor with a wooden railing, which now lay in deep shadow. Still, it was dead quiet and the picnic area appeared to be empty. No time to stop now, he thought, so he decided to make a break for it. He got to his feet, lowered his head, and set off toward the pavilion at a dead run. When he reached it, he tried to take the stairs two at a time and jump onto the raised wooden dance platform, but his middle-aged legs were too tired and wouldn't jump that high anymore. The toe of his shoe caught the edge of the top stair and he stumbled, crashing painfully onto the dance floor. As he did, he lost his grip on the shotgun and heard it skitter away into the darkness.

Scalese was a big man, and the deck was hard. He lay motionless for a moment, trying to catch his breath, before he finally rolled over and got up shakily onto his hands and knees. He crawled slowly to the closest of the decorative, wooden posts that surrounded the platform and paused to look back to the wood line. Straining to see into the dark, he saw nothing and heard even less. That only made Scalese more and more nervous. He knew that prick Burke was out there somewhere, and he felt naked without his shotgun. At his size, Tony was used to dealing with problems up close with his fists or maybe a knife. He had never been a very good shot with a handgun; but with the Lupara, he didn't have to be. Close enough was good enough with a 12-gauge scattergun.

Finally, he turned and looked around the dark platform, certain that the sawed-off shotgun lay somewhere on the other side of the dance floor. There was a thick, wooden post in the center, which carried most of the weight of the heavy roof. He figured the shotgun must have slid behind it, so he crawled across the pitch-black platform, feeling his way across the floor with both hands out ahead of him like a blind man navigating by braille, hoping his fingers would find it. Finally, his right hand touched the shotgun's barrel and he breathed a sigh of relief. However, when he wrapped his fingers around the short handgrip and pulled up, the shotgun wouldn't move.

"Looking for something, Tony?" A voice spoke to him from the darkness. It was Burke! His boot rested on top of the Lupara, pinning it down.

Scalese looked up and saw Burke's dim outline a foot or two away, leaning casually against the pavilion's center post. He was nearly invisible, dressed in black from head to foot, with a black ski mask, black gloves, and a strange-looking contraption on his head. The bastard must be some kind of Ninja with goddamn night vision goggles. No wonder he took his crew apart so easily. Worse, he held some kind of high-tech automatic rifle in his gloved hands. The Italian was much larger than Burke, almost twice his size, more muscular, and with broad shoulders. However, on his knees with a gun pointed at his head, there wasn't much Scalese could do about it. He could feel the .45-caliber Colt tucked in the small of his back. Maybe, if he could work his right hand around his hip and grab it, he might stand a chance. Then, to his surprise, Burke took his foot off the shotgun.

"Is this what you want?" Burke asked as he took a step back, inviting him to try.

"What's the trick? I go for it, and you shoot me in the head?"

"Nope," he answered as he lowered the rifle. He also pulled off the night vision goggles, the headset, and the ski mask, and tossed them all behind him, too.

Scalese still wasn't buying it. Ever so slowly, his fingers closed around the Lupara's handgrip and he stood up, straightening himself to his full height until he towered over Burke. A thin smile finally crossed Scalese's lips. "You're a fool," he mumbled between clenched teeth. The little man had thrown away his advantage, and he had no idea who he was dealing with. Scalese's smile slowly faded and his eyes turned cold and hard, as he raised the sawed-off shotgun with his right hand and pulled back on its twin hammers with his left, intending to cut Burke in half with a blast from both barrels. However, as Scalese swung the Lupara around, Burke stepped in close, grabbed the barrel, twisted, and snatched the shotgun out of Tony's hands. Burke then tossed it behind him with the other gear, as if Scalese were a naughty child playing with a dangerous toy. With a lightning-fast move, Burke then stepped in even closer and slammed his elbow across the bridge of Scalese's nose. The big Italian's head snapped back, and Burke immediately brought the elbow down on Scalese's left collarbone, breaking it with an audible 'snap!'

Scalese tried to respond. He balled up his right fist and took a swing at Burke's head, but it was too little and he was too slow. Burke caught Scalese's right wrist, slipped under the punch, got the big man on his hip, twisting and lifting as he flipped him high in the air with apparent ease. It all happened in the blink of the eye, as Scalese crashed down on the hard wooden deck, landing on his head and left shoulder. The fall from six feet up knocked the wind out of him and left him stunned and in pain.

That was when Scalese heard several other men laughing at him from the deep shadows. "Krav Maga?" one of them asked, referring to the deadly Israeli hand-to-hand fighting system, at which Bob Burke was an expert. "Nice to see you've been working on your game, Major."

"Don't screw with him, Ghost. Kill him and let's get out of here," another added.

"Not yet," Burke stepped over Scalese and searched his pockets. He pulled out the stiletto, flicked the blade open, and closely examined the blade. "Is this what you used to kill my wife, Tony?" he asked as he tossed the knife behind him with the other stuff.

"That wasn't me. It was Greenway. I had nothin' to do with that." Scalese shook his head and tried to clear the cobwebs, only to feel a sharp, stabbing pain in his chest and shoulder.

"What about the little girl? You had nothing to do with that either?"

Scalese looked up at him defiantly and said nothing; so Burke placed his boot on the big man's upper left chest, where the broken collarbone was located, and pressed down.

"Ah! You son of a bitch!" Scalese screamed at him and tried to push the boot away, but it wouldn't budge.

"Where is she, Tony?" He lifted the boot from Scalese's chest. "I can play this all night, but you can't; you'll bleed to death internally. Tell me where the girl is and I'll let you walk out of here. That's the best offer you're going to get."

Scalese's head dropped back to the deck. "She's in the back seat of my Lexus in the North lot with Patsy Evans and Greenway," he finally said. "Don't worry, my guy Jimmy's guarding them. I'm not that stupid."

"Ah, crap," one of the other voices called out from the darkness. "We put the guard down and somebody drove the Lexus out of the parking lot a couple of minutes ago."

Scalese looked up at him and laughed. "I guess you shot the wrong man, Burke. Jimmy was there to watch Greenway, not the girls."

"All right, where did he take her? Back to the CHC office?"

"Probably. If he's running, he's going to need a lot more than my freakin' Lexus," Scalese conceded painfully. "I think he's got a bunch a' money squirreled away somewhere in the building, so that's where he'll go." Scalese rolled over and slowly got to his feet, bent over like an old man, his left arm hanging limp. "One thing though, when you get the girl, do us both a favor and kill him."

"Don't worry, Tony, if he's touched her I will; and then I'll be back for you," he said as he turned to walk away. "Count on it."

As he did, Scalese's right hand slipped behind his back and came out holding his Colt .45 automatic. The big Italian smiled as he raised it toward Burke, knowing that the powerful handgun would blow a hole through the little man big enough for him to put his fist through. That was when the loud Boom! of a 12-gauge shotgun lit up the night. The blast caught Scalese in his right shoulder, blew the .45 out of his hand, and nearly took his arm off. Scalese staggered backward as a second blast hit him in his chest and sent him tumbling over the wooden railing. He ended up lying on the ground below, eyes wide open, looking up at the surrounding canopy of trees above him, very much dead.

Bob turned and saw Ernie Travers step out of the deep shadows holding the Benelli shotgun. "I guess you really don't have to be a very good shot with that thing, do you?" Bob asked.

"Nope. Shotguns or horseshoes — close enough is close enough," Travers grinned as he jacked in a fresh round. "You know, we really gotta get some of these." Satisfied, Travers turned and walked back to the tree line to retrieve the ghillie suit and the rest of the army gear he left there. He picked it up and returned to the pavilion, expecting to find Bob and his men standing there; but the dance floor was empty, and Bob and the others were gone. Travers stepped to the railing and looked out into the clearing that surrounded the pavilion. Except for Tony Scalese's body, it was empty too. To the south, he heard the muffled sound of boots running away down a gravel trail.

"Goddamnit, Bob," he shouted as loud as he could. "You can't go in there alone," he added as he set off after them at a dead run.

CHAPTER TWENTY-EIGHT

As he, Ace, and Vinnie ran down the path toward the South parking lot, Bob put on his headset and radioed, "Koz, stay put, we'll come around and pick you up in five. Chester, pack up. We're headed your way and then we're out of here."

Bob turned to Ace and Vinnie and told them, "All that fireworks is bound to draw attention, so we need to double time back to the SUVs." When they reached the South parking lot, Chester and Linda had already packed their gear and were throwing it in the back of one of the Chicago Police Department SUVs as Bob and the other two came out of the woods.

When Linda saw three men in camouflage gear carrying automatic rifles, but no six-year-old girl, she screamed, "Where's Ellie, Bob? Where's Ellie?"

"Greenway got away from the North parking lot in Scalese's gold Lexus. Scalese told us Patsy and Ellie are in the back seat."

Linda dropped to her knees shaking her head, screaming, "That bastard, that bastard! When I get my hands on Scalese... I swear, I'm going to kill him myself."

"You won't have to. He's dead. So are all the rest of them."

"But you promised me you'd get her back! God, I should have never..."

"He's headed for the CHC building, so that's where we're going. And I'll get her back, Linda, like I told you I would. Now get in the car," Slowly, as if on wooden legs, she got up, sobbing, and sat on the rear seat of the big SUV, holding her head in her hands.

That was when Ernie Travers burst out of the woods carrying his shotgun, the ghillie camouflage suit, and an armful of gear. Bob turned and looked at him, and frowned. "I didn't want you involved in the rest of this, Ernie."

"It's a little late to worry about that isn't it, Bob? I'm already 'a little bit pregnant.' Besides, you've got my two vehicles, and I've got all this gear that Ace signed for," Travers answered as he threw the Benelli and the other equipment in the back of the SUV.

Bob quickly turned to the three men around him. "Okay, Chester, do you still have the Semtex and detonators?"

"Roger that. It's in my gear bag, ready to go," Chester nodded.

"Semtex?" Ernie Travers looked askance at Bob.

"I'll explain it later, Ernie. For now, you don't want to know," Bob added

"Okay, but I'm not going; I'm staying here," Travers told him as he took off the dark overalls they gave him and he shoved them in the back of the SUV with the rest of the gear. "As soon as you guys clear the area, I'm calling it in. That way, I can feed the reporters what I want and get ahead of the story. By the time I get done, this'll look like a Mafia turf war gone bad; and believe me, Chicago's had enough of those to know what they look like. The woods are strewn with the bodies of a dozen or more gunmen from different parts of the DiGrigoria crime family, armed to the teeth, with their cars sitting in both parking lots. To cap it all off, Tony Scalese himself is lying back there by the Pavilion. Nobody's going to be looking for much more of an explanation than that."

"You're sure you can pull this off?" Bob asked.

Ernie laughed. "Who would ever believe the truth — a telephone guy, a receptionist, an old CPD cop, and a squad of Deltas from Fort Bragg cleaned out the Chicago mob?"

"Well, when you put it that way..."

"Besides, I know a couple of really good crime reporters with the *Sun Times* and *Tribune*. Between the bodies out here and the stuff they're still untangling about Bentley and the DiGrigorias, it shouldn't be hard to get all the charges against you and Linda dropped, and all the rest of it shoved off on Scalese and DiGrigoria. Now get the hell out of here, 'before I runs the lot of youse in,' as my sainted patrolman father would've said."

"Great, that solves another problem for me," Bob said as he reached into his pants pocket, pulled out the computer flash drive, and handed it to him. "The reports and stuff we printed out are in a thick manila envelope in the back seat of that old Taurus. I wasn't sure what to do with it or whom I could trust, but if your *Sun Times* and *Tribune* pals are good at forensic accounting, they should be able to milk this for a long series of articles on Organized Crime in Chicago and probably win a Pulitzer Prize. My suggestion is to give half of it to each of them, and watch the feeding frenzy. In particular, tell them to follow the links between Greenway, the DiGrigorias, Tony Scalese, and a prominent local US Attorney."

Travers looked at him for a moment, and then nodded. "In Cook County? Wouldn't surprise me one damned bit. But the Taurus? Isn't that Linda's?"

"No, we stole it from one of your lots at O'Hare, where we left her car. By the way, we're taking your two SUVs, and Linda left the keys to the Taurus in the ignition."

"Wonderful," Travers shook his head and stepped over to where Linda sat in the SUV and knelt down next to her. "You should stay here with me until the shooting stops. I can put you and your daughter in protective custody."

"Until the shooting stops?" Her eyes flashed as she reached into the SUV and pulled out one of the 9-millimeter Berettas lying in back with the other equipment, and jacked a fresh round into the chamber. "You let me know when that happens, Ernie. Until then, I'm not leaving my daughter alone with that animal Greenway for one second longer than I have to. Enough talk, let's go!" she turned toward Bob with a look of angry determination.

As he opened the driver's side door and got behind the wheel, Bob turned to Chester and said, "Take the other SUV, pick up Koz and The Batman in the north lot, and the three of you take care of that little errand we discussed before. They can provide you cover and run interference. Ace, Vinnie, and I are headed back to the CHC building in Indian Hills to make a house call on Dr. Greenway," he said as he looked at his watch. "I'm showing 23:30. I want everyone back at the airplane by 01:00. That gives both teams 90 minutes to execute before it's wheels up and back to Bragg. Chester, if it gets hairy over there, I want you to abort. I can go back and take care of that later. And Ernie, we'll leave the SUVs at the airfield. When you get a chance, check them out yourself. You might find a couple of new presents inside."

Lawrence Greenway sped through the dark, empty streets of Indian Hills in Tony Scalese's blood-spattered Lexus at over 90 miles an hour. He had used the windshield washers to get the worst of the gore off, so he could at least see to drive; but he wasn't too worried about being stopped by the town police tonight. With Chief Bentley and his nephew Bobby Joe in the morgue and the rest of the department being grilled by State Police investigators, his other 'nephews' weren't bothering anyone tonight. If they did, he held Jimmy DiCiccio's .357-Magnum Colt Python revolver in his right hand, and what would one or two more of them matter. When he ran around the car in the Forest Preserve parking lot and got behind the wheel, he saw the big pistol lying on the ground and picked it up. Now, he wasn't about to stop for anything.

In the back seat, Patsy Evans sat with her arms around a terrified Ellie

Sylvester, holding her close, trying to comfort her. "Let us go," she pleaded with him. "You don't need us."

"Oh, I *need* you more than you know, my dear. But you will. I promise you that."

"Then let her go. I'll come with you and do whatever you want... I... I won't even fight you. Please, but let her go."

"How noble of you, Patsy. But, no. You'll do that anyway; and frankly, I always prefer it when you girls fight me. I know that's how you like it too."

He raced into the Hills Business Park and was going far too fast when he turned into the CHC office-building parking lot. The Lexus bounced over the curb, lost a hubcap, and skidded to the left before he was finally able to bring it to stop in the handicapped spaces near the building's front entry. Greenway grabbed the revolver off the passenger seat and got out, leaving the engine running. He intended to be back down in a few minutes, no more, and get the hell away from the building, Indian Hills, and Chicago as quickly as he could.

Greenway pulled the rear car door open. "Get out," he looked in and shouted at Patsy.

"No!" she shouted back and clutched Ellie even tighter.

"Out, now," he ordered as he pointed the .357-Magnum Colt at Ellie and dared Patsy to keep arguing with him. There was something about looking straight down the barrel of a very large handgun like that, which sapped the courage from even the bravest. Reluctantly, Patsy edged across the seat toward him, until Greenway reached inside, grabbed her by the forearm, and dragged both her and Ellie out of the car. "You can save the petulance for later, *Patsy*. If you don't do exactly what I tell you, neither you nor the little girl leaves this building alive. Do you understand me?"

The roads leading away from the Park District Forest Preserve parking lot and the Interstate were dark and empty, until a line of police cars and ambulances raced past them in the opposite direction, lights flashing and sirens wailing. It looked like Ernie Travers was about to have his hands full, Bob thought. For the first few miles, he tried hard to keep his speed within ten miles per hour of the posted limits. With all the weapons and tactical gear in the back, the last thing he wanted was to pop up on some cop car's radar and be stopped.

Ace laughed. "Bob, wake up. We don't need to worry about cop cars;

we are one."

Bob slapped his forehead. "Jeez, am I stupid, or what?" he said as he looked around the dashboard, flicked on the SUVs rooftop emergency light bar and siren, and pressed the accelerator to the floor. The big engine roared and in less than a minute, he reached the entrance ramp to Route 53. The big, black, Chicago Police Department SUV accelerated to 120 miles an hour, blowing through the express I-Pass tollbooth lanes without slowing down.

"This is fun!" Ace laughed as the rearview mirror on the passenger side clipped the backside of the tollbooth and went flying across the road. "We gotta come back and do this again."

Patsy kept her arms around Ellie and kept herself between the little girl and Greenway's gun as the doctor dragged them up the sidewalk to the front door. He punched his access code into the keypad with his index finger, pulled the door open, and shoved Patsy and Ellie inside.

"Let us go," Patsy screamed. "I won't say anything. I promise."

"Shut up!" he said as he dragged her across the lobby.

They were halfway to the elevators when two of Scalese's security men ran into the lobby from the side corridor with their guns drawn. From their expressions, they had been taking one of their usual long breaks in the employee lounge, and had been startled by loud voices arguing in the front lobby. Greenway rarely came to the building at night, but from the bad haircuts, cheap, ill-fitting blazers with "S-D Security" logos on the breast pockets, he recognized them as two of Tony Scalese's newer hires. If he looked closer, he'd probably see their prison tattoos, as well. What they weren't, however, were older, experienced thugs from one of Salvatore DiGrigoria's regular crews, who might not listen to him. The nametag on the man in front read "Costanza." The one in back read "Bitaglia."

"What are you cretins looking at?" Greenway snarled as he pulled Patsy and the little girl toward the elevator.

"Uh, sorry, Dr. Greenway." Bitaglia stepped forward, clearly uneasy about what was going down. "We heard a bunch of noise out here and… Hey, is that a gun you got there?"

The two guards looked back and forth between Greenway, Patsy, and the little girl and frowned, until Costanza, the other guard, said, "Yeah, it's a .357 Mag, ain't it? Big sucker. Jimmy DiCiccio's got one like that."

"It *is* Jimmy's!" Patsy screamed at them. "You've got to help us, he's..."

"Shut up, I told you," Greenway hissed as he squeezed her arm hard and pulled her toward the elevator. "And you two guard the doors," Greenway ordered.

"Uh, wait a minute, Doc," Bitaglia apologized, clearly uneasy about the situation.

"Do what I said. Tony's coming back here any minute now, and we're expecting big trouble. You two know what to do with those things?" Greenway asked, looking at their pistols.

"You bet we do, Dr. G., Tony himself gave us these here Glocks." Costanza grinned as he held up his boxy semi-automatic. "But what's this about trouble?"

"Tony and his men were ambushed in that park tonight. He's coming back here, and trouble might be coming right behind him, trying to finish the job. Your job's to keep them out. You got that?"

"Yes, Sir! Yes, Sir, Dr. Greenway. We won't let anyone..."

"There's only two of you on duty here tonight?" he asked as the elevator door opened.

"No, Freddie Fortuno's here, too. I, uh, I think he went upstairs to check on..."

"You mean he's taking a nap, don't you? Well, get him down here. I want all three of you keeping a close eye out, or I'll have you fired. Understand!" Greenway ordered as he shoved Patsy and Ellie into the elevator car and waited impatiently for the doors to close. "I'll be in my office, and I don't want to be disturbed."

Three minutes later, the black SUV passed the white Indian Hills water tower and entered the Hills Business Park. Bob cut the emergency lights and siren while Ace and Vinnie checked the magazines in their weapons. As they approached the office building, Bob pulled into the parking lot of the building across the street, where the well-lit façade of the CHC building was clearly visible through the fringe of small trees.

"That's Scalese's Lexus." Linda pointed. "Greenway's here, what are we waiting for?"

"Hang on a minute," Bob quickly answered as he detached the night vision telescopic sight from his SCAR sniper rifle and scanned the parking lot. "Looks like he was in a big hurry." Greenway had left the Lexus sitting at an odd angle near the building's front entrance, spilling over the white lines on the two adjoining spaces. Its driver's side and left-rear door hung wide open, the engine was running, and the lights were on, further illuminating the building's lobby."

"But he has Ellie in there!" Linda pleaded.

"His office is on the third floor, on the back side to the right?" Linda nodded as he turned the scope on the building itself, scanning it slowly, floor by floor. "The lobby is lit up as usual, but the second and third floors are dark, at least this side." Looking more closely at the first floor, Bob said, "I see two guards on the first floor, but there could be more. Here," he said as he handed the scope to Linda. "Recognize them?"

"I think so," she answered as she focused on their faces. "I'm not positive, but they look like a couple of new hires on the night crew."

"I assumed Scalese took his best men to the forest preserve, but you never know."

"It don't make no never-mind," Vinny commented as he snapped a fresh magazine in his M-110. "We're takin' 'em out no matter who they are, but Linda's right. Let's get this done, before they get any more ready."

"Agreed," Bob answered. "Greenway's arrival must have shaken them up. They're standing in the back of the lobby, looking none too happy."

"Like I care," Ace said, as he put on his headset.

"True. Ace, you set up here with the SUV. You have a clear shot at the front of the building and can cover the entry roads. Linda, you stay here with him. Prepare to engage in two minutes. Vinny, work around back and find a spot where you can cover the rear — the lobby and Greenway's office if you can. I'll head for the side employee entrance. Chester left me a small piece of Semtex, so when you two have clear shots on the guards, take them out and I'll blow the side door and head up. Vinny, when I get the girl, bring the SUV around to the side door, and I'll meet you all there."

"There's not going to be any 'I' in this thing," Linda leaned forward and glared at him. "I'm coming with you. It's going to be 'we,' or I'll go by myself, you got that?"

Greenway kept a firm grip on Patsy's arm as he dragged her and Ellie out of the elevator and down the third floor corridor to his office. He opened the door, turned the lights on, and threw them on the couch.

"Stay there!" he said as he pointed a long finger at Patsy. "That is, unless you'd like me to come over there and visit with you for a while?"

He watched as Patsy pulled Ellie close and shrank away from him. "I didn't think so," he leered at her, pausing for a brief moment to consider what a luscious young thing she was going to be. Unfortunately, there had to be some business before pleasure, he realized as he returned to his desk.

Earlier, he saw that bastard Scalese had broken into his desk and credenza and searched the drawers. Greenway shook his head and laughed. Well, the dumb, musclebound Italian could have torn the entire desk apart, for all it mattered; but he wouldn't find Greenway's "good stuff," because Greenway no longer kept it there. He turned around, pulled the credenza away from the wall, and saw an innocuous 18" x 18" louvered AC vent. One weekend when Scalese was off on a "business trip," drinking and whoring with his boys in Las Vegas, Greenway brought in his own contractor who installed a high tech safe there. He bolted it into the building's structural steel, and it featured a nearly un-crackable six-digit combination lock. He opened it and pulled out a thick, hand-tooled leather briefcase made in Florence. Ironically, it was a gift from old Sal DiGrigoria himself, and using it to hide his "getaway" stash was the perfect way to get even with the senile old bastard.

The briefcase was his "travel bag." Greenway set it on his desk and turned the lock dials to his preset code and popped the top open. He raised it far enough to take a quick look inside. There was no time to count everything, but he saw that nothing appeared to be disturbed. His three foreign passports still lay on top — one British, one Canadian, and one Dutch, his personal favorite. Given the sudden downturn in his prospects here in Chicago, the briefcase would be very helpful for his imminent long-term retirement plan.

He snapped the case shut. The past few years had been very good, but everything was unravelling now, all because of that nosey bastard Burke. Scalese and his men must have taken some losses in the Forest Preserve tonight, but surely they had eliminated that meddlesome young man by now and would be heading back here. Greenway knew he must be long gone before Tony and his thick-skulled Mafiosi returned, but with his stash, Jimmy DiCiccio's revolver, Tony's Lexus, and a soft "squeeze" to keep him company for a few nights, it would be a nice trip. No one was looking for him yet. As long as he had the little girl, Patsy would be far more submissive and do whatever he wanted; and together, they would make excellent hostages if trouble should rear its ugly head along the way.

Yes, it was time to say goodbye to Indian Hills and head north.

Montreal was worth an extended stay. There were a dozen ways to sneak across the border through the back woods of upper Maine, and a hundred places to get rid of two slightly used dead bodies. Greenway licked his lips. After that, perhaps Rio de Janeiro, Copenhagen, or Bangkok. Those were progressive cities, where a gentleman of means could indulge his fantasies and minor peccadillos without being interrupted by little men with narrow minds.

"Time to go, Patsy," he said as he picked up the briefcase and motioned her toward the door with the big revolver.

"Where are you taking us?" she glared up at him.

"On an adventure," he said with big eyes and a crocodile smile. "And, oh my, but we shall have so much fun; won't we, Ellie?"

"Ghost, Vinny. I have one target at the rear lobby door."

"And I have the other one at the front door."

"On my mark then, Five... Four... Three... Two... One... Mark."

With almost simultaneous precision, the two sniper rifles fired, emitting muted 'coughs.' The high-velocity, specialty bullets struck the building's thick, floor-to-ceiling, reflective-glass windows with what sounded like one loud Palang! Small, round, spider-webbed holes appeared in both the front and rear exterior glass of the lobby, knocking both guards backward. They now lay motionless on the lobby floor, as Bob heard "Target one down," and, "Target two down," in his earbud, in voices so calm, the speakers might have been reading the local weather report. He immediately pressed the button on his remote detonator and the ounce of Semtex blew a large hole in the reinforced metal door of the employee entrance, destroying the heavy, magnetic lock with a loud Bam!

Bob ran forward and pulled the outer door open with Linda following right behind. The fire stairs were inside and to the right. He yanked the emergency door open, but Linda didn't wait. She held her Beretta in a two handed grip, cut ahead of him, and ran up the stairs. She was fast, and the best that Bob could do was to reach out with his free hand and grab her by the seat of her pants and stop her.

"No! Stay behind me!" he ordered.

"But it's my daughter!"

"This is no time to argue, Linda. Stay back. I'd rather you weren't here at all, much less carrying that handgun; but if you are coming with me, keep it at your side and pointed down," he told her as he pushed the barrel aside. "If you can't do that, wait downstairs." Reluctantly, she nodded, so he sprinted ahead of her up the steep flight of stairs, taking them two at a time.

Both M-110 sniper rifles carried noise suppressors, and the "Palang!" of a high-velocity bullet hitting the plate glass window followed by the faint 'tinkle' of small shards of glass falling on the lobby's hard travertine floor was all that could be heard inside the building's first floor atrium lobby, until Bob detonated the Semtex charge on the rear door. It shook the building and even rattled the windows on the third floor. Greenway felt the explosion through the soles of his shoes. It caused him to pause halfway across the office floor and listen intently for any other sounds. His hearing was excellent, and he immediately detected the sound of doors banging in the emergency stairwell several floors below. Tony and his guys? That made no sense.

"Go, out the door!" he growled as he grabbed Patsy by her arm. "And keep a firm grip on that brat!" he said as he shoved them out the office door and down the hall toward the elevator, "

As he passed the metal door to the emergency stairwell, Greenway heard footsteps running up the stairs toward him. They hadn't gotten this high yet, but Greenway knew he had to slow them down if he hoped to get away. He pointed the big Colt at the metal emergency stairwell door and fired three shots, Blam! Blam! Blam! The .357-Magnum slugs punched holes through it as if it weren't there, and he heard the big slugs ricochet off the stairwell's bare concrete walls below. Hopefully, that would scare the hell out of whoever was coming up, he thought.

As Greenway turned and headed for the elevator, he found himself face to face with yet another of Scalese's security guards, who came running out of one of the empty offices with his gun drawn. From the panicked look in the man's eyes, it was obvious the gunshots woke him from a sound sleep.

"What the hell… Who…?" The guard tried to ask as he waved his gun around.

"You!" Greenway shouted at him. "You're Fortuno, aren't you?"

"Uh, yeah… Freddie Fortuno, Dr. Greenway, what…?"

"No time for that now. Men are coming here to kill Tony and me. While I get these girls to safety, you keep that fire door covered and shoot anyone who tries to come up here. You got that?"

"Uh, yeah, sure. I can do that," Fortuno said as he crouched down in the corridor and pointed his gun at the fire door. "You can tell Mr. Scalese, they won't get past me."

Greenway ran on to the open, third-floor elevator lobby, where Patsy picked up Ellie and held her in her arms. The lobby was like a narrow bridge that connected the left and right wings of the building and gave him a clear view into the front and rear sides of the first floor atrium below. He ran to the railing, looked down, and saw one of the security guards he had talked to only moments before — was his name Bitaglia? — sprawled on the floor with a large pool of blood around his head. Greenway turned to the rear railing and saw the other guard, Costanza, lying in a similar state. In that instant, he realized it wasn't Tony. It was that bastard Burke again!

Greenway backed his way to the elevator doors as more gunfire erupted at the end of the hall and the emergency door flew open, and crashed against the sidewall.

Like Wyatt Earp at the O.K. Corral, Freddie Fortuno stood in the hall outside Greenway's office. He dropped into a classic, knees-bent, two-handed, shooting stance with his Glock pointed across the hall at the center of the stairwell door only ten feet away. When Freddie saw the emergency door fly open in front of him, he closed his eyes and opened up, pulling the trigger and firing off all ten rounds in his magazine until the Glock clicked empty. When he finally dared to open his eyes again, he saw he actually put most of the bullets through the open doorway. Yep, he shot that sucker dead, he grinned.

Experience matters, in cards, horseshoes, and being shot at with semi-automatic weapons. Bob Burke had run up two flights of stairs and turned the corner toward the third floor, when three bullets ripped through the metal fire door up ahead. He pulled Linda down and ducked as the slugs ricocheted back and forth off the concrete walls. From the sound of the gunshots, he guessed them to be from a .357-Magnum, probably a revolver, fired "blind" to slow them down while the shooter ran away. So, Bob immediately got to his feet and took the remaining stairs, two at a time. When he reached the third-floor landing, he pulled Linda behind the concrete sidewall with him, and kicked the door. It crashed against the opposite wall with a loud, echoing Boom! He expected to hear several individual shots from a .357 Magnum; instead, he was greeted by a fusillade of bullets flying in through the open doorway.

Those shots bore the distinctive sound of a 9-millimeter, most likely a Glock. Bob had fired enough rounds with one of them to know what they sounded like, and had had enough bullets of every size and shape fired at him over the years that the counter in his head immediately switched on. Most of the rounds smacked into the concrete wall on the other side of the stairwell and lost their energy. A few ricocheted around the stairwell, but none came close to him or Linda. The standard Glock magazine held ten bullets, which is what he counted. If that was the case, the shooter was now empty, Bob thought, as he dropped to the floor and rolled into the open doorway, ready to fire before the shooter reloaded. However, if the guy carried an extended 17-round magazine, then he was screwed.

With his head on the floor and his Beretta out in front of him, he acquired a target — a man standing not twelve feet away across the hallway in a solid, knees-bent, two-handed shooting stance. His Glock was still pointed at the open doorway and he continued to pull the trigger with an audible Click! Click! Click! Before the guy figured out he needed a fresh magazine, Bob put three quick rounds in the center of his chest. It was a tight shot grouping, the kind the instructor at Bragg would have laid a quarter over on the paper target and smiled. These shots, however, punched Freddie Fortuno back through Greenway's doorway, where he collapsed on the floor.

Bob stuck his head an inch or two farther out and looked down the corridor toward the elevator lobby. Greenway had reached the elevators and was now standing in front of the polished brass doors. That, and the other emergency stairwell at the far end of the hall, were Greenway's only way out now, and they both knew it.

Greenway held Patsy Evans in front of him and pulled Ellie Sylvester in front of her, with his right forearm wrapped tightly around Patsy's throat. A large-caliber revolver dangled from Greenway's right hand, pointing down at Ellie's head. In his left dangled a big, leather briefcase. At first glance, Burke recognized the revolver as a .357-Magnum Colt Python, which squared with the sounds he had heard from the three earlier gunshots into the stairwell door. Greenway looked down the corridor, saw Burke looking up at him from the floor of the stairwell, and saw the Beretta in Burke's hand, which was now pointed at him. Greenway bent even lower, now almost completely hidden behind them.

"Greenway, give it up," Bob shouted at him. "My men are outside, and the only way you're getting out of this building is through me."

"I don't think so," Greenway shouted back. "Tony Scalese and his men should be here any minute."

"They're dead, Scalese and all the rest of them. Stop now or you're going to join them."

Greenway blinked as he realized the magnitude of what Burke just said. Dead? All of them? This couldn't be happening, he thought. His eyes flared as he pointed the Colt revolver down the hallway and fired a shot in Bob's general direction. The .357-Magnum handgun sounded like a cannon in the tight hallway, and both Patsy and Ellie began to scream. Bob pulled his head back as he heard the counter inside his head speaking to him, "That was four — four down, and two to go."

True to his character, Lawrence Greenway immediately ducked back down behind Patsy and Ellie. Bob was a crack shot with a pistol, but he couldn't risk firing at the doctor, as much as he would dearly love to. However, Greenway was in an equal bind. He needed to get into the elevator and the hell away from here, so he bent down, set the briefcase on the floor next to him, and reached his left hand out toward the elevator button. His eyes were locked on Bob Burke, as his fingers ran up and down the wall, trying unsuccessfully to locate the elevator buttons. Finally, he took his eyes off the emergency stairwell, turned his head, found the Down button, stretched his arm out even further, and pushed the button.

As he did, the muzzle of the big Colt turned away from Ellie. Bob immediately took careful aim with the Beretta and fired off three 9-millimeter rounds. At least one tore through the back of Greenway's left hand, and all three rounds smashed into the elevator's control box, putting the machinery out of operation.

"Ah!" Greenway screamed and pulled his shattered hand back, but it no longer mattered. That elevator wasn't going anywhere, not tonight, and neither was Lawrence Greenway. Only then did Bob pull his head back into the stairwell and look up at Linda standing over him. "Don't worry," he told her. "We have him trapped up here now and that bastard's not going anywhere."

"But he has Ellie!"

"Not for long."

CHAPTER TWENTY-NINE

Lawrence Greenway raised his shattered left hand and his eyes went wide as he saw the large, ragged hole in the center of the back of his hand. He was a doctor. He had finished in the top ten of his medical school graduating class. In the abstract, he knew the human hand was a prehensile organ with one of the most complicated physiologies in the human body. He could name the twenty-seven bones it contained, not to mention the numerous muscles, tendons, nerves, veins, and arteries around them, even without having one of his med school cheat-sheets tucked up his sleeve. Fortunately for him, the bullet struck his left hand, not his right; but even a high school dropout could see the jagged bones and pieces of flesh protruding from the hole and the blood running down his forearm, and know it would require extensive surgery and a goddamned miracle if it was ever to function properly again.

It usually takes a few seconds for the excruciating pain from a wound like that to travel from the injury to the brain. However, with a half dozen shattered bones, torn muscles, shredded tendons, and raw nerves, this pain immediately began at the tips of his fingers, shot up his hand to his arm, up his spine, and intensified as it blew through the top of his head. He pulled the hand away and ducked down behind Patsy again. He screamed. Patsy screamed, Ellie screamed, and he screamed again as murderous waves of pain washed over him. "Burke, you bastard! I'll kill you; I'll kill you!"

"Let them go and I'll let you try. Come on, I'll even stand up and let you take a free shot at me," Burke shouted back, but Greenway was not listening. Like a wounded animal, every fiber of his being was now concentrated on survival. The elevator controls had shorted out and that escape route was closed to him now. Somehow, though, he had to get away from this maniac Burke and out of the building. That was his only hope, so Greenway tightened his grip around Patsy Evan's neck and dragged her away down the hall toward the other emergency stairs.

That was when he heard voices in the open atrium below. "Ghost, you okay up there?" he heard another man call out.

"We're fine," Bob Burke answered. "You and Vinny block the other staircase. Greenway's headed that way."

"Roger that," still another voice answered.

"You hear that, Greenway?" Bob called out to him again. "Those guys are two of the most talented killers our government has ever produced, and they'll drop you in your tracks before you even know they're there. So let the girls go, and I'll let you live. Jail's a whole lot better than dead."

Greenway growled and ignored him. Jail was *not* better than dead! Not to a man like him. He pulled Patsy and Ellie down the hallway toward the emergency door, careful to stay behind them. Burke might be lying about the skills of the other two men; but he had already proved he was a crack shot with a pistol, and Greenway was not about to give him a second chance. When he reached the door at the end of the hall, he pushed his butt against the panic bar to open it. The hand throbbed with a murderous pain now. Ah!" he groaned as he stepped through the door onto the third floor landing, keeping the two girls behind him.

"Ghost!" he heard that voice call out again, even louder now as it echoed up the stairwell. "Someone's in the west stairwell above me. If I get a shot, you want me to take him out?"

"Only if it's 'can't miss.' He's got the two girls with him."

Greenway did not dare look over the side to see what he was dealing with, but he knew in his gut he could not go down. For the past few years, he heard Salvatore DiGrigoria's thugs and paid gunmen talk and yell amongst each other, but Burke and his men were strangely different. There was no loud bravado or threats here. The tone of their voices was so terrifyingly calm and matter-of-fact that they might be tailors fitting a suit, statisticians delivering a report, or morticians measuring a man for a coffin. As Burke said, however, these men were killers — real killers — and Greenway knew they were his worst nightmares.

With no other options left to him, Greenway shoved Ellie and Patsy up the stairs, keeping himself pressed against the outside wall until they reached the first landing and turned the corner. "Go, go, faster!" he prodded them on with the revolver. Running and stumbling, their footsteps scraped and echoed off the bare metal stairs and concrete like an invading army. Finally, they turned the final corner, and found themselves on the small landing in front of the roof access door.

It was strangely ironic how life sometimes looped round and round in little circles, Greenway thought. Only three days before, he had run up these very stairs and through this door, chasing that bitch Eleanor Purdue out onto the roof. It was three days and a lifetime ago, he thought, all because of that damned O'Malley. If he hadn't goaded Eleanor into stealing still more documents, none of this would have happened — Eleanor would still be alive, there would have been nothing on the roof for Burke to see, his airplane would have landed quietly at O'Hare, and Doctor Lawrence Greenway, MD, would have continued on with his comfortable life, complete with its foibles and minor peccadilloes. How unfortunate, he thought.

He pressed against the panic bar to open the door to the roof, as he did three days before, but nothing happened. The door did not budge. Below him, he heard the third floor door open and knew Burke was down there, hot on his heels. Greenway backed off a half step and kicked the door again, even harder, but the damned thing still would not open. In the dim light, he looked down and saw that someone had installed a hasp and thick Master padlock on the panic bar, no doubt some 'eager beaver' in maintenance, to keep people like him and Eleanor Purdue off the roof. Well, it was a little late for that, Greenway concluded, as he placed the muzzle of the colt Python against the lock where the semicircular shackle entered the body of the lock, and pulled the trigger. The sound of the .357-Magnum going off at the top of the narrow confines of the concrete stairwell was more deafening than before, but the bullet blew the lock apart.

The little girl screamed even louder now, as Greenway shoved her and Patsy out of the small stairwell penthouse and onto the roof. "Shut her up! Shut her up, or I swear…"

As Bob Burke passed the elevator, he saw blood splattered all over the control panel, and followed a long trail of it to the fire door and up the emergency stairs. It was easy to see that Greenway had already lost a lot of blood and must be in pain. He held Linda back to keep her behind him on the third floor landing, as he peeked around the door frame and up the staircase. But he could only watch helplessly as Greenway disappeared around the next turn of the stairs with Ellie and Patsy. Again, he couldn't risk taking the shot. He hoped Greenway would finally decide to quit, but the good doctor appeared to be a tough sell on that point.

He started up the next flight of stairs toward the roof, when he heard a booming gunshot in the stairwell above him. He pulled back, but quickly realized the shot wasn't aimed at him. Nonetheless, the counter inside his head told him, "That's five! Five down and only one left in the cylinder," — unless Greenway brought some extra ammunition along and reloaded — leaving Burke to wonder how long it would be before the law of averages and his luck would run out.

"Ghost. What's going on up there? You okay?" he heard Ace's

voice in his earbud.

"That was Greenway, but he wasn't shooting at me," Bob explained. "From the sound, I'd guess he shot the access door. Maybe it had a lock. Anyway, he went up on the roof, and I'm going on up with Linda. You follow and provide backup. Vinny, stay down on the first floor and cover the lobby and the other stairs," Burke ordered.

"Roger that, Ghost," Vinny answered. "But be careful; that body armor you've got on might be bullet proof, but large parts of you ain't."

The last time Greenway was on this roof it was late afternoon. The sun was setting, but there was plenty of daylight as he closed in on Eleanor. Then, Greenway was the hunter. Tonight, he was the hunted, and the dark roof was his dead-end. It was flat and rectangular, with a three-foot high parapet wall that ran around the outer edge to screen the jumble of standpipes, risers, air conditioning ducts, water cooling tower, elevator equipment room, and the two emergency stairwell penthouses from the ground. This jumble of walls, pipes, and ducts might provide a myriad of wonderful hiding places for a child playing hide and seek; but if you are an adult being chased by men with guns, the mechanical equipment only got in the way.

Worse still, every step he took and every move he made caused the shattered bones in his left hand to move and scrape together. The pain was excruciating. He groaned and watched helplessly as the blood flowed even faster. Ordinarily, Lawrence Greenway had a very high threshold for pain. In fact, some thought he was a masochist. Tonight, this bullet wound dominated his every thought and sensation, and he knew he was no longer thinking clearly. The only way he could stop the broken bones from moving was to press his hand against his chest with his right forearm, while he continued to hold the Colt in his right hand. That stopped the left hand from shaking and moving, but he could feel his blood soaking into his shirt and running down his chest.

Greenway slammed the roof access door shut behind him with his shoulder, knowing full well he had just stepped into trap of his own making. The only way down now were the two flights of emergency stairs. Burke was waiting in the one behind him, and that was out. That only left the stairs at the far end of the roof, the ones Burke had come up from the lobby. The roof was dark. If Greenway could get across the roof to that other staircase, they might think he was still hiding up here in the jumble of ducts and pipes. He could run back down the stairs and get to

Tony's car before they knew he was gone.

Patsy and the little girl stood huddled together in the thick gravel a few feet away. "Go! Go!" he screamed and waved the pistol at them, tying to get them moving, only to have his shattered hand explode in pain again. "Ah!" he moaned

"I'm glad it hurts!" Patsy glared at him as she picked Ellie up and shielded her, shuffling away through the slippery pea gravel. "And I hope he shoots you again you, you… bastard!" she screamed at him again. "When he does, I'm going to laugh."

In a rage, Greenway pointed the big Colt at her again, but stopped and pulled his arm back to cradle his left hand before the pain got worse. "When I finish with you, you won't be laughing at anything. Now move!"

Burke took the stairs two at a time, with Linda close on his heels. When he reached the door to the roof, he paused to listen and then turned toward her. "Linda, I want you to stay here in the stairwell. But I know you won't do that, will you?"

"You got that right," she quickly answered as she tightened her grip on the Beretta. "He has Ellie and I'm going out there."

"Linda, have you ever even fired a big handgun like that?"

"I hate guns, especially handguns."

"Then stay behind me. He's only got one bullet left. If you go up there waving that big 9-millimeter around, you're as likely to hit me or one of the girls as you are to hit him. So, let me handle it. All right?"

Reluctantly, she lowered the Beretta. "Get Ellie back, Bob," she said as she reached out and touched his arm. "And don't go getting yourself shot; I couldn't handle that either."

Bob nodded and pushed her back a few paces behind the sidewall before he shoved the door open, and dove through the opening. He executed as good of an acrobatic somersault as a tired and badly out-of-practice, middle-aged ex-Ranger was likely to do, rolling over and coming back up in a solid kneeling position with his Beretta extended in front of him, seeking a target. As he expected, some thirty feet away he saw Lawrence Greenway heading for the other stairwell. Greenway was close to the narrow, center section of the building, a few feet from the perimeter parapet wall, but he had a long way to go before he reached that other door. The sound of the fire door slamming against the outer wall provided all the warning Greenway needed to turn and hide behind the girls again. His right arm was draped over Patsy's shoulder and the

Colt revolver was pointed down at Ellie again. On the dark roof, that left Bob with no shot.

"Give it up, Greenway" Bob called out to him. "The building's surrounded, and you're not going anywhere. Better to be a one-armed doctor, than a dead one."

"That's not going to happen, *Major* Burke," Greenway glared back at him, grimacing in pain. "This is a monstrously large pistol and it will blow a very large hole in little Ellie if you don't let me get out of here."

"Doc, there's two problems with that," Burke answered as he got to his feet and began to walk toward Greenway at a slow but steady pace, his Beretta straight out in front of him, aimed unwaveringly at Greenway's head. "First, you're bleeding to death and you need a hospital. You're a doctor, and you know that. Second, that's a revolver you're holding, not an automatic. It only holds six bullets and you've already fired five — three into the fire door, one at me, and one back there into the door lock. That only leaves you with one bullet left."

Greenway blinked, and that was a dead giveaway. He dipped back and forth behind Patsy, so as not to give Burke a clear shot. As he did, Bob could almost hear the little wheels going around inside the doctor's head as he also counted the shots he took. Unfortunately, he kept coming up with the same number Burke had. There was one bullet left in the big Colt, and they both knew it. That was why Burke continued walking slowly toward him, closing the gap to twenty feet and then fifteen. Behind him, he heard Linda's footsteps in the gravel, and in his earbud, he heard Ace's reassuring voice tell him, "I'm in the doorway at your Seven, Ghost, ready when you are."

Burke was close enough now to see that the front of Greenway's white shirt appeared dark and shiny. So did his pants. At night, everything wet appears black and shiny, especially blood, and Greenway was covered with it now.

"Look at your shirt, Doc. You've lost a lot of blood," Burke told him. "As I see it, you have two choices. If you use that last bullet to shoot one of the girls, I'm going to unload the nine rounds I have left into you, one soft painful body part at a time." As he spoke, he closed the gap to ten feet and then five, drifting slightly to the right, and causing Greenway to turn with him, exposing more of himself to Ace. "Don't worry, though. I'll make sure none of those bullets actually kill you; but if you think one bullet wound hurts like hell, you have no idea what eight or nine new ones are going to feel like."

Burke saw the sweat running down Greenway's forehead. "Or, you can use that last bullet and take a shot at me!" Burke shouted at him as he lowered his Beretta, tossed it aside, and threw his arms out wide. "It's your last bullet, Doc. If you shoot me, you can make a run for the other stairs and maybe make it down to your car. Come on! That's your best chance; hell, it's your *only* chance."

Greenway stared back at him, blinking even faster as he began to wobble.

"Come on, Doc!" Burke shouted at him again as he spread his arms even further apart. "Take the shot!" he shouted and stepped closer. "It's your big chance, take it!"

Greenway's eyes suddenly grew wide and he flew into a rage. He could see the blood on his own arm, he could feel himself growing weak, and he knew they would never let them off the roof. It *was* his only chance. "You…!" he screamed and shoved Patsy aside, turned, and swung the Colt Python toward Burke. As he did, Patsy wrapped her arms around Ellie and pulled her down, shielding the little girl with her body as Bob Burke leaped at Greenway.

Two gunshots rang out almost simultaneously, followed quickly by a third. The first was the loud, base roar of Greenway's 357-Magnum as it spit six inches of blue-white flame and a very powerful bullet at Bob Burke. It struck him in the center of his chest like a heavyweight's body punch, stopping him in midair and knocking him backward onto on the roof. The second and third gunshots came from a 9-millimeter Beretta. The first caught Greenway in the gut and bent him over at the waist. His eyes dropped to his stomach and he saw a large hole at the center of his pain. Stunned, he looked up and saw Linda Sylvester standing in front of him with a large smoking automatic in her hand and the angriest, most vengeful eyes he had ever seen. That was when a second bullet from her Beretta hit him in the chest. It punched him backward on rubbery legs until they reached the knee-high parapet wall and he lost his balance. He toppled backward off the roof, cartwheeling through the air until he landed on the concrete sidewalk in front of the building's revolving doors, far below.

Linda was the first to react to Bob being shot. "No! Oh, God, no!" she screamed as she ran to his side and raised his unconscious head in her lap.

Ace reached him at the same time, dropping his rifle on the roof. He knelt next to Bob, tearing at his black over-shirt to reveal the tactical protection vest he wore underneath. There was a tear in the center of the vest. Ace immediately ripped open the overlapping high tech panels, expecting the worst. "You damned fool!" he growled.

Finally, Burke emitted a painful groan, grabbed his chest, and began to cough. "It's 'you damned fool, *Sir*,' " he managed to correct the senior enlisted man.

"Don't pull that *Sir* crap with me, you're retired," Ace fired back. "And that vest ain't rated for no .357-Magnum. You took it right to the edge, my man, and then some." He felt around under the panels, but found no blood, only the spent .357 slug, which he pulled out and pressed into Bob's palm. "Here's your souvenir for the evening, *Major.*"

"God, that hurts!" Bob said as his fingers probed his own side. "I think I have a couple of broken ribs."

Patsy rushed over and lowered Ellie to the ground next to her mother. "That was the bravest thing I've ever seen anyone do," Patsy said to Bob.

"And the dumbest!" Linda added angrily.

"Not really," Bob shrugged. "It was a... well-calculated risk."

"Calculated risk? Like I haven't heard that one before!" Ace grumbled.

"Hey, he only had one bullet, I had the vest, and you were behind me, Ace, ready to take him out as soon as he moved. So, where's the risk?"

"The risk? Well, for starters, I didn't have a shot; Linda got in the way. She took it, not me," Ace said, as he looked at Linda with newfound respect. "But Greenway fired first, and you almost bought the farm."

"Details," Bob dismissed the thought as he turned and looked up at her. "I thought you said you couldn't shoot."

"I said I hate guns, I never said I couldn't shoot one," Linda admitted, embarrassed. "My husband — my *ex-husband* — kept dragging me out to the range and insisted I learn."

"Well, it was a sweet shot, and I guess I have one thing to thank him for, anyway," Bob said.

Linda continued to glare at him, and then turned toward Patsy. "Besides, what you did was almost as brave as what he did." Linda held out her arms to Patsy. The two women gathered Ellie between them, wrapped their arms around each other, and began to cry.

Finally, she turned back to Bob Burke. "Robert, half of me wants to strangle you, right here and now, while the other half wants to hug you too. Oh, hell," she said as she leaned forward with Patsy and Ellie and they all wrapped their arms around him and squeezed.

"Ah! Watch the ribs, the ribs!" he groaned. "Look, I'd love to stay here and get more of this tender, loving care, but we need to get moving. Ace..."

"Vinny and I will police our way down to the lobby and meet you at the SUV in Three."

"In Three," Bob confirmed. "Girls, a little help up here," he added as he reached his arms out to Linda and Patsy, and let them pull him up to his feet. "Lord, I hope no one else needs saving tonight, because they're gonna have to call someone else."

By the time Ace and Vinny finished policing up their shell casings, Linda, Patsy, Ellie, and Bob were already in the SUV's two rear seats, waiting. When Ace came out the building's side employee door, he placed a beautifully hand-tooled leather briefcase in Bob's lap. "We found this on the third floor landing in front of the elevator doors," he said.

Bob looked at it and said, "It's Greenway's. I remember he sat it down there just before I shot him."

"I think that's why he came back here," Patsy said.

"Scalese told us that Greenway was headed back here to get his stash," Bob said as he examined the briefcase's hinges and locks and checked for any wires or signs the case had been tampered with or booby-trapped, but he saw nothing.

"It must be important," Patsy added. "He dragged us up to his office to get it, when he could've just taken off and run."

Bob assumed the case was locked, but he pressed the two buttons anyway. To his surprise, they snapped open. "Looks like he was in a big hurry and didn't even lock it."

Linda was sitting next to him as he raised the top, and she pressed closer for a better look. "Wow!" she exclaimed. Inside the briefcase they saw dozens of stacks of hundred-dollar bills, four black-velvet bags with drawstrings, and a thick folder of papers. Bob picked up the folder as Linda's forefinger probed the stacks of cash. She picked up one of the velvet bags, pulled the drawstring open, and peeked inside. "It's full of diamonds," she whispered.

Meanwhile, Bob looked inside the folder and saw a stack of multicolored certificates. He fanned the stack with his fingernail. "Bearer Bonds, in one-thousand-dollar denominations. They're as good as cash."

"Looks like 'doctoring' pays pretty good these days," Linda said.

Bob poked Ace in the shoulder and said, "Let's get out of here. I don't know if Indian Hills has any cops left; but if they do, they should be here soon, so let's get back to the airport."

"Roger, that," Ace answered. "I'll get a Sit Rep and ETA from Chester and Koz and call the pilot too. I'll tell him wheels up in Fifteen."

"By the way, where are Chester, Koz, and the Batman?" Linda asked as they drove out of the business park. "I didn't see them after we left the Forest Preserve."

"They're off taking care of a few things for me."

"Chester says everything's copacetic," Ace spoke up. "They have the stuff and they're on schedule to meet us at the airplane."

"Outstanding! Call Ernie Travers, too," Bob leaned forward and said. "Ask him if he can meet us at the plane. Tell him I have some more presents for him. That should get him moving."

"Is that where we're going? That private airport in Mount Prospect? But what about..."

"You, Ellie, and Patsy?" Bob cut her off and slowly, painfully, turned so he could see her face and Patsy's, "I was hoping all three of you would come with us for a while."

"You mean to North Carolina?" Linda asked. "Bob, I can't take off like that. Ellie has school, and there's my job, and I've got to get my car back, and..."

"Look, CHC is as dead as Greenway and Scalese now. You need to be away from here and someplace else for a few days until Ernie can work some of his police magic. He's giving Eleanor's reports and the flash drive to some *Tribune* and *Sun-Times* reporters. That will blow the lid off their operation, including the cops and politicians they've been paying off. In a few days, we'll be cleared and DiGrigoria and his pals will be the ones on the run, not us."

"But North Carolina? I don't even have a toothbrush," Linda argued, and Patsy agreed.

"Linda," Bob patted the top of the briefcase. "There's... I don't know, a million dollars? Maybe a whole lot more in here, and none of it belongs to anyone anymore. That'll buy you a whole bunch of toothbrushes, a new wardrobe, a couple swimming suits, some nice party clothes, and a *new* car. The O'Hare Parking Authority can keep the old one.

And, when we're done we can make big contributions to the Disabled American Vets and the Fisher House Foundation with what's left."

"But what about the investigations and O'Malley?" Linda continued to argue.

Bob smiled. "Mr. O'Malley is about to have more problems than he can imagine. As for tonight, I know a dozen guys and their wives, including the Commanding General, who'll swear on a stack of Bibles that we've been down there all week. Besides, there's no place on earth where you and Ellie will be safer for the next few days than inside the gates of Fort Bragg with 40,000 of my close personal friends to keep an eye on you."

"You can arrange all that?" Linda asked. "I… I don't know."

"Linda, get real!" Patsy said. "Think of what almost happened to us — you, Ellie, *and* me. Besides, neither of us has a job or anyone else to go back to now."

"And don't worry about your jobs," Bob told both of them. "By the end of the week, after Ernie gets all those bogus charges dropped, I'll have my company back and you two can come to work for me."

"Oh, that wouldn't be right, Bob. People might get the wrong idea," Linda answered.

"Let's worry about that later," he told her as he pulled Ellie up into his lap. "For now, I think we all need a little vacation, don't we, Ellie? A little quality time around the pool, with lots of ice cream and funny drinks with umbrellas?" he asked, and the little girl quickly smiled and nodded. "Besides, with these ribs, you're pretty safe. Even so, I'd like to spend some time getting to know the two of you better, if that's okay with you."

This time it was Linda's turn to smile and nod. "You're right, that does sound good."

"Look," Patsy interjected, "I know what you two will be doing for R&R, not that it's any of my business, but what does that make me? The babysitter?

"Patsy, we're throwing a big party tonight after we all get some sleep," Bob told her.

"And I can think of at least two dozen guys who will be happy to fill your dance card, girl," Vinnie laughed. "You'll have no shortage of your own R&R, believe me."

"Mommy, what's R&R?" Ellie asked, and the big kids all cracked up laughing.

CHAPTER THIRTY

Salvatore DiGrigoria was forty-five minutes late arriving at the office the next morning. Mr. D was punctual to a fault and was never late for anything. This unheard-of tardiness brought his older sister and longtime secretary, Gabriella, to the verge of a nervous breakdown. Salvatore had a housekeeper, a cook, a driver, and two bodyguards to watch over him; so, when he was suddenly late like this at his age, she feared the worst. Finally, she heard the elevator "Ding!" When her brother stepped out, she breathed a sigh of relief and mumbled a quick "Hail Mary." He hurried on past, completely ignoring her, which was even more unusual, appearing distracted, and from his expression, more than a little angry. Worse still, Salvatore was a proud little man who resembled a beer keg on legs, but he was always well groomed. Today however, his hair was a mess, he hadn't shaved, and his herky-jerky stride resembled a bowling ball careening down a flight of stairs. This was not good, Gabriella thought.

"Salvatore, are you alright?" she called out to him. "I was worried that..."

"Da goddamned reporters woke me up. Dere must 'a been a hundred of 'em camped out around da house. I could hardly get out 'a dere. It's dat goddamned Enzo, I'm gonna kill 'im!"

The grim expression on his face told her not to ask anything more. Something was seriously wrong. As he passed her desk, he jabbed a stubby finger on the fresh, neatly folded copy of the *Chicago Tribune*, which Gabriella dutifully placed there for him each morning. "I already read da goddamn thing," he growled, pointing to a battered copy under his arm, which someone must have given him. "Did you read it?" he asked gruffly, knowing she never read the newspaper. "Well, today, you better! Dat goddamned Enzo!"

Now, Gabriella was truly flustered. Sal never swore, at least not in front of her, and he only talked about his brothers behind closed doors. "I'll bring you your espresso," she called to him as he went into his office and slammed the door behind him. Between the newspaper and a jolt of Sicilian espresso, she could only imagine what his blood pressure would be this morning.

The old man threw the battered copy of the *Tribune* on his desk and quickly sat down. He opened it to the front page and looked at it again, although he already knew what it said, word for word. The banner headline was all he needed to see to know today would be a fiasco:

MOB SHOOTOUT IN SUBURBS

> Sixteen members of the warring North and South Side branches of the DiGrigoria crime family died in a bloody shootout as their long-simmering gangland turf fight exploded in a pitched gun battle last night in the Parker Woods Forest Preserve ...

" 'Da warring North and South side branches...?' 'Long-simmering...?' What da hell are dey talking about," old Sal mumbled, growing angrier and more confused as he read on:

> According to State Police sources, the dead included long-time DiGrigoria underboss Tony Scalese, as well as underbosses Eddie Fanucci, Johnny Corso, Jimmy DiCiccio, and others...

DiGrigoria blinked, stunned as he re-read the long list of names. In the sidebar articles accompanying the main story, the news was infinitely worse.

LOCAL DOCTOR FOUND SHOT TO DEATH

> Prominent local doctor Lawrence Greenway, President and founder of Consolidated Health Care (CHC) in suburban Indian Hills was found shot to death outside his company offices early this morning. Inside, police found the bodies of three DiGrigoria gunmen. Greenway has been linked to organized crime, and CHC is long believed to be a mob front according to Chicago Crime Commission sources. Financial documents obtained last night by the *Tribune* reveal a pattern of corruption and fraud in Federal Medicare and Medicaid programs and insurance billing...

Even that pervert Greenway got it! Well, at least there was one spot of good news, DiGrigoria reluctantly admitted as his eyes turned to another sidebar.

US ATTORNEY LINKED TO MOB

Documents obtained by the *Chicago Tribune* reveal substantial payments from Consolidated Health Care and DiGrigoria crime family underboss Tony Scalese to Peter O'Malley, US Attorney for Northern Illinois. Records show cash and campaign contributions in excess of $1 million dollars this year alone. Phone calls to O'Malley, the local office of the FBI, and O'Malley's Justice Department superiors in Washington D.C., were not returned.

Salvatore sat back in his chair, stunned. Tony? *My* Tony paying off O'Malley? Salvatore knew nothing about any of that. Tony? One million dollars? "Dat son-of-a-bitch!" Salvatore screamed as he suddenly realized Scalese cut a deal with that bastard and sold him out. "Dat rat!" he fumed as he re-read the story and still couldn't believe it. How could things possibly get any worse? Then he saw the next sidebar story, and realized they had.

REPORTERS OBTAIN DIGRIGORIA FINANCIAL DOCUMENTS

In an unprecedented joint investigation, The *Chicago Tribune* and *Chicago Sun-Times* have acquired detailed financial records of Federated Environmental Services and Federated Investments in Evanston, the parent corporations of Consolidated Health Care, all owned by reputed mob boss Salvatore DiGrigoria. They show payoffs to dozens of local law enforcement officials, including Indian Hills Police Chief Cyrus Bentley, found shot to death last night. The documents obtained by the *Tribune* and *Sun-Times* include ledger books hand-written by DiGrigoria himself...

The old man's eyes grew wide. "What?" he screamed as he jumped to his feet, shaking with anger as he read and re-read that last sentence. "My 'hand-written' ledger books?" he said as he stared at Uncle Luigi's five-foot-high Yale safe sitting against the far wall. It looked exactly as it had when he locked it and left the office yesterday. Those liars! That goddamned newspaper lied, as usual. They didn't have his ledger books; they couldn't, because that safe was impregnable.

Salvatore crossed the room, stood next to it, reached out, and touched the door. Its surface was cool, thick, and reassuring, as usual; but he knew he must be certain. He bent down in front of the safe as quickly as his aching old knees and back would allow, entered the five-number combination, and turned the locking handle with a soft click! He swung the door wide open and stuck his head inside. To his horror, he saw that the top half of his stack of ledger books, the ones for the past fifteen years, were indeed gone! In their place sat a single sheet of heavy, white stationery with something written on it. He leaned closer and read the large printed letters, which said, "Fry in Hell, you old bastard! The Telephone Guy."

It would be nice to think the "old bastard" actually read the entire note; but the truth was, unless he was a speed-reader, he was unlikely to have read more than the first half before the eight ounces of Semtex plastique at the back of the safe exploded. It lifted the six-hundred-pound safe off the floor, shattered its steel plates and welds, and blew what was left of Salvatore DiGrigoria across the room and out his office window. Later, a few cynical cops wondered if any pieces of the old man might have carried far enough to reach his private burial ground in Lake Michigan. However, most realized that they were unlikely to have made it much farther than Sheridan Road.

XXX

If you enjoyed the read, I would appreciate your going to the
Burke's War Kindle Book Page

http://www.amazon.com/dp/B00TXZYQWG

and posting a rating and comment. Just click the link below,
click on the blue "467 Customer Reviews," then on the bar
that says, "Write a Customer Review."

■■■

Also, if you'd like a FREE copy of another of my

fan-favorite thrillers, *Aim True, My Brothers*, with

4.6 stars on 252 Kindle Ratings, copy and paste

this link into your browser:

https://dl.bookfunnel.com/3uu04iwhsd

Preview of *Burke's Gamble*, Book #2 in the
Bob Burke Action Thriller Series

Welcome to 'American Sniper' meets 'The Godfather,' Round #2, an action suspense thriller novel. Bob Burke is an ex-Army Ranger and Delta Force commander. When one of his former NCOs is thrown out the fifth floor window of an Atlantic City casino run by the New York mob, Bob's going to hit them where it hurts the most, and payback's going to be a hoot!

CHAPTER ONE

Atlantic City, New Jersey, 12:30 a.m.

To paraphrase the Russian writer Leo Tolstoy, "All winning gamblers are alike; each losing gambler is unhappy in his own way." If US Army Sergeant First Class Vinnie Pastorini had ever read Tolstoy or had even heard of him, he probably would have agreed, but Vinnie knew nothing about Russian literature. What he did know a lot about was Special Operations, 'asymmetrical' warfare, weapons, fighting, drinking, gambling, and losing.

Vinnie had spent countless hours at the tables in Las Vegas, Monte Carlo, Biloxi, the Indian casinos in North Carolina and northern California, and here in Atlantic City. Along the way, he experienced his share of long winning streaks and even longer losing streaks, but the past few months were his all-time worst. As they say, bullets miss, hand grenades can be fickle bitches, life's short, sometimes the wrong guy gets killed, and sometimes "shit happens." For all that, Vinnie knew his luck was about to change. He knew it! What goes up must come down, and what goes down must always come back up. One hand! One big hand was all he needed for his luck to snap back and get the juices flowing again. It was going to happen, here and now, in Atlantic City. He could *feel* it!

On his previous trips to Atlantic City, Vinnie had played in most of the casinos, but he had never played at Caesars down on the Boardwalk before. When he walked inside, it was almost midnight and he immediately liked what he saw. The big action never got going in any of them until at least 11:00 p.m., when the heavy hitters came out and a guy could win some serious money. Vinnie hoped that was the case, because he was in dire need of winning some "very serious money," and they said Caesars was the classiest casino with the best-healed clientele on the Boardwalk. That didn't include the Bimini Bay, the Tuscany Towers, or the Siesta Cove casinos up in northeast Atlantic City, all of which were owned by Boardwalk Investments, but he couldn't go back there until he recouped at least a major down payment on what he owed them. It also did not include the Borgata or Harrah's either. He didn't owe them anything, but they were too close to the Bimini Bay for comfort. They would be the first places that Shaka Corliss and his goons would look for him, and that was far too risky. No, he had to try the casinos on the south side along the Boardwalk and win his stake back before they caught up with him. If not, he'd be a dead man walking.

Strolling casually through the front doors of Caesars, he glanced at the gambling tables. The maximums here were higher here than at Resorts or Bally's, and that was good. Even still, they weren't high enough. He put his hand in his pants pocket and felt what was left of his cash. No need to count. He knew he had a shade over $7,000 left, which meant he had already lost the $100,000 he brought back from North Carolina earlier that day, plus another $100,000 he had conned two other casinos out of. Vinnie shook his head and laughed at himself. Somehow, he'd managed to blow $218,000 in a little over seven hours. That was a record even by his standards, and now he owed a lot of money to the wrong people.

So what, he thought. Oh, Patsy was going to be super pissed at him, and Shaka Corliss and his goons would talk tough and shove him around a bit. In the end, however, they wanted their money back; and a dead man couldn't do that. Oh, he'd have to sell the new house and sign some promissory notes, but that would only put him back where he started three months before. The Army? What could they do? Bust him a grade? "Send him to Iraq?" as the old running Army joke had gone since Vietnam, or so someone once told him. Well, he had been there and done that too; and he was still on the right side of the grass looking up at all of them.

Vinnie's slide began two weeks before, when he and Patsy came up here for a little R&R. They had just bought the new house, paid cash, and had $30,000 left over. That was the perfect number for an insane weekend in Atlantic City, he thought, so they hit the road. Insane? You could say that, Vinnie knew better than most. In two days, he blew through the $30,000 plus two $50,000 advances he talked the casino out of. It never ceased to amaze him what people would do for a Vet, if he flashed a big smile and an Army ID card. Unfortunately, that bill came due like any other; and when you owe the money to New Jersey casino operators, they came collecting with a baseball bat. So, he and Patsy drove back down to Fort Bragg, saw the Credit Union, and took out a $100,000 loan on the house to pay them off.

A week later, they drove back up to Atlantic City with the best of intentions of getting a nice room for the night, paying off the sharks, having a good meal, and driving back south, suitably embarrassed and chagrined the next morning. And it almost worked. The Bimini Bay even comped him a room. After all, he'd racked up enough Gold Club Points for a top-floor suite with a nice view of the marina. Then, he took Patsy to Ruth's Chris for a great steak, and told her there was no need for her to go down to the casino office with him. It would only take a minute for him to drop off the money and return to the room. Unfortunately, the guys in the Unit didn't call him "double-down Vinnie" for nothing, but he knew his luck had changed. He could feel it, and there was no sense in giving all that money to those clowns when he *knew* he could win it back. That was seven hours ago.

Vinnie wasn't stupid. When he left Patsy up in the room, he didn't run straight to the tables downstairs at the Bimini Bay. Instead, he drove south to the Boardwalk and began at The Trump Taj Mahal. He then tried his hand at Resorts, Bally's, the Tropicana, and finally at Caesars. Of the large, mainline casinos, this was the end of the line. By the time he left the Taj and Resorts, the $100,000 from North Carolina was gone. With his patented smile, Army ID, and a signature, they gave him lines of credit for another $50,000 at Bally's, plus two $25,000 advances at the Tropicana. Now he was at Caesars with his remaining $7,000.

There was no time to waste. Vinnie quickly walked around the table groupings and saw most of the usual games — craps and roulette on the ends, and a long, double line of semi-circular card tables in between. Each table had its own dealer, tabletop graphics, and an illuminated, glass sign, which named the game being played — Three Card Poker, Blackjack, Caribbean Stud, Texas Hold 'em, Crisscross, Let it Ride, Spanish 21, even Casino War. They had them all, and he had enjoyed playing most of them on his last few trips here, winning and losing a pile at each. Tonight, those games were tempting, but their stakes were far too low and he did not have all night. Maybe he had two or three hours at best. By then, Shaka Corliss and the goons would track him down, and he had better have enough cash to buy that bastard off. Patsy was sitting in that hotel room back at the Bimini Bay, *their* Bimini Bay, and the two of them would be in deep trouble if he didn't.

Vinnie's eyes finally came to rest on the Texas Hold 'em Parlor on the back wall of the casino. It wasn't his favorite game, but they had unlimited stakes tables there, and that was what he desperately needed. He walked over and stepped inside and saw that it was a big room with dozens of tables, most of which were already full. Giving it no further thought, Vinnie stepped over to the control desk and told the man what he was looking for.

"You sure you want 'no limit,' young man?" the man asked

Vinnie nodded, so the man pointed down the side wall. "A seat just opened up at table 22. But I'll tell ya, that's a fast crowd down there, so good luck."

Vinnie smiled, walked down the table, and took his seat. Fast crowd? Looking around at the nine other players, all he saw was the usual collection of *World Series of Poker* wannabes: seven men and two women. Most of the men wore the usual de rigueur combination of black sunglasses, "Beats" earphones, layers of gold chains around their necks, and backward baseball hats. The others wore western shirts, bolo ties, and cowboy hats. The former stared at him with blank expressions, while the cowboys at least said, "Howdy." The women were another matter. One was bright-eyed and straight out of a Dolly Parton look-alike contest; while the other had dark, dead, "shark" eyes. She had body art up and down both arms and her neck, big loop earrings, studs, and about anything else that could be stuck through her nose, lips, tongue, ears, and probably a few uncomfortable places he couldn't see. Vinnie never could figure out what any of that had to do with the luck of the draw, much less beauty; but then again, if that was "normal," then the world was in big trouble.

The next hour went about as he had learned to expect. He started winning big early and got his $7,000 up to $35,000, before it all slowly went to hell again and he found himself staring at the small pile of $2,200 in front of him. The dealer button was Vinnie's, not that it mattered. The house dealer was a woman for this set, and she seemed to know what she was doing when she opened a new deck and shuffled. The "blinds" were posted, the chips were down, and Vinnie was staring vacantly at the table as she began to deal the first-hand. She got halfway around the table, when she froze in mid card. That never happened. Vinnie looked up and saw the pit boss and one of their big, uniformed security guards standing to her right and left. Surprisingly, they weren't looking at Vinnie or anyone else at the table. They were looking behind Vinnie, over his shoulder.

That was when he felt a not-so-gentle tap on his shoulder. He turned his head and looked up to see two more beefy Caesars security guys flanking him. Behind them were Shaka Corliss and his twin goons. They were hard to miss. Corliss was black, with a gleaming, shaved head, white-capped teeth, wraparound Oakley sunglasses, a huge chrome-plated revolver in a shoulder holster, and a terminal case of arrogance and anger. Little more than average height, he rippled with the kind of phony muscles you get from too many hours lifting weights at a gym.

Between him and Vinnie, it had been mutual dislike at first glance. Maybe Corliss didn't like white people, or Army sergeants, or just losers, but Vinnie doubted Corliss got along with anyone. The two look-alike, baby-faced goons standing on each side of him looked like they ran 6' 6" and around 270 pounds each, like football players from some small town in Nebraska. Corliss got off by ordering them around and being rude, arrogant, and insulting whenever he could. Vinnie guessed he must pay them a ton of money to put up with that crap, because they towered over him and either one of them could break him in half.

The Caesars security guy was nothing but polite. "I hate to interrupt, Sir, but if you'd come with us, please?" he asked Vinnie.

"You're kidding, I'm in the middle of a hand here," he complained.

"We'll hold your seat and your chips. It'll just be a minute."

"Like hell it will!" Corliss shoved the Caesars guy aside. "Tha's *our* chips and *our* money, Sucker, and you already burned through all you're gonna burn through!"

Vinnie looked up at Corliss and thought about it as he slowly got to his feet. Obviously, the game was over and he wasn't recouping any of the money he owed them. However, "in for a penny, in for a pound," he thought as his right hand shot up in a perfect uppercut — compact, explosive, and straight to the ceiling. It caught Corliss under his chin and sent him flying back into his twin goons. All things considered, other than the Ruth's Chris steak, the surprised, open-mouthed, stupid expression on Corliss's face was the most satisfying highlight of the evening.

At 6' 2" and a solid, athletic 200 pounds, Vinnie was no small man himself, but after he got in that first punch, all he remembered was a blur of more punches, counter punches, kicks, and a good bit of pain. He had fought his way through six combat tours in two different official wars, and a lot more nonofficial ones as an Army Ranger and Delta Force upper-level NCO Operator, although membership in that elite fraternity would always be top secret and never to be acknowledged. He was considered an expert with most weapons in the Army inventory and just as good in no-holds-barred, hand-to-hand combat, and had been in more than his share of old-fashioned bar fights at one Army post after another. Tonight, he was able to get in a dozen good shots at one goon after another. He even tossed one security guard onto a nearby poker table, breaking it in half, and tossed one of Corliss's goons upside down into the wall. In the end, however, six to one, almost all of whom were bigger than he was, usually won. When someone broke a chair over his head and he went down for the count, that was all she wrote.

If you enjoyed this Preview of **Burke's Gamble,** the Author's newest political action thriller, you can download a Kindle copy at

http://amzn.to/2lORmXJ

***

Also, if you'd like a FREE copy of another of my fan-favorite thrillers, **Aim True, My Brothers**, with 4.6 stars on 252 Kindle Ratings, copy and paste this link into your browser:

https://dl.bookfunnel.com/3uu04iwhsd

THE AUTHOR
WILLIAM F. BROWN

Burke's War is the first story in the three-book Bob Burke suspense thriller series, followed by Burke's Gamble and Burke's Revenge. They are exciting, fun reads. I'm the author of nine mystery and international suspense thrillers, exclusively available on Kindle.

A native of Chicago, I received a BA from The University of Illinois in History and Russian Area studies, and a Masters in City Planning. I served as a Company Commander in the US Army and later became active in local and regional politics in Virginia. As a Vice President of the real estate subsidiary of a Fortune 500 corporation, I was able to travel widely in the US and now travel extensively abroad, particularly in Europe and the Middle East, locations which have featured prominently in my writing. When not writing, I play bad golf, have become a dogged runner, and paint passable landscapes in oil and acrylic. Now retired, my wife and I live in Florida.

In addition to the novels, I've written four award-winning screenplays. They've placed First in the suspense category of Final Draft, were a Finalist in Fade In, First in Screenwriter's Utopia — Screenwriter's Showcase Awards, Second in the American Screenwriter's Association, Second at Breckenridge, and others. One was optioned for film.

The best way to follow my work and learn about sales and freebees is through my web site http://billbrownthrillernovels.com.

DEDICATION

To the three best proofreaders a writer can have: my wife, Elisabeth Hallett in far away Montana, and Loren Vinson. To Hitch and the staff of Booknook Biz for their help with processing, file conversion. And to Todd Hebertson at My Personal Art for the cover art.

Burke's War

Copyright 2015 by William F. Brown

This is a work of fiction. Names, characters, places, and incidents either are the product of the author's imagination or are used fictitiously.

Cover Design by Todd Hebertson
Digital Editions produced by: Booknook.biz.